book 2 in the dare to love series

dare to FALL

AMBER NICOLE

Dare To Fall

ISBN paperback: 979-8-9897939-9-0

Cover Design by Amber Nicole

Also by Amber Nicole

Dare To Love Series

Dare To Hold

A Season To Hold

Dare To Fall

A Season to Fall

Dare To Stay

A Season to Stay

Standalones

Gabby Wallace Skips Valentine's Day

To every woman keeping the streaks, the schedules, and the smile, exhausted from trying to be enough—He is the vine. You are the branch. You can let go and remain in Him.

Dear Reader,

Before you dive in, I want to take a moment to share a few things about the heart behind this story.

Dare to Fall is a clean Christian romance, filled with swoony moments, real struggles, and deep faith themes. It's a love story—but more than that, it's a story about abiding. About grace that doesn't have to be earned. About what it means to stop striving long enough to remain in the One who has been holding you all along.

You'll meet Harper, a woman who keeps the streaks, the schedules, and the smile—convinced that if she just does enough, serves enough, is enough, then maybe she'll finally feel close to God. And Micah, a man whose faith is steady and strong, and who sees Harper more clearly than she sees herself. Their story doesn't begin with easy answers. It begins in the striving. In the pretending. In the questions.

You'll see flawed characters hide behind good intentions. You'll watch them wrestle with what it really means to abide.

Dear Reader,

And—my prayer—you'll watch them learn that love, real love, isn't something you perform your way into. Because this story reflects what I believe to be true: that God isn't asking us to hold it all together, that striving was never the point, and that the invitation has always been to simply remain.

If you're looking for a Christian romance with real heart, real struggle, and real hope—this one's for you.

With love and gratitude,
Amber Nicole

Content Warnings

This story gently touches on the following themes:

- Emotionally distant parents
- Past relationship hurt
- Faith struggles and spiritual doubt
- ADHD representation
- Mild romantic tension/temptation
- Brief mentions of alcohol

These elements are not graphic in nature, but they are noted here so readers can feel informed and safe before diving in.

Chapter 1
Harper

"This one isn't working either."

I tug at the zipper of this champagne-colored gown and catch Ivy's eye in the boutique mirror. She's perched on the velvet bench beside Olivia, both of them watching me with the patience only genuine friends possess after enduring thirty-plus dress changes without complaint.

"It's pretty," Ivy offers, tilting her head.

"Pretty isn't enough." I twist toward the mirror, studying my reflection. The dress is classy. Sophisticated. But it doesn't pop. It doesn't demand attention, or turn heads, or make anyone stop mid-conversation to stare.

And that's the problem.

"You look beautiful, Harp." Olivia says between sips of her iced coffee.

"Beautiful doesn't cut it," I mutter, smoothing the fabric over my hips. "I need unforgettable."

Because if I'm going to walk into The North Texas Education Gala in three weeks and face Collin for the first time since he ended things, I need more than beautiful. I need a dress that makes him question every decision he's ever made. I need him to see what he walked away from—not just the surface, but the woman who would have stood by him, who would have chosen him over and over. I need him to feel the loss, to wonder if letting me go was the biggest mistake of his life.

Ivy stands, moving behind me to help with the stubborn zipper. Her fingers are gentle as she tugs it the rest of the way up. "Harper, you know this gala isn't really about Collin, right? It's about the kids. Raising money for after-school programs, getting new books in classrooms—"

"I know, I know." I turn back to the mirror, tugging at the neckline of the champagne dress.

I let out a breath. This gala was supposed to be simple. Collin and I had talked about going together for months—it's the biggest fundraiser of the year for our district, the type of event that actually gets measurable results for after-school programs, new books in classrooms, the things my kids need and never quite have enough of. I'd been excited about it, genuinely. And then Collin happened, and now I'm standing in this boutique in Downtown Dallas in a dress that makes me look like a hotel curtain, trying to remember why I cared in the first place.

"This really isn't the one, is it?" I turn back to the mirror.

"Definitely not," Olivia says. "Too safe."

"Safe," I echo, and the word tastes bitter.

Collin was safe.

No questionable past, no red flags that would make my father raise an eyebrow over Sunday dinner. My parents didn't just like Collin—they loved him. My mother asked about him on every phone call; my father actually smiled when he walked through the door. He was everything they wanted for me, everything they thought I needed. He checked every box on their list, even though I was realizing he didn't check all of mine.

Why do I feel the need to play it safe? Being the obedient daughter. Dating a respectable man. Checking all the boxes on my parents' perfect checklist.

And where did that get me?

Dumped during dessert at a restaurant where the wine list cost more than my rent, while other diners pretended not to notice my world falling apart over white tablecloths and candlelight.

"I cannot show up to this gala alone," I say, more to myself than to them. "Not when Collin is going to be there."

There. I said it.

The real reason I'm drowning in tulle and silk on a Tuesday afternoon in February. The real reason I've been spiraling for the past two months. I can't let him see me still single, still stuck exactly where he left me. I can't give him the satisfaction of knowing that dumping me over dessert actually hurt.

"So, what's the plan?" Olivia asks gently. "Find a date in three weeks?"

"I don't know," I admit, my voice small. "I just... I need someone. Anyone who can help me walk in there looking like I've moved on. Like I'm fine. Like I don't need him."

Silence.

Not regular silence. Scheming silence.

I catch their reflections in the mirror—Ivy and Olivia exchanging one of those looks that says they're having an entire conversation without words. One that makes my stomach drop.

"What?" I ask, suspicious now.

"Nothing," Ivy says too quickly, but her lips are twitching as if she's fighting a smile.

I narrow my eyes at both of them. "You're doing that thing."

"What thing?" Olivia asks, all innocent.

"That thing where you two plot something without including me. I can literally see it happening."

They exchange another glance, and this time they don't even try to hide their grins.

My stomach twists. "Oh no. Whatever you're thinking, the answer is no."

"We haven't even said anything yet," Ivy protests.

"You don't have to. I know that look."

Behind me, that scheming silence returns. I catch Ivy leaning toward Olivia in the mirror's reflection, whispering something that makes Olivia's eyes light up.

"Okay, seriously," I spin around. "What are you two—"

"We dare you to ask Micah to be your date to the gala," Ivy blurts out, her grin spreading like wildfire.

My whole body goes rigid. The champagne fabric suddenly feels too tight. "Excuse me?"

"You heard us." Olivia straightens, matching Ivy's smile.

"Absolutely not." The words come out faster than I can think them. "Are you insane?"

"Think about it—" Ivy starts.

"I don't need to think about it. The answer is no."

"He's perfect for this," Olivia presses. "Single, good-looking. Respectable—"

"Micah makes everything weird," I cut in, crossing my arms. "Existing in his presence is weird."

Ivy's grin widens. "He's funny."

"Dad jokes are not funny. They're torture."

"He's trustworthy," Olivia continues.

"So are serial killers until they're not."

Olivia snorts into her coffee. "Micah's not a serial killer, Harper."

"He once set the church parking lot on fire with a grill," I counter, jabbing a finger at them.

"That was an accident—" Ivy protests.

"A grill, Olivia. An outdoor grill. How do you even manage that?"

"He's single," Ivy cuts in, using that patient voice she reserves for when she thinks I'm being stubborn. "He cleans up nice. He's safe. And most importantly, Collin barely knows him."

That stops me cold.

My arms drop slightly. "What?"

"Think about it," Ivy continues, stepping closer. "Yeah, Collin met him once at our Christmas thing, but he has no idea who Micah really is. He doesn't know about the dad jokes or the awkwardness, or the church parking lot fire. All Collin will see is you walking in on the arm of a good-looking guy."

Olivia slips into full therapist mode now. "And when Collin sees you with someone like Micah? He'll instantly want you back. That's how men work. They don't value what they have until someone else has it."

My pulse kicks up. "You really think so?"

"I know so," Olivia says with complete confidence.

I turn back to the mirror, my mind racing.

Micah.

Micah, who runs the entire children's ministry at New Chapter Church without fail. Micah, who shows up when someone's moving and actually lifts the heavy boxes instead of pretending to carry the pillows. Micah, who fixes things that don't belong to him just because he can't stand to see them broken.

Micah, who's...annoyingly decent.

And yes, fine. He's good-looking. More than good-looking. Broad shoulders, an easy smile, hair that somehow always looks like he just rolled out of bed, but in that unfair shampoo-commercial way. And those thick-framed glasses? Half nerd, half heartthrob, and wholly unfair.

Put him in a suit and tie, and even Collin would do a double-take.

Not that I'd ever admit that out loud.

The idea settles over me slowly, piece by piece clicking into place.

All Collin would see is me, looking stunning, on the arm of another man.

A nice-looking man.

I could convince Collin that I've moved on. That I'm fine. That I don't need him.

Even if none of it's true.

But then reality crashes back in.

Micah. The guy who thinks puns are peak comedy. The guy who can recite every VeggieTales episode by heart and considers it a professional skill as the children's ministry director. The guy who unironically wears socks with sandals and sees nothing wrong with it.

I'd have to ride in the car alone with him—trapped in close quarters with nowhere to escape. Introduce him to everyone as my date; watch him shake hands and charm people with that calm smile of his. Laugh at his dad jokes all night. Smile through his overly enthusiastic commentary about everything from the appetizers to the centerpieces. Pretend to find it endearing when he inevitably makes some terrible pun about "raising the steaks" at a fundraiser.

And worse—I'd have to pretend to like him. Actually like him. Gaze up at him adoringly like he hung the moon. Let him hold my hand, his fingers laced through mine. Lean into him when we pose for photos. Act like his presence doesn't make me want to simultaneously roll my eyes and scream into a pillow.

Would people expect us to kiss?

I shake off the thought immediately. No. Absolutely not. That definitely cannot happen.

I'd need to set some serious ground rules before agreeing to any of this.

I don't know if pretending for an entire evening is even physically possible.

I straighten my spine, suddenly hyperaware of how boring this champagne dress really is—and how insane this entire plan sounds.

"Over my dead body," I say, but even I can hear the wavering in my voice.

Ivy's smile turns triumphant. "Too late. We already dared you."

"You can't just—"

"You know the rules, Harp." Olivia folds her arms, her expression serious now. "None of us has ever turned down a dare. Not once."

My jaw clenches. She's right.

The dare tradition started back when Ivy and I were in high school—stupid, silly challenges to make us brave when we felt small. Singing too loudly in a crowded room. Ordering the weirdest thing on the menu. Slipping notes to boys we liked and running before they could read them. When we met Olivia in college, she joined in, and the three of us turned it into something bigger. A pact. A promise.

The dares have gotten us through breakups, job

changes, and moments when we needed each other most. They pushed Ivy to grab a stranger's hand on a crowded street in New Orleans—and that stranger turned out to be Gray Bennett, her now husband. They pushed us all to dare something bigger at New Year's: *never lose faith, love without pretending, be brave even when it's scary.*

And then at Ivy's wedding, while I was too busy arguing with Micah Sanders near the drink station, Ivy turned to me with that look, the one I now recognize as dangerous, and dared me to dance with him.

I danced to one song with Micah. One song. And for those three and a half minutes, he didn't annoy me even once. He just wove me through the crowd, kept me close, and somehow gave me the one quiet moment I'd had all night in the middle of a hundred maid-of-honor disasters. Like he knew I was running on fumes and just... let me breathe. Didn't say a word about it.

And then the song ended, and he went right back to being insufferable.

"And if I do?" I challenge anyway. "If I just say no?"

They exchange another look, identical grins forming.

"Then you break a tradition," Ivy says softly. "But you won't."

The weight of those words settles over me. She knows me too well.

I want to argue. Want to storm out of this boutique and pretend this conversation never happened. Want to tell them that asking Micah, of all people, is a terrible, ridiculous, completely insane idea.

But I can't.

Because deep down, beneath all the protests and panic, I know they're right.

Ivy goes quiet for a moment, browsing a rack of dresses with a small, knowing smile.

"You know it was almost exactly two years ago, on our girls' trip to New Orleans, when you told me: 'Ivy Taylor, you are one yes away from something good.'"

I freeze. "That is not fair."

"It's completely fair. You and Olivia dared me to grab a stranger's hand in that crowd." A soft laugh. "Deep down, I think you both knew it would lead to something good."

I knew. We all did, even if we were pretending it was just a silly dare. And then Gray Bennett walked into her life because she said yes.

I glance away from Ivy's expression, which is doing something unbearably gentle.

"You can't use my own words against me," I say.

"I just did." She holds up a new dress—deep emerald, structured, the kind that doesn't apologize for itself. "Now try this one."

I retreat into the dressing room before either of them can say another word. My hands shake slightly as I peel myself out of the champagne gown. The zipper sticks at first, and I yank it harder than I need to. The fabric finally gives, sliding off my shoulders and pooling at my feet, lifeless and dull.

I kick it aside.

The relief is immediate. Like I'd been holding my breath in that dress without realizing it.

That dress wasn't mine. It was safe and beige and careful, and I've spent the last two months being all of those things already. I don't need to wear them to a gala.

If I'm going to do this—if I'm really going to walk back into Collin's orbit with Micah on my arm and pretend I've moved on—I need a dress that backs up the story. A dress that says thriving, not trying too hard. A dress that makes Collin remember exactly what he gave up over a five-star dessert.

I reach for the one Ivy handed me.

Sparkly, emerald green. I step in slowly, almost nervous, and reach back for the zipper.

It molds to my curves as if it were made for me. The fabric feels like armor and confidence wrapped into one.

I turn toward the mirror.

Oh.

The color makes my red hair look like fire, and the sequins shimmer under the dressing room lights like tiny captured stars. I look...I look like myself. Not the version of me that spent two months second-guessing every text, replaying every dinner, wondering what I did wrong.

This version stands up straight without being told to.

I reach up and pull the clip out of my hair, letting it fall loose around my shoulders. My eyes sting, just for a second—not from sadness, but from the strange, unexpected relief of recognizing yourself in a mirror again.

I look like a woman who is going to be fine.

More than fine.

I smooth my hands down the fabric once, slowly, and lift my chin. Then I take a breath and step out of the dressing room.

Ivy's jaw actually drops. "Oh my..."

Olivia sets down her coffee so fast it nearly spills. "That's the one."

I turn toward the full-length mirror, and for the first time all afternoon, something shifts inside me.

I don't see the girl who got dumped. Not the girl scrambling to meet impossible standards. Not the girl trying to fix something that was never whole to begin with.

I see Harper.

Bright. Fiery. Unapologetic.

The girl who walks into rooms and makes people look twice.

"If this dress doesn't convince Collin to take me back," I say slowly, my voice steadier now as I meet Ivy's eyes in the mirror, "then Micah better."

Ivy's grin could light up the whole boutique. "Deal."

I take a deep breath, the weight of the dare settling over me—dangerous, thrilling, and exactly what these dares are supposed to do: push us beyond our limits into something we never saw coming. After all, we dared Ivy to hold a stranger's hand, and now she's married to him.

Olivia raises her coffee cup as if she's making a toast. "To fake dating."

"To ending up exactly where you're supposed to be," Ivy adds, and there's something in her smile I can not analyze right now.

"To Collin seeing what he lost," I say, because someone has to.

They exchange a look. The kind that has an entire conversation inside it.

I turn back to the mirror, heart pounding against my ribs, smoothing my hands down the emerald fabric one more time.

To making Collin regret every single thing. I think.

And to getting through one evening with Micah Sanders without wanting to strangle him.

Chapter 2
Harper

Wednesday night arrives faster than I am ready for.

I light the last candle on the terrace of my apartment and step back to look at everything.

String lights crisscross overhead, casting a warm glow over the mismatched patio furniture I've spent the last hour arranging. The fire pit crackles in the center, flames dancing against the cool March evening. And the s'mores station—complete with three types of chocolate, giant marshmallows, and graham crackers arranged in a wicker basket—sits on the table like a Pinterest board come to life.

A chalkboard sign leans against the railing:

S'MORE OF JESUS LESS OF ME

Okay, so maybe I went a little overboard. But if we're going to do a Bible study, we might as well have a theme.

I adjust the sign one more time, then step back to admire my work. The clipboard in my hand holds tonight's itinerary—color-coded, of course—with time slots for fellowship, s'mores making, icebreaker questions, and finally, the actual Bible study portion.

"Harper, this is amazing!"

I turn to see Ivy stepping onto the terrace, Gray trailing behind her with an amused smile. She's carrying a bowl of what looks like fruit salad, and Gray's got a cooler that probably holds enough drinks to hydrate a small army.

"You think so?" I can't help the grin spreading across my face. "I wanted it to feel...intentional. You know, like we're creating space for community."

"Mission accomplished," Ivy says, setting the bowl on the snack table. "So...have you asked Micah yet?"

"No, not yet, I've been too busy."

"Don't wait too long; the gala is just over two weeks away."

"Ugh," I pick up a stack of napkins that absolutely do not need rearranging and start rearranging them. "Don't remind me."

Gray sets down the cooler, perfect timing to change the subject, and glances at the chalkboard. "S'more of Jesus. Nice."

"Thank you." I gesture to the fire pit. "I figured if we're going to study the Word, we might as well enjoy it. Faith doesn't have to be boring."

"It definitely won't be boring with you in charge," Gray says, and I'm pretty sure that's a compliment.

People trickle in over the next fifteen minutes, and I let the hosting instincts take over—pointing people toward the snack table, making introductions, keeping my hands busy so I stop thinking about the fact that I still need to ask Micah to be my fake date.

The Bible study started back in January. Gray and Ivy had floated the idea on New Year's Eve, and by the second week of the month they'd pulled together maybe eight people around their kitchen table. No agenda, just open Bibles and honest conversation and whatever snacks someone remembered to bring.

Then twelve people showed up the following week. Then sixteen.

Now it rotates—someone different opens their home each Wednesday, and every time we think the group has settled, a few more faces appear. I love that I get to host tonight. I love that this exists at all.

I'm refilling the drink station when Ivy sidles up beside me, her voice low. "Did you invite Olivia?"

"I texted her." I sigh.

"And?"

"She never responded."

Ivy's expression softens, that look she gets when she's trying not to show how worried she is. "She'll come around. She just needs time."

"I know." I force a smile. "She always does."

But I'm not sure anymore. Olivia's been pulling away for months—skipping church, dodging plans, making excuses. And every time I reach out, it feels like she's slipping further through my fingers.

Before I can spiral too far into that thought, a familiar, irritating voice cuts through the chatter.

"So, are we actually going to talk about the Bible at this Bible study, or just eat s'mores?"

I whip around to see Micah Sanders standing by the fire pit, arms crossed, one eyebrow raised behind those stupid, perfectly clear-framed glasses. He's got that dark, slightly too-wavy hair that looks like he ran a hand through it once and called it styled, and the kind of easy smile that probably works on everyone except me. A few days of stubble that he clearly has no intention of dealing with. A hoodie and jeans, because Micah Sanders has never once dressed for the occasion in his life and somehow always looks infuriatingly comfortable doing it.

"Excuse me?" I march over, clipboard in hand. "Of course we're going to talk about the Bible. Do you think I'd call it a Bible study if we weren't going to study the Bible?"

He shrugs, a smirk tugging at his lips. "I don't know. I've seen you get pretty distracted by aesthetics."

"Aesthetics are important," I fire back. "Creating an atmosphere where people feel welcomed and comfortable is part of hospitality. Which, by the way, is biblical."

"So is studying the Bible."

"We *will* study the Bible. There's an itinerary." I wave the clipboard at him. "Color-coded. With time slots."

His eyes flick to the clipboard, and his smirk deepens. "Of course there is."

"Fellowship comes first," I continue, defensive now. "People need to connect before they can be vulnerable enough to dig into Scripture. That's basic discipleship."

"Or," Micah counters, leaning against the patio railing, "you could just open with prayer and jump in. Keep it simple."

"Simple is boring."

"Simple is effective."

"You're—"

"Hey, Harper." Gray's voice interrupts, and I turn to see him approaching. "Don't you have something to ask Micah?"

My thoughts screech to a halt. "Um, no? Why would I—"

I pause.

Wait.

"How did you know about that?"

Gray just shrugs, already backing away.

I narrow my eyes at him, but he's already gone, disappearing into the small crowd with a stealth that only comes from years of avoiding awkward conversations.

Micah's looking at me now, curiosity replacing the teasing. "What did you need to ask me?"

"Nothing." I turn abruptly, heading back toward the snack table. "Absolutely nothing."

But of course, he follows me.

"Harper."

"I'm busy." I grab the box of graham crackers, even though the basket is still half full.

"Busy avoiding my question."

"Busy being an excellent host." I shove a few more crackers into the basket, then move to check the chocolate supply.

"You're a terrible liar."

"I'm not lying. I'm hosting."

"Harper."

His voice is closer now, lower than the surrounding noise, and something about the way he says my name sends a shiver down my spine that I absolutely did not ask for and immediately resent.

I blow out a breath, glancing around. People are laughing, conversing, completely oblivious to the mild panic attack I'm currently having.

Without thinking, I grab Micah's arm and pull him toward the kitchen.

"Whoa, where are we—"

"Shh," I tug him through the sliding door, past the kitchen island, and straight into the pantry. The door clicks shut behind us, and suddenly we're standing in a space barely big enough for one person, let alone two.

The single overhead bulb casts harsh shadows, and I'm acutely aware of how close he is.

Micah glances around, then back at me, a slow smile spreading across his face. "This is cozy."

"Don't." I point a finger at him. "Don't make it weird."

"I'm not the one who dragged us into a pantry."

"I needed privacy."

"For what?" His tone shifts, teasing fading into something more genuine. "Harper, what's going on?"

I take a breath, steeling myself. "I need you to do something for me."

He blinks. "Okay..."

"Do you remember Collin?"

His expression hardens almost instantly. "Yeah. The guy who couldn't be bothered to look up from his phone at Christmas?"

"That's not—" I stop myself. "I mean, yes. But that's not the point."

"Then what is?"

I fidget with the edge of my sweater, suddenly wishing I'd rehearsed this better. Or at all. "Are you free on Friday March 21st?"

Micah pulls out his phone, scrolling through his calendar. "I've got dinner with Gray and the guys, but other than that—"

"Reschedule it."

He looks up, eyebrows raised. "What?"

"Reschedule it. Because you're going with me to the North Texas Education Gala."

Silence.

He stares at me as if I've just spoken an unfamiliar language. "I'm...what?"

"The gala. It's a fundraiser for the school district. Formal event. Dinner, dancing, speeches. Very boring, very necessary. And I need a date."

"And you're asking me?"

"Yes."

"Why?"

Because Ivy and Olivia dared me. Because I can't show up alone. Because Collin will be there and I need to prove I've moved on, even though I haven't.

But I don't say any of that.

"Because you're available," I say instead. "And you clean up nicely."

Something shifts in his expression. "You think I clean up nice?"

"I think you own a suit and you know how to wear it," I say, keeping my voice completely even. "I was at the same wedding you were."

The corner of his mouth tugs upward.

"So you noticed."

"I noticed you didn't embarrass yourself. That's all." I straighten. "So you'll do it?"

He studies me for a long moment, and I can practically see the gears turning in his head. "What's the catch?"

"There's no catch."

"Harper."

"Fine." I cross my arms, defensive. "Collin is going to be there. And I don't want to show up alone. Happy?"

Something flickers across his face. Surprise? Concern maybe? I can't tell in the dim light of the pantry. The space suddenly feels smaller than it did thirty seconds ago. Or maybe Micah is just—closer. I'm not sure which one it is and I don't love that I can't tell.

"So this is about your ex."

"It's not *about* him. It's just...easier if I have someone with me. And you're—"

"Convenient?"

"Available," I correct. "And trustworthy."

He says nothing. Just looks at me in that quiet, unhurried way he has, and I become suddenly, uncomfortably aware of how close we're standing. Close enough that I can smell him—something warm, like cedar and laundry detergent—and that is not information I needed tonight. The pantry hums with a silence that feels louder than the party outside, and I realize I've stopped breathing at a normal rate.

I force myself to look back up at him.

That was a mistake.

He's looking down at me with an expression I don't have a name for. Not his usual smirk. Not the raised eyebrow. Something quieter than both, and significantly more inconvenient.

Stop it, I tell myself. This is Micah.

"Just please don't make it weird," I say, mostly to fill the silence.

The corner of his mouth lifts, and there it is—that dimple. Just one, tucked into his left cheek, appearing only when his smile is real instead of practiced. It is, without question, the single most disarming thing about Micah Sanders, and I have spent the better part of two years pretending it doesn't exist.

I look away.

"I'm literally standing in a pantry with you right now. It's already weird."

Before I can respond, the door swings open.

Ivy stands in the doorway, eyes wide, a half-eaten s'more in one hand. "Um...what are y'all doing?"

I step back so fast I nearly knock over a bag of flour. "Nothing."

"Doesn't look like nothing."

"We were just—" I glance at Micah, who looks far too amused by this entire situation. "Talking."

"In the pantry?"

"It's quiet in here."

Ivy's gaze bounces between us, a slow grin spreading across her face. "Right...quiet. Got it."

She backs out of the doorway, still grinning, and I resist the urge to throw something at her.

When I turn back to Micah, he's already moving toward the door. "We should probably get back out there before people talk."

"You worry too much." I mutter.

He pauses in the doorway, glancing back at me. "For the record. I didn't say no."

My heart does this weird little flip. "You didn't say yes either."

"I'll think about it."

And then he's gone, slipping back onto the terrace as if nothing happened.

I stand there for a second longer, staring at the space where he just was, my pulse still racing.

I'll think about it.

Not a yes. But not a no either.

I grab the box of graham crackers—to make it appear as if I wasn't in the pantry for nothing—and head back outside.

The rest of the evening passes in a blur. We eventually make it to the actual Bible study portion, though I'm pretty sure I spend more time watching Micah across the fire than actually paying attention to the discussion. He's sitting next to Gray, laughing at something someone said, completely at ease in a way I've never been able to manage.

And when he catches me staring, I look away.

By the time everyone leaves, I'm exhausted. Ivy and Gray are the only ones left—perks of being married, I guess. They don't have to awkwardly figure out who's leaving with whom.

Gray's stacking chairs on the terrace while Ivy helps me gather trash, and I can feel her watching me. Waiting.

The second I toss the last stack of paper plates into the trash bag, she pounces.

"So," she leans against the counter, arms crossed, that knowing smile already forming. "Pantry. Micah. Spill."

I groan. "There's nothing to spill."

"Oh come on."

"I asked him to the gala. He said he'd think about it. End of story."

Gray walks in from the terrace, wiping his hands on his jeans. "Wait, you actually asked him?"

"Yes."

"In the pantry?"

"It was private."

He exchanges a look with Ivy, and they both start grinning like idiots.

"What?" I demand.

"Nothing," Gray says, far too innocent. "Just...an interesting choice of location."

"It was the only quiet place."

"Uh-huh." He leans against the counter beside Ivy. "And how'd he take it?"

"He said he'd think about it."

Gray nods slowly, as if he's processing this. "That's Micah-speak for '*yes, but I need to pretend I'm being thoughtful about it.*'"

"Really?" The word slips out before I can stop it.

"Oh yeah." Gray grins. "He does that thing where he acts all logical and measured, but he's already made up his mind. He's likely to text me in approximately twenty minutes to ask for advice on what to wear. Don't worry, I'll act as if I'm unaware of this entire situation."

Ivy laughs. "That's actually accurate."

"It is not," I protest, even though my heart's doing that annoying flutter thing again.

"Harper," Ivy's tone shifts, gentler now. "Did you see the way he looked at you when he left?"

"He didn't look at me in any specific way."

"He definitely did," Gray says. "I was standing right there. Dude looked like someone had just handed him a winning lottery ticket and he's trying to play it cool."

I throw a dish towel at him. He catches it, laughing.

"I'm serious," he continues, tossing the towel back at me. "Micah does nothing halfway. If he said he'd think about it, he's already thinking about it. Probably planning the entire night in his head."

"Or he's trying to figure out how to say no without hurting my feelings."

Ivy shakes her head. "He's not going to say no."

"You don't know that."

"I know Micah," Gray says. "And I know that look. Trust me, Harper. He's in."

"He's in for a fake date to make my ex jealous," I clarify. "That's it."

Gray and Ivy exchange another look—one of those

married-couple silent conversations that somehow communicates an entire thesis.

"What?" I demand.

"Nothing," Ivy says, her smile soft. "Thanks for hosting tonight. Those s'mores were incredible."

"Perfect addition to Bible study," Gray agrees, grabbing his jacket from the back of a chair. "Though I think Micah ate about seven of them."

I can't help but laugh. "He definitely did. I watched him."

Ivy loops her arm through Gray's. "Well, we should get going. Early morning tomorrow."

"Of course," I say, walking them to the door.

Gray pauses in the doorway, turning back with that serene smile. "Good luck with everything, Harp. See you Sunday."

And then they're gone, leaving me standing in my kitchen surrounded by s'mores supplies and the lingering feeling that I've just started something I have absolutely no idea how to finish.

I grab my phone, checking for texts I know aren't there yet.

Nothing from Micah.

But my thumb hovers over Collin's name in my contacts. The urge hits me hard and fast—to text him, to ask how his day was, to fall back into the comfortable rhythm we used to have.

Miss you. Can we talk?

I start typing, then stop. Delete it. Start again.

Hey, how have you been?

Delete.

I go completely still. It's been two months, and I still

reach for him like muscle memory. Like my heart hasn't caught up to the fact that he's gone.

But he is gone. He chose to leave. He walked out of that restaurant without looking back, and I sat there like an idiot, staring at a half-eaten chocolate soufflé while the server awkwardly asked if I wanted a to-go box.

I lock my phone and set it facedown on the counter.

No.

I'm not texting him. I'm not giving him the satisfaction of knowing I'm still thinking about him.

Instead, I'm showing up to that gala in two weeks looking absolutely stunning, with Micah on my arm, and I'm going to make Collin Matthews regret every single decision he made that night.

I take a breath, squaring my shoulders.

Game on.

Chapter 3
Micah

Harper Mitchell doesn't know I'm in love with her. And I need to keep it that way.

Harper, with the wild red hair and opinions about everything. Harper, who has lodged herself somewhere in my chest since she first snapped at me about background checks.

I've told no one.

Not Gray, even though he acts like he has me figured out—which, technically, he does, but I'd never admit that out loud. Not my mom, who keeps asking when I'm going to "find a nice girl" and settle down. Not the guys I meet with for accountability every other Thursday, even though we're supposed to be honest about temptation and all that.

Because Harper Mitchell scares me.

Not in a bad way. More like how standing at the edge of a cliff scares you—like one wrong step and you're free-falling with no idea if there's anything to catch you at the bottom.

She's loud. I'm quiet.

She's spontaneous and colorful and takes up space as if

she was born to own every room she walks into. I'm the guy who sets reminders for his reminders and panic-orders the same coffee every morning because choosing is stressful.

She's a wildfire.

I'm...I don't know. A box of matches, maybe. Useful in theory. Boring in practice.

And she's so far out of my league, we're not even playing the same sport.

I pull into the driveway of my bungalow—tucked into a neighborhood just outside of Downtown Dallas where people actually know their neighbors' names—and kill the engine. But I don't get out. I just sit there, hands gripping the steering wheel, staring at my front porch light like it holds the answers to every question scrambling my brain.

She asked me.

Harper asked me.

To the gala. As her date.

Fake date. To make her ex-boyfriend jealous.

I drop my head against the steering wheel and let out a long breath.

This is a catastrophic idea.

Because she's not asking me to the gala because she likes me.

She's asking because I'm convenient.

I groan and force myself out of the truck.

Get it together, Micah.

The front steps creak under my weight. The door sticks a little—I keep meaning to fix it—and I shove it open with my shoulder.

Silence has fallen over the house. It's too quiet.

"Biscuit, I'm home!"

A blur of brown and white fur rockets toward me from the hallway. My ferret—all two pounds of pure chaos—

comes bounding across the hardwood like he's been waiting for me to get home for hours. Which, knowing him, he probably has been.

I crouch down, and Biscuit immediately climbs up my arm, perching on my shoulder like some kind of weasel-parrot. He chitters softly in my ear, his tiny nose twitching as he investigates my hair.

"Yeah, I missed you too, buddy."

Most people think ferrets belong in cages. But Biscuit's been free-range since I adopted him three years ago. He's litter-box trained and has the run of the house. His favorite spots include the tunnel system I built him in the living room, the drawer in my dresser where he's hoarded approximately seventeen socks, and anywhere I happen to be sitting.

He's weird. High-maintenance. Requires more patience than most people have.

But I love him.

I scratch behind his ears as I head to the kitchen, Biscuit clinging to my shoulder like a fuzzy scarf. He lets out a happy squeak when I open the treat jar, and I toss him a salmon-flavored puff. He catches it mid-air and scurries down my arm to devour it on the counter.

"You know you're not supposed to be up here," I tell him. He ignores me, as usual.

At least someone's life is simple.

I pull out my phone, my thumb hovering over Gray's name in my contacts.

I should text him. Ask for advice. Maybe get some perspective before I do something stupid like agree to fake-date the girl I've been quietly in love with for months.

But my thumb doesn't move.

Because I already know what I'm going to do.

I'm going to say yes.

Not because it's smart. Not because it makes sense. But because Harper asked, and I've never been able to say no to her.

Even when I should.

I stare at the screen for another moment, then set the phone down on the counter.

Gray can wait.

I need to take this to God first.

Biscuit follows me down the hallway, scampering along the baseboards before darting into my room ahead of me. By the time I walk in, he's already curled up in his favorite spot on my bed—right behind my pillow.

The space is simple. Bed. Dresser. A chair by the window where I do my morning quiet time. My Bible sits on the nightstand, a dozen sticky notes marking passages I've been working through, and my journal is open to this morning's entry.

I sink into the chair, elbows on my knees, and close my eyes.

"Okay, God. Let's talk."

I sit there for a moment, eyes closed, trying to find the right words.

But that's the thing about prayer—there are no right words. Just honest ones.

"Okay," I start again, quieter this time. "I know You already know what happened tonight. You were there. In the pantry. Which...okay, I liked more than I should have."

I open my eyes, staring at the worn pages of my Bible on the nightstand.

"She asked me to be her date to the gala. Her fake date. And I know this is a terrible idea. Fake dating her to make her ex jealous? That's a disaster waiting to happen. I should say no. I should tell her to find someone else. Someone who doesn't..."

I trail off, rubbing a hand over my face.

"Someone who doesn't have feelings for her."

There it is. Out loud. To God, at least.

"I've had a thing for her for months now. And I've tried to ignore it, tried to focus on other things, tried to convince myself it would fade. But it hasn't. If anything, it's gotten worse."

I lean back in the chair, letting my head rest against the wall.

"And the thing is... I don't even know where she's really at with You. She shows up to everything—Bible studies, volunteering in children's ministry so much I have to physically stop her and tell her no, go sit in the service instead. She knows all the right answers. Says all the right things. But does she actually have a relationship with You? Or is she just going through the motions?"

I pause, the question hanging heavy in the quiet room.

"Because I see her serving constantly, running herself ragged trying to do all the things, but I don't know if she's ever just... sat still long enough to actually be with You. To know You, not just know about You."

Biscuit stirs on the bed, stretching before curling back into a tighter ball.

"But God, when I'm around her, I see glimpses of something real. Something deeper than she's willing to admit. Like there's this whole part of her that's searching for You, even if she doesn't realize it yet. And I keep thinking...maybe I could help. Maybe I could show her what it looks like to actually know You, not just serve You."

I pause, knowing how that sounds.

"But that's probably just me making excuses, isn't it? Trying to justify wanting something I shouldn't want."

I close my eyes again, the weight of it pressing down on me.

"Or maybe...maybe it's not just me. Maybe You're pulling me toward her for a reason. Maybe there's something here I'm supposed to walk through, even if it scares me. Even if I don't understand it yet."

The thought settles somewhere deep, equal parts terrifying and hopeful.

"The thing is, I'm going to say yes. I already know I am. Because she asked, and I can't say no to her. Which is probably a problem. Actually, it's definitely a problem."

I absently stroke Biscuit's fur when he climbs into my lap, the motion calming.

"So I guess what I'm asking is...what do I do with this? How do I spend time with her—pretending to be her boyfriend, no less—without falling harder than I already have? How do I protect my heart when she's going to walk away the second Collin takes her back?"

The room is quiet except for Biscuit's soft breathing.

"And God, if I'm honest...I don't want her to go back to him. Collin doesn't value her. Doesn't show up. She deserves someone who actually sees her. Who thinks she's worth the effort. Who—"

I stop myself.

"Who loves her the way You love her."

That's the actual issue, isn't it?

"I want to be that person. I want to be the one who shows her what genuine love looks like. But I'm terrified that I'm not enough. That she'll always see me as the awkward guy who makes bad jokes and sets grills on fire—even though that was one time and it was an accident. That even if she doesn't go back to Collin, she'll never choose me."

My voice drops to barely a whisper.

"So I'm asking for wisdom. And strength. And maybe a miracle, because I'm going to need all three to get through this without completely wrecking myself. Help me honor You in this. Even if it costs me everything."

I sit there in the silence, waiting. Not for an audible voice—I've never heard one of those. But for that quiet sense of peace that settles when I've finally stopped trying to control everything and just surrendered it.

It doesn't come immediately.

But slowly, like dawn breaking, something shifts. Not answers. Not a clear path forward. Just...peace. It makes little sense, but somehow holds me steady anyway.

"Okay," I whisper. "I trust You. Even when I don't understand."

I open my eyes, reaching for my phone.

Time to text Gray.

I stare at my phone screen, Gray's name in my contacts staring back at me.

I should call him instead. Get this over with. Hear him say whatever it is he's going to say—probably something annoyingly wise that I don't want to hear but desperately need to.

Before I can overthink it, I hit call.

He picks up on the second ring.

"Took you long enough."

I blink. "What?"

"Dude, Ivy told me about the pantry the second you left. I've been sitting here waiting for you to call." There's a grin in his voice—I can hear it. "Actually, I told her you'd call within twenty minutes. She said thirty. I win."

"You were betting on when I'd call you?"

"We're married. We bet on everything."

I lean back in the chair, rubbing a hand over my face. "How much did Ivy tell you?"

"Enough to know something happened." His tone shifts, more serious now. "But I saw the way you two were looking at each other when you came back out. And the way Harper was definitely not paying attention to the actual Bible study portion because she kept staring at you across the fire."

My pulse quickens. "She was not."

"She absolutely was. Ivy noticed too. We had a whole silent conversation about it." He laughs. "So, are you going to tell me what she wanted, or do I have to guess?"

I blow out a breath. "She asked me to go to the gala with her."

"The gala? Her school thing?"

"Yeah."

"As her date?"

"Fake date," I clarify quickly. "To make her ex jealous."

Gray lets out a low whistle. "Oh man."

"I know."

"No, I don't think you do." He's definitely grinning now. "Micah, this is the best thing that's ever happened to you."

"How is this the best thing?" I stand up, pacing across my room. Biscuit chitters from the bed, annoyed that I've disturbed his nest. "She wants me to pretend to be her boyfriend to make her ex jealous. That's a disaster waiting to happen."

"Or," Gray counters, "it's an opportunity."

"An opportunity for what? Heartbreak?"

"An opportunity to show her what she's been missing."

I pause. "That's not what this is about."

"Isn't it, though?"

"Gray."

"Micah." His voice is steady now, the teasing gone. "Come on. You've been into this girl for how long now?"

I don't answer.

"Exactly," he continues. "And yeah, she's asking you to fake it. But dude, she asked you. Not some random guy from our friend group. Not one of her teacher friends. You."

"Because I'm convenient," I mutter, sinking back into the chair.

"Or because she trusts you."

I pause, letting that sink in.

"She's trying to win back Collin," I say finally, quieter now.

"And you're going to show her why Collin isn't worth winning back."

"That's manipulative."

"No, that's being a good friend. There's a difference." He pauses. "Look, I'm not saying go in there trying to sabotage her plan. I'm saying show up. Be yourself. Let her see what it's like to be with someone who actually values her. Who shows up."

"She doesn't want that from me."

"She doesn't know she wants it yet," Gray corrects. "But trust me, once she sees the difference between you and Collin? She's going to notice."

I lean forward, elbows on my knees. "Or she's going to go back to him the second he shows interest again, and I'm going to be the idiot who agreed to help her do it."

Gray's quiet for a moment. When he speaks again, his tone is softer. "You know what Ivy said to me after you left?"

"What?"

"She said it was the first time she's seen Harper relaxed since the breakup. And you were the reason."

My throat feels constricted. "Ivy's a romantic. She sees what she wants to see."

"Maybe. Or maybe she's right." He pauses. "Micah, I bet you've been praying about this girl for months. That you've been asking God for clarity, for direction, for some kind of sign that you're not crazy for feeling what you feel?"

"Am I that easy to read?"

"And now she's literally walked up to you and asked you to spend an entire evening with her. As her date. Fake or not, that's still a date."

"It's not a proper date—"

"Maybe this is your answer," Gray cuts in. "Maybe God's opening a door you didn't expect. And yeah, it's messy. It's complicated. But some of the best things God does in our lives are messy. Look at me and Ivy. That was a disaster at first."

"You two are married now. That's different."

"It's different because we didn't give up when it got hard. We leaned into it. We trusted God with the outcome." His voice steadies.

I close my eyes, his words sinking deeper than I want them to.

"So you think I should say yes."

"I think you're going to say yes whether I tell you to or not."

A laugh escapes before I can stop it. "You're not wrong."

"But yeah," Gray continues. "I think you should say yes. Not because it's going to be easy. Not because you're going to walk away from this unscathed. But because maybe God's putting you in her life for a reason."

I sit there for a moment, letting the weight of his words settle.

"Also, Ivy says to tell you she's already planning double dates in her head, so you better not mess this up."

"We're fake dating. There will be no double dates."

"Sure, Micah. Keep telling yourself that."

I shake my head, smiling despite everything. "I don't like you."

"Love you too, man." His tone shifts again, becoming serious. "But, real talk? Go tell Harper yes before she asks someone else."

My stomach drops. "You think she'd actually ask someone else?"

"If you take too long? Absolutely. Harper doesn't sit still. You know this," he pauses. "And Micah?"

"Yeah?"

"Pray about it. But also trust that maybe God's already been answering your prayers. You just didn't expect the answer to come in a pantry."

I huff out a quiet laugh. "Yeah. Maybe."

"Call me tomorrow. Let me know how it goes."

"Thanks, man."

"Anytime."

The line clicks off, and I sit there in the quiet for a moment, phone still in my hand.

Gray's right.

I've been praying for clarity. For direction. For some kind of sign that I'm not completely off-base with these feelings.

And Harper literally walked up to me tonight and asked me to spend an entire evening with her.

Maybe that is my answer.

Chapter 4
Micah

New Chapter Church on a Thursday has its own particular rhythm. Quieter than Sunday but never quite still, more like a house between meals than an empty one. I've learned over the years that children's ministry runs on two things in roughly equal measure: good logistics and stubborn love. The logistics I handle on a spreadsheet. The love shows up on its own, which is the part that still gets me after all this time.

By lunchtime, I am in back-to-back conversations, then running an errand, then back at my desk working through the tasks that require just enough concentration to keep my hands busy.

I am thankful it is busy enough to distract me.

Most of the morning, anyway.

My phone rings at half past noon, and I already know before I look at it that it's my mother. Sandra Sanders has always had a God-given sixth sense when one of her children is overthinking something. With four of us to keep track of, she's had a lot of practice.

"You sound distracted," she says before I've finished saying hello.

"I'm fine, Mom."

"That is exactly what you said when you were fourteen and trying to hide that you'd backed the car into the mailbox."

I lean back in my office chair. "The mailbox was already leaning."

"Micah Allen Sanders."

"Structurally compromised before I got there," I say. "I maintain that."

She laughs, which is the intended effect, and then she waits. My mother has always known the best way to get one of us to talk is simply to stop filling the space. It's a technique I've borrowed more times than I've credited her for.

"There is something on my mind," I finally say.

"Is it a girl?"

The pause lasts exactly long enough to be incriminating.

She makes a sound that lands somewhere between delight and victory, and in the background I can hear the familiar noise of my parents' kitchen—someone talking over the television, something on the stove, at least two separate conversations happening simultaneously. I am the third of four, raised in a house where silence was a scheduling conflict and the front door was functionally always unlocked. My parents built something large and warm and slightly overwhelming, and all four of us turned out, in different ways, to love people loudly because of it.

"Tell me," she says.

"There's not much to tell yet." I give her the careful version—a friend who needs help, an event, a question I'm still sitting with. I leave out the pantry and focus on the practical question of whether helping someone is wisdom or just a dream dressed up nicely.

She goes quiet for a bit after I'm done talking, and that means she's genuinely thinking things over, not just gathering her thoughts to answer.

"Wait," she says slowly. "Is this Harper?"

I say nothing.

"Micah. Is this the Harper you've been talking about for two years?"

"I haven't been—"

"The kindergarten teacher."

"Mom."

"I'm adding this to my Sunday school prayer group."

"Please do not do that."

"Honey, those women are powerful intercessors—"

"Those women will start texting me," I say. "Once you tell them, the next thing I know I'm getting prayer emojis from Miss Carol at seven in the morning."

She dissolves into laughter, and I wait it out, rubbing the bridge of my nose.

"Fine, I'll keep it between me and the Lord. For now." A pause that I do not trust. "Have you talked to your accountability group about this?"

I sigh, long and resigned. "I meet with them tonight, actually."

"Good." Her voice carries the deep satisfaction of a woman who has just learned everything is going according to plan. "Then you have people who will tell you the truth, and I don't have to worry."

"You were never going to stop worrying."

"That's true," she agrees cheerfully. "But now I can worry with less urgency."

I can't help but laugh.

"Micah." Her voice softens into the register she uses when she means something. "Just lead with kindness. Whatever this turns into, whatever it doesn't. Just lead with that."

I stay at my desk for a while after we hang up, turning that over quietly. It is so simple it almost feels insufficient. But my mother has built four reasonably functioning people on that principle alone, so I figure she knows something I am still learning.

My hand taps the steering wheel to a rhythm that has nothing to do with the song on the radio.

We meet every other Thursday, the seven of us, in the back corner booth that Rosie's Diner holds for us without being asked anymore because we have been coming long enough that Linda, the Thursday night manager, just puts the reserved sign out automatically. Three older men and four younger ones gathered around terrible coffee and honesty that most people spend their whole lives avoiding.

It was Pastor David, the missions pastor, who initiated it, and he has the distinctive trait of a man who has weathered life's trials and emerged with gentleness rather than bitterness—a quality I hope to cultivate in thirty years. The others bring their own versions of that. Between the seven of us there is more accumulated wisdom than I sometimes know what to do with, and also enough combined stubbornness that none of us lets anyone get away with performing fine when they are not actually fine.

It is the most important two hours of my week, and I

have been looking forward to tonight and dreading it in equal measure.

Because tonight I am going to say something out loud that I have never willingly admitted to another person.

I have been falling for Harper Mitchell for nearly two years.

Not the version I could pass off as a casual observation or a vague awareness. The real version.

Her red hair is the first thing anyone notices, and it suits her in a way that feels almost intentional, like God matched the outside to the inside and knew exactly what He was doing. The freckles across her nose are the second thing, if you're paying attention. She is sharp and has a comeback for nearly everything, and her default setting in my presence has always been somewhere between mildly combative and genuinely entertaining, which I have come to understand is actually one of her higher forms of comfort.

She does not bicker with people she does not trust. I figured that out about six months in and filed it away.

But underneath all of that fire is someone who stays late to label things on Sunday's after church, who sits on the floor with a crying kid without being asked, who shows up for the people she loves in ways she never once announces or takes credit for. She is beautiful in a way that catches you off guard because she is so busy being everything else that it almost sneaks up on you.

That version. The one that has been growing slowly and stubbornly through every Sunday hallway conversation and group chat argument and moment where she did something quietly generous when she thought nobody was paying attention. I have been carrying this with a lid on it for a long time, and tonight I am going to take the lid off in front of six men who will not let me put it back on without actually dealing with it first.

Some of them know who she is. She has volunteered in the kids' wing, served at enough church events, been enough of a fixture in the New Chapter orbit that her name is not unfamiliar. Which means when I say it, a few of them will already have a picture in their minds, and the conversation will be real from the first sentence.

I pull into the diner parking lot and sit in the truck for a moment with the engine running.

Once I say this out loud, I cannot take it back.

Not to these men. They will ask questions and pray hard and tell me the truth even when it is inconvenient, and I will leave tonight knowing more clearly which direction I am supposed to walk than I do right now.

That is exactly what I need.

The diner filled up around us as soon as the seven of us settled into the corner booth and placed our orders. The four of us on the younger end of the table are still finishing the catching-up that happens in the first ten minutes, the easy back-and-forth about the week, about work, about nothing in particular.

Then David sets down his mug.

It is a minor gesture, almost imperceptible, but the table knows it. It means we are starting.

We go around the way we always do, each man recounting where he is this week. Not a performance, not a highlight reel. Just the truth.

I listen to all of it. I contribute where I can. And when the table lands back on me with the patient collective attention that these men have perfected over years of doing this together, I put both forearms on the table and say the thing I drove across town to say.

"I have something I need to admit."

Nobody rushes me. That is one thing I have learned to trust about this room.

"There is a woman; I have known her for almost two years. She attends New Chapter, volunteers in the kids' wing sometimes, which means some of you know who I'm talking about." A beat. "Her name is Harper."

David nods once, slowly. Across the table, James leans back in his chair and folds his hands, and waits.

"It has not been a single moment, just two years of small ones stacking up, and somewhere in the middle of all of them I realized that I had stopped thinking of her as just a friend and started thinking of her as someone I wanted to know more deeply than I currently do." I pause. "I have told no one the full version of this until tonight."

"Why tonight?" Robert asks. His voice is quiet and unhurried, the voice of a man who has heard a lot of confessions and treated all of them with the same steady care.

"Because something happened that is forcing me to stop carrying it privately and actually figure out what I believe about it." I wrap both hands around my mug. "She asked me to be her fake date."

The table is quiet for exactly two seconds.

"Tell us what that means," David says.

So I do. I give them the version with all the relevant details and tell them I already said yes.

"I should have come to you all first," I say. "I'm sorry

that I didn't. But I've already committed, and I don't intend to go back on it."

The table sits with that for a moment. Food arrives, and nobody rushes to fill the silence.

It is Scott who speaks first, cutting his food with the unhurried ease of a man who knows he does not need to compete for airtime. "Let me ask you something. When you said yes to her, were you saying yes to the favor or to the feelings?"

I consider that honestly. "Both."

James leans forward. "And does she know?"

"No."

"Does she have any indications?"

"If she does," I say, "she has worked very hard not to show it."

A small sound from Robert that might be a laugh. He covers it with his coffee.

"What you are doing for this woman is a genuinely kind thing. She asked for a friend to show up for her in a hard moment, and you said yes. This is not complicated. That is just good," David says, setting his fork down and giving me the kind of direct eye contact that has never once failed to make me sit up slightly straighter. "The part that becomes complicated is what happens after."

"One evening is a gift," Scott says. "You show up, you be her friend, you do not make it about your feelings."

"But if it goes beyond one evening, if this fake arrangement turns into something that feels real on either side of it, then you owe her a direct, honest conversation about where you actually stand." James holds my gaze. "You cannot keep saying yes to being near her without eventually telling her why you keep saying yes. That is not fair to her, and it is not fair to you."

"And it is not honoring to God," Robert adds quietly, not as a rebuke but as a reminder. "You are a man who knows how to lead with integrity. Lead with it here too."

I nod, turning all of it over slowly.

"One more thing," David says, and his voice shifts into the gentler register he reserves for the things that matter most. "You have been carrying this for two years. That is a long time to hold something without bringing it to God fully and openly and asking Him what to do with it." He tilts his head. "Have you done that?"

The question lands the way the true ones always do, quietly and right in the center.

"Not the way I should have," I admit.

"Then that is where this starts. Before the gala, before the coffee tomorrow, before any of the rest of it. You take this to God, and you hold it open-handed and you ask Him what He wants to do with it." A pause. "Can you do that?"

"Yes," I say.

"Good," he picks up his fork again. "Then we'll pray over it before we leave tonight, and you'll come back and tell us how it goes."

Laughter moves around the table, easy and real, and something in my chest loosens in a way it has not all day. I lean back in the booth and let it settle, grateful for the particular gift of being known by people who will not let you get away with being less than honest, and who will pray over your mess without once making you feel smaller for having brought it.

Chapter 5
Harper

My alarm goes off at six forty-five, and I silence it with the particular efficiency of someone who has been doing this for years, which is the only efficient thing that happens for the next forty minutes.

I am sitting on the edge of my bed in yesterday's oversized t-shirt, one sock on, watching a TikTok about a woman who turned her garage into a reading nook, when my thumb slows on the scroll.

The next video is a girl, probably my age, sitting in soft morning light with her Bible open on her lap. She looks unhurried in a way that feels almost aspirational.

I watch it twice without meaning to.

I wish that could be me.

But I'm always in a hurry.

Then my phone buzzes with a notification from my Bible app.

Don't break your streak, Harper!

The little flame icon pulses at me with the cheerful

urgency of something that knows me better than I'd like to admit.

"Oh—" I sit up. "I almost forgot."

I tap the app open. Twenty-six days. The flame is orange and proud, and I feel a small, genuine satisfaction at the number.

I navigate to the daily devotional tab, and the short video auto-plays, a calm voice reading the daily Bible verse and a short context behind it. *Be still and know that I am God.*

A quick thirty-second video. My daily dose of Jesus.

There is a longer reading below the video. Its multiple paragraphs, a reflection, and a prayer prompt. I scroll past all of it with my thumb, scanning the text quickly.

I should read it. I want to read it, actually, which is a surprising thing to notice at six fifty-two in the morning. I want to close TikTok and open my actual Bible and sit with this for a few minutes. How the girl in the video looked as she was sitting with it.

Later, I tell myself. I'll do it properly later, when I have time to actually focus.

I press the green check mark at the bottom of the screen.

Twenty-seven days.

I set my phone down with the satisfied feeling of a completed task and immediately forget what I was doing before it.

I need to get ready for work.

I make it to the bathroom, apply foundation, get distracted by a dry patch near my chin that sends me to the cabinet under the sink looking for the good moisturizer, which is not under the sink, which means I spend three minutes looking for it before finding it on my nightstand where I left it two days ago. I go back to the bathroom. Start on mascara. Run out to the kitchen because I just remembered I never made my lunch.

The kitchen is only slightly better than the bathroom situation. I get out the bread, the turkey, the mustard. I make the sandwich, set it on the counter, open the fridge to get the cheese, and notice the leftover pasta from Tuesday that I keep meaning to finish. I should really eat that tonight, or it will go bad. I make a mental note. The cheese is behind the pasta. I get the cheese. I put it on the sandwich.

I should finish unloading the dishwasher from last night while I'm in here. I open it and start pulling out the bottom rack—plates, bowls, the big pasta pot—and I get about halfway through before my brain registers that I still have no mascara on one eye.

I abandon the dishwasher and go back to the bathroom.

Mascara. Blush. The earrings I set out last night because past-me was optimistic about morning-me's ability to function. Lip gloss. I look at myself in the mirror and decide I look like a kindergarten teacher who has it mostly together, which is accurate.

I grab my bag, my keys, my coffee thermos, and I am almost to the door when something stops me.

A feeling, specific and nagging. The kind my body sends when my brain has dropped something important.

I stand in the doorway and mentally retrace my steps.

Lunch.

I left the sandwich on the counter.

I walk back to the kitchen, and there it is, half-assembled next to the mustard and the cheese I never put away, sitting in front of the refrigerator that is standing wide open and has been for approximately fifteen minutes.

"Harper," I say to myself, in the voice I use for my

kindergartners when they try to walk out without their backpacks.

I finish the sandwich in forty-five seconds, wrap it, put it in my bag, put away the mustard and the cheese, and close the refrigerator. I close the dishwasher too, still half-full, because it will have to wait until tonight.

I'm out the door by seven twenty-three, which is fine. I can make it.

The smell of Elmer's glue and crayons hits me the second I step into my classroom—a scent I associate with both chaos and comfort in equal measure.

A verse flickers through my mind, the one I read during my thirty-second devotional this morning before my coffee finished brewing.

Standing here now, in the quiet before the chaos, it nudges at me again.

Be still.

I should probably get better at that.

I set my oversized teacher tote on my desk and bow my head for half a second, a quick, almost reflexive gesture. *God, please let today be a good day.*

And then I'm already mentally running through the day's lesson plan. Letter recognition. Counting to twenty. A craft project involving glue sticks, which is always a gamble in a kindergarten classroom.

My phone buzzes, and I dig through my tote bag, finally finding it buried at the bottom. It's the group chat.

IVY

Have you heard from Micah yet?

I stare at the message, then type back quickly.

HARPER

If he says no, does that mean my end of the dare is complete?

OLIVIA

He said no??

HARPER

He hasn't said anything. He probably forgot.

IVY

I promise. He did not forget.

HARPER

Then why hasn't he reached out?

OLIVIA

Just text him. It's not that hard.

IVY

Ya, I'm sure he's doing this on purpose to freak you out.

I shove my phone into my desk drawer before they can push further.

The morning flies by in a blur of sight words, snack time negotiations, and a minor crisis involving a glue stick and someone's hair. By the time the lunch bell rings and I've walked my kids to the cafeteria, I'm already mentally drained.

I'm heading back toward my classroom when I see him.

Collin.

He's coming down the hallway from the opposite direction, tablet in hand, with that focused expression he gets when he's problem-solving. His tie is a bit loose—navy blue with thin gray stripes—and his sleeves are rolled up to his elbows, as if he's been busy dealing with problems all morning.

Which, knowing him, he probably has been.

He glances up and sees me, and his expression softens, just slightly. "Hey Harper."

"Hey." I stop a few feet away, clutching my water bottle like it's a lifeline. "Busy morning?"

"Always." He exhales, running a hand through his hair. "Had back-to-back parent meetings, then a discipline issue in the fourth-grade hallway. You know how it is."

I do know. That's the thing about Collin—he cares. Maybe too much. He's the type of assistant principal who remembers students' names, checks in on struggling teachers, and stays late to make sure every detail is handled. He's good at his job. Really good.

It's the reason I fell for him in the first place.

"Sounds rough," I say, and I mean it.

He shrugs, but there's a weariness in his eyes. "It's the job. Someone's gotta do it."

There's a beat of silence—not awkward, exactly, but weighted with all the things we're not saying.

"Well," I say finally, "don't work too hard."

His mouth quirks into a small smile. "I could say the same to you."

"Kindergarteners *are* exhausting."

"I don't doubt it." He glances at his tablet, then back at me. "Hey, I've been meaning to ask—how's everything going? With... life?"

The question catches me off guard.

"Good," I blurt out. "Superb, actually."

"Yeah?" There's something in his tone—curiosity, maybe? Or is that hope?

"Yeah." I force a smile. "I've been keeping busy. You know me."

He nods slowly, like he's processing something. "That's good. I'm... I'm glad."

His phone buzzes, killing the moment like it has so many other times in the past. He glances at the screen and sighs. "I gotta take this. Superintendent's office."

"Of course." I step aside, giving him space.

He walks past, then pauses. "It was good seeing you, Harper."

"You too."

I watch him disappear around the corner, phone already pressed to his ear, and I let myself smile.

Because that? That felt like progress.

He asked how I was. He said he was glad I'm doing well. Those aren't the words of someone who's completely moved on.

I pull out my phone and text the group chat again.

HARPER

Just ran into Collin. I think he still cares.

IVY

Harper...

HARPER

Don't "Harper" me. I know what I'm doing.

I shove my phone back into my pocket, that familiar spark of determination flaring in my chest.

This is going to work.

It has to.

By the time I'm driving home that afternoon, the March sun is already dipping low, casting everything in shades of orange and pink. I crank up the heat in my car—because an unexpected cold front came in—and tap Micah's name on my CarPlay before I can overthink it.

It rings once. Twice.

Then, "Yeah?"

His voice is strained. Breathless.

I frown. "Uh, are you okay?"

There's a grunt on the other end. "Yeah. Why?"

"You sound like you're dying."

"I'm..." Another grunt. "working out."

I blink. "Wait. You work out?"

There's a pause. Then, in the most offended tone I've ever heard from him, "Why do you sound so surprised?"

"I don't know." I can't help the grin spreading across my face. "I just didn't picture you as a gym guy."

"What did you picture me as?"

"Someone who listens to podcasts about time management."

He huffs out what might be a laugh. "I can do both, Harper."

"Multitasking. Impressive."

"Did you call just to insult me, or—"

"I wanted to see if you've made up your mind," I say, cutting to it. "About being my date to the gala. Because if it's a no, I need to find an alternative."

A pause. The clank of weights. "Do you have a backup in mind?"

"Well, yeah. Duh. An entire list."

"You do not have a list."

"Yeah huh."

"Harper." His voice drops into that low, unbothered register that makes me want to argue with him on principle. "You know Jesus knows when you're lying."

"Then I'll repent later." I wave a hand at the windshield even though he cannot see me. "Anyway. Seriously, Micah. Yes or no."

Silence. Then another grunt, and a noise that sounds like he's setting down equipment, and then the ambient gym sounds fade slightly, like he's stepped outside. A door closing. Quieter now.

"I guess I can do it."

I sit up straight. "Really?"

"But I have some terms and conditions."

I settle back into my seat. "Of course you do. When can we go over them?"

"Can you do lunch after church on Sunday?"

"I'm serving at nine-thirty and eleven."

A pause that feels pointed. "I didn't approve that."

"I don't need your approval."

"Harper." There's something in the way he says my name when he means business, careful and direct, that makes me pay attention even when I don't want to. "You're serving both services again?"

"Someone has to."

"Someone does," he says, "but it doesn't have to be you every single week. When's the last time you actually sat in a service?"

I open my mouth. Close it. The honest answer is that I

genuinely cannot remember, and I am not about to tell him that.

"I know enough," I say instead.

"That's not what I asked."

"Micah."

"I'm serious. There's a difference between serving the church and being fed by it. You can't keep pouring out if you're never sitting down long enough to—"

"Can we please focus on the gala?" My voice comes out sharper than I intend. I soften it slightly. "I appreciate the pastoral concern. Truly. But I know my faith and I know where I stand with God, and right now what I need is for you to tell me your terms and conditions so we can get this settled."

He is quiet for a moment. Not the sharp, silent kind. The kind that means he heard me, filed it away, and has decided this is not the hill he wants to die on today.

"First service ends at ten forty-five," he says finally. "I can do lunch after that if you want to meet me there."

"Fine," I say.

I can hear him breathing—still a little heavy from the workout. My brain unhelpfully produces an image of him outside the gym, t-shirt probably damp, running a hand through that already-unreasonable hair. I shove the thought sideways immediately.

Absolutely not.

"So Sunday," I say, snapping myself back. "Lunch after the first service."

"I'll text you where."

"I'll text you where," I correct. "You're the one doing me a favor. The least you can do is let me pick the restaurant."

"Fine."

"Fine," I pause. "Was that so hard?"

"Incredibly."

I grin despite myself. "See you Sunday, Sanders."

I hang up before he can get the last word, the only way to reliably end a conversation with Micah, and I'm still smiling as I pull into my apartment complex.

I drop my bag by the door, kick off my shoes, and collapse onto the couch.

The remote is exactly where I left it—wedged between two throw pillows—and I grab it without thinking, flipping on the TV.

The screen lights up with the familiar intro to *The Bachelor*.

I should turn it off.

I know I should.

This show is... well, it's not exactly spiritually edifying. It's dramatic and shallow and promotes a version of love that's about as real as the rose ceremonies. Ivy's mentioned more than once that she doesn't watch it anymore—says it messes with her perspective on relationships.

And she's probably right.

But I don't turn it off.

Instead, I pull a blanket over my legs and settle in, letting the drama wash over me. Two women fighting over the same guy. Someone crying in a confessional. The lead looking tortured as he hands out roses like they're life-or-death decisions.

It's ridiculous.

And I can't look away.

Halfway through the episode, my eyes drift to the coffee table.

My Bible is sitting there—right where I left it after church on Sunday. The leather cover catches the light from the TV, and I feel that familiar tug.

One that says: *you should read it.*

The one that whispers: *when's the last time you actually opened it?*

I stare at it for a long moment.

Then I look back at the TV.

The contestant on screen is sobbing now, mascara running down her face as she talks about how she's '*never felt this way before*' and how the lead is '*everything she's ever wanted*'.

I should turn it off.

I should pick up my Bible instead. Spend time in the Word. Pray. Do literally anything that doesn't involve watching strangers make out on national television.

But I don't.

Because it's easier this way.

Easier to zone out. Easier to let the noise fill the silence. Easier to avoid the uncomfortable questions that always seem to surface when I actually sit still long enough to listen.

The Bible stays on the coffee table.

The show keeps playing.

And somewhere deep down, beneath all the noise and distraction, I feel it—conviction.

The kind that's easy to ignore if you try hard enough.

So I do.

I ignore it.

Chapter 6
Harper

Saturday is the one day that belongs entirely to me, and I protect it with the energy of someone who has earned it.

I have a system. I have always had a system. The week is for my students—twenty-three kindergartners who need everything I have and several things I don't. Sunday is for church, which takes up the entire morning and most of the afternoon once you factor in setup and teardown. Sunday evenings I give myself permission to do absolutely nothing, which I have decided counts as observing the Sabbath.

But Saturday. Saturday is mine.

I wake up at eight-fifteen, which feels luxurious, and by eight-thirty I am sitting cross-legged on my bed with my coffee and my phone and my Saturday list pulled up in the notes app, because there is something deeply satisfying about a list with checkboxes and I refuse to apologize for it.

The list reads, in order of priority:

> *Clean bathroom.*
> *Change sheets.*

Laundry – fold, put away.
Grocery run.
Meal prep for the week.
Call mom back.
Wipe down kitchen counters.
Vacuum.
Water the plants.
Find the source of the weird smell in the hall closet.

I look at the list. I feel the particular pleasure of having written it. Then I open TikTok for twenty minutes before I start.

By nine-fifteen, I am in full motion. There is a version of being busy that feels genuinely good, productive, and purposeful, and satisfying in a way that not much else replicates. I am that version of busy right now. I strip the sheets and start the laundry and put on the podcast while I clean the bathroom, because if I am going to scrub a toilet, I am at least going to be enriched while I do it.

The podcast is called *Unbothered* and the host is a woman named Jenna who has the type of organized, intentional life that I find both aspirational and mildly stressful. Today's episode is called "*How to Protect Your Energy Like a CEO.*" Jenna has a morning routine that starts at five-fifteen and includes a cold plunge, which I respect in theory but will never do in practice.

"*The most successful women I know,*" Jenna says, while I scrub the grout with a toothbrush I designated for exactly this purpose, "*have learned that nobody is coming to save you. You are your own answer. Be your own foundation.*"

I nod along, rinsing the toothbrush.

"*You don't wait for rest,*" Jenna continues, her voice bright and certain. "*You don't wait to be poured into. You generate your own energy. You fill your own cup.*"

"Yes," I say out loud, to nobody. "Exactly."

"*Every yes to something is a no to something else. So the question I want you to sit with today is this—what are you saying yes to? What are you building? Because a life worth living doesn't happen to you. You happen to it.*"

I pause for half a second, toothbrush hovering over the grout.

The verse from yesterday morning flickers at the edges of my brain uninvited. Be still and know that I am God. Which is a beautiful sentiment, I think, but Jenna makes a compelling point about the cup.

Then I keep scrubbing.

Staying focused would have prevented the grocery store from taking fifty minutes. The store's layout, which forces a walk past the candle display to get to the produce section, made this easier.

I have a list. I always have a list. My notes app displays the list, organized by section. My numerous grocery store experiences have taught me that to survive one with

ADHD, you must enter with a plan and execute it with military discipline.

I execute it with something closer to enthusiastic chaos.

The produce section is fine. The dairy section is fine. I am moving well; I am focused; I am a woman with a list and a purpose, and then I turn the corner toward the pantry aisle and there is the seasonal display, which has apparently been restocked since last week and now features a candle called Sunday Morning that smells like vanilla and cedar and something warm I cannot name.

I pick it up to look at the label.

Eleven minutes later I set it back down, because I already have four candles at home, which I think about for approximately three seconds before putting it back in my cart, because five candles is also a reasonable number of candles and I deserve something nice.

I found everything on my list except the eggs, which were on the list, and somehow I walked directly past twice before ending up at the self-checkout without them.

I go back for the eggs.

I also come back with a bag of the chocolate-covered almonds that were on an end-cap between the eggs and the checkout, which were not on the list but which I have now added to the list retroactively so I can check them off.

The second podcast episode starts while I'm putting groceries away. This one is called "*Stop Playing Small: Unlocking Your Full Potential,*" and the host spent the first ten minutes talking about a vision board she made in January that has already manifested three of its seven goals, which I find genuinely impressive even though I have complicated feelings about the word manifest.

I switch to a playlist while I meal prep. Something

upbeat. Something that keeps my hands moving and my brain just occupied enough to stay in the kitchen.

The laundry gets switched. The counters get wiped. I find the source of the weird hall closet smell, which turns out to be a forgotten bag of potatoes beginning their journey toward becoming something else entirely, and I deal with it with the grim efficiency of a woman who has made this exact mistake before and will almost certainly make it again.

By eleven-thirty, I have checked off nine things.

I feel fantastic.

Ivy is already at a booth when I arrive at Si Señor just after noon, with Olivia sliding in across from her a minute behind me. The restaurant is busy the way it always is on a Saturday, warm and a little loud. The smell of sizzling fajitas hits me and I decide immediately that I made the right lunch choice.

We order without looking at the menus because we have been coming here long enough that the menus are mostly ceremonial. We share a bowl of queso. Olivia gets the chicken enchiladas. Ivy gets the tacos, which she has ordered every single time, and I get the burrito bowl.

"We need to talk about the girls' trip," Olivia says, wrapping both hands around her water glass with the expression of a woman about to deliver a verdict.

Ivy makes a face. "I know."

I look between them. "That's the thing. We always go in the spring."

"I know," Ivy says again. "But Gray's got the worship

conference in April and I told him I'd go with him, and May is already looking—"

"What about June?" Olivia asks.

"School doesn't let out until the second week," I say. "And then I usually do the summer reading program the last two weeks."

We are all quiet for a moment, looking at our drinks, silently acknowledging that we are the kind of busy that has started to eat the things we said we'd never let it eat.

"This is how it starts," Olivia says eventually, in the voice she uses when she's making a clinical observation about something that is actually making her sad. "You reschedule the things that matter, and then one day you realize you haven't done them in three years."

"That will not happen to us," Ivy says firmly.

"July," I say. "What about the last week of July? I'm free, school's out, and if we book it now, we'll actually do it instead of just talking about doing it."

Ivy pulls out her phone. Olivia pulls out hers. We spend the next twenty minutes with calendars open, talking over each other, narrowing it down to a four-day window that works for all three of us, and by the time the food arrives we have a date locked in.

"Where are we going?" Ivy asks, picking up a taco with both hands.

"Somewhere warm," Olivia says.

"Somewhere with good food," I say.

"Somewhere that is not New Orleans," Ivy says, "because I cannot be held responsible for what happens to my marriage if Gray finds out I'm going back without him."

We laugh, and the afternoon stretches out around us the way good Saturday afternoons do, unhurried and easy, the food warm and the salsa bottomless and the conversation moving the way it only moves between people who have known each other long enough to skip the surface and go straight to the real things.

I drive home an hour later with a full stomach and a full heart and the windows down, even though it is only technically warm enough for that if you commit to it fully.

By four o'clock I have finished the list.

I stand in the middle of my living room and look at the list.

Every box checked.

I wait for the feeling that is supposed to come with that.

It doesn't quite arrive. Not fully. There's something that resembles satisfaction, thin and surface-level, the way a snack resembles a meal—enough to quiet the feeling for a moment but not enough to actually address it. I set my phone on the couch cushion beside me and try to figure out what I am waiting for.

I worked all week. I had a wonderful lunch with my people. I cleaned my home and meal prepped and protected the girls' trip, and dealt with the potato situation. I was, by any reasonable measure, productive.

I feel vaguely, inexplicably hollow.

I pick my phone back up.

The evening goes quickly, the way evenings do when you are not doing anything that requires your full attention. I scroll for a while; the feed moving under my thumb in a pleasant, frictionless blur. I switch to a game I downloaded two months ago, a word puzzle thing that I'm embarrassed by how often I open, and I play three rounds without really engaging, just going through the motions of tapping letters while the television plays something in the background that I chose and immediately stopped watching.

I check Instagram. I check it again fifteen minutes later. I open TikTok, watch four videos, close it, and open it again.

At some point I pick up the throw blanket from the end of the couch and wrap it around myself, and in the process my hand knocks my Bible off the end table where it's been sitting since Wednesday's Bible study. It lands cover-up on the rug, and I lean over and pick it up and set it back on the table.

My hand rests on it for a second.

The cover is soft and slightly worn at the corners, the good kind of worn that means it has been used and loved, which is mostly true from a few years ago when I went through a season of actually reading it regularly. There is a faint coffee ring on the back cover from sometime last fall that I keep meaning to address and haven't.

Be still and know that I am God.

The verse from yesterday morning nudges at the edges of my brain, quiet and patient, the way it has been nudging all day between the podcast episodes and the grocery run and the meal prep containers and the game and the scroll.

I could read it. I have the time. I have nothing but time right now, which is the whole point of Saturday, and the apartment is clean and the list is finished and there is no reason I could not sit here for thirty minutes with this Bible open and actually do the thing I told myself I'd do later.

My phone lights up on the cushion beside me. A notification from the game. Your daily streak is waiting!

I reach for my phone.

I'll do the Bible tomorrow. I'm at church tomorrow, anyway. That counts.

Chapter 7
Harper

I pull into the New Chapter parking lot at seven forty-eight, travel mug in one hand and my clipboard in the other.

The morning air still has that cool edge to it, and I pause for just a second outside the side entrance to the children's wing and breathe it in. This is the part I love best. Before the drop-offs, before the noise, before any of it. Just the quiet knowledge that in about an hour this hallway is going to be full of kids who have no idea how to be anything other than exactly what they are, and I get to be here for that.

I push through the door.

The hallway smells like carpet cleaner and the lingering scent of goldfish crackers, which is honestly the most comforting smell I know.

Micah is already at the check-in station when I round the corner into the main preschool area.

He is bent over the tablet at the check-in desk, scrolling through something, his glasses falling down his nose, and he pushes them back up with his pointer finger. He has his church lanyard on, and his hair is doing that thing where it looks like he ran his hand through it in the car and then forgot about it.

Not that I am looking.

I just need to verify that he has arranged the check-in tablet, which fully justifies looking in his direction for legitimate operational reasons.

He looks up when I walk in. "Morning."

"Morning." I set my clipboard down on the nearest table and start counting the crayon bins. "Tablet working?"

"Already updated the check-in list." He holds it up briefly, then sets it back down. "You're twelve minutes earlier than last week."

"I have a lot of crayons to count."

He gives me a look that is both patient and faintly amused, which is something he does constantly, and I used to despise, but now...now I have mixed feelings about it. Then he goes back to his tablet, and I go back to my crayons.

By eight forty-five, the drop-off rush has hit its stride, and the children's wing is exactly as loud as it is supposed to be. I am stationed in the preschool room, crouched at table height while seventeen three-year-olds watch me with the intensity that only tiny people and large dogs are capable of.

"Okay," I spread my hands out on the table. "Who knows what rain is?"

Every hand goes up. Three kids also stand up. One child named Beau, who has been wearing the same fire truck shirt every Sunday since September, raises both hands.

"It comes from the sky," he says with enormous authority.

"It does. It comes from the clouds." I make a loose, falling-fingers motion with both hands, and they mimic me, which is the other thing I love about this age group. They just do what you do. No self-consciousness, no second-guessing. "And a long, long time ago, the Bible tells us it rained for a really, really long time. Like, way more rain than we've ever seen."

"How long?" a girl named Clara asks. She has two braids and a very serious expression.

"Forty days and forty nights." I say.

I walk them through it the same way I walk kindergartners through their reading groups with total conviction that this is the most important information they will receive today.

Noah was warned. Noah listened. Noah built something enormous even though it probably seemed strange to the neighbors. I asked them to name animals that might have been on the Ark. We get dogs, cats, elephants, and one impassioned pitch for a dinosaur from a boy named Miles. We talk about what it means to trust in God, even when you can't see the complete picture.

I am good at this. I know I am good at this, not arrogantly, but in the same matter-of-fact way I know I am good at parallel parking and making pie crust from scratch. Some things you just know because you have put in the hours.

I grew up in the church. I know these stories the same way I know the alphabet or my multiplication tables. Noah, Moses, Jonah, Ruth. The Sermon on the Mount. The Great Commission. I have heard them all so many times that they have settled into something comfortable and familiar, like a sweater I have owned for years. Which means I do not need to sit in service and hear them again.

I am better used here, in this room, watching these kids absorb something real and good and true for the very first time. Which is arguably more important than sitting in a padded chair and taking notes.

I pass out the animal stickers for the craft and feel completely settled in this conclusion.

Somewhere between the craft and the song, I become aware that Micah has appeared in the doorway.

He does this periodically, doing his walking rounds, checking in on each room to make sure everything is running smoothly. I have watched him do it enough times that I know his pattern: he appears in the doorway, scans the room, makes a note on his clipboard if anything needs addressing, and moves on. He is not intrusive about it. He is just quiet and thorough.

He stops in the doorway of my room for approximately five seconds.

I am leading the kids through the closing song, which involves hand motions, so I do not stop. But I am aware of him standing there in my peripheral vision, arms loosely crossed, watching the room run exactly the way a room is supposed to run.

He makes another note on his clipboard.

Then he moves on.

I file this away as operationally irrelevant and go back to the hand motions.

What I do not file away, unfortunately, is the moment right before he moves on when the light from the hallway catches his profile and I think, in a way that is mostly involuntary, that Ivy was right. He is good-looking.

Not in a way I had ever thought to pay attention to before.

I am resetting the tables for second service when Jade, another volunteer, starts gathering her bag from the back corner. She is newer, probably in her mid-twenties, a genuinely warm person who always remembers your name and brings enough snacks to share. I like her.

"Okay, I'm heading out," she says, zipping up her bag. "You coming, Harper? I heard this week is a fantastic message. Something about time management, how we fill our hours." She tilts her head. "Or are you serving both hours again?"

I smile. "Oh, no, actually. I'm going to lunch."

"Oh, fun!" she brightens. "Well, be sure to watch the stream online later."

"Oh, yeah." The words are out before I have finished the thought. "Of course. I always do."

She squeezes my arm on her way past. "Have fun at lunch!"

She disappears into the hallway.

I pick up a stray crayon from the floor and set it back in its bin.

The truth is I have watched approximately one service stream in the last four months, and that was only because it was playing on Ivy's laptop when I walked into her apartment.

I tell myself I am going to watch the stream every single Sunday, and then I get home and there is laundry and a book I am three chapters into and a very insistent need to make something for dinner that takes longer than it should, and by Tuesday the idea has passed.

But it would have made Jade feel bad to say that.

I straighten the final crayon bin and tell myself the guilt sitting just beneath my sternum is just hunger.

The hallway is buzzing with people. Families, regulars, people stopping to talk to people who are stopping to talk to other people. The lobby area outside the children's wing becomes a slow-moving river of Sunday clothes and stroller traffic, and I am weaving through it toward the side exit when I nearly walk directly into Micah.

He catches himself first, stepping slightly to the right, which means I narrowly avoid full impact but still end up closer to him than intended because someone with a double stroller has just merged into the space behind me and there is nowhere to go.

"Hey," he says.

"Hi." I shift sideways to let a family pass on my left. "Ready?"

"Yeah." He glances over my head at the crowd. "I guess I'll meet you there?"

"Yep." I move toward the exit. "I'll probably beat you there."

"That is an interesting thing to be competitive about."

"I'm not competitive. I'm just stating a likely outcome."

"Those are the same thing."

Someone cuts between us going in the opposite direction, which briefly separates us by about four people. I resurface on the other side and find him still standing roughly where I left him, looking unbothered by the foot traffic.

"Okay," I say, because I am closer to the door and there is a clear path opening up. "Whoever gets there first chooses the appetizer."

He raises his eyebrows, solemn acknowledgment. "Try not to get too far ahead of me."

"No promises."

Chapter 8
Micah

The server arrives with our food, setting down Harper's turkey club and my chicken wrap with practiced efficiency. "Anything else I can get you two?"

"We're good, thanks," Harper says, already reaching for a fry.

The server walks away, and then it's just us.

Harper takes a bite of her sandwich, and I unwrap my food slowly, buying myself time.

"So," she says after swallowing, "what are your terms and conditions?"

"Right." I set down my wrap, folding my hands on the table. "I have just one."

"One? That's it?"

"Yep."

"Well...what is it?"

I hold eye contact. "No more grill jokes."

She stares at me. "That's your condition."

"The parking lot thing was an accident."

"Micah, you set asphalt on fire."

"I set a small section of asphalt on fire." I pick my wrap back up. "Anyway. That's the condition."

Harper looks at the ceiling for a moment, like she's asking God for patience. "I have spent a week wondering what your conditions were going to be, and it's the grill."

"It's important to me."

"Fine." She points at me. "Done. No more grill jokes."

"Thank you."

"You're a strange person."

"I've been told." I take a bite.

"My turn." She says, "I have some ground rules."

"Let's hear them."

She pulls out her phone, swiping to what looks like a notes app. Of course she has notes.

"Okay, first things first." She looks up at me, her expression all business now. "The gala is on March 21st. It's the North Texas Education Gala—a big fundraiser, very formal. Dinner, dancing, silent auction. The whole thing."

"Got it." I lean back slightly. "And Collin will be there."

"Yes." Something flickers across her face—determination mixed with something else I can't quite read. "He's an assistant principal at my school, so he's pretty much required to attend these things."

"And the goal is...?"

She hesitates, then lifts her chin slightly. "To make him realize what he's missing."

I nod slowly, ignoring the way my stomach twists at that. "Okay. So we need to look like a couple. A convincing couple."

"Exactly." She takes another fry, pointing it at me for emphasis. "Which means we need to figure out what we're comfortable with. Boundaries. Limits. You know."

"Right." I pick up my wrap, mostly to give my hands something to do. "So, what are you thinking?"

She scrolls through her notes. "Holding hands is fine. That's like baseline couple behavior."

"Agreed."

"Arm around the waist, shoulder, that kind of thing—also fine."

"Okay."

"Dancing." She glances up. "There will be dancing. Slow dancing. Are you okay with that?"

The image of Harper in a formal dress, my hand on her waist, swaying to music in a room full of people—yeah, I'm more than okay with that. But I can't say that.

"I can handle dancing," I say instead.

"Good." She makes a note on her phone. "Because Collin hates dancing. He always made excuses to avoid it, and I love dancing."

"Then we'll dance," I say, and something in my tone makes her look up.

Our eyes meet, and for a second, neither of us says anything.

Then she clears her throat and looks back at her phone. "Right. Okay. Um... terms of endearment?"

"What about them?"

"Do we use them? Like, do you call me *babe* or *honey*?"

I consider this, taking a bite of my wrap to buy time. "What did Collin call you?"

Her nose wrinkles slightly. "Nothing, really. Just Harper."

"Freckles."

The word comes out before I can stop it, and Harper's head snaps up.

"What?"

"Freckles," I repeat, committing to it now. "That's what I'd call you."

She blinks, clearly thrown off. "Why?"

I gesture vaguely toward her face. "Because you have them. Right here." I point to my nose and cheeks. "They're...I don't know. They're you."

Her mouth opens, then closes. "That's...that's what you'd call me?"

"If this situation wasn't fake," I clarify, feeling my neck heat. "That's what I would call you."

She stares at me for a long moment, and I can't read her expression.

Then she says quietly, "But it is fake."

"Right." I clear my throat, looking back down at my wrap. "So maybe something else. Something more...generic."

"No."

I glance up. "No?"

She picks up a fry, not meeting my eyes. "It's... it's actually kind of perfect. Different from what Collin would've done. Personal. People will believe it."

"You sure?"

"Yeah." She finally looks at me, and there's something soft in her expression. "Freckles works."

"Okay. Freckles it is."

We sit there for a moment, the weight of that decision settling between us.

Then Harper's eyes narrow slightly, and she tilts her head. "Wait. So what do I call you?"

"What?"

"If you get to call me Freckles, I should get to call you something. Make it fair."

I hadn't thought about that. "You can just call me

Micah."

"Boring." She taps her fingers on the table, studying me. "Have you ever had a girlfriend?"

"Yes, Harper, what kind of question is that?"

"Well, what did your ex call you?"

The question catches me off guard. "Uh...Micah. Just Micah."

"See? Boring." She leans forward, eyes scanning my face as if she's searching for something. "You need something good. Something that matches Freckles."

"I really don't need—"

"Four eyes," she announces, grinning.

I blink. "Excuse me?"

"What? It's accurate."

"It's also what bullies called me in middle school."

Her grin falters. "Oh. Really?"

"Really."

"Well, that's...unfortunate." She sits back, reconsidering. "Okay, fine. Not four eyes."

"Thank you."

She goes quiet for a moment, still studying me, and I'm feeling like a specimen under a microscope.

Then she smiles. "Dimples."

I freeze. "What?"

"You have them." She points to her own cheeks. "Right here. When you smile. Which, by the way, you don't do nearly enough."

I know acutely that my face is heating. "You've been watching me smile?"

Her cheeks flush. "I'm observant. It's a teacher thing."

"Uh-huh."

"So? Dimples. It's only fair. You get Freckles, I get

Dimples." She leans back in her chair, looking entirely too pleased with herself. "It's perfect, actually. Symmetrical."

I should say no. Should tell her it's unnecessary. Should point out that we're supposed to be keeping this simple.

But the way she's looking at me—like she's genuinely proud of herself for coming up with it—makes it impossible to argue.

"Fine," I say finally.

"You don't sound very enthusiastic about it, *Dimples*."

Her playful teasing, accompanied by that tiny smirk, evokes an unfamiliar reaction in me.

"It's fine," I manage.

"Just fine?"

"It works."

She grins, victorious. "Good. Then it's settled. Freckles and Dimples."

There's a beat of silence, then Harper clears her throat and looks back at her phone. "Right. Next thing on the list."

But I can still see the faint blush on her cheeks.

And I know she's thinking the same thing I am—that "Freckles" and "Dimples" doesn't feel fake at all.

She makes another note, then pauses. "Okay, next thing. This is important."

I straighten slightly. "What?"

She meets my eyes, her expression serious now. "Kissing."

Every coherent thought scatters. "What about it?"

"We're not doing it."

Oh. Right.

"Okay," I say, keeping my voice carefully neutral.

"I mean, like, on the cheek is fine. That's normal couple stuff. But nothing... you know." She waves her hand vaguely around her face. "Anything more than that is off-limits."

"Got it. No kissing."

"Because this is fake. And kissing would make it...not fake."

"Makes sense."

"Good." She nods, as if she's convinced herself as much as me. "So we agree. No kissing."

"No kissing," I repeat.

"Great."

"Perfect."

I clear my throat. "So, tell me about the gala. What's the actual plan? Besides, you know, looking like a couple."

She seems relieved by the subject change. "Okay. So the night starts with a cocktail hour—that's when people mingle, check out the silent auction items, that kind of thing. That's prime time for introducing you to people."

"Who specifically?"

"My principal, definitely. Dr. Bailey. She's great, very supportive. And probably the superintendent, if he's there. Some of my colleagues." She pauses. "And obviously Collin will see us during cocktail hour. That's when we make the first impression."

"First impression," I echo. "So we need to look..."

"Happy," she finishes. "Like we're completely into each other. Like I've totally moved on and you're the reason."

"No pressure."

She shoots me a look. "Do you want to help me or not?"

"I'm helping. I'm just clarifying expectations."

"The expectation is that you look at me like I'm the best thing that's ever happened to you."

The words hang between us, and I have to fight the urge to say, *that won't be hard.*

Instead, I take another bite of my wrap.

Harper continues, oblivious to the minor crisis

happening in my head. "After cocktail hour, there's dinner. Assigned seating, so we'll be at a table wherever they place us, most likely with people I work with. More opportunities to sell the relationship."

"Sell the relationship," I repeat. "You make it sound like a business transaction."

"It kind of is." She shrugs. "I'm trading your time and acting skills for a chance to make my ex jealous. That's a transaction."

"Wow. Romantic."

"It's not supposed to be romantic, Micah. It's supposed to be strategic."

"Right. Strategic." I lean forward slightly. "So what does strategic look like? During dinner, I mean."

She thinks for a moment, twirling a fry between her fingers. "Little touches. Like, you can put your hand on mine when we're talking. Or lean in close, like you're telling me something private. Laugh at my jokes."

"What if they're not funny?"

"They're always funny."

"Debatable."

She throws a fry at me. I catch it.

"See?" I pop it in my mouth. "Good reflexes. That'll come in handy when you inevitably throw something at me during the gala."

"I will not throw anything at you."

"You just threw a fry at me."

"That was different."

"How?"

"It was a strategic fry throw."

I laugh and she grins, clearly pleased with herself.

"Okay," I say, composing myself. "So dinner. Subtle

touches, fake laughter, general couple behavior. What else?"

"Dancing," she says. "After dinner, there's a live band. That's when we really need to turn it up."

"Turn it up how?"

"Dance close. Look at each other as if we're the only people in the room. Make it impossible for Collin to look away."

"And you think that'll work? Making him jealous?"

Her jaw tightens slightly. "It has to."

She makes another note on her phone, then looks up at me. "Okay, I think that covers the basics. Anything else you want to add?"

I should say no. I should leave it at that and let this stay simple.

But instead, I hear myself ask, "What happens after?"

She blinks. "After what?"

"After the gala. After we've successfully convinced everyone we're dating. What then?"

"Oh." She sets down her phone, suddenly very interested in her sandwich. "I don't know. I guess we just...see how it goes."

"With Collin."

"Yeah. With Collin."

I nod, ignoring the way my stomach twists. "And what if he wants you back?"

"I haven't thought that far." She pauses. "I guess I would consider taking him back."

"And us?" I change the subject.

She looks up sharply. "What about us?"

"We just...stop? Go back to how things were before?"

For a second, she doesn't answer. Just looks at me with an expression I can't quite read.

Then she says quietly, "That was always the plan, Micah."

"Right." I pick up my wrap, even though I've suddenly lost my appetite. "Just making sure we're on the same page."

"We are."

"Good."

Silence stretches between us, heavier than before.

Harper clears her throat. "So. March 21st. You'll pick me up at five?"

"I'll pick you up at five."

"And you'll wear the suit you wore to Ivy and Gray's wedding?"

"Yes."

"Good." Her lips curve into something that's definitely not innocent. "The navy one with the dark green tie? The one that actually fit your shoulders properly?"

My pulse quickens. She remembers how it fit?

"You...noticed my suit?"

"Hard not to." She shrugs, but there's a spark in her eyes now. "The way it fit when you lifted those chairs during cleanup? Pretty sure half the reception noticed."

Heat crawls up my neck. "Harper—"

"I'm just saying," she continues, leaning slightly closer, "if you're wearing that suit, we'll be fine. The green tie will match my dress perfectly."

I level her with a look. "Are you flirting or starting a fight?"

The words come out before I can stop them, and her eyes widen slightly.

Then she grins—slow and dangerous. "Maybe both."

"What does your dress look like?"

"You'll have to wait and see."

And just like that, the tension shifts.

Not gone. Just...different.

"You're going to be a nightmare at this gala, aren't you?" I say.

"Probably."

"Great. Can't wait."

"Liar. You're totally looking forward to it."

"I'm looking forward to it being over."

"Sure you are." She dips a fry into the ketchup. "Admit it, Micah. Part of you is excited."

"Part of me is terrified."

"Of what?"

Of falling harder than I already have. Of watching you walk away when this is over. Of pretending I'm fine when I'm not.

But I don't say any of that.

Instead, I say, "Of you stepping on my feet during the slow dance."

She gasps. "I'm an excellent dancer."

"We'll see."

She narrows her eyes, but she's smiling. And for just a second, sitting here in this sandwich shop with glitter in her hair and a half-eaten turkey club in front of her, I let myself believe that maybe this won't destroy me.

We finish our food; the conversation drifting to safer topics—her students, my plans for the upcoming kids' ministry event, whether the silent auction will have anything worth bidding on.

The server drops off the check, and Harper reaches for it immediately.

"I've got it," I say, pulling it toward me.

"Micah, you're doing me a huge favor. I should pay."

"You're not paying."

"It's the least I can do."

"Harper." I hold the check out of her reach. "I've got it."

She crosses her arms. "This feels like toxic masculinity."

"This is called being polite."

"It's my lunch invitation."

"And it's my decision to pay."

We stare at each other, and I can see her deciding whether to fight me on this.

Finally, she sighs. "Fine. But I'm getting the next one."

"The next one?"

"Yeah. After the gala. When we debrief."

"We're debriefing?"

"Obviously. We'll need to discuss what worked, what didn't, and how convincing we were."

I shake my head, smiling despite myself. "You really have thought of everything."

"That's what the notes are for."

"Right. The notes."

I leave cash on the table, and we both stand, gathering our things.

As we walk toward the door, Harper glances up at me. "Thanks. For doing this. I know it's weird."

"It's definitely weird."

"But you're still doing it."

"I said I would."

"I know. But still. Thank you."

"You're welcome," I whisper.

We step outside; the March air hits us immediately. Harper pulls her cardigan tighter, and I resist the urge to offer her my jacket because that feels like crossing a line we haven't established yet.

"See you Friday!" She turns toward her car. "Don't be late."

"I'm never late."

"Good," she smiles. "See you later, Micah."

"See you, Harper."

I watch her walk away, glitter still catching the light in her hair, and I pull out my phone.

One new text from Gray.

GRAY

How'd it go?

I stare at the message for a long moment.

MICAH

I have no idea what I just agreed to.

GRAY

That good, huh?

MICAH

That complicated.

GRAY

Welcome to Harper Mitchell.

I slide my phone back into my pocket and head to my truck, already replaying the entire lunch in my head.

The way she smiled. The way she threw that fry. The way she remembered my suit from the wedding.

And the realization, settling heavy in my chest, that I'm not playing dumb at all.

I know exactly what I'm doing.

I'm falling for her.

And I have no idea how to stop.

Chapter 9
Micah

My alarm goes off at five-fifteen, and I turn it off before the second pulse.

I've been waking up before it for the last three days. I'd like to blame the season—children's ministry ramps up in the spring, the programming calendar gets heavy, there's always something—but if I'm being honest, it's not the calendar keeping me up.

I reach for my Bible before I reach for my phone.

This is the third time I've done the year-in-the-Bible plan. Every time I start over, I'm a different person sitting down with the same words, and the same words land differently. Something I read at twenty-three hits a lot differently five years later. I've stopped being surprised by it and have counted on it.

I read until the room gets lighter. Biscuit shifts in his cage, rustling around with the quiet industry of an animal who has very important things to do at five-thirty in the morning, and when I close my Bible, I pray—then I lace up my shoes and go for a run.

The neighborhood is still mostly dark; the sky doing

that gray-blue thing it does right before the sun commits. I hit my usual pace, the kind where my body knows what to do and my brain gets left alone, which is the part I need.

Left alone with what, exactly, is a fair question.

Lunch had been completely fine. A sandwich place on Main, midday, a table near the window. Nothing remotely unusual about two friends setting parameters for a favor one of them is doing for the other. Harper had her notes. She'd been efficient and clear and professionally businesslike about the whole thing, which was exactly what the situation called for, and I had matched her energy because that was the right thing to do.

The problem wasn't the conversation.

The problem was that sitting across from her had been the most settled I'd felt in a while. And I hadn't expected that. I'd expected the low-grade ache I usually carry around when she's in the room. What I hadn't expected was how easy it was.

I'd driven home afterward and sat in my driveway for four minutes before going inside.

I run an extra block. Then I turn around and head home.

The Monday morning staff meeting wraps up at ten, and I stay at the table after everyone else filters out, spreading the volunteer schedule across the conference room table like it's a map I can navigate my way out of something with. March is tight. Two of my lead volunteers have a wedding the same weekend as the spring family event, my curriculum order is a week behind, and I've got three new families coming through the intake process for our mother's day out program who need to be placed in the right classrooms before they slip through the cracks.

I work through it methodically. Make the calls. Send the emails. Draft a note to a parent who had concerns last Sunday about her son's classroom transition—careful language, warm, direct. This is the part of the job that nobody outside of ministry really thinks about: the back-channel logistics that keep the whole thing from quietly falling apart, and I don't mind it. I've always been better with systems than most people expect from someone who spends his Sundays on the floor with four-year-olds.

I'm halfway through the supply order when someone knocks on the open door.

It's one of my volunteers—a college junior who's been helping in the elementary room on Sundays since September. Good kid. A little too much energy before nine a.m., but he loves the work and the kids know it, which matters more than anything else.

He leans against the doorframe with the specific posture of someone who wants to ask something but hasn't figured out how to start yet.

"You got a minute?"

I set the supply order aside. "Yeah. Sit down."

He spends about thirty seconds doing the thing young men do where they try to make the question sound smaller than it is. Then it comes out: there's a girl. They've been friends for a while. He doesn't know what to do with that. What if he says something, and it changes everything? What if she doesn't feel the same? What if he waits too long, and she moves on?

I lean back in my chair and listen until he runs out of words.

"Here's the thing," I say. "You're asking the wrong question. You're asking *what if it goes wrong*, when the question you actually need to answer is whether you're willing to keep pretending it's something smaller than it is just because that feels safer?"

He looks at me.

"You can't protect yourself into honesty," I tell him. "At some point, you have to stop managing the risk and just tell the truth. The fear doesn't go away first. You move anyway."

He nods slowly, the way people do when something lands. Thanks me. Pushes his chair back and heads out.

I look at the supply order sitting open on the table in front of me.

I let the quiet sit there for a moment.

That was an impressive speech, Micah.

After he leaves, I pull the supply order back toward me and get back to work.

It happens again on Tuesday. Different guy, different details, same essential architecture—someone who cares about a person and has built an elaborate internal structure around all the reasons he shouldn't say so. I give him a version of the same counsel, and mean every word, which is the part that makes the irony almost funny.

Almost.

By Wednesday morning, my prayer is less organized than usual.

With my Bible closed on my lap, I sit on the edge of my bed in the early darkness, staying quiet for longer than usual. I know what the right thing is. I just don't know how to do it when it's her. When the stakes are this specific.

There's no audible answer. But I've been doing this long enough to know that the absence of an answer isn't the absence of presence, and I sit there until I feel less like I'm talking to a ceiling and more like I'm being heard.

Then I get up. Feed Biscuit. Make coffee.

Two days until the gala.

I change my shirt twice before I leave for Bible study.

The first one is fine. The second one is also fine. I change back to the first one, tell myself I'm being ridiculous, and then stand in front of my closet for another ninety seconds before putting on a different one entirely. Biscuit watches this from the bed.

"Not a word," I tell him.

He blinks.

The drive over takes twelve minutes. It's Daniel's place this week—a townhouse off Legacy with decent parking and a tendency toward snack spreads that outperform the occasion. The group rotates through houses, which means the vibe shifts slightly depending on whose living room you're in, and Daniel's is comfortable and low-lit and usually smells like whatever his roommate has been baking.

I park, grab my Bible off the passenger seat, and go in.

I administer the usual greetings as I ease into the room and tell myself I'm not watching the door.

I watch the door.

Two more people walk in. Then another. Then a couple I recognize from the young adults group, and then the door doesn't open again for a while.

I do the rounds. Ask a question I don't remember asking, laugh at something in the right place. I'm fine. I'm good at this.

Then Gray walks in.

Alone.

I keep my face easy. Give it a few more minutes. I refill my water. Circle back toward the living room.

Gray's already watching me when I look up.

I hate that he clocked it that fast.

He waits, letting me come to him.

"Where's Ivy?" I ask, keeping it conversational.

He takes a sip of his drink. "Women's serving event. Her and Harper went together."

I nod. "Right."

Gray says nothing else. He just looks at me with that expression he has, the one that has been perfecting itself over the years into something that communicates '*I see exactly what's happening here*' without requiring him to say a single word out loud.

The study is good. Someone brings up a passage that sparks genuine conversation, and I'm present for it, really present, because that's what this is for. This is what Wednesday nights are for. I don't half-attend things. I don't know how.

But on the drive home, the city quiet outside my windows, I let myself sit with it.

Two days.

Two days of knowing exactly what I feel and exactly what this arrangement is and exactly how those two things do not fit together, and then Friday night, I'm going to put on a suit and pick her up and spend an entire evening at her side.

Pretending.

I merge onto the highway; the lights spreading out ahead of me.

God, I really hope You know what You're doing.

It's not a complaint. It's not even doubt. It's just honest.

And somewhere between the exit ramp and my parking lot, the same quiet that's been there all week settles back over me like it always does—not because anything has been resolved, but because I know Whose hands it's in.

That has to be enough.

For now, it's enough.

Chapter 10
Harper

It's Thursday afternoon, and my kindergarteners are finally walking in a somewhat straight line toward the cafeteria for dismissal.

I say "somewhat" because Mia is currently spinning in circles while holding Jackson's hand, and Lucas has decided that hopping on one foot is the superior method of transportation.

"Mia, feet on the ground, please," I call out, trying not to laugh.

She stops spinning long enough to give me a dizzy grin before resuming her pirouette.

By the time I've dropped them off with their parents and made it back to my classroom, I'm exhausted. But also weirdly energized.

Because tomorrow night is the gala.

Tomorrow night, I'll walk into that ballroom on Micah's arm, in my emerald dress, and show Collin exactly what he's missing.

I'm tidying up the reading corner—picking up scattered

board books and re-fluffing the bean bags—when I hear a knock on my doorframe.

"Hey, stranger."

I look up to see Anna leaning against the doorway, her arms full of construction paper and what looks like the stapler I definitely lent her three weeks ago.

"Hey!" I straighten, brushing glitter off my hands. "Is that my stapler?"

"Maybe." She grins, walking in and setting everything on my desk. "In my defense, you have the good stapler. Mine jams every five seconds."

"Uh-huh. Likely story."

She laughs, then tilts her head, studying me. "Okay, what's going on with you?"

"What do you mean?"

"You've been glowing all day. Like, genuinely smiley. And you keep checking your phone."

I feel my cheeks heat. "I am not."

"You absolutely are." She perches on the edge of my desk, eyes sparkling with curiosity. "So spill. What's happening?"

I try to play it cool, reorganizing the pencil jar that doesn't need reorganizing. "Nothing. Just... excited for the weekend."

"You're a terrible liar."

I laugh despite myself, setting down the pencil jar. "Fine. Maybe I'm in a good mood."

"Because...?" she drags out the word, clearly not letting this go.

I bite my lip, then glance toward the door to make sure no one's listening. "Okay, but you can't tell anyone."

Anna leans forward, delighted. "Oh my gosh, this is good. What is it?"

"The gala's tomorrow night."

"Right, I know. We're all going. What about it?"

I take a breath, then admit, "I have a date."

Anna's jaw actually drops. "What?! Who?!"

"His name's Micah." The name feels strange and right all at once on my tongue. "He works with kids. Super patient. Really sweet."

"Wait, wait, wait." Anna waves her hands like she's trying to catch up. "Back up. When did this happen? How long have you been seeing him?"

And here's where I should probably tell the truth—that it's fake, that we're just pretending, that this whole thing is an elaborate scheme to win back my ex.

But instead, I hear myself say, "A few weeks now."

Anna gasps. "A few weeks?! And you didn't tell me?!"

"I didn't want to jinx it." The lie comes easier than it should. "We've been taking it slow. He's... he's really great, actually."

"How did you meet?"

"Through mutual friends." That part's true, at least. "He's got this calm, steady vibe. Like, nothing rattles him. And he's got the best smile—kind of dorky but in this adorable way. With these dimples that—"

I stop myself.

Anna's grinning now, leaning forward. "Dimples? Oh, you've got it bad."

"I do not have it bad."

"You're blushing."

"I'm not—" I touch my cheeks, which are definitely warm. "It's just hot in here."

"Uh-huh. Sure." She's practically bouncing now. "This is amazing! I'm so happy for you. What does he do?"

"He runs the children's ministry at my church." Also true.

"A church guy. I love that for you."

I grin, unable to help myself. "Yeah, he's... he's pretty great."

"And he's going to the gala with you tomorrow?"

"Yep!"

Anna squeals and grabs my hands. "Harper, this is perfect. You're going to have the best time. And Collin's going to lose his mind when he sees you with someone else."

My stomach flips at that, equal parts excitement and guilt.

Before I can respond, a voice from the doorway makes us both freeze.

"Hey, Harper. Anna."

Collin.

He's standing there in his usual work attire—dress shirt, tie slightly loosened, that focused expression he always wears by the end of the day.

Anna and I both straighten, and I'm suddenly hyper-aware of how giddy we probably look—two teachers giggling in a classroom on a Thursday afternoon.

"Oh, hey, Collin!" Anna says brightly.

"Hey." He glances between us, something unreadable in his expression. "Just wanted to drop off the updated schedule for next week's assembly." He sets a flyer on my desk. "Make sure your class is ready by 9:15."

"Got it. Thanks."

There's a beat of silence.

He shifts his weight, like he wants to say something else, then just nods. "Alright. Have a good weekend."

"You too," I manage.

He turns and disappears down the hallway, his footsteps fading.

Anna waits exactly three seconds before turning to me with wide eyes. "Okay, that was awkward."

"Was it?"

"Harper. The tension in here was suffocating." She lowers her voice. "Does he know? About your date tomorrow?"

"No. Why would he?"

"I don't know. I just thought maybe..." She trails off, then shakes her head. "Never mind. Doesn't matter."

I fidget with the assembly schedule, not meeting her eyes. "Do you know if he's bringing anyone? To the gala?"

Anna pauses, considering. "I don't know, actually. I haven't heard anything." Then she grins, squeezing my shoulder. "But it doesn't matter, because you have a date."

"Right." I force a smile. "I do."

"With the dimple guy."

"With the dimple guy," I echo, and despite everything, I feel the tension in my shoulders release slightly.

Anna checks her phone. "Okay, I really need to go. But seriously—I can't wait for tomorrow!"

"Yeah, I'm so excited."

She grabs her construction paper and my stapler, waving as she heads out. "See you tomorrow night!"

Once she's gone, I sink into my desk chair, grab my phone and open the group chat with Ivy and Olivia.

HARPER

Need you both to come over no later than 3pm tomorrow to help me get ready for the gala.

Three dots appear almost immediately.

IVY

Obviously.

OLIVIA

I'll be there!

I smile, pocketing my phone.

Tomorrow night, everything changes.

I stare at the ceiling of my apartment for what feels like a very long time.

The dress is hanging on the back of my closet door, and I made the mistake of leaving the curtains open, so the emerald fabric keeps catching the light every time a car passes outside. Like it's reminding me it's there. Like it needs the attention.

I pull my blanket up and roll onto my side.

It's fine. Everything is fine. I have a plan, and the plan is solid, and tomorrow night I'm going to walk into that ballroom looking like the best decision Collin Matthews ever let walk out of his life, and he's going to feel it. He's going to see me on Micah's arm and remember exactly what he gave up, and then...

And then what?

I roll onto my other side.

This is the part I keep skating over when I run through it in my head. Because there are two versions of the story I've been telling myself, and lately they've started to feel like they are fighting for the same ending.

Version one: Collin sees me. Collin remembers. Collin

realizes he made a mistake. We talk and we find our way back to what we had before things got complicated, and I spent two months pretending I wasn't waiting for a text that wasn't coming. That version has a shape I recognize. It's familiar in a way that comfortable things are familiar, even when comfortable and good aren't exactly the same thing.

Version two is harder to look at directly.

Version two is just: *jealousy*. Making him watch. Making him feel a fraction of what I felt the night he broke up with me. Version two has nothing at the end except the satisfaction of being seen as something worth wanting, even if only for one night.

I'm not sure which version I actually believe in anymore.

I stare at the ceiling again.

The honest answer is that somewhere between planning this whole thing and sitting across from Micah at that sandwich place going over ground rules, the two versions got blurry. I wanted Collin to see me happy, and then I started running my mouth to Anna about his dimples like someone who wasn't talking about their fake boyfriend, and now I'm lying here at eleven-thirty on a Thursday night and I can't tell if I'm nervous about seeing Collin tomorrow or nervous about something else entirely.

I press the heels of my hands against my eyes.

Don't, I tell myself. *Don't make this complicated. You know what this is. You set the ground rules yourself.*

Right.

Ground rules. Professional. Platonic. Temporary.

I reach for my phone out of habit, then put it back down before I can open anything. I don't need to scroll myself into a spiral. I need to sleep.

Tomorrow I have to be *on*. Hair, makeup, the dress, the

shoes that are going to destroy my feet by nine o'clock but look incredible so they're worth it. I have to walk in like I belong there, like this is easy, like I've moved on.

I can do that.

The dress catches the light one more time.

I pull the blanket over my head.

Chapter 11
Harper

Friday morning, I wake up at 5:47 a.m.

Which is ridiculous because the gala isn't until tonight and I have literally the entire day to get ready.

But my brain doesn't care about logic.

I lie in bed for exactly four minutes, staring at the ceiling, trying to convince myself to go back to sleep.

It doesn't work.

By 6:15, I'm out of bed and stress-cleaning.

I start with the kitchen—wiping down counters that are already clean, reorganizing the spice rack even though it's fine, scrubbing the sink until it gleams.

Then I move to the living room. Vacuum the rug. Fluff the couch pillows. Rearrange the throw blankets in a way that looks effortlessly casual but actually took me ten minutes to perfect.

I'm on my third pass over the same spot on the carpet when I finally stop and realize what I'm doing.

Spiraling.

I set down the vacuum and collapse onto the couch,

staring at the emerald dress hanging on my closet door across the room.

It's beautiful. Stunning, really.

But looking at it now, all I feel is nerves.

What if this doesn't work?

What if Micah and I look awkward together?

What if Collin doesn't even care?

I close my eyes, trying to breathe through the panic.

It's going to work. It has to work.

When I open my eyes again, my gaze lands on the coffee table.

My Bible is sitting there, right where it's been for weeks now.

That familiar tug hits me—the one that whispers, *read it.*

I stare at it for a long moment.

Then I reach over and pick it up; the worn cover soft under my fingers. I flip it open to a random page—Psalms—and start reading.

"The Lord is my shepherd; I shall not want..."

The words are familiar. I've known them since I was five years old, reciting verses in Sunday school for gold star stickers. I could probably quote half of this chapter from memory.

"He makes me lie down in green pastures..."

It's spring in Texas, which means the bluebonnets will be out soon. It would be fun to get with the girls and do a mini photo shoot...

Oh, right, back to the Bible.

But what's the point?

I already know what it says. I've heard every sermon, attended every Bible study, grown up singing the songs, and checking all the boxes. Rereading it isn't going to magically make me feel better. It's not going to fix the mess I'm in or tell me what to do about my relationship crisis.

My mind wanders.

To what Collin's face will look like when he sees me. To whether Micah will actually pull this off or if the entire night will be a disaster.

I read the same verse three times and still don't absorb it.

Guilt prickles at me, but I push it away.

I close the Bible and set it back on the table, telling myself I'll try again later.

After the gala. When things calm down.

When it might actually help.

Instead, I grab my phone and pull up Spotify, scrolling until I find an upbeat playlist.

Music fills the apartment—something pop and loud and energetic—and I let it drown out the quiet.

IVY

On my way!

I glance at the clock.

2:40 p.m.

How is it already 2:40?

I've been stress-cleaning and overthinking for over eight hours.

HARPER

Hurry

I yank open the door as soon as the doorbell rings, and there she is—smiling, calm, carrying a massive tote bag that's almost as big as her.

"I came prepared," she announces, stepping inside.

I hug her immediately. "Thank goodness. I've been spiraling."

She pulls back, studying me. "I can tell. Your apartment is suspiciously clean."

I find myself laughing unintentionally. "Is it that obvious?"

"Harper, I can see vacuum lines on your carpet. You never vacuum."

"That's not true."

"When's the last time you vacuumed?"

I pause. "Okay, fine. Maybe I've been stress-cleaning."

She grins, setting her bag on the couch. "It's going to be fine. You're going to look amazing tonight."

"Promise?"

"Promise."

I exhale, some of the tension easing.

Twenty minutes later, the doorbell rings again.

Olivia. Late per usual.

I open the door to find her holding a tray of iced coffees, looking effortlessly put-together in jeans and an oversized sweater.

"Sorry I'm late," she says, stepping inside. "Traffic was—"

"You live ten minutes away," I interrupt.

She grins sheepishly. "Okay, fine. I couldn't decide what to wear."

"To help me get ready?"

"Presentation matters, Harper."

Ivy snorts from the couch.

Olivia hands out the coffees—caramel macchiato for me, iced vanilla latte for Ivy, brown sugar cinnamon latte for herself. "Okay, let's do this. Where are we starting?"

We migrate to my bedroom, and I immediately feel better with both of them here.

Ivy unpacks her bag—hair tools, face masks, nail polish in about fifteen different shades.

Olivia sets up her makeup kit on my dresser with the precision of a surgeon.

And I sit on the edge of my bed, sipping my coffee, watching them work.

"Okay," Ivy says, plugging in a curling iron. "Hair first. What are we thinking?"

"Something elegant," I say. "But not too formal. I don't want to look like I'm trying too hard."

Olivia glances over her shoulder. "You're definitely trying hard. That's the whole point."

"Okay, but I don't want it to *look* like I'm trying hard."

"Got it. Effortless effort." She turns back to her makeup kit. "The cornerstone of every great lie."

I throw a pillow at her.

She catches it without looking.

"Alright," Ivy says, gesturing to the chair in front of my vanity. "Sit. Let me work."

I sit, and she gets to work sectioning my hair.

Olivia perches on the edge of my bed, scrolling through her phone. "So. Are we more nervous about the gala or about seeing Micah in a suit?"

I meet her eyes in the mirror. "The gala. Obviously."

Ivy and Olivia exchange a look.

"What?" I demand.

"Nothing," Ivy says innocently, wrapping a section of hair around the curling iron.

"You're doing that thing again."

"What thing?"

"That thing where you two have an entire conversation without words."

Olivia grins. "We're not doing anything."

"You're absolutely doing something."

Ivy releases the curl, and it falls in a perfect ringlet. "We're just wondering if you've thought this through."

"Thought what through?"

"The Collin thing," Olivia says carefully. "Trying to win him back."

My jaw tightens. "Of course I've thought it through. That's literally the entire plan."

"Right. But..." Ivy hesitates. "Are you sure that's what you want?"

"Yes. Obviously."

"It's just—" Olivia sets down her phone. "He dumped you at a restaurant, Harp. Over dessert. That's not exactly—"

"I know where he dumped me," I cut in. "I was there."

"We know. And we love you. Which is why we're asking if maybe...you deserve better than a guy who couldn't even wait until you got home."

I twist in the chair to glare at her. "Collin was good to me. My parents loved him. He was stable and—"

"Boring," Ivy finishes gently.

"He wasn't boring."

"Harper," Olivia's voice softens. "You used to complain that he never wanted to do anything spontaneous. That he made you feel like you had to be perfect all the time."

"That's not—I never said that."

"You did. Multiple times."

Ivy gently turns my head back toward the mirror. "Stop moving or I'm going to burn you."

I huff but stay still.

For about thirty seconds.

"He wasn't perfect, okay?" I blurt out. "But at least he wanted me. At least he chose me—until he didn't."

Ivy's hands pause. "Harper. That's not—"

"And maybe if I can just show him I've changed, or that I'm doing fine without him, he'll realize he made a mistake."

"But what if he didn't?" Olivia asks quietly.

I blink. "What?"

"What if breaking up with you wasn't a mistake? What if you two just... weren't right for each other?"

My stomach twists. "We were right."

"Were you, though?" Ivy's voice is gentle but firm. "Because from where we were sitting, you seemed like you were trying really hard to be someone you're not."

"I wasn't—"

"You stopped posting on social media because he thought it was 'attention-seeking,'" Olivia says. "You started wearing more neutral colors because his mom made that comment about your 'bold choices.' You—"

"Can we please just focus on getting me ready?" I snap, louder than I mean to.

Silence.

Ivy's hands are gentle in my hair. "Okay. Yeah. Let's focus on that."

But the words hang in the air between us, heavy and uncomfortable.

Olivia nods, turning back to her makeup kit without another word.

I feel bad immediately, but I don't apologize.

Because if I apologize, I'll have to admit that maybe they're right.

And I'm not ready to do that.

An hour later, my hair is done.

Ivy's somehow created this elegant updo with loose curls framing my face, and it looks like something out of a magazine.

"Ivy, this is incredible," I breathe, turning my head to see it from different angles.

She smiles, softer now. "Remember when I used to do hair as a side gig in college? Paid for textbooks."

"Why did you stop again?"

She shrugs. "Graphic design paid better."

Olivia's moved on to makeup now, dabbing foundation on my face with a damp sponge.

"Close your eyes," she instructs.

I do, letting her work.

The room is quiet except for the soft music playing from my phone, and for a moment, it feels peaceful.

Then Ivy breaks the silence.

"Oh, I forgot to tell y'all—there's a women's brunch next Saturday at the church. It's a panel on finding purpose in your calling. I think you'd love it."

I open one eye. "Oh, that sounds great! Are you going, Liv?"

There's a pause.

Too long of a pause.

"Uh, probably not," Olivia says finally, her tone carefully casual. "I've got a thing. A work thing."

"On Saturday?" Ivy nudges.

"Client emergency. Could happen any time."

I open both eyes now, looking at Olivia in the mirror.

She's focused intently on organizing her makeup brushes, not meeting my gaze.

"You've had a lot of weekend work emergencies lately," I say carefully.

"It's the nature of the job, Harp." Her voice is tight.

"We miss you at church, Liv." Ivy says.

Olivia's jaw tenses. "I know. I'll try to make it soon."

But we all know she won't.

The air in the room shifts—heavier now, weighted with things we're not saying.

I want to push. Want to ask what's really going on. But before I can, Olivia reaches for my chin abruptly.

"Okay, tilt your head back. I need to do your eyeshadow."

And just like that, the moment's gone.

By 4:15, we're almost done.

My hair is perfect. My makeup is dewy and natural. And I'm standing in front of my full-length mirror in my pink silk robe, staring at the emerald dress hanging on the closet door.

"Alright," Ivy says, unzipping it carefully. "Moment of truth."

I step into it, and she and Olivia help me pull it up, zipping it slowly.

The fabric settles against my skin like it was made for me.

I turn toward the mirror.

And I barely recognize myself.

The dress hugs my curves perfectly, the emerald color making my red hair look like fire. The sequins catch the light, shimmering with every movement.

I look... stunning.

Ivy's eyes well up. "Harper, you're gorgeous."

Olivia whistles low. "Collin's going to regret everything."

"That's the plan," I say, but my voice sounds far away.

Because looking at myself now, I'm not thinking about Collin.

I'm thinking about Micah seeing me like this.

I shove the thought away immediately.

Stop it. This is about Collin. Focus.

"Okay," Ivy says, checking her phone. "It's 4:30. Micah will be here in half an hour."

My stomach does a full somersault.

"We should probably finish getting you ready," Olivia says, handing me a pair of earrings.

I put them on, my hands shivering.

Ivy watches me in the mirror. "Should we pray before he gets here? Over the night?"

I actually love that idea. The thought of praying with Ivy.

"Yeah," I say. "I'd like that."

But before we can, Olivia stands abruptly. "Oh, actually I need to run to my car. I think I left my phone charger."

She's out the door before either of us can respond.

Ivy and I sit in silence for a moment.

"Is she okay?" I ask quietly.

Ivy sighs, sinking onto the edge of my bed. "I don't know. She won't talk about it."

"How long has she been avoiding church?"

"Weeks. Maybe longer." Ivy looks up at me, worry etched across her face. "She's been dodging Sunday service. Bible study. Everything."

Guilt twists in my chest. "I've been so wrapped up in my own drama, I didn't even notice how bad it's gotten."

"Don't," Ivy says firmly. "She's good at hiding it. But yeah... I'm worried."

"Should we say something?"

"I've tried. She just shuts down."

I glance toward the door where Olivia disappeared. "She's struggling with something."

"I know."

"We need to help her."

"I know." Ivy stands, taking my hands. "But right now, let's focus on tonight. And we can still pray. Just us."

I nod, bowing my head.

Ivy's voice is soft but steady. "Father, thank You for this friendship. Thank You for Harper and her brave, beautiful heart—even when she's scared. I pray You'd cover her tonight. Give her peace, wisdom in every conversation, and confidence that comes from You, not from a dress or a plan or anyone's approval."

She squeezes my hands.

"I pray this night would go better than she's imagining. That You'd protect her heart and show her what she really needs—not what she thinks she wants. And God, please be with Micah too. Give him grace and patience and... just be in the middle of whatever happens tonight."

A pause.

"And Lord, we lift up Olivia. Wherever she is right now—physically, emotionally, spiritually—meet her there. We don't know what she's going through, but You do. Draw her close. Remind her she's loved. Help us to love her well, even when we don't have the right words."

Another squeeze.

"We trust You with tonight. With all of it. In Jesus' name, amen."

"Amen," I whisper.

When I open my eyes, there are tears threatening to spill, but I blink them back.

Ivy pulls me into a hug, and for just a moment, I let myself believe that maybe everything really will be okay.

Chapter 12
Micah

I've changed my shirt three times.

Which is ridiculous because it's a navy suit. The shirts are all white. There are exactly zero creative decisions to be made here.

But somehow, the first shirt felt too formal. The second one had a wrinkle I couldn't get out. And now I'm standing in front of my bathroom mirror in shirt number three, wondering if I should just give up and wear a paper bag.

Biscuit chitters from his perch on the bathroom counter, watching me with what I swear is judgment.

"Don't look at me like that," I mutter, adjusting my collar for the fourth time.

He sniffs, then scurries down and disappears into the hallway.

Even my ferret thinks I'm being ridiculous.

I stare at my reflection, trying to recognize the guy looking back at me.

Navy suit. White shirt. Tie that I wore to Ivy and Gray's wedding that apparently Harper says will match her dress perfectly. Hair that I've tried to style three different ways and finally gave up on.

I look... fine.

Not great. Not impressive. Just fine.

And somehow, I'm supposed to walk into a gala full of Dallas's education elite and convince everyone that Harper Mitchell—brilliant, beautiful, completely-out-of-my-league Harper...chose me.

God, I really hope You know what You're doing here.

I check my watch. 4:12 p.m.

Harper's expecting me at five.

Flowers. I should bring flowers.

The thought settled in my mind sometime around 2 a.m. last night when I couldn't sleep. Because showing up empty-handed to pick up your fake girlfriend for a gala feels wrong, even if the relationship isn't real.

I do the mental math quickly. Ten minutes to the florist on Main Street. Maybe another ten to pick out flowers—no, probably fifteen because I have no idea what I'm looking for and I'll definitely overthink it. Then five minutes to wait in line and pay, assuming there's not a crowd. Then another ten minutes from the florist to Harper's apartment, but it's Friday evening, so traffic could add another five or ten minutes.

I check my watch again. 4:18 now.

If I leave right now, I'll have just enough time. Forty-five minutes should cover it. But barely. And I'd rather show up five minutes early than five minutes late.

I walk back to my bedroom and catch my reflection in the mirror above my dresser.

Navy suit. White shirt. Green tie perfectly straight.

And my glasses—thick clear frames that Gray once described as "*aggressively nerdy in the best way possible.*"

I've worn glasses since middle school. They're part of my face at this point. I don't even think about them anymore.

But tonight...

I stare at my reflection, studying the guy looking back at me.

He looks like Micah. Regular, everyday Micah who runs children's ministry and makes dad jokes and color-codes his calendar.

But tonight, I need to be the version of Micah who belongs on Harper Mitchell's arm at a fancy gala. The version who doesn't look out of place next to a girl who makes heads turn.

I walk to my bathroom and grab the contacts from the drawer, then reach up and slowly take off my glasses, setting them on the counter.

I almost never wear contacts. They're annoying, and honestly, I like my glasses. But something about tonight feels different. Like I need to show up as a different version of myself.

The version that belongs on Harper's arm.

I wrestle the contacts in—blinking about seventeen times and nearly poking myself in the eye twice—and finally straighten to look in the mirror.

Different.

Definitely different.

I'm not sure if it's better, but it's something.

My phone buzzes on the counter.

GRAY

You good?

I huff out a laugh and type back.

MICAH

Define good.

GRAY

Not having a panic attack.

MICAH

Then no. Not good.

GRAY

You're going to be fine. Just be yourself.

MICAH

What if myself isn't enough?

Three dots appear, then disappear. Then appear again.

GRAY

Micah. She asked YOU. Not anyone else.
You. That means something.

I stare at the message, wanting to believe it.

MICAH

She asked me to make her ex jealous.
That's different.

GRAY

Is it though?

I don't respond.

GRAY

Look, I'm not saying this is going to be easy. But you're going to show up, be the guy you've always been, and let God handle the rest. Trust the process.

MICAH

I hate when you're right.

GRAY

Get used to it. Now go pick up your girl and stop overthinking.

MICAH

She's not my girl.

GRAY

Sure, Micah. Keep telling yourself that.

I pocket my phone, take one last look in the mirror, and start out the door.

Then I pause.

My glasses.

I turn back and grab them from the counter. The last thing I need is these contacts irritating my eyes on the drive home later. I tuck the case into my jacket pocket, just in case.

Now I'm ready.

Biscuit appears out of nowhere, weaving between my feet like he's trying to trip me.

"I'll be back later," I tell him, crouching down to scratch behind his ears. "Behave."

He chitters, which I'm choosing to interpret as agreement.

I grab my keys, check my reflection one more time in the entryway mirror, and step outside.

The March evening air is crisp; the sky already darkening into shades of purple and orange. I unlock my truck and slide into the driver's seat, gripping the steering wheel for a moment before starting the engine.

Okay, God. Here we go.

I pull out of the driveway and head toward the florist, my mind racing through every possible scenario for tonight.

What if we look awkward together?

What if I say something stupid?

What if Collin takes one look at us and knows we're faking?

What if Harper realizes halfway through the night that this was a terrible idea and bails?

I force myself to take a breath, loosening my grip on the steering wheel.

One step at a time. Just show up. Be present.

By the time I pull into Harper's apartment complex, my heart is pounding so hard I can feel it in my throat.

4:58 p.m.

I'm late.

Two minutes isn't technically late, but to me it feels like a catastrophic failure of planning.

Which is entirely the florist's fault.

Closed for a private event.

That's what the sign on the door said when I showed up at 4:30. Apparently, some wedding reception booked out the entire shop for the evening, and I stood there on the sidewalk for a solid thirty seconds just staring at the sign like it might change if I willed it hard enough.

It didn't.

So I panicked.

And when you panic on Main Street at 4:30 on a Friday evening with no backup plan, you make questionable decisions.

Like walking into the bookstore next door.

I glance at the passenger seat where a small gift bag sits, tissue paper sticking out the top.

It's not flowers.

But it's something.

I grab the bag, kill the engine, and step out of the truck, my pulse still doing something erratic.

Please let this not be weird. Please let this not be weird.

I head toward her building, the gift bag clutched in one hand like it might explode if I hold it wrong.

The elevator ride up feels like it takes approximately seventeen years.

When I finally reach her door, I stand there for a second, smoothing down my jacket, checking my breath, looking down at the gift bag and wondering if I should just leave it in the truck and pretend I didn't bring anything at all—the door swings open before I can knock.

Olivia stands there, iced coffee in hand, and her eyes widen slightly.

"Wow." She blinks. "Okay. Yeah, you clean up nice."

I feel my neck heat. "Thanks. Is Harper ready?"

"Almost. Come in."

She steps aside, and I walk into Harper's apartment.

It smells like lavender—probably whatever candle she has burning on the coffee table. The space is tidy, everything in its place, and I'm momentarily distracted by how very Harper it all is.

Colorful throw pillows. Books stacked on the side table. A half-empty coffee mug that says:

I TEACH TINY HUMANS, WHAT'S YOUR SUPERPOWER?

"She'll be out in a second," Olivia says, studying me with an expression I can't quite read.

"Okay. Yeah. No rush."

Except there's definitely a rush and I'm pretty sure I'm going to pass out if I have to stand here much longer.

Ivy appears from the hallway, smiling warmly. "Micah! You look great."

"Thanks." I shift my weight, suddenly hyperaware of how formal I feel. "You too."

She laughs. "I'm in jeans and a sweater, but I appreciate the sentiment."

Olivia leans against the wall, still watching me. "So. You ready for this?"

"As ready as I'll ever be."

"Good answer." She takes a sip of her coffee. "Because Harper's been spiraling all day, so you're going to need to be the calm one."

"Got it. Calm. I can do calm."

Ivy grins. "You look calm."

"I'm faking it."

"Aren't we all?" Olivia mutters.

Before I can respond, I hear footsteps from the hallway.

And then Harper appears.

And I forget how to breathe.

Chapter 13
Micah

She's wearing an emerald dress that fits her like it was designed specifically to destroy me.

My eyes go to her neckline. I attempt to correct course, but it's too late.

The neckline drapes low enough that I notice, high enough that I feel guilty for noticing. Thin straps. A lot of bare shoulder. A gold bracelet stacked on her wrist that she's already fidgeting with.

I look at her shoes. Strappy black heels that bring her almost level with my chin.

Her hair is swept up, soft and elegant, with loose curls escaping to frame her face in a way that makes my fingers ache to tuck them back. Her makeup is understated but flawless—just enough to highlight the green of her eyes and the shape of her lips, but not enough to hide the freckles scattered across her nose and cheeks like constellations I could spend a lifetime mapping.

And when her eyes meet mine, I swear the entire world tilts sideways.

She's breathtaking.

No—she's more than that.

She's the kind of beautiful that makes you forget how to speak. How to breathe. How to do anything except stand there like an idiot and wonder how you got lucky enough to be standing in her doorway.

"Hi," she says, a little breathless.

"Hi," I manage, though it comes out rougher than I intended.

She steps further into the room, smoothing down the dress nervously. "So. What do you think? Too much?"

Too much?

She looks like she walked out of a dream.

"No," I say, finding my voice. "You look... perfect."

Her cheeks flush, and she glances away. "Thanks. You clean up pretty nice yourself."

"Thanks."

There's a beat of silence, and I'm acutely aware of Ivy and Olivia watching us like we're a live performance.

Then Harper's eyes narrow slightly, and she tilts her head. "Wait. Where are your glasses?"

I blink. "What?"

"Your glasses." She steps closer, studying my face like she's trying to solve a puzzle. "You're not wearing them."

"Oh." I reach up automatically, like I'm going to adjust frames that aren't there. "Contacts. I thought... I don't know. Thought I'd switch it up."

She's close now. Close enough that I can smell whatever perfume she's wearing—something floral and warm that's making it hard to think straight.

Her hand lifts, almost without thought, and her fingers brush along my jaw, tilting my face down toward her.

I freeze.

Her touch is featherlight, but it sends electricity straight through me as her eyes scan my face.

"You look..." she trails off, her thumb grazing my cheekbone, and something flickers in her expression. Surprise. Maybe confusion. Maybe something else entirely that makes my heart kick against my ribs.

"Different," she finishes quietly.

Her hand drops, but the heat of her touch lingers.

I'm still trying to remember how to breathe when I manage, "I didn't realize they had such an effect on you, Harper."

Her eyes snap to mine, and her cheeks flush. "They do not."

"Clearly they do if you're asking where they are."

She opens her mouth, then closes it, then crosses her arms. "I was just making an observation."

"Uh-huh."

"It's not like I care whether you wear glasses or contacts."

"Right. You sound very indifferent."

"I am indifferent."

"You're blushing."

"I am not—" She catches herself, then narrows her eyes at me. "You're enjoying this."

I grin despite myself. "Maybe a little."

Then her gaze drops to the gift bag still clutched in my hand. "What's that?"

My stomach drops. "What's what?"

"That," she points. "The bag. Is that for me?"

"Oh. Uh. Yeah." I hold it out awkwardly. "I was going to get flowers, but the florist was closed, and I panicked, so I went to the bookstore next door, and—" I'm rambling. "It's nothing. Just... here."

She takes the bag, eyebrows raised, and pulls out the tissue paper.

Inside is a simple leather journal. Brown cover, unlined pages, nothing fancy.

She opens it, flipping through the blank pages, and I see the exact moment she reaches the inside front cover.

Where I wrote something.

In pen.

That I can't take back now.

Her eyes scan the words, and I want to disappear into the floor.

She looks up at me, blinking. "You got this for me?"

"I—yes. Maybe. I don't know." I run a hand through my hair. " I thought maybe you could use it for... I don't know, notes or something, and then I was standing in line and I had a pen and it felt weird to give you a completely blank journal so I just—" I stop myself. "I'm sorry. That was probably weird. I can get you something else—"

"Micah." Her voice is softer now, and when I finally look at her, she's smiling. "This is really sweet."

"It is?"

"Yeah." She runs her fingers over the cover. "I've been meaning to get a new journal anyway. For...studying. And stuff."

There's something in her tone—something almost vulnerable—that makes me pause.

"Are you sure it's not weird?" I ask.

"It's a little weird," she admits. "But in a good way. A very you way."

Ivy appears beside her, peeking at the journal. "What'd he write?"

Harper angles it so she can't see, her cheeks flushing slightly. "Nothing. Just... something nice."

"Let me see—"

"Nope." Harper closes the journal quickly, clutching it to her chest. "This is mine now. No looking."

Olivia leans against the wall, grinning. "He wrote something sappy, didn't he?"

"I did not write something sappy," I protest.

"You totally did," Harper says, but she's smiling. "Thank you. Really. This is... it's perfect."

Ivy clears her throat loudly, though she's smiling too. "Okay, lovebirds. You should probably get going, or you're going to be late."

Harper shoots her a glare. "We're not—"

"Yeah, yeah. Fake dating. We know." Olivia waves her hand dismissively. "Now go. Have fun. Don't do anything we wouldn't do."

Harper grabs her clutch from the coffee table, and I move toward the door.

But before we leave, Ivy catches my arm. "Take care of her," she says quietly.

"I will," I promise.

And I mean it.

The elevator ride down is quiet.

Harper's fiddling with her clutch, and I'm trying not to stare at her in the reflection of the elevator doors.

When we step outside, the cool evening air hits us, and Harper shivers slightly.

I immediately shrug off my jacket. "Here."

"Micah, you don't have to—"

"I know." I drape it over her shoulders anyway. "But I want to."

She looks up at me, and for a moment she looks almost vulnerable. "Thanks."

We walk to my truck, and I open the passenger door for her.

She pauses. "You know I can open my own door, right?"

"I know you can. But let me."

She studies me for a moment, then smiles. "Okay."

She climbs in, and I close the door behind her, taking a second to collect myself before walking around to the driver's side.

When I slide into the seat, she's adjusting the jacket around her shoulders—and then I catch it.

She leans in slightly, nose practically touching the lapel, and takes a deliberate breath.

I blink. "Did you just... smell that?"

Her head snaps up, eyes wide. "What? No."

"You absolutely just smelled my jacket."

"I did not."

"Harper."

"I was just—" she stops, her face flushing. "It's not my fault you smell good."

A laugh escapes before I can stop it. "I smell good?"

"Don't let it go to your head."

"Too late. It's already there."

She glares at me, but there's no heat behind it. "Can we just go?"

"Sure," I say, grinning like an idiot. "But for the record? You could've just asked what cologne I'm wearing."

"I wasn't—" she huffs, sinking deeper into my jacket. "Just drive, Micah."

"Whatever you say, Harper."

I start the engine and pull out of the parking lot, heading toward the hotel hosting the gala.

For the first few minutes, neither of us says anything.

Then Harper breaks the silence. "So. You ready for this?"

"Are you?"

She laughs, but it sounds nervous. "Not even a little."

"Well, that makes two of us."

She glances over at me. "Really? You seem so calm."

"I'm very good at faking calm."

Harper's quiet for a moment, then says, "Thank you. For doing this. I know it's a lot."

"It's not that much."

"Micah, you're spending your Saturday night pretending to be my boyfriend at a work event. That's definitely a lot."

I glance at her, then back at the road. "Maybe I don't mind."

She doesn't respond right away, and when I glance over again, she's looking out the window.

"Why are you doing this?" she asks quietly. "Really."

I grip the steering wheel a little tighter. "Because you asked."

"That's not a reason."

"Sure it is."

"Micah."

I take a breath. "Because I don't like the idea of you walking into that gala alone and feeling like you have to prove something to people who don't deserve it."

She turns to look at me, and I can feel the weight of her gaze.

"That's..." she pauses. "That's really sweet."

"Don't sound so surprised."

"I'm not surprised. I just..." She trails off, then shakes her head. "Never mind."

"What?"

"Nothing. Just... thank you."

We fall into silence again, but this time it feels different. Lighter, somehow.

The drive is familiar—streets I've driven a hundred times, buildings I know by heart. But tonight, everything feels different.

The hotel comes into view—a massive, glittering building in the heart of downtown, all glass and lights and elegance.

I pull up to the valet station, and a guy in a uniform steps forward immediately.

Harper's eyes widen. "Valet. Fancy."

"It's a gala. We need to go all out."

"Clearly."

I put the truck in park, and the valet opens Harper's door before I can get out.

She steps onto the curb, smoothing down her dress, and I hand the keys to the valet before walking around to meet her.

The hotel entrance is lit up with string lights and lanterns.

Harper takes a breath, slipping my jacket off and handing it to me, her hand tightening around her clutch.

"Are you okay?" I ask quietly, feeling her warmth as I slip my jacket back on.

"Yeah. Just... nervous."

"Me too."

She looks up at me, surprised. "Really?"

"Really."

For a moment, we just stand there, looking at each other.

Then I hold out my arm. "Ready?"

She loops her arm through mine, and the contact sends a jolt through me that I try very hard to ignore.

"Ready," she says, though her voice wavers slightly.

We walk toward the entrance together, the sounds of music and laughter drifting through the open doors.

And as we step inside, I send up one more prayer.

God, please let me not mess this up.

The lobby is even more extravagant than I expected.

Chandeliers hang from the ceiling, casting warm golden light over everything. There's a massive staircase leading up to the second floor, where I assume the actual gala is happening. And everywhere I look, there are people—dressed to the nines, laughing, holding champagne glasses, looking like they belong here.

Harper's grip on my arm tightens slightly.

"You good?" I murmur.

"Yeah. Just...a lot of people."

"We don't have to stay long if you don't want to."

She glances up at me. "Micah, we just got here."

"I know. I'm just saying. If it gets overwhelming, we can leave."

Something softens in her expression. "Thank you."

We make our way toward the staircase, Harper's heels clicking against the marble floor.

Halfway up, she stumbles slightly, and I catch her elbow.

"Careful."

She laughs, embarrassed. "These heels are a death trap."

"Then why wear them?"

"Because they make my legs look amazing."

I glance down automatically—and immediately understand what she means.

The dress has a slit. A high slit that reveals way more leg than I was prepared for. Smooth, pale skin that disappears under emerald silk, and I have to physically force my eyes back up because looking is not appropriate. Not even close to appropriate.

Especially not when I'm supposed to be her fake date, not some creep who can't control himself.

"Eyes up here, buddy," she teases, and there's laughter in her voice.

My face heats. "I wasn't—"

"Relax. I'm messing with you."

We begin to climb the staircase toward the ballroom.

Harper exhales slowly. "Okay. Here we go."

"Here we go," I echo.

She looks up at me, her eyes bright and nervous and determined all at once.

"Remember," she says. "We're a couple. We're falling in love. We're disgustingly happy."

"Got it. Disgustingly happy."

"And if you see Collin—"

"I know. Make him regret everything."

She grins. "Exactly."

We're almost at the top when she pauses.

"Wait."

I look down at her. "What's wrong?"

"Hold my hand, Dimples."

The nickname catches me completely off guard.

"What?"

"We're supposed to be a couple, remember? Couples hold hands." She says it matter-of-factly, but I can see the slight flush creeping up her neck. "So. Hold my hand."

"Right. Yeah. Of course."

I reach for her hand, and the moment our fingers touch, something shifts.

Her hand is smaller than mine—delicate, warm, soft in a way that catches me off guard. My palm engulfs hers easily, but when her fingers slide between mine, lacing together with a confidence that feels both natural and terrifying, it's like every nerve ending in my body wakes up at once.

Her skin is impossibly soft. I can feel her pulse fluttering against my palm, quick and unsteady, matching the erratic rhythm of my own heartbeat.

This is fake, I remind myself. *Just for show*.

But the way her hand fits against mine—like two puzzle pieces that were always meant to click together—doesn't feel fake. It feels right. Dangerously, overwhelmingly right.

She glances up at me, something unreadable flickering in her green eyes, and I wonder if she feels it too. This pull. This shift.

I squeeze her hand gently, and she squeezes back.

And I have to remind myself to breathe.

"Okay," she says, looking up at me with those bright, determined eyes. "Now we look like a couple."

You look like you belong on my arm, I think. *Like you've always belonged there.*

But I don't say that.

Instead, I squeeze her hand gently. "Ready, Freckles?"

Her breath catches—sharp and surprised, and her fingers tighten around mine. When she looks up at me, there's something in her eyes I can't quite read. Something that wasn't there a moment ago.

"You can't just—" she stops, shaking her head slightly. "That felt real."

It was real, I think.

But out loud, I force a casual shrug. "I'm just practicing this whole fake date thing, Harper. It's not real."

The lie tastes bitter on my tongue.

Her expression flickers before she nods. "Right. Of course. Just practicing."

She squares her shoulders, and just like that, the walls go back up.

"Ready?" I ask again, softer this time.

She takes a shaky breath. "Ready."

And together, hand in hand, we step into the ballroom—toward Collin, who is somewhere in this room, toward the plan, toward whatever happens next.

I just hope I survive it with my heart still intact.

Chapter 14
Harper

The ballroom is breathtaking.

Crystal chandeliers hang from the ceiling, casting warm golden light across white-linen-covered tables. Centerpieces of roses and candles create little pockets of intimacy in the massive space. A jazz band plays softly on the stage at the far end, and everywhere I look, people are laughing, drinking champagne, looking like they belong in a magazine spread.

And I'm walking into it hand-in-hand with Micah Sanders.

His palm is warm against mine, steady and grounding, and I'm hyperaware of every point of contact—his thumb brushing against my knuckles, the way his fingers lace through mine like they've done this a thousand times before.

This is fake, I remind myself. *Remember that. This is all fake.*

But it doesn't feel fake.

"Are you okay?" Micah murmurs, leaning down so only I can hear.

I glance up at him and force a smile. "Yeah. Just taking it all in."

"It's a lot."

"Understatement of the year."

He squeezes my hand gently, and we move further into the room, and I scan faces, looking for someone I know.

"Harper!"

I turn to see Dr. Bailey, my principal, making her way toward us with a warm smile. She's in her early thirties—a powerhouse in a navy gown with the presence that makes you want to be a better human just by being near her. Mariah Bailey is the kind of woman who runs a school like it's a Fortune 500 company and still remembers every student's name.

"Dr. Bailey, hi!" I let go of Micah's hand just long enough to give her a quick hug, then immediately reach for him again. "I'd like you to meet Micah. Micah, this is Dr. Mariah Bailey, my principal."

Micah extends his free hand. "It's nice to meet you, Dr. Bailey. Harper talks about you all the time."

"Oh please call me Mariah." She shakes his hand, her smile widening. "All good things, I hope."

"Only the best," he says smoothly, and I have to fight the urge to stare at him.

Since when is Micah smooth?

Mariah turns to me, eyes twinkling. "Well, Harper, you've been holding out on us. I didn't know you were seeing anyone new."

Her emphasis on the word *new* makes me nervous. Of course she knew about Collin. She had to approve our relationship disclosure form when we started dating—standard protocol when two staff members are involved. The breakup, which was all anyone whispered about in the halls the first week after it happened.

"It's still pretty new," I say quickly, feeling heat creep up my neck. "But I feel like I've known him forever! Everyone says we're rushing things, but...we like to say... umm."

I glance up at Micah, panicking slightly, praying he'll follow my lead.

He doesn't miss a beat. His expression shifts, and he looks down at me like I just said something profound. "We like to say you can't rush true love."

Oh. That's... actually fantastic.

Mariah's face lights up. "Aw, you two finish each other's sentences! That's adorable."

Micah squeezes my hand, playing the part perfectly. "Harper makes it easy."

"Well, good for you, Harper," she says, her tone genuine. "I'm glad to see you moving on. You deserve someone who makes you happy."

There's weight behind those words—an unspoken acknowledgment that Collin didn't.

"Thank you," I manage.

She glances at Micah. "What do you do, Micah?"

"I run the children's ministry at a church here in Dallas," he says. "So I guess you could say Harper and I both work with kids. Just differently."

"How wonderful." Mariah looks genuinely pleased. "It's always nice to meet someone who understands the calling."

Micah smiles, and I catch a glimpse of those dimples. "Harper's one of the best. Her kids are lucky to have her."

My cheeks heat. "He's biased."

"I'm honest," he corrects, squeezing my hand.

Mariah excuses herself to greet other guests, and I'm left standing there with Micah, trying to process what just happened.

"That went well," I say.

"She seems great."

"She is." I glance around the room again, scanning. "Okay, so far so good. We look like a couple. We're believable. This is—"

"Harper Mitchell!"

I turn to see James Flintlock, the superintendent of Dallas ISD, approaching with a broad smile. He's tall, gray-haired, and has the type of commanding presence that makes everyone stand a little straighter.

"Mr. Flintlock!" I straighten automatically. "It's so good to see you."

"Likewise. I was hoping you'd be here tonight." He shakes my hand warmly. "I wanted to personally congratulate you again on Teacher of the Year last spring. Your classroom observation was the highlight of my year."

Pride swells in my chest. "Thank you so much. That means the world."

His gaze shifts to Micah, curious. "And who's this?"

"This is Micah Sanders, my boyfriend." I loop my arm through Micah's. "Micah, this is Mr. Flintlock, our district superintendent."

Micah extends his hand. "It's an honor, sir. Harper speaks highly of your school district."

"Does she?" he chuckles. "Well, any man who can keep up with our reigning Teacher of the Year must be something special."

"I like to think so," Micah says, glancing down at me with a soft smile.

James nods approvingly. "Well, don't let me keep you two. Enjoy your evening. And Harper—keep up the excellent work."

"Thank you, sir."

He moves on, and I exhale slowly.

"Teacher of the Year?" Micah says, impressed. "You didn't mention that."

"It didn't come up."

"That's a pretty big deal, Harper."

I shrug, but I can't help smiling. "I'm good at my job."

"You're more than good."

And the way he says it—like he genuinely means it—makes something warm bloom in my chest.

I'm starting to relax. Starting to breathe normally. Starting to think that maybe this night won't be so bad after all.

And then I see him.

Collin.

He's standing near the bar, laughing at something someone said, and he looks... good. Really good. Black suit, perfectly tailored, hair styled just right.

But something else grabs my attention.

It's the girl next to him.

She's beautiful—blonde, elegant, wearing a stunning red dress. And she's draped over him like she belongs there, her hand resting possessively on his arm, her laugh bright and easy.

As I watch, she leans up and kisses him.

Not a quick peck. A real kiss. The kind that says, *mine.*

And he kisses her back.

My entire world tilts sideways.

He moved on.

He moved on fast.

Like I wasn't good enough to remember. Like six months together meant nothing. Like he could see me every single day at work and just... forget.

"Harper?"

Micah's voice sounds far away, muffled, like I'm underwater.

"Harper, are you okay?"

I force myself to look away from Collin, to focus on Micah's concerned face.

"I'm fine."

"You don't look fine."

"I'm fine," I repeat, sharper than I mean to. Then I plaster on a smile that feels like it might crack my face in half. "I just need champagne."

"Harper—"

"Champagne, Micah. Please."

He studies me for a long moment, then nods slowly. "Okay. Stay here. I'll be right back."

He heads toward the bar, and I stand there alone, trying very hard not to look at Collin again.

But I can't help it.

My gaze drifts back, and this time, the girl is laughing at something he said, her hand on his chest, and they look... comfortable.

Like I never mattered at all.

Micah returns with a champagne flute, handing it to me. "Here."

I take it and down half the glass in one go.

His eyebrows raise. "Easy."

"I'm fine."

"You keep saying that."

"Because I am."

He doesn't look convinced. He glances across the room,

following my earlier line of sight, and I watch as his expression shifts—understanding dawning.

"That's him, isn't it? Collin."

I nod, taking another sip.

"And that's...?"

"Someone he moved on with. Apparently." I drain the rest of my glass and set it down on one of the tall cocktail tables scattered around the perimeter for mingling. "Fast, too."

Micah's quiet for a moment, then says gently, "Harper, we don't have to do this. If you want to leave—"

"No," I cut him off, my voice firmer than I feel. "No, I don't want to leave."

"Are you sure?"

"Yes." I look up at him, squaring my shoulders. "I'm here. You're here. We have a plan. And I'm not letting him ruin this night. Besides—" I glance back at Collin, trying to convince myself. "We don't even really know that they're actually together. What if he's doing the same thing? Trying to make me jealous?"

Micah just nods, but I can tell he doesn't believe it for a second.

"Okay," he says carefully. "But if you change your mind—"

"I won't."

He nods slowly, then holds out his hand. "Then let's give them something to talk about."

I take his hand, lacing my fingers through his, and let him lead me further into the ballroom.

This is fine. Everything is fine.

And I'm going to make sure Collin sees exactly what he's missing.

The next hour passes in a blur of introductions and small talk.

I introduce Micah to everyone we pass—teachers, administrators, district officials. And every single time, I gush.

"This is Micah, my boyfriend. Isn't he wonderful?"

"Micah runs the entire children's ministry at his church. He's so dedicated."

"We met through mutual friends. He has the biggest heart—you should see him with kids. And his faith? Incredible. He loves Jesus more than anyone I know."

And Micah? He plays along perfectly.

He shakes hands. Smiles warmly. Asks thoughtful questions. Rests his hand on my lower back in a casual, yet possessive way.

He's good at this.

Too good.

"You're laying it on pretty thick," he murmurs during a lull in conversation.

"That's the point, isn't it?"

"I thought we were trying to prove to Collin that we're dating," he says quietly. "Not convince the entire Dallas Independent School District."

"We have to make it believable," I counter. "All these people know him. If we don't sell it to everyone, it won't work."

He considers this, then nods. "Fair point."

We're making our way toward the cocktail hour area

when I spot Anna near the appetizer table. She waves enthusiastically, and I wave back, steering Micah in her direction.

"Anna! Hey!"

She beams, setting down her plate to hug me. "Harper! Oh my gosh, you look stunning. That dress is everything."

"Thanks. You look amazing too." I gesture to Micah. "This is—"

"The boyfriend!" Anna interrupts, turning to Micah with a grin. "The one with the dimples. I've heard so much about you."

Micah's eyebrows raise slightly, and I feel my cheeks heat.

"Have you?" he says, glancing at me with amusement.

"Don't listen to her," I mutter.

"Oh, I'm definitely listening," he says, turning back to Anna. "What exactly did Harper say?"

Anna laughs. "Just that you're sweet and patient and have a great smile. Oh, and that you work with kids, which is adorable."

"Adorable," Micah repeats, smirking. "Hear that, Harper? I'm adorable."

"I never said adorable."

"You definitely implied it," Anna says, grabbing another appetizer.

Micah leans down, his breath warm against my ear. "I'm never letting you live this down, Freckles."

The nickname sends a shiver down my spine, and I have to fight to keep my composure.

"Behave, Dimples," I murmur back.

Anna's eyes widen. "Wait, Dimples? That's your nickname for him?"

"It's—" I start.

"It's perfect," Anna finishes, grinning. Then she turns to Micah. "Wait, what do you call her?"

"Freckles," Micah says, and the way he says it—soft and warm—makes my pulse skip.

Anna nearly squeals. "Oh my gosh, you two are disgustingly cute."

Before I can respond, a man approaches carrying two drinks. He's tall, dark-haired, wearing a charcoal suit that fits him well.

"Here you go, babe," he says, handing Anna one of the glasses.

Anna lights up. "Perfect timing! Harper, Micah, this is my husband, Tim. Tim, this is Harper—we teach together—and her boyfriend, Micah."

Tim shakes both our hands. "Nice to meet you both. Anna's told me a lot about you, Harper."

"Good things, I hope."

"Mostly complaints about the copy machine," he says with a grin.

Anna swats his arm. "That copy machine is a menace, and you know it."

"How long have you two been married?" Micah asks.

"Six months," Tim says, pulling Anna close. "Still in the honeymoon phase."

"Barely," Anna teases, but she's smiling.

They're sweet together. A couple that makes marriage look simple.

Micah chuckles, and I'm about to respond when he glances toward the bar. "I'm going to grab a water. Harper, do you want anything?"

I should say water. I should pace myself.

But my eyes drift across the room to where Collin is still

standing with that girl, and before I can stop myself, I say, "Champagne."

Micah hesitates. Just for a second. But I catch it.

And I wonder—does he disapprove? He's so godly, so deeply rooted in his faith. He probably thinks drinking is worldly or irresponsible.

"Sure," he says finally, his tone neutral. "I'll be right back."

He squeezes my hand once, then heads off, leaving me with Anna and Tim.

Anna immediately leans in, lowering her voice. "Okay, spill. He's even better in person. How long have you two been together again?"

"About a month," I say automatically.

"And it's serious?"

"Yeah. Really serious, actually."

Anna squeals, pulling me into another hug. "I'm so happy for you! This is amazing!"

"Thanks," I manage, even though my stomach is churning.

When Anna finally lets go, I spot Micah returning from the bar, water bottle in one hand, my second glass of champagne in the other. He's scanning the room, and when our eyes meet, he smiles.

That soft, genuine smile that does something complicated to my heart.

And I realize with sudden, terrifying clarity: *I'm in way over my head.*

Anna and Tim excuse themselves to mingle, and Micah appears at my side, handing me the water bottle first, then the champagne.

"Stay hydrated in between," he says gently. "If you're going to drink."

"Thanks." I take a sip of water, trying to calm my racing heart.

"So, what's next?" he asks.

"Dinner, I think. They should seat us soon."

He studies me for a moment, like he's trying to read between the lines, but before he can say anything, the lights dim slightly and someone announces dinner is being served.

"Come on," Micah says, offering his arm. "Let's find our table."

I loop my arm through his, and we make our way toward the seating chart.

And as we walk, I catch movement out of the corner of my eye.

Collin.

He's watching us from across the room.

Not the girl. Not the champagne in his hand.

Us.

And for just a second, our eyes meet.

There's something in his expression—surprise, maybe? Or regret?

I can't tell.

But I lift my chin, tighten my grip on Micah's arm, and smile.

Let him watch, I think. *Let him see exactly what he's missing.*

Just because he's with some girl tonight doesn't mean I can't still win him back. If anything, it proves he's trying to move on—which means maybe he hasn't yet.

Maybe there's still a chance.

I recalibrate my plan, my determination solidifying.

This is still doable. I just have to be better. Smarter. More convincing.

And with Micah by my side, looking at me like I'm the only person in the room?

I can do this.

I will do this.

Collin will regret ever letting me go.

Chapter 15
Micah

We're weaving through the ballroom toward the seating chart, her arm looped through mine, when she halts.

"There," she says, pointing to a display board near the entrance. "Table seven."

I scan the list of names under Table 7, and my stomach sinks.

Harper Mitchell, Micah Sanders, Dr. Mariah Bailey, Shawn Bailey, Collin Matthews, Jessica Brennan

Harper sees it at the same moment I do.

"No." Her voice is tight. "No, no, no. We're sitting with Collin?"

"Looks like it."

"And Dr. Bailey." She's spiraling now, her breathing picking up. "Oh my gosh, Micah, I can't—I can't sit through an entire dinner with both of them watching us. What if we mess up? What if they notice we're faking? What if—"

"Harper." I turn to face her, gently taking both her hands. "Breathe."

"I am breathing."

"You're panicking."

"I'm not—" she stops, exhaling shakily. "Okay, maybe I'm panicking a little."

"We're going to be fine," I say, squeezing her hands. "We've been doing great so far. Everyone believes us."

"But, Collin—"

"Collin is just another person at the table. That's it."

She looks up at me, her eyes wide and uncertain, and I can see her trying to convince herself. But the panic is still there, written all over her face.

I need to get her out of her head. Give her something else to focus on.

My gaze drifts across the room, and I spot it—a small photo booth tucked between two floral arrangements, velvet curtain drawn back, a sign reading:

CAPTURE THE MOMENT.

Perfect.

"Come on," I say, tugging her hand gently.

"What? Where—"

"Photo booth." I nod toward the corner. "We're doing it."

She blinks. "Right now?"

"Yes, now. Before dinner. Before you spiral any more than you already have." I pull her toward it. "Come on, Freckles. You need a distraction."

"Micah, I don't think—"

"Too late. Already decided."

Her resistance falters, and I catch the tiniest hint of a smile breaking through her panic. "You're ridiculous."

"And you're overthinking." I guide her toward the

booth, and she doesn't pull away. "Let's go be a fake couple and take some terrible photos."

She laughs—actually laughs—and just like that, some of the tension drains from her shoulders.

"Okay," she says, squeezing my hand. "Let's do it."

The photo booth is smaller than it looked from across the room.

Harper slides onto the bench first, tugging me in after her, and suddenly we're pressed together in a space that feels about two sizes too small.

"Okay," she says, slightly breathless. "How does this work?"

I lean forward and press the *start* button on the screen. "Looks like we get four photos. Three seconds between each one."

"Perfect." She shifts closer, and I keenly notice her shoulder touching mine and the floral, sweet smell of her hair.

The screen counts down.

3... 2... 1...

FLASH.

For the first photo, Harper makes a silly face—crossing her eyes and sticking out her tongue. I laugh and throw up bunny ears behind her head.

3... 2... 1...

FLASH.

Second photo: she's mid-laugh, and I'm grinning at her instead of the camera because watching her laugh is better than any photo.

3... 2... 1...

FLASH.

Third photo: we both try to do serious faces, but she cracks first, and we're both laughing again.

Then the countdown starts for the fourth photo.

3…

Harper turns to look at me, still smiling.

2…

And suddenly, we're very close.

Close enough that I can see the flecks of gold in her green eyes.

1…

FLASH.

The camera captures us like that—staring at each other, caught in a moment that feels too real, too charged, too much like something that shouldn't be happening in a fake relationship.

Harper doesn't move.

Neither do I.

We just sit there, looking at each other, the sounds of the gala fading into background noise.

"Harper," I say quietly, though I'm not sure what I'm planning to say next.

She blinks, breaking the moment, and quickly slides out of the booth. "We should grab the photos."

"Right. Yeah."

I follow her out, and we wait by the printer as it spits out two strips of photos.

Harper grabs hers first, studying them with a soft smile.

I take mine and look at the sequence: silly, laughing, serious, and then… that last one.

The one where we're looking at each other a little too long to be just friends.

Harper tucks her strip carefully into her purse, and I slide mine into my jacket pocket.

"Okay," she says, smoothing down her dress. "I'm ready now. Let's go face the table of doom."

I chuckle despite myself. "Table of doom?"

"You'll see."

Table seven is already partially occupied when we arrive.

Mariah is there, along with an older couple I don't recognize. And across from them, sitting side by side, are Collin and the girl from earlier.

Harper's hand tightens around mine as we approach.

"Harper!" Mariah says, smiling warmly. "We were wondering when you'd make it over. Please, sit."

We take the two empty seats—Harper next to Mariah, me beside her.

Which puts us directly across from Collin and the blonde in the red dress.

Up close, I can see Collin more clearly. He's polished, put-together, the kind of guy who looks like he stepped out of a business magazine.

I met him once—briefly, at Gray and Ivy's Christmas party. He'd been Harper's boyfriend then, standing at her side with his phone glued to his hand and barely making any conversation.

But now, looking at him across this table, I see him differently.

There's something guarded in his expression as he looks at Harper—like he's already regretting coming over here. Like seeing her with someone else makes him uncomfortable in a way he wasn't prepared for.

Good.

"Collin," Harper says, her voice carefully neutral. "Hi."

"Harper." He nods, then glances at me, his brow furrowing slightly. "And you must be...?"

"Micah Sanders," I say, extending my hand across the table. "Harper's boyfriend."

He shakes my hand, and his grip is firm. Professional. "Collin Matthews. Assistant principal at Harper's school."

His eyes narrow slightly, studying my face. "Haven't we met before?"

I pause, pretending to think about it. "Don't think so."

"I'm pretty sure we have. Last Christmas? Gray and Ivy's party?"

"Doesn't ring a bell," I say with a casual shrug.

Collin's jaw tightens slightly, and I can see it register—the sting of being forgettable. Not worth remembering.

"Huh," he says, releasing my hand. "Must be mistaken."

There's a beat of awkward silence, and I can feel Harper's eyes on me, but I don't look at her.

Good. Let him feel what it's like to not matter.

Then the blonde speaks up, her voice bright and loud. "I'm Jessica! Collin's girlfriend. Well, technically we've known each other since we were kids, but we just started dating recently, which is so funny because—"

She keeps talking, but I'm watching Harper.

She's staring at Jessica like she's seeing a ghost. Or maybe like she's solving a puzzle she doesn't want the answer to.

I reach under the table and squeeze her hand.

She squeezes back, hard.

"Anyway," Jessica finishes, laughing at her own story, "it's so great to finally meet you, Harper! Collin's mentioned you."

"Has he?" Harper's smile is plastic.

Mariah, bless her, jumps in with a question about the silent auction, and the conversation shifts.

But I can feel the tension radiating off Harper.

Dinner is served shortly after—some kind of chicken with roasted vegetables I'm sure is delicious, but I can barely taste it.

Because Harper is watching me.

Every time I answer a question from Mariah or make small talk with the older couple, I can feel her eyes on me. Studying. Assessing.

And I can feel Collin's eyes on us too.

Finally, during a lull in conversation, I lean close—close enough that my breath brushes her ear—and murmur, "You know, I enjoy catching you looking at me."

Her eyes widen, snapping to mine. "I wasn't—"

"You were," I say, letting my voice drop lower, more intimate. Playing it up for the audience I know is watching.

Her cheeks flush pink, and she looks away, but I catch her chin gently, tilting her face back toward mine. Making sure Collin can see every second of this.

"You're imagining things," she whispers, but her voice is breathless now.

"Am I?"

She doesn't answer, but the blush deepens, spreading down her neck, and I catch the exact moment Collin's jaw tightens across the table.

Perfect.

I let my thumb graze her cheek once before pulling back, and when I glance at Collin, he's staring at us like he's trying to figure out what we just said.

Mission accomplished.

Across the table, Jessica is back to talking—something

about a trip she and Collin took to Austin—and I notice Harper's gaze drift toward them.

She's comparing herself. I can see it in the way her shoulders tense, the way her smile doesn't quite reach her eyes.

And I hate it.

Because Harper is brilliant. Funny. Fiery. She lights up every room she walks into, challenges everyone around her to be better, and has more life in her little finger than most people have in their entire bodies.

And she has no idea.

She's sitting here, doubting herself, measuring her worth against someone else—when the truth is, there's no comparison. Not even close.

But she doesn't see that.

She only sees what she thinks she's missing.

After dinner, the band starts playing, and couples filter onto the dance floor.

Mariah and her husband are one of the first. Then the older couple. Then Jessica practically drags Collin out of his seat.

"Come on," she says, laughing. "You promised you'd dance with me tonight."

Collin looks reluctant but follows.

And then it's just Harper and me, sitting at an empty table.

"We should dance," I say.

She looks at me, surprised. "You want to?"

"That's the point, isn't it? Put on a show?"

"Right." She stands, smoothing down her dress. "The show."

I offer my hand, and she takes it.

The dance floor is crowded, warm, and filled with couples swaying to a slow jazz standard. I guide Harper to a spot near the edge, then pull her close.

One hand on her waist. The other holding hers.

She fits against me perfectly.

We start to sway, moving in time with the music, and for a moment, it's just us.

No Collin. No Jessica. No performance.

Just Harper in an emerald dress, looking up at me with those bright green eyes.

"Thank you," she says suddenly.

"For what?"

"For being here. For doing this. For not making me feel crazy."

"You're not crazy."

"I feel crazy."

"You're not," I repeat, more firmly this time. "You're hurt. There's a difference."

Her eyes soften, and she rests her head against my chest.

And I let myself have this.

Just for a moment.

I let myself imagine that this is real. That we're not pretending. That when the night ends, she'll still look at me like this.

But then I catch movement out of the corner of my eye.

Collin.

He's dancing with Jessica a few feet away, but he's not looking at her.

He's looking at us.

At Harper.

And there's something in his expression—regret, maybe. Or longing.

Harper must notice too, because she shifts slightly, pressing closer to me.

"He's watching," she murmurs.

"I know."

"Good."

The song ends, and another begins.

We keep dancing.

And I keep wishing this was real.

Chapter 16
Harper

I've lost count of how many glasses of champagne I've had.

Three? Four? Enough that my body is tingling, and the tension that's been coiled in my chest since we arrived has finally started to unwind.

I'm not drunk.

Just... loose. Bold. The kind of confidence that only comes from excellent champagne and the knowledge that Collin Matthews has been watching me all night.

Micah and I are still on the dance floor, swaying to another slow song, and I can feel Collin's eyes on us from across the room.

Let him watch.

Let him see what he gave up.

"Are you doing okay?" Micah asks, his hand warm on my lower back.

"I'm great." I smile up at him. "Why?"

"You've had a lot of champagne."

"I'm fine, Dimples. I can handle my alcohol."

He doesn't look convinced, but he doesn't push. Just

keeps dancing with me, steady and grounding, like he's been doing all night.

And I realize—again—how good he is at this.

Too good.

The way he holds me. The way he looks at me. The way he says my name, like it means something.

It all feels so real.

"Harper?"

I blink, refocusing on his face. "Yeah?"

"You zoned out."

"Sorry. Just thinking."

"About?"

About how you're better at being my fake boyfriend than Collin ever was at being my real one.

But I don't say that.

"Nothing important," I say instead.

The song ends, and Micah guides me off the dance floor toward one of the tall cocktail tables. I grab another glass of champagne from a passing server, and Micah watches me with that careful, protective expression he's been wearing all night.

"Maybe slow down," he suggests gently.

"Micah, I'm an adult. I can handle—"

"Harper."

The voice makes me freeze.

I turn slowly, and there he is.

Collin.

Standing right behind me, hands in his pockets, looking at me with an expression I can't quite read.

"Collin." My voice comes out steadier than I feel. "Hi."

"Hey." His gaze slides down my body—slowly, deliberately—before coming back up to meet my eyes. "You look...

incredible. That dress is stunning on you. Really shows off your figure."

Heat floods my face, but not the good kind.

"Thank you," I manage.

His eyes linger a little too long on the neckline. "Seriously, Harper. You look amazing. I don't think I've ever seen you look this good."

There's an awkward beat of silence, and I'm suddenly very aware that he has a girlfriend standing twenty feet away, I have a date standing right next to me and this is wildly inappropriate.

"I appreciate that," I say carefully, taking a small step back.

But Collin doesn't seem to notice—or care.

Then Micah is there—stepping into the space between us, his hand settling possessively on my lower back. The warmth of his palm burns through the silk of my dress.

"Everything okay here?" His voice is calm, but there's steel underneath it.

Collin's eyes flick to Micah, and something shifts in his expression. "Yeah, of course. Just catching up with Harper."

"Right," Micah's hand doesn't move from my back. "You were saying something about her dress?"

Collin clears his throat. "Just that she looks great. That's all."

"She does." Micah's tone is pleasant enough, but the message is clear: Back off.

Collin straightens slightly, like he's trying to reassert himself. "So, Micah. Children's ministry director, wasn't it?" He says it with just enough condescension to make it sound less impressive. Like he's reminding everyone in earshot that he's an assistant principal—a real professional—and Micah just plays with kids for a living.

"That's right." Micah doesn't rise to the bait. His hand stays steady on my back.

"Must be... rewarding work." Collin's smile doesn't reach his eyes.

"It is."

Another silence—this one thick with tension.

I take a sip of champagne, mostly to give my hands something to do.

Collin clears his throat. "So, uh, Jessica and I... we're actually pretty serious." He grins, that proud, showing-off kind of grin. "She's incredible, you know? She runs marathons, volunteers at the animal shelter every weekend, and just got promoted to senior account manager at her firm. And she's hilarious—like, genuinely the funniest person I've ever met. Everyone loves her."

The words hit me like a punch to the stomach.

He's listing her accomplishments like he's reading off a résumé. As if he's trying to prove something. Like he needs me to know just how amazing his new girlfriend is.

Like he's rubbing it in my face.

"We actually grew up together," Collin continues, and there's something wistful in his voice now. "Known each other since we were kids. Lost touch for a while, but we reconnected about two months ago and... I don't know. It just clicked. Like it was meant to be, you know?"

Two months ago.

Two. Months. Ago.

The same time he dumped me.

My chest tightens, and I feel like I can't breathe.

"Wow," I manage, forcing a smile that feels like it might crack my face. "That's... that's great, Collin. Congratulations."

"Thanks." He shifts his weight. "What about you two? How long have you been together?"

"About a month," I say, and I feel Micah's hand tighten slightly on my back, steadying me. "But honestly? It feels like so much longer. Like we've known each other forever."

I glance up at Micah, and he's looking down at me with this soft expression that makes my heart stutter.

"When you know, you know," Micah adds, his voice warm.

Collin's jaw tightens slightly. "Right. Yeah, I guess so."

"Micah's incredible," I continue, emboldened by champagne and adrenaline. "He's patient and kind and actually listens when I talk. He shows up. He's present. He makes me feel..." I pause, searching for the right word. "Seen."

Collin nods slowly, and there's something in his expression now—regret, maybe? Or jealousy?

I can't tell.

"Well," he says finally, shifting his weight awkwardly. "I'm glad you found someone. You deserve to be happy, Harper."

"Thanks. You too."

There's an uncomfortable pause where none of us seem to know what to say next.

Then, from across the room, I catch Jessica waving at Collin—big, enthusiastic gestures, pointing at something near the stage. She mouths something I can't make out.

Collin glances over his shoulder and nods at her, then turns back to us. "I should—Jessica's calling me over. But, uh, yeah. Good seeing you both."

"You too," I manage.

Collin walks toward Jessica, who immediately loops her arm through his and pulls him into conversation with another couple.

I let out a breath I didn't realize I was holding.

"Are you okay?" Micah asks quietly.

"Yeah. I just need—" I set down my champagne glass. "I need air. Or space. Or something."

"Come on." He takes my hand. "Let's get out of here for a minute."

He leads me away from the dance floor, weaving through clusters of people until we reach a set of large French doors at the far end of the ballroom. Through the glass panels, I can see a balcony overlooking the gardens below, lit by soft string lights.

Micah pushes open the doors, and the cool night air hits my face immediately.

I step outside, gripping the railing, and take a deep breath.

The noise from the ballroom fades to a muffled hum behind us—laughter, music, the clink of glasses—but out here, it's quieter. Calmer.

Micah closes the doors behind us but stays close, hands in his pockets.

"Well," he says after a moment, "that was odd."

I let out a breath that's half laugh, half something else entirely. "That's one word for it."

"He basically gave you her résumé."

"I know."

Micah steps closer, leaning against the railing beside me. "Harper."

"I'm fine."

"You keep saying that."

"Because I keep meaning it."

"Do you?"

I open my eyes and find him watching me with that

same careful expression. Like he's trying to figure me out. Like he actually cares.

"He's really moved on," I whisper, my voice barely above a whisper. "Like... completely moved on."

"I know."

"They grew up together. She's got this perfect job, runs marathons, volunteers every weekend—" I stop, shaking my head. "We were together for six months, and he never looked at me the way he looked when he was talking about her. Never bragged about me like that. And now, two months later, he's acting like she's the best thing that ever happened to him."

My throat tightens. "There's no winning him back, is there?"

"Hey," Micah turns to face me, his voice firm but gentle. "Don't say that."

"But—"

"Harper, look at me." He waits until I meet his eyes. "Did you see his face when you walked into that ballroom tonight? When he saw you in that dress, on my arm, looking like you were doing just fine without him?"

I swallow hard. "I don't know. Maybe?"

"I saw it," Micah says with certainty. "He noticed. Trust me. And yeah, maybe he's moved on with Jessica. Maybe he thinks she's great. But you know what? You're great too. And if he had half a brain, he'd realize what he lost."

"Micah—"

"I'm serious. Tonight isn't over yet. You're stunning, you're confident, and you've got everyone in that room believing we're crazy about each other." He squeezes my hand. "If you want him back, Harper, we can still make this work. We just have to keep doing what we're doing."

I search his face, looking for any sign that he's just saying what I want to hear.

But all I see is conviction.

"Do you really think so?"

"I know so." He gives me a small smile.

"I just—" I push off the wall, pacing. "I thought tonight would feel different. I thought seeing him would give me closure or clarity, or something. But all I feel is—"

I stop.

Because through the doorway, I can see into the ballroom.

And Collin is standing there, near the edge of the dance floor, looking directly at us.

Not at Jessica. Not at the crowd.

At us.

My heart starts racing.

"He's watching," I mumble.

Micah follows my gaze, then looks back at me.

"Kiss me."

His eyes widen. "What?"

"Kiss me." I step closer, my pulse pounding. "He's watching. We need to sell this."

"Harper, the rule was no—"

"I know what the rule was." I reach up, cupping his face. "I'm breaking it. Kiss me, Dimples."

He hesitates, his eyes searching mine. "Are you sure?"

"Yes."

"This isn't just the champagne talking?"

"No," and I mean it. "Please."

For a moment, he doesn't move.

Then he exhales slowly, and his hand comes up to cradle the back of my head.

"Okay," he whispers.

And then he kisses me.

It's not tentative. Not careful. Not the kind of kiss you give someone when you're pretending.

It's real.

His lips are warm and firm against mine, and the second we connect, everything else disappears. The gala. The music. Collin. All of it fades into the background.

There's only Micah.

His hand tangled in my hair. His other hand on my waist, pulling me closer. The way he tastes of mint and something uniquely him.

I reach up, threading my fingers through his hair, and he makes this low sound in the back of his throat that sends electricity down my spine.

He tilts his head, deepening the kiss, and I forget how to breathe.

Forget how to think.

Forget that this is supposed to be fake.

Because nothing about this feels fake.

His thumb brushes against my jaw, gentle and reverent, and I press closer, needing more of this, more of him.

Time stops.

The world narrows to the space between us—the warmth of his body, the steady thrum of his heartbeat against my chest, the way he's holding me like I'm something precious.

When we finally pull apart, we're both breathless.

I stare up at him, and he stares back, and neither of us says anything.

Because what is there to say?

"Harper," he says finally, his voice rough.

"Yeah?"

"That was—"

But before he can finish, the sound of applause erupts from the ballroom.

We both turn toward the doorway as the announcer's voice comes over the speakers.

"Ladies and gentlemen, thank you so much for joining us on the dance floor tonight! Now, we'll be moving into the fundraising portion of our evening. Please take your seats as we highlight the incredible work of the Dallas Independent School District."

The moment breaks.

Reality crashes back in.

I step back, smoothing down my dress, suddenly very aware of how close we were. How close we still are.

"We should—" I gesture vaguely toward the ballroom. "We should probably go back."

"Right. Yeah."

But neither of us moves.

We just stand there, staring at each other, the kiss hanging between us like a question neither of us knows how to answer.

Finally, Micah clears his throat. "For the record?"

"Yeah?"

"That definitely sold it."

A laugh bubbles up before I can stop it. "You think?"

"Yeah." His lips quirk into a small smile. "Pretty sure everyone in a ten-mile radius believes we're together now."

"Good. That's... that's what we wanted."

"Right. What we wanted."

There's something in his tone—something that makes my stomach flip.

But before I can figure out what it is, he holds out his hand.

"Come on, Freckles. Let's go watch people bid ridiculous amounts of money on silent auction items."

I take his hand, lacing my fingers through his, and let him lead me back into the ballroom.

Chapter 17
Micah

I can't think straight.

Harper kissed me.

Or I kissed her.

Or we kissed each other.

I don't even know anymore.

All I know is that a few minutes ago, I had Harper Mitchell pressed against a wall on a quiet balcony, her hands in my hair, her lips on mine, and every single rational thought I've ever had completely evaporated.

And now we're back in the ballroom like nothing happened.

Like the world didn't just tilt off its axis.

Like kissing her didn't just confirm everything I've been trying to outrun.

She's laughing at something Mariah just said, her hand resting lightly on my arm, and I'm trying to focus on the conversation. Trying to nod at the right moments. Trying to act normal.

But all I can think about is the way she tasted sweet, like

something I was never supposed to have. The way she made this little sound when I deepened the kiss. The way her fingers tightened in my hair like she didn't want to let go.

That wasn't fake.

I know it wasn't fake.

She has to know it wasn't fake.

Right?

But she's acting like everything's fine. Smiling. Mingling. Sipping another glass of champagne like we didn't just cross a line we explicitly agreed not to cross.

And I don't know what to do with that.

"Micah?"

I blink, realizing Harper's looking at me expectantly.

"Sorry, what?"

"Mariah asked how long you've been running the children's ministry."

"Oh. Right." I force myself to focus. "About three years now. Started as a volunteer and worked my way up."

"That's wonderful," she says warmly. "It takes a special person to work with children full time."

"Harper does it every day," I say, glancing down at her. "I just get them on Wednesday nights and Sunday mornings."

Harper beams up at me, and I wonder how long I can keep this up.

God, help me.

Mariah excuses herself to check on the silent auction, and suddenly it's just us again.

Harper sways slightly, and I steady her with a hand on her elbow.

"You okay?"

"I'm perfect." She grins up at me, her eyes bright and unfocused. "Absolutely perfect."

She's definitely had too much champagne.

"Maybe we should get some water," I suggest.

"I don't need water. I need—" She spots someone across the room and waves enthusiastically. "Anna! Anna, come here!"

Anna makes her way over, Tim trailing behind her, and Harper immediately loops her arm through mine.

"Anna, have you met Micah? Of course you have. Isn't he amazing?"

Anna grins. "You've mentioned that. A few times."

"Because it's true." Harper leans into me, and I can smell the champagne on her breath. "He's so amazing. And patient. And kind. And he has these dimples—" She reaches up and pokes my cheek. "Right here. See them?"

"Harper—"

"And he kisses like—" She stops herself, eyes widening slightly. "Never mind."

Anna's eyebrows shoot up. "Oh really?"

"Harper," I say quietly, "maybe we should—"

"I'm fine, Dimples." She pats my chest. "Completely fine."

But she's not fine.

She's drunk.

Not falling-down drunk, but definitely past the point of making good decisions.

And Collin and Jessica have already left, anyway. There's no one left to perform for. No reason to stay.

I need to get her out of here before she says something she'll regret tomorrow.

"Actually," I say, addressing Anna and Tim, "I think we're going to head out. It's getting late."

"Aww, but the auction isn't over yet," Harper protests.

"I know, but you have to teach on Monday. Early morning." I lower my voice. "And Collin already left, so..."

Understanding flashes in her eyes—brief and sharp—before she nods. "Fine. But only because you're very convincing, Dimples."

I guide her toward the exit, one hand on her lower back, the other ready to steady her if she stumbles.

She waves at approximately seventeen people on the way out, calling out goodbyes and compliments and something about "seeing everyone Monday."

By the time we make it to the valet stand, I'm exhausted.

And Harper is leaning heavily against my side.

"You're warm," she mumbles.

"Thanks?"

"And tall. You're very tall."

"I'm aware."

"I like that about you."

My heart does something stupid. "Harper—"

"And you smell good. What is that? Your cologne?"

"I don't know. Probably."

"It's nice. You're nice."

The valet pulls up with my truck, and I help Harper into the passenger seat. She sinks into it with a sigh, and I reach for her seatbelt, clicking it into place.

But then I notice her hair.

The elegant updo from earlier is coming undone—pins slipping, curls falling loose around her face. Without thinking, I reach up and gently tuck a strand behind her ear, my fingers grazing her temple.

She watches me with soft, unfocused eyes.

There's a smudge of mascara under her left eye—probably from rubbing it earlier when she was upset. I brush my thumb across it carefully, wiping it away, and her breath catches.

"Micah," she whispers.

I should step back. I should close the door and walk around to the driver's side.

But I don't.

Instead, I lean in—just slightly—and press my forehead to hers.

Her eyes flutter closed, and for a moment, we just breathe. The noise of the valet stand fades. The world narrows to just this.

I could kiss her.

I want to kiss her.

But she's drunk. And vulnerable. And this—whatever this is—can't happen like this.

So instead, I close my eyes and just stay there for one more second. Two. Three.

"You take care of me," she breathes, her voice barely above a whisper.

"Someone has to," I manage, my voice rough.

"Collin never did."

The words hit me harder than they should.

I pull back slowly—reluctantly—and every instinct in me screams to stay close. But I force myself to straighten up, to let go, to step back.

"Let's get you home," I mumble.

Then I close the door—carefully, gently—and stand there for a moment, one hand still on the truck, trying to remember how to breathe.

Finally, I walk around to the driver's side and slide in.

But the warmth of her forehead against mine still lingers.

For the first few minutes, Harper is quiet.

She stares out the window at the Dallas skyline, the city lights reflecting in the glass, and I can't tell what she's thinking.

Then, so softly I almost miss it, she says, "He moved on like I was nothing."

My hands tighten on the steering wheel.

"Harper—"

"Six months together, and he moved on in like, what, two weeks? Maybe less?" Her voice cracks. "How does someone do that? How do you just... forget someone?"

I glance over at her, and my chest aches at her expression.

"You're not nothing, Harper."

She turns to look at me, and there are tears in her eyes. "Then why does it feel like I am?"

I don't have an answer.

Not one that will fix this. Not one that will take away the hurt.

So I just reach over and take her hand, lacing my fingers through hers.

"You're not nothing," I repeat, quieter this time. "Collin's an idiot for not seeing what he had. But that doesn't mean you're not enough. It just means he wasn't right for you."

She stares at our joined hands for a long moment.

Then she whispers, "What if no one is?"

"Someone is."

"How do you know?"

Because I would be, I want to say. Because I see you, Harper. All of you. The messy parts and the beautiful parts, and everything in between. And I wouldn't forget you in two weeks or two months or two years, or ever.

But I don't say any of that.

Because she's drunk and hurting and trying to get over someone else.

And I'm just the guy pretending to be her boyfriend.

So instead, I squeeze her hand and say, "Because you're worth being right for."

She doesn't respond.

And when I glance over a few minutes later, she's asleep, her head resting against the window, her hand still in mine.

The drive to her apartment feels both too long and not long enough.

Too long because I keep replaying the entire night in my head, torturing myself with the memory of how right it felt.

Not long enough because I don't know what happens when we get there. I don't know if she'll remember this conversation tomorrow. Don't know if she'll remember the kiss.

Don't know if she'll regret it.

When I pull into her parking lot, Harper stirs slightly but doesn't wake.

"Hey," I say softly, gently shaking her shoulder. "Harper. We're here."

She blinks awake, disoriented. "What?"

"Your apartment. Come on, let's get you inside."

She tries to unbuckle her seatbelt, fumbling with the latch, and I reach over to help her.

"I can do it," she mumbles.

"I know you can."

She manages to get the door open but nearly trips over her own feet trying to step down from the truck.

I'm out of my seat and around to her side in seconds, catching her before she face-plants into the pavement.

"Okay, new plan," I say. "I'm carrying you."

"You don't have to—"

"Harper."

She looks up at me, and something in my tone must convince her, because she just nods.

I scoop her up—one arm under her knees, the other around her back—and she immediately wraps her arms around my neck.

"You're strong," she murmurs against my shoulder.

"You're light."

I carry her up the stairs to her apartment, and she digs her keys out of her clutch with one hand while still holding onto me with the other.

Her apartment is dark when we walk in, and I fumble for the light switch with my elbow.

"Bedroom?" I ask.

"Down the hall. First door on the right."

I navigate carefully, trying not to bump into anything, and finally make it to her room.

It's exactly what I expected—organized chaos. Colorful throw pillows on the bed. Books stacked on the nightstand. A bulletin board covered in photos and postcards.

I set her down gently on the edge of the bed, and she immediately flops backward with a sigh.

"My feet hurt."

"I bet." I kneel down and carefully unbuckle her heels, slipping them off one at a time.

She watches me through half-closed eyes. "You're too good to me, Dimples."

"Just taking care of you, Freckles."

I grab the blanket folded at the foot of her bed and drape it over her.

She's still in her dress, still has her makeup on, but I'm not about to try to navigate that situation.

"Sleep," I say. "You'll feel better in the morning."

"Don't leave."

The words are barely a whisper, but they stop me in my tracks.

"Harper—"

"Please." She reaches out, her hand finding mine in the dark. "Don't leave."

I should leave.

But the way she's looking at me—vulnerable and small and scared—makes it impossible.

"I'm not leaving," I say quietly.

Relief floods her face. "Promise?"

"Promise."

She closes her eyes, still holding my hand.

I wait for a moment, then carefully reach for the reading chair in the corner of her room—one of those oversized ones with a cushion. I drag it closer to the bed, trying not to make too much noise, and sink into it.

But I don't let go of her hand.

I can't.

So I sit there, our fingers intertwined, watching as her breathing gradually slows.

With my free hand, I reach over and gently brush a strand of hair away from her mouth.

She doesn't stir.

Just keeps breathing, soft and steady, her features relaxing more with each passing minute.

The tension in her shoulders eases. The worry lines between her brows smooth out. The tight set of her jaw softens.

She looks peaceful.

Beautiful.

Completely unaware that I'm sitting here falling apart.

Her thumb twitches slightly against my palm—a small, unconscious movement—and the ache intensifies.

I run my thumb over her knuckles, just once, memorizing the way her hand feels in mine. The warmth of her skin. The delicate bones beneath. The way our fingers fit together like they were designed for this exact moment.

Minutes pass. Maybe ten. Maybe twenty. I lose track.

All I know is that I'm watching her breathe. Watching the rise and fall of her chest. Watching the way her eyelashes flutter slightly in sleep.

And I'm holding her hand like it's the only thing keeping me anchored to the earth.

My suit jacket is wrinkled. My tie is crooked. I'm pretty sure I have lipstick on my collar from when she hugged me earlier.

And I don't care.

Because this—sitting here in the dim light, holding Harper Mitchell's hand while she sleeps—this is everything.

Even if she'll never know.

Even if tomorrow she wakes up and goes right back to trying to win Collin back.

Even if this is the only moment like this I'll ever get.

I close my eyes for just a second, letting myself feel the weight of it.

Then I open them again because I don't want to miss a single moment of watching her.

"God," I whisper into the darkness. "I'm asking You to help her see how special she is. How much she's worth. How beautiful and brilliant and fierce she is, even when she doesn't believe it herself."

Then I let go of her hand, take a deep breath and run my hands over my face.

"I'm asking You to heal her heart. To take away the pain of losing Collin. To help her see that it's okay to move on. That she deserves someone who sees her. Someone who shows up. Someone who won't forget her in two weeks or two months or ever."

I pause, my chest aching.

"And I'm asking You to help her find that someone. Someone who will love her the way she deserves to be loved."

I lift my eyes, staring at the ceiling.

"Can I ask a selfish prayer, Lord?"

Silence.

Just the sound of Harper breathing and my own heartbeat pounding in my ears.

"Can that someone be me?"

The words hang in the air, heavy and terrifying, and true.

"I know I shouldn't be asking this. I know she's not ready. I know she's still trying to get over him. But God... I think I'm in love with her. And I don't know what to do about it."

I drop my head into my hands.

"So if You could make a way... if You could show her that I'm not just pretending... if You could help her see that this—" I gesture vaguely at the space between us. "that this could be real..."

I trail off.

Because I don't know how to finish that prayer.

Don't know how to ask for something I want so badly it physically hurts.

So I just sit there in the darkness, listening to Harper breathe, and hope that God heard me anyway.

Hope that somehow, someday, this won't just be pretend anymore.

Chapter 18
Harper

My head is pounding.

That's the first thing I'm aware of—a dull, throbbing ache that seems to pulse in time with my heartbeat.

The second thing I'm aware of is that I'm still wearing my dress.

The emerald sequined dress that cost me way too much money and is now twisted around my body at an uncomfortable angle, digging into my ribs.

I groan, forcing my eyes open, and immediately regret it.

Sunlight streams through my bedroom window like a personal attack, and I throw my arm over my face.

What happened last night?

Fragments come back in pieces. The gala. Champagne. Lots of champagne. Collin with Jessica. Dancing with Micah.

The kiss.

Oh, the kiss.

I kissed Micah.

Or he kissed me.

Or—honestly, I'm not entirely sure who started it, but it definitely happened, and now I need to get up and figure out what that means.

I blink at the ceiling, my mind still fuzzy with sleep. Sunlight streams through the window, way too bright for whatever time it is. I rub my eyes with the heels of my hands, trying to clear the fog from my brain.

One problem at a time, Harper.

First: Get out of bed.

I stretch my arms overhead, feeling my spine pop in three places, then slowly swing my legs over the side of the mattress. Both feet touch the floor—solid ground, thank goodness—and I take a steadying breath.

Okay. You've got this. Just stand up like a normal person who didn't kiss her fake boyfriend last night.

I push myself up and take one step forward.

My foot catches on something warm and solid, and suddenly I'm pitching forward, arms windmilling uselessly as gravity does its thing.

I land hard.

On something that definitely isn't the floor.

What the...?

My brain scrambles to process. Warm. Solid. Moving?

Then a very male grunt sounds directly beneath me, and I freeze.

Oh no.

Oh no, no, no.

I lift my head, and Micah's eyes fly open inches from mine.

For one horrible, suspended moment, neither of us moves. Neither of us breathes.

Pure panic floods his face as he seems to fully register

our position—me sprawled on top of him, my hands braced against his chest, our faces way too close.

"What are you doing in my apartment?!" I blurt out, my voice climbing about three octaves. "On the floor! Next to my bed!"

I brace my hands against his chest for balance, and that's when I notice the blanket has slipped down to his waist.

And his chest is...bare.

Completely bare.

And—oh my word—he has abs.

Like, actual defined abs.

I blink down at him, my brain completely stalling out.

This is Micah. Sweet, awkward, always-wears-button-ups Micah, and he apparently has a six-pack hiding under all those oxford shirts.

When did this happen?

"I—you—we fell asleep, and I didn't want to..." He's stammering, his hands hovering uselessly near my shoulders like he's not sure whether to push me off or steady me.

I scramble off him, my face burning as I push myself to standing.

"You have abs?" The words come out as nearly a yell before I can stop them.

Micah stands up too, shirtless in only his dress pants from the gala, disoriented movement, squinting at me like he's trying to bring me into focus. He immediately crosses his arms over his stomach. "Harper—"

"Why are you shirtless in my bedroom?!"

"I can explain—"

"And why do you have abs?!" I'm gesturing wildly now, my brain trying to keep up in real time.

"Can we maybe focus on one crisis at a time?"

He's squinting around the room now, one hand still covering his abs while the other fumbles through the air like he's searching for something. "Where are my glasses?"

"Your glasses?" I'm still staring at him—at his abs, at his bare chest, at the fact that he slept on my floor. "Micah, why are you on my floor?"

"My glasses, Harper." He takes a stumbling step forward, nearly running into my nightstand. "I can't see anything without them."

Oh. Right. He's basically blind without those things.

"Don't you have contacts?" I ask because I need this to not be entirely my fault.

"Daily lenses. I threw them away last night."

"Who throws away perfectly good contacts?"

"People who follow the instructions on the box, Harper." He pinches the bridge of his nose.

I take a step back to scan the floor, trying to locate them, and my heel comes down on something.

Crack.

I freeze.

Oh no.

I lift my foot and stare down at the mangled frames—broken clean in half at the nose bridge.

"Did you find them?" he asks hopefully.

"Um." I stare at the two separate pieces in my hands—the lenses still intact, but the frames snapped clean apart at the nose bridge. "Yes?"

"Can you hand them to me?"

"About that..."

I walk over to my desk and grab the tape dispenser, holding one half of the frames in each hand. I start frantically winding tape around the broken nose piece, trying to hold both halves together. The tape overlaps in lumpy layers, getting thicker with each desperate wrap.

It looks absolutely ridiculous.

Like something a kindergartener would bring home from craft time.

But maybe if I fix them, he won't be mad?

I turn back around and hold them out. "Here."

Micah takes them, squinting as he examines the tape-covered mess. "Harper… what happened?"

"I stepped on them."

"You stepped on them."

"I'm so sorry!" The words tumble out in a rush. "I didn't see them, and I was confused because you're on my floor—shirtless, by the way, which we still need to talk about—and I tripped, and I'm so, so sorry. I'll go with you today to get them fixed. Right now. We can go right now. It's the right thing to do. The least I can do, really, considering I broke them and you were—" I gesture vaguely at the floor. "—doing whatever you were doing down there."

"Harper." His voice is calm, cutting through my spiral. "Breathe."

I take a breath.

Then another.

"It's okay," he says gently, putting them on. "They're just glasses."

"But I broke them."

"Accidents happen."

"But—"

"Harper." He steps closer to me, and I'm suddenly very aware of how tall he is. And how shirtless he still is. "It's fine. I promise."

I force myself to breathe normally, counting to five like my therapist taught me.

One. Two. Three. Four. Five.

My heart rate slows.

And then my eyes drift down to his stomach again.

"Those are pretty nice abs, Micah," I hear myself say.

He gives me the most bewildered look I've ever seen. "What?"

"I just—" I gesture vaguely at his torso. "I didn't know you worked out. Like, really worked out."

"I go to the gym sometimes."

"Clearly."

He grabs his white dress shirt from the chair and quickly pulls it on, fumbling with the buttons.

And I finally remember the actual important question.

"Why are you here?"

He pauses mid-button. "You don't remember?"

"Remember what?"

His expression softens. "You got pretty drunk last night. Like, really drunk. And you got sick. A few times, actually. I didn't feel right leaving you alone, so I made a bed on the floor."

Oh no.

"You could have at least slept on the couch," I say weakly.

"Yeah, no. Not with how much I was up helping you last night."

A flash of memory hits me—Micah's hand holding my hair back, his voice low and soothing, telling me it was okay.

I press my hand to my forehead; the headache intensifying. "Oh no."

"Hey." He steps closer, concern written all over his face. "It's okay."

"I threw up in front of you."

"Technically on the toilet, but yes."

"Multiple times."

"Three, to be exact."

I groan, sinking onto the edge of my bed. "I'm so sorry."

"Don't be."

"I don't normally drink," I blurt. "Like, ever. And I definitely never drink that much. Last night was just... a lot. With Collin and Jessica and the whole—" I wave my hand vaguely. "Everything."

"I know."

"And I probably said a bunch of stupid things and made a complete fool of myself—"

"You didn't."

"—and now you've seen me at my absolute worst, and I'm still in this stupid dress—" I look down at the wrinkled, twisted emerald fabric. "Oh my gosh, I'm still in my dress."

I stand up abruptly and immediately regret it as the room spins slightly.

Micah's hand is on my elbow instantly, steadying me. "Easy."

"I need to change."

"Okay."

"And shower."

"That's probably a good idea."

I start toward the bathroom, then stop. Turn back around.

Micah's standing there in his wrinkled shirt and dress slacks, hair still a mess, squinting slightly out of his broken glasses.

And despite everything—despite the headache and the embarrassment and the fact that I apparently threw up three times in front of him—I feel this overwhelming wave of gratitude.

"Thank you," I say quietly. "For staying. For taking care of me."

His expression softens. "Anytime, Freckles."

The nickname makes my stomach flip.

And suddenly, another memory surfaces.

The kiss.

His hands in my hair. My hands on his chest. The way the world disappeared.

I stare at him, and he stares back, and I wonder if he's thinking about it too.

But before I can say anything—before I can figure out what to say—I blurt out, "Can you make breakfast?"

He blinks. "What?"

"There's bacon and eggs and stuff in the fridge." I'm already backing toward the bathroom. "Can you start making it?"

"Uh... sure?"

I pause at the bathroom door. "And can you pretty please start a pot of coffee?"

"Harper—"

But I'm already closing the door, leaning against it, my heart racing.

What am I doing?

I catch a glimpse of myself in the mirror and nearly scream again.

Mascara is streaked down my face in dark trails. One of my false eyelashes is completely missing—just gone, presumably lost somewhere between the gala and my bed. And my hair, which was elegantly pinned up last night, is now half-fallen, sticking out at odd angles like I stuck my finger in an electrical socket.

I look like a disaster.

I am a disaster.

I peel off the dress, letting it fall to the floor in a sparkly heap, and turn on the shower.

As steam fills the bathroom, I stand under the hot water and try to piece together last night.

The gala. The introductions. Collin introducing me to his girlfriend.

The photo booth.

The dancing.

The kiss.

And then... champagne. Lots of champagne. Talking to Anna. Talking to random people. Everything getting blurry.

Micah taking me home.

Micah carrying me inside.

Micah taking care of me while I was sick.

Micah sleeping on my floor because he didn't want to leave me alone.

I press my forehead against the cool tile wall.

What does this mean?

I finish showering, wrap myself in a towel, and stare at my reflection again.

Clean face. Wet hair. No makeup.

Just me.

And somewhere in my kitchen, Micah Sanders is making me breakfast.

I take a deep breath.

Okay, Harper. You can do this. Just go out there, eat breakfast, and pretend like everything is normal.

Even though nothing about this is normal.

Even though I can still feel the ghost of his lips on mine.

Even though I'm pretty sure last night changed everything.

I slip on a sweatshirt, my favorite pair of leggings, and open the bathroom door.

The smell of coffee hits me immediately.

And despite the confusion and the embarrassment, and the massive hangover—I smile.

Because Micah stayed.

And somehow, that feels like the most important thing in the world.

Chapter 19
Micah

I'm standing in Harper Mitchell's kitchen, cooking breakfast, trying to remember how to be a functional human being.

My hands are shaking.

Get it together, Micah.

But I can't stop thinking about last night.

The way she looked at me right before she said it.

Kiss me, Dimples.

So I did.

And it was everything I knew it would be and nothing I was prepared for.

I can still feel the ghost of her hands in my hair. Still taste the champagne on her lips. Still hear that little sound she made when I pulled her closer.

The coffee maker beeps, startling me back to reality.

Focus. Breakfast. You're making breakfast.

Cooking has always calmed me. Something about the routine, the steps, the way everything has a place and a purpose.

Unlike whatever is happening between Harper and me right now.

The bacon is sizzling; the pancakes are stacking up on a plate, and I'm just scrambling the eggs when I hear the bedroom door open.

I freeze.

Harper walks into the kitchen, and my brain just...blanks.

She's in an oversized sweatshirt and leggings, her wet hair pulled back in a low bun, no makeup, looking nothing like the polished girl from last night.

And somehow, she's even more beautiful.

"Wow," she says, surveying the spread on the counter. "Impressive. You can cook too."

"It's just breakfast," I say, plating the eggs.

"That's a whole meal, Dimples. Not just breakfast." She grabs two mugs from the cabinet and pours coffee for both of us.

I set the plates on her small dining table, then turn back to grab the bacon.

And that's when the guilt hits me.

Because I'm standing in Harper's apartment. Alone. After spending the night.

And yeah, I was on the floor. And yeah, she was sick. And yeah, nothing happened.

But it still feels...wrong.

"Harper." I set down the bacon platter. "I don't really think this is appropriate for me to be here. You and me. Alone in your apartment."

She pauses mid-sip of coffee. "What?"

"I just—" I run a hand through my hair. "I stayed last night because you needed help. But now it's morning, and we're having breakfast, and I don't—"

"Micah." She sets down her mug. "It's not like we're actually dating."

The words hit me like a punch to the gut.

It's not like we're actually dating.

Right.

Because this is fake.

All of it is fake.

The hand-holding. The dancing. The way she looked at me last night before she kissed me.

Fake.

"Right," I say, forcing my voice to stay steady. "Yeah. Of course."

She doesn't seem to notice the shift in my tone. Just grabs a pancake and drowns it in syrup. "Besides, you've already seen me at my worst. Throwing up. Mascara everywhere. Missing a fake eyelash. If that doesn't kill the romance, nothing will."

I should laugh. Make a joke. Keep things light.

But all I can think is that nothing could kill the romance for me. Not the throwing up. Not the mascara. Not any of it.

Because I'm pretty sure I'm in love with her.

And she thinks this is all pretend.

"So," Harper says, cutting into her pancakes. "Last night went pretty well, right? I mean, aside from the whole me-getting-drunk part."

"Yeah," I manage. "It went well."

"Collin definitely noticed us. Did you see the way he kept looking over?"

"I saw."

"And Dr. Bailey loved you. Everyone loved you, actually." She takes a bite, chewing thoughtfully. "We're pretty convincing as a couple."

Because it's not fake for me, I want to say.

But I don't.

"We did good," I say instead.

"These pancakes are really good," Harper says as if this situation is completely normal.

"Thanks."

"Seriously. Where'd you learn to cook like this?"

"My mom. She made me learn before I moved out for college. Said no son of hers was going to survive on ramen and pizza."

Harper smiles. "Smart woman."

"She has her moments."

We eat in relative quiet, and I try to focus on the food instead of the way Harper's looking at me. Like she's trying to figure something out but doesn't quite know what.

When we finish, I stand to clear plates, but Harper waves me off.

"No, I got it. You cooked, I clean. That's the rule."

I want to argue, but that's when I catch my reflection in the mirror above her couch.

The taped-up glasses.

I'd almost forgotten.

"Okay, well, I'm gonna get going—" I stand.

And Harper bursts out laughing—doubled-over, tears-in-her-eyes laughing.

"What?" I ask, completely confused.

"Your glasses!" She points at my face, still laughing. "Oh my, I forgot about the tape. You look ridiculous."

I touch the frames self-consciously. "They're fine."

"They're held together with half a roll of Scotch tape, Micah."

"It's functional."

"It's a disaster." She wipes her eyes, finally composing herself. "I'm so sorry. Again. Where did you get those?"

"LensCrafters. The one down the street."

"Okay," she nods decisively. "You go home and change —because I'm sure you want to get out of that suit, and then meet me at LensCrafters in an hour?"

"Harper, you really don't have to—"

"Micah." Her voice is firm now. "I'm going to get your glasses fixed. End of discussion."

I open my mouth to argue, then close it.

Because the look on her face tells me, there's no point.

"Fine," I say. "One hour."

"One hour," she confirms.

I grab my jacket from the chair, slip on my shoes, and head for the door.

But before I leave, I glance back.

Harper's standing in the middle of her living room, arms crossed, hair still damp, looking stubborn and absolutely beautiful.

And all I can think is: *I'm so screwed.*

My house feels too quiet when I get home.

I drop my keys on the counter, and Biscuit immediately appears, chittering indignantly.

"Yeah, I know," I mutter, crouching down to scratch behind his ears. "I was gone all night."

He climbs up my arm, perching on my shoulder, and I make my way to the bedroom.

"Long night, buddy," I say, stripping off the wrinkled dress shirt. "Really long night."

Biscuit chitters again, like he's asking for details.

"Okay, fine. You want the full story?" I toss the shirt into the hamper and head to the bathroom. "Harper asked me to be her fake date to this gala. Which, yes, I know, was a terrible idea. But I did it anyway because apparently I'm incapable of saying no to her."

I turn on the shower and wait for the water to heat up.

"And then—" I pause, running a hand over my face. "Then she kissed me. Or I kissed her. I don't even know anymore. But it happened. And it was..."

I trail off because I don't have words for what it was.

"And now I'm supposed to just pretend like everything's normal. Like I didn't spend all night praying that she could be mine. Like I'm not completely in love with her."

Biscuit squeaks, and I glance at him.

"You think I'm being dramatic?"

He tilts his head.

"Yeah, well, you're probably right."

I shower quickly, throwing on jeans and a t-shirt, and fish out a backup pair of dailies from the drawer. I keep extras for emergencies. Apparently, this qualifies.

The broken glasses sit on my dresser, still wrapped in tape, and I carefully place them in their case.

When I'm ready to leave, Biscuit follows me to the door.

"I'll be back soon," I tell him. "And when I get back, we're having a serious conversation about boundaries and emotional self-preservation."

He chitters, completely unbothered.

I grab my keys and head out, trying to ignore the nervous energy buzzing under my skin.

Because in twenty minutes, I'm meeting Harper at LensCrafters.

Just the two of us.

In broad daylight.

With absolutely no excuse to hold her hand, or call her Freckles, or pretend that last night meant something.

God, give me strength.

I climb into my truck and head toward the store, already bracing myself for whatever comes next.

Chapter 20
Micah

Harper is already waiting outside LensCrafters when I pull into the parking lot.

She's changed into jeans and a cream-colored sweater, her hair now dry and falling in loose waves around her shoulders. She's scrolling through her phone, and when she spots my truck, she waves.

I take a steadying breath before getting out.

Just act normal. This is normal. Two friends getting glasses fixed. Completely normal.

"Hey," she says as I approach. "Ready to fix the damage I caused?"

"It's really not a big deal."

"Micah, they're held together with tape. It's a big deal." She walks toward the door. "Come on. Let's get you sorted out."

The store is bright and modern, with rows and rows of frames displayed on sleek white shelving. A cheerful employee—name tag reading Mary—greets us immediately.

"Hi! How can I help you today?"

I pull out the taped-up glasses from their case, and her eyes widen slightly.

"Oh. Wow. Those are... um..."

"A disaster," Harper supplies. "Total disaster. My fault. Can they be fixed?"

Mary takes the glasses carefully, examining them from multiple angles. She pokes at the tape, tests the bent frame, and her expression grows increasingly sympathetic.

"I'm really sorry," she says finally. "But these are beyond repair. The frame is completely warped. You'd need a whole new pair."

Harper's face falls. "Oh no."

"It's fine," I say quickly. "I have contacts."

"But you need backup glasses," Harper insists. "What if you run out of contacts? What if your eyes get irritated? What if—"

"Harper—"

She turns to Mary. "He needs new glasses. What do you have?"

Mary perks up immediately. "Well, we have a great selection! What kind of frames do you prefer?"

"Clear," I say. "Just... basic clear frames like the ones I had before."

"Boring," Harper mutters.

"Practical," I correct. "They match everything."

Mary smiles diplomatically. "Why don't we look at a few options? We can start with something similar to what you had and branch out from there."

She leads us over to the men's section, and suddenly I'm surrounded by hundreds of frames in every shape, size, and color imaginable.

"Okay," Mary says, pulling down a pair of clear plastic

frames. "These are close to your original style. Want to try them?"

I slip them on and look in the mirror.

They're fine. Perfectly adequate. Exactly like my old ones.

"What do you think?" Mary asks.

"They're good—"

"Next," Harper says immediately.

I turn to her. "What's wrong with these?"

"Nothing's wrong with them. They're just... boring. You can do better."

"I don't need better. I need functional."

"You need both." She's already scanning the wall, her eyes lighting up when she spots something. "Ooh, try these."

She hands me a pair of tortoiseshell frames—rounded, slightly vintage-looking.

I put them on skeptically.

"Oh no," Harper says, wrinkling her nose. "You look like a hipster English professor."

"Is that bad?"

"Do you want to look like you spend your weekends at poetry readings talking about Kerouac?"

"I don't even know who that is."

"Exactly. Next."

Mary is clearly enjoying this, pulling down pair after pair while Harper provides running commentary.

Wire frames. "Too serious. You look like you're about to audit someone's taxes."

Bright blue frames. "Too much. You're a children's pastor, not a rapper."

Square gray frames. "Getting warmer, but still not quite right."

After the tenth pair, I'm losing patience.

"Harper, can we just pick something? They're glasses. They all help me see."

"But they also frame your face, Dimples. First impressions matter." She's studying the wall again, tapping her chin thoughtfully. "We need something that says 'approachable but confident.' 'Friendly but put-together.'"

"That's a lot to ask from glasses."

"Fashion is communication."

"Since when do you care about my fashion?"

She pauses, and something flickers across her face. "I don't. I just...I broke your glasses. The least I can do is help you find a suitable replacement."

Before I can respond, Mary returns with another pair.

"These just came in," she says. "They're really popular right now."

They're dark-rimmed glasses. Thick, bold frames in matte black. Nothing like what I usually wear.

I shake my head immediately. "Those aren't really my style."

"Just try them," Mary encourages.

"I don't think—"

"Micah." Harper crosses her arms. "Try them."

"They're too much."

"You don't know that until you try them."

"I know my own taste—"

"Humor me."

She's got that stubborn expression I'm recognizing. The one that means she's not backing down.

"Fine," I mutter, taking the glasses from Mary.

I slip them on and turn toward the mirror.

And—oh. Wow.

They're actually really nice.

The thick frames make my face look more defined somehow. More mature. And the dark color contrasts with my hair in a way the clear frames never did.

I look like a different person.

Not boring, put-together Micah who blends into the background.

Someone who might actually belong on Harper Mitchell's arm.

"Oh my," Harper breathes.

I glance at her reflection in the mirror.

She's staring at me, her lips slightly parted, and I swear her cheeks are flushed.

And...did she just bite her lip?

"What?" I ask.

"Those are—" She clears her throat. "Those are the ones."

"You think?"

"I know." She steps closer, studying my face. "They're perfect. Like, really perfect. You look..."

"I look what?"

She meets my eyes in the mirror, and something passes between us. Something that makes the air feel thicker.

"You look really good, Dimples," she whispers.

"Yeah?"

"Yeah." She's still looking at me, and I can't read her expression. "Like, dangerously good."

"Dangerous?"

A smile tugs at her lips. "You're already hard enough to ignore without looking like that."

The words hang between us, and I'm not sure if she meant to say them out loud.

Her eyes widen slightly, like she's just realizing what she said.

"I mean—" She steps back quickly. "I mean, you know. For the fake dating thing. When we have to convince people. You'll be very convincing. Looking like that."

"Right," I say, even though my brain is currently unable to think. "The fake dating thing."

"Exactly."

Mary, who has been watching this entire exchange with barely concealed amusement, jumps in. "So we're going with these?"

I look at myself one more time.

The glasses do look good. Really good.

And the way Harper's looking at me...

"Yeah," I say. "We'll go with these."

"Perfect!" Mary beams. "I'll just need to get your prescription information, and we can have these ready in about an hour."

I take off the glasses and hand them back to her as she walks away to grab paperwork, catching Harper's eye.

She's biting her lip again, looking anywhere but at me.

"Thanks," I mumble. "For helping me pick them out."

"It's the least I could do." She's still not looking at me. "Since I destroyed your old ones."

"Harper."

She finally meets my gaze, and there's something vulnerable in her expression.

"You didn't have to come with me," I continue. "But I'm glad you did."

A small smile. "Yeah, well. Somebody has to make sure you don't walk around looking like a tax auditor."

And just like that, the moment breaks.

But as Mary returns with forms for me to fill out, and Harper wanders off to look at sunglasses, I can't stop replaying what she said.

You're already hard enough to ignore.

I fill out the paperwork, trying to focus on the words instead of the hope blooming in my chest.

Because I'm already in too deep.

And if I'm not careful, I'm going to drown.

An hour later, I'm walking out of LensCrafters with new glasses and a receipt I didn't pay for.

We'd argued about it. I insisted it wasn't necessary, that accidents happen, that I could handle it.

Harper crossed her arms and gave me that look.

And once again, I can't say no to Harper.

So now I'm wearing glasses I didn't pay for, and I have absolutely no idea what happens next.

Do I just leave? Say thanks and drive away?

Do I ask if she wants to grab lunch?

"Well," Harper says, breaking the silence. "Mission accomplished. You have glasses again."

"Thanks to you."

"Thanks to my clumsiness, you needed them in the first place."

"Harper—"

"I know, I know. Accidents happen." She smiles, but it doesn't quite reach her eyes. "You should probably get going. I'm sure you have church stuff to prep for tomorrow."

Tomorrow.

Sunday.

Church.

Right.

"Actually," I hear myself say, "I was wondering if you'd want to... I don't know. Grab lunch or something?"

Her eyes widen slightly. "Lunch?"

"Yeah. If you're not busy. We could—" I stop myself before I say something stupid like *keep hanging out* or *pretend this morning isn't ending*. "We could debrief. About the gala. Make sure we're on the same page for... whatever comes next."

It's a terrible excuse.

But she doesn't call me on it.

Instead, she just looks at me, her expression unreadable. The silence stretches between us, and I can feel my heart hammering against my ribs.

Say something, Harper.

Please.

Chapter 21
Harper

The food truck park is buzzing with Saturday afternoon energy.

Families with kids. College students. Couples on dates.

And me and Micah, sitting at a picnic table with tacos from the best truck in Dallas, pretending like this morning didn't happen.

Pretending like I didn't see him shirtless on my bedroom floor.

Pretending like he didn't take care of me all night while I was sick.

Pretending like I didn't say he looked "dangerously good" in those glasses an hour ago.

"These are incredible," Micah says, taking another bite of his carne asada taco. "How did I not know about this place?"

"Because you live under a rock," I say, biting into my al pastor taco. "This is like, the best food truck park in Dallas."

"I don't live under a rock. I'm just... busy."

"With church stuff?"

"With church stuff," he confirms.

We eat in comfortable silence for a moment, the sounds of the park filling the space between us—music from one truck, kids laughing, the sizzle of grills.

It feels natural.

Easy.

Which is dangerous because nothing about this situation is supposed to be easy.

My phone buzzes on the table, and I glance down.

DR. BAILEY

Hi Harper! Quick question. What's the name of your church again? Shawn and I are looking to try somewhere new tomorrow, and I remember you mentioning yours is great!

I freeze, taco halfway to my mouth.

"What's wrong?" Micah asks.

"Nothing. Just—" I set down the taco and pick up my phone, typing quickly.

HARPER

New Chapter Church! It's on Main Street downtown. Service starts at 9:30.

"Harper, you look like you just saw a ghost."

"Not a ghost. Worse." I show him the screen. "My principal wants to visit my church. Tomorrow."

Micah's eyes widen slightly. "Oh."

"Yeah. Oh."

My phone buzzes again.

DR. BAILEY

Perfect! Maybe we'll see you there?

I type back before I can overthink it.

HARPER

Yes! Definitely. I'll be there. Meet me in the lobby, and we can sit together!

DR. BAILEY

Wonderful! I do hope Micah will be with you. He's quite the catch. Shawn was impressed with him at the gala.

I stare at the screen.

Then I slowly look up at Micah.

He's watching me with a cautious expression. "What?"

"She wants you to be there."

"At church?"

"At church. Tomorrow. She said," I glance back at my phone. "She said you're '*quite the catch*' and her husband was impressed with you."

Micah blinks. "He was?"

"Apparently." I set my phone down, my mind already racing. "Okay. Okay, this is fine. We can work with this."

"Harper—"

"You just have to come and sit with us during the service. Maybe we grab lunch after with Mariah and her husband. Easy."

"Harper."

"It'll be fine. You're great with people. Everyone loved you last night. This is just an extension of that—"

"Harper." His voice is firmer now. "I can't."

I stop mid-ramble. "What?"

"I have to work."

My brain blanks. "Work?"

"Sunday mornings. I'm the children's ministry director, remember?"

Oh crap.

"I forgot." I press my hand to my forehead.

"How did you forget my job?" He's trying not to smile.

"I don't know! I was—" I gesture vaguely with my taco. "I was thinking about the fake dating thing, not your actual job!"

"Which is running the children's ministry."

"At the church we'd be attending."

"On Sunday morning."

"When you're working."

"Exactly," he says. "Wait, aren't you scheduled to serve both hours tomorrow?"

"Crap, yes. I'll have to swap with someone." I glance at him hopefully. "Can you swap me?"

"Me?"

"Yeah, don't you have a fancy app or something with all the volunteer schedules?"

"Harper, it's not that simple. Text your pod leader."

I stare at him.

He stares at me.

"Micah. You are the leader of all the pods."

He pinches the bridge of his nose. "Fine, just text me. Officially. So I have it in writing."

"That is the most bureaucratic thing you've ever said to me." I drop my head into my hands. "This is a disaster."

"It's not a disaster."

"Yes, it is. Dr. Bailey is expecting to see you, and now I have to tell her you won't be there, and she's going to think we broke up or that I lied about having a boyfriend—"

"Harper." Micah reaches across the table and gently pulls my hands away from my face. "Breathe."

I take a shaky breath.

"Okay," he says calmly. "Here's what we do. You tell her the truth. That I work Sunday mornings because I run the children's ministry. That makes sense. It's not suspicious."

I blink. "That's...actually smart."

"Right? And honestly, it makes me look better."

"How?"

"Because I'm a great, godly man who's so dedicated to his faith that he works at the church every Sunday."

I stare at him. "Did you just call yourself a great, godly man?"

"I'm quoting you. From about thirty seconds ago."

"I didn't say that."

"You definitely implied it."

"I did not—" I stop, realizing he's messing with me. "Are you enjoying this?"

"Maybe a little."

"I'm having a crisis here."

"I can tell." He's full-on grinning now. "But it's kind of fun watching you spiral."

I grab a tortilla chip and throw it at him. He catches it easily, still grinning.

"Okay, fine," I say, picking up my taco again. "So you'll be working during the service. That's actually fine. Great, even. Very respectable."

"Wow. What a compliment."

"I'm serious. It shows you're committed. And very responsible."

"All the qualities you want in a fake boyfriend."

"Exactly—" I pause. "Wait. Are you mocking me?"

"Would I do that?"

"Yes. You absolutely would."

He laughs, and despite my panic, I feel myself smiling.

Goodness, I enjoy making him laugh.

Wait. No. Stop that thought immediately.

"Okay," I say, refocusing. "So you're working during the service. That's covered. But—" I hesitate. "What about after?"

"After?"

"Lunch. With Dr. Bailey and her husband." I look at him hopefully. "Could you swing that?"

He's quiet for a beat, studying me.

"You want me to have lunch with your principal and her husband."

"Yes."

"After I've already worked all morning."

"Yes."

"To keep up the fake dating charade."

"Yes."

He leans back, considering. "This wasn't part of the original deal."

"I know."

"The deal was just the gala."

"I know that too."

"And now you're asking me to extend it."

"I know, I know. I'm asking a lot. But Micah, she's my boss. If she thinks I lied about having a boyfriend, it's going to be so awkward at work, and..."

"Okay."

I stop. "Okay?"

"Yes. I can do lunch."

Relief floods through me. "Really?"

"Really. But you're paying."

"Done. Absolutely. I'll pay for lunch every day for a week if you want."

"Let's start with tomorrow and see how it goes."

"Thank you." I reach across the table and squeeze his hand without thinking. "Seriously. Thank you. You're a lifesaver."

His expression shifts slightly, something I can't quite read passing across his face.

"Just a fake lifesaver," he mumbles.

"Right. Fake. Obviously." I pull my hand back, suddenly very aware of what I just did. "Anyway. Tomorrow. Lunch. You'll be there."

"I'll be there, Freckles."

The nickname. He keeps using it like its nothing, and every single time, I like it a little more than I should.

We finish our tacos, falling back into easier conversation about the food trucks, the weather, random things that don't involve fake dating or feelings or the way my heart keeps doing weird things when he looks at me.

But as we're gathering our trash to leave, I catch myself watching him.

The way he smiles. The way his hair falls slightly over his forehead. The way he carefully stacks all our trash so it's easier to throw away.

And I realize something terrifying.

This has nothing to do with Collin.

Inviting Micah to lunch tomorrow? That's not about making my ex jealous.

That's about wanting to see Micah again.

That's about not wanting this—whatever this is—to end.

"You okay?" Micah asks, and I realize I've been staring.

"Yeah. Fine. Just thinking."

"About?"

About how I might be falling for you and I have no idea what to do about it.

"About tomorrow," I say instead. "But all is fine."

"Gotcha."

We walk to the parking lot, and when we reach our cars,

there's this awkward moment where neither of us knows how to say goodbye.

"So," I say. "I'll see you tomorrow?"

"See you tomorrow."

"Thanks again. For doing this."

"Anytime, Harper."

He climbs into his truck, and I watch him drive away, my heart doing that stupid flutter thing again.

I get in my car and pull out my phone. The group chat is already a disaster—twenty-seven unread messages, the most recent being Olivia sending a single question mark at 11:43 this morning.

HARPER

Can you guys come over? Like now?

IVY

I have been waiting for this text. On my way.

OLIVIA

Already in my car.

They arrive within ten minutes of each other, which means they were both already close, which means they were both already waiting. Olivia has a Sonic bag. Ivy has that look on her face—the one that means she has questions and has been physically restraining herself from asking them.

I barely get the door open before she says, "Finally."

"Hello to you too."

"Harper," Olivia sets the Sonic bag on my counter and

turns to face me with her full therapist posture, which she claims she doesn't do outside of work. "We have been texting you constantly."

"I was a bit busy."

Ivy lowers herself onto the couch, one hand at her side. "Start from the beginning. From when you left your apartment. Leave nothing out."

So I don't.

I tell them everything—the gala, the kiss, Collin, the drive home, the next day, the glasses, all of it. Ivy asks three follow-up questions. Olivia asks none, which means she's already forming opinions she's waiting to share.

When I finish, the room is quiet for a beat.

Then Ivy says, "Okay. What's the emergency?"

I open my mouth. Close it. Try again.

"I invited Micah to lunch tomorrow. With my principal. After church."

Olivia is very still in the way she gets when she's listening hard.

"And that's the problem?" Ivy asks.

"That's the problem." I press my fingers to my forehead. "Because this whole thing started because of Collin. That was the point. Make him think I'd moved on, get through the gala, done. That was it."

"But?" Olivia says.

"I don't know." And that's the honest answer. "That's what's freaking me out. I don't know."

Chapter 22
Micah

I'm standing in the church lobby thirty minutes before service starts, and I still can't believe I'm doing this.

Yesterday, after our lunch at the food truck park, I went straight to Marcus, our youth pastor, and asked if he could cover children's ministry this morning.

"You're taking a Sunday off?" He'd looked at me like I'd grown a second head. "You haven't taken a Sunday off in... what, two years?"

"Two and a half," I'd corrected. "But yeah. I need tomorrow."

"Everything okay?"

"Yeah. I just... I have something I need to do."

Something I need to do. Like I'm running errands or going to the dentist.

Not surprising the girl I'm fake-dating-but-actually-falling-for by showing up when she thinks I'll be working.

Marcus had agreed immediately—probably because I've covered for him about seventeen times—and now here I am, dressed in dark jeans and a button-down, wearing my new glasses, waiting for Harper.

I can't say no to her.

That's the problem.

She asks, and I say yes. Every single time.

Even when I should say no. Even when it would be smarter to put some distance between us. Even when I know I'm just digging myself deeper into feelings, she doesn't return.

I check my phone. 9:02 a.m.

Service starts in twenty-eight minutes.

The lobby is filling up with people—families, college students, regulars I recognize, and visitors I don't.

And then I see her.

Harper walks through the front doors, and my breath catches.

She's wearing a floral dress that hits just above her knee, her hair in loose waves, with minimal makeup. She looks beautiful and nervous, scanning the lobby like she's searching for someone.

For Dr. Bailey, probably.

Not for me.

But when her eyes land on me, they widen in shock. And then, she smiles.

She weaves through the crowd, stopping a few feet away. "Micah? What are you doing?"

"Good morning to you too, Freckles."

"You're supposed to be working. With the kids. In children's ministry."

"I got someone to cover."

"You—" she blinks. "You got someone to cover?"

"Yeah."

"But you said—"

"I know what I said."

"So why are you here?"

I shove my hands in my pockets, trying to look casual, even though my heart is hammering. "Because you asked."

The words hang between us, more honest than I intended.

Harper stares at me, something unreadable flickering across her face.

"You didn't have to do that," she whispers.

"I know."

"Seriously, Micah. I would've been fine explaining to them you were working—"

"I wanted to be here."

That stops her.

We stand there for a moment, the noise of the lobby fading into the background as she looks at me like she's trying to figure out what I mean.

Before either of us can say anything else, a voice calls out.

"Harper!"

We both turn to see Dr. Bailey and her husband walking toward us, all smiles.

Harper's expression shifts immediately—from confused to bright and welcoming.

"Mariah! Shawn! You made it!" She gives them both quick hugs, then gestures to me. "You remember Micah."

"Of course!" Mariah beams. "Micah, it's so good to see you again. I wasn't sure if you'd be here since Harper mentioned you usually work Sundays."

"I asked someone to cover," I say, sliding my hand to Harper's lower back. "Couldn't miss the chance to sit with Harper during service."

The way Harper glances up at me—surprised and

maybe a little pleased—hits me somewhere I wasn't prepared for.

"Well, we're so glad you did," Shawn says, shaking my hand. "This place is incredible. Harper wasn't kidding about the building."

"Would you like a tour before service?" Harper asks. "We have a few minutes."

"That would be wonderful!"

For the next ten minutes, Harper and I lead them through the church—showing them the coffee bar, the bookstore, the kids' area where I usually spend my Sunday mornings.

Harper's in full teacher mode, animated and enthusiastic, and I find myself just watching her.

The way she gestures when she talks. The way she lights up when they ask questions. The way she keeps glancing at me like she still can't believe I'm here.

We make it to the sanctuary, and Harper slides in first, and I sit beside her, Mariah and Shawn taking the seats to her right.

"This is beautiful," Mariah says, looking around at the high ceilings, the stage with its warm lighting, the screens displaying the morning's welcome message.

"It really is," Harper agrees.

The lights dim slightly, and Gray steps up to the mic, guitar in hand.

"That's Gray," she whispers. "My friend Ivy's husband."

"Oh yes! I remember her." Dr. Bailey whispers.

"Good morning, New Chapter!" Gray's voice fills the sanctuary. "Let's stand and worship together."

He strums the opening chords to a familiar song—upbeat and joyful—and around us, people begin to sing.

I glance at Harper.

Her eyes fixed on the screen displaying the lyrics, and she's singing along. Quietly at first, then a little louder.

But she looks stiff. Like she's performing rather than worshiping.

During the second song—a slower, more intimate one—people around us start raising their hands.

Harper glances around, then shifts beside me, her arms crossing and uncrossing like she can't quite settle.

I lean close. "You okay?"

"I don't know what to do with my hands," she admits, voice low.

I almost smile. "Some people raise them. It's called outward worship—a physical way of surrendering, opening yourself up to God." I pause, watching her process that. "But it's not required. There's no right way to do this."

She glances sideways at me. "Then what do you do when you don't feel it?"

"Close your eyes," I say simply. "Block everything else out. Sometimes the most honest thing you can offer is just... stillness."

She's quiet for a second, like she's weighing that. Then, almost imperceptibly, her eyes flutter shut.

I look back at the stage.

But a moment later I glance over again—and the sight of her stops me mid-breath. Her hands have stopped fidgeting. Her shoulders have dropped. Her expression, usually so animated and searching, has softened into something I haven't seen on her before.

She sways, just barely, with the music.

Like she forgot she was performing for anyone.

Pastor Jack opens the way he always does—with a question nobody's ready for.

"I want you to do something for me," he says, stepping to the edge of the stage. No Bible yet. Just him and the quiet. "Take a minute. Right now. Make a mental list of everything you want to accomplish this week. Your priorities. The things you're going to spend your time on."

The room settles.

"Got your list?"

A few people nod. Someone near the back laughs a little, like the list is already too long.

"Good." He tilts his head. "Now go back through it. How many of those things required spending time with God?"

Silence.

I shift in my seat. Because if I'm being honest, my own list this week looked a lot like logistics. Children's ministry schedules. Volunteer coordination. The craft supply order I'd been putting off since February. I had prayed. I had read. But had I wanted it, the way you want water when you've been thirsty all day?

I'm not sure I had.

Pastor Jack picks up his Bible.

"Psalm 42," he says. "The writer compares himself to a deer that's longing for water. Not wandering toward water. Not thinking about water. Longing. Parched. Bone-dry and desperate for the one thing that will actually fix it."

He reads the verse aloud, and something about the plainness of the image—an animal, a stream, a need that simple—cuts right through all the complexity I've been carrying.

I glance at Harper.

She's writing.

I do a double take because for a second I think I imagined it. But no, she has the journal open in her lap, the brown leather one I gave her, and she is writing. Her pen is moving fast, trying to keep pace with Pastor Jack, and from the way she's angled toward the stage, I can tell she's not taking polite notes. She's trying to get it all down.

She underlines something. Hard. Twice.

I look back at the stage before she can catch me staring.

"The psalmist," Pastor Jack continues, "is exhausted. He is under pressure. He is running on empty—and not because his life is falling apart, but just because life is a lot. Sound familiar?"

Quiet laughter ripples through the congregation.

"And yet, in the middle of all that, his deepest cry isn't for relief. It isn't for answers. His innermost desire is for God. Not what God can fix. Not what God can provide. Just...God."

Harper's pen scratches across the page.

I find myself thinking about the last few months. How I'd been so busy doing ministry that I'd maybe stopped experiencing it. How I could talk about God's presence in a small group setting, could teach it, could lead accountability around it—and still manage to skip right past actually sitting in it myself.

"Here's the thing about presence," Pastor Jack says, coming back to center stage. "We treat it like a reward. Like something we get to access once we've handled everything else on the list." He shakes his head. "But God isn't waiting at the bottom of your productivity. He's not limited to a building, or a service time, or a quiet morning when everything lines up perfectly. He is Spirit. He is here. Right now, in this room, with every single person who walked through those doors today."

I hear Harper exhale beside me.

"So what does it actually take?" Pastor Jack opens his hands. "Desire. That's it. A want. A willingness to draw close—through His Word, through prayer, through just sitting still long enough to let Him in." He pauses. "And here's the promise: as you draw close to Him, He is ready and willing to draw close to you. He will restore your soul. Not because you earned it. Because He is that kind of God."

I glance over again.

Harper has stopped writing. She's just listening now, pen hovering over the page, like the words came too fast and she decided to feel them instead of chase them.

Pastor Jack paces slowly. "Spending time with God is a basic need. Like water. Like air. And we treat it like a bonus—like something we'll get to when the week slows down." He stops. "The week doesn't slow down. You already know that. But God doesn't need a slow week. He just needs your desire. Your willingness to say: this is my priority. This is what I want most."

He lets that sit.

I let it sit.

Because I needed that as much as anyone in this room. Maybe more, given how easy it is to dress busyness up in ministry clothes and call it devotion.

When the message ends and heads bow, I close my eyes

and offer something quieter than I usually pray. Not a list. Not an intercession for my volunteers, or my curriculum, or the three kids I've been watching closely this semester.

I want to want You most. Teach me what that looks like.

When I open my eyes, Harper is still looking down at the journal. She's reading back over what she wrote, her finger tracing a line she underlined. Slowly, she closes the cover.

I smile before I can stop myself.

She brought it to church.

She's not going through the motions today.

After service, we all stand in the lobby, and Mariah is glowing.

"That was incredible," she says. "The worship, the sermon—all of it. Shawn, we have to come back next week."

"Absolutely," Shawn agrees. "Pastor Jack is an engaging speaker. And the community here feels so warm."

"That's one of the things I love about New Chapter," Harper says. "Everyone's so welcoming."

"And Micah," Mariah says, turning to me. "You work here every weekend?"

"I do. Usually, I'm knee-deep in crafts and Bible stories on Sunday mornings, but I made an exception today."

"For Harper," she says knowingly.

"For Harper," I confirm, squeezing Harper's hand.

She blushes slightly, and I file that reaction away for later.

"Well," Shawn says, checking his watch. "We'd love to

take you two out for lunch if you're available. Our treat. We want to hear more about this church—and about you two."

Harper glances at me, and I nod.

"Lunch sounds great," she says.

Chapter 23
Micah

We end up at a bistro a few blocks from the church—a cozy spot with white tablecloths and a brunch menu that makes my mouth water.

Once we're settled with drinks and have ordered, Mariah leans forward with a smile.

"Okay, I have to ask. How did you two actually meet? Harper's been vague about the details."

Harper and I exchange a glance.

"At church, actually," I say.

"Really?" Shawn raises his eyebrows. "That's sweet."

"It wasn't sweet at first," Harper admits, laughing. "We actually got off on the wrong foot."

"Oh, this I have to hear," Mariah says, clearly delighted.

Harper looks at me. "You want to tell it, or should I?"

"I'll start. You can correct me when I get it wrong."

She grins. "Deal."

"So Harper came in with her friend one Sunday morning," I begin, reaching for my water glass. "And there was a little boy in the hallway—one of her former students—upset and separated from his dad."

"He ran straight to me," Harper adds. "Like a full sprint, arms out. What was I supposed to do, sidestep him?"

"She didn't sidestep him," I confirm. "She also didn't have a name tag, a visitor badge, or any record on file in our system."

Mariah's eyes are already dancing. "Oh no."

"Oh yes," Harper says. "And this one comes around the corner like he's about to make a citizen's arrest."

"I was doing my job," I say, keeping my voice even, which only makes Harper laugh harder.

"He literally said, 'And I'm just supposed to take your word for that?'" Harper widens her eyes, doing a passable impression of my tone. "To a kindergarten teacher. About being a kindergarten teacher."

Shawn lets out a laugh. "That's rough, man."

"In my defense," I say, holding up a hand, "we have policies for a reason. I didn't know her."

"So what happened?" Mariah leans forward, chin in her hand.

"She filled out the background check," I say.

Harper lifts her fork. "Out of spite."

"Completely out of spite," I agree.

"And then I looked him dead in the eye and told him I'd see him next weekend." Harper smiles at the memory, something almost fond in it. "He told me they'd contact me if it was approved."

Shawn shakes his head, grinning. "And you still ended up together?"

Harper glances at me, just for a second. "Eventually, we figured out how to be in the same room without arguing."

"Mostly," I add.

Mariah laughs, reaching for her glass. "I love that. The best ones always start a little sideways."

"That's a great story," Shawn says. "You two seem great together."

"We are," Harper says, glancing at me. "He keeps me grounded. And I... well, I keep things interesting."

"That's one word for it," I tease.

She kicks me lightly under the table, and I grin.

Our food arrives, and the conversation shifts to lighter topics—Mariah and Shawn's own relationship story, their thoughts on the sermon, recommendations for other things to check out at New Chapter.

But at some point, Harper turns to me and whispers, "You know, you didn't have to give up your Sunday morning for this."

"I wanted to."

"Still. It's a big deal. Don't you, like, never take Sundays off?"

"Congratulations," I say, leaning back in my chair. "You've found my weakness."

She raises an eyebrow. "And that is?"

I look at her, and for once, I don't hide what I'm feeling.

"You." I wink, keeping my tone light and teasing, but there's truth underneath.

Harper's cheeks flush pink, and she looks away, flustered.

"You're just being funny," she mutters.

"Maybe."

But as she bites her lip, trying not to smile, I know she felt it too.

The truth buried in the joke.

Because she is my weakness.

And every time I'm around her, it gets harder to pretend she's not.

By the time lunch ends, I'm exhausted in the best way.

The conversation has been easy. Laughter has been frequent. And Harper's been leaning into me all afternoon—little touches, shared glances, the kind of comfortable intimacy that makes Mariah and Shawn exchange knowing smiles.

We walk them to their car, and Mariah pulls Harper into a hug.

"Thank you so much for today. We loved the church. And we love seeing you so happy."

"Thank you for coming," Harper says. "It means a lot."

Mariah pulls back, keeping her hands on Harper's shoulders for just a moment, the way people do when they mean what they're about to say. Then she looks over at me.

"I hope we'll see you at the open house next month, Micah. After all, her classroom is like her second home—I think you'd love seeing it."

"I wouldn't miss it," I say, and I mean it.

Something flickers across Harper's face—quick enough that I almost miss it. A softness she doesn't quite have time to hide before she looks away.

Shawn steps forward and shakes my hand, his grip firm and warm. "Take care of her, Micah."

"I will."

They drive off, and suddenly it's just Harper and me, standing in the parking lot, the afternoon sun warm on our faces.

"That went well," she says.

"It did."

"Thank you."

"Anytime, Freckles."

She looks up at me, and there's something soft in her expression. Something I don't know what to do with.

"You know, I had a very productive day off planned," I say. "Yard work. Groceries. Very exciting stuff."

She laughs. "And?"

"And somehow I ended up here." I shake my head slowly. "You are my weakness."

Harper doesn't laugh.

Doesn't roll her eyes or fire something back. She just looks at me for a half second, something shifting behind her expression—and then she steps forward and wraps her arms around me.

I freeze for half a second, then wrap my arms around her too, holding her close.

She fits perfectly against me. Her head tucked under my chin. Her hands pressed flat against my back like she's steadying herself. The faint scent of her shampoo, something floral and sweet, curling around us both.

We stand like that for a long moment, and I let myself have this.

Just this.

The parking lot is quiet. Somewhere down the street, a bird calls once and goes still. The afternoon light has gone golden and warm, and I'm hyperaware of every single point of contact between us—her fingers curled against my back, the soft rise and fall of her breathing, the way she hasn't moved.

Neither have I.

Then she pulls back slightly. Just enough to look up at me.

And the way she's looking at me; her eyes are soft. Searching. Like she's trying to figure something out she's been turning over for weeks. Like maybe she's finally letting herself look.

My hand moves before I've made the decision to move it, reaching up to brush a strand of hair away from her face. My fingers linger against her cheek, and I feel the moment her breath catches—a small, quiet thing that undoes me completely.

"Harper," I whisper.

I don't even know what I'm asking.

But she seems to.

Because she doesn't step back. Doesn't pull away. Doesn't deflect with a joke or a grin or one of the hundred ways she usually keeps the world at arm's length.

She just looks at me with those bright green eyes, and I can see the exact moment she realizes what's about to happen — and chooses not to stop it.

I lean in. Slowly. Deliberately. Giving her every chance to pull back.

She doesn't.

Her chin tilts up, almost imperceptibly. Her eyes flutter closed. The space between us shrinks to nothing...

WAAAAH! WAAAAH! WAAAAH!

A car alarm detonates through the quiet parking lot, loud and jarring and absolutely merciless.

We fly apart as if electricity shocked us.

Harper's hand flies to her chest. "Oh my."

I run a hand through my hair, my heart pounding. "That's—"

"Loud. That's really loud."

Across the parking lot, someone's frantically clicking their key fob, trying to shut off the alarm on a silver sedan.

Whatever that moment was, it has completely shattered.

Harper takes another step back, wrapping her arms around herself. "I should—I should probably get going."

"Right. Yeah. Of course."

"I have lesson plans to finish. For tomorrow."

"Sure."

She's not looking at me now. Just staring at her car keys like they're the most fascinating thing in the world.

"Harper—"

"Thank you again," she says quickly. "For today. It really meant a lot."

"I'm glad I could be there."

"Yeah. Me too."

The car alarm finally stops, leaving an awkward silence in its wake.

Harper gestures toward her car. "I'm just gonna—"

"Go. Yeah. I'll see you later?"

"See you later."

She walks to her car, and I watch as she gets in, starts the engine, and pulls out of the parking lot.

She doesn't look back.

And I'm left standing there, hand still tingling from where I touched her face, wondering what the heck just happened.

We almost kissed.

No.

I almost kissed her.

And she didn't stop me.

She was going to let it happen.

Which means—I press my hands to my face, trying to get my racing thoughts under control.

God, what am I doing?

This is fake. It's supposed to be fake.

But nothing about the way she looked at me just now felt fake.

Nothing about the way my heart is currently trying to beat out of my chest feels fake.

I climb into my truck and sit there for a moment, gripping the steering wheel.

Then I pull out my phone and call Gray.

He answers on the second ring. "Hey, man."

"I almost kissed her."

Silence.

"Gray?"

"Define 'almost.'"

"Like, hand-on-her-face, both-leaning-in, would-have-happened-if-not-for-a-car-alarm almost."

"A car alarm?"

"Don't ask."

More silence.

"Micah."

"I know."

"You're supposed to be fake dating."

"I know."

"This doesn't sound fake."

"I know Gray, hence why I am calling you."

I hear him exhale slowly. "Okay. What do you need from me?"

"I don't know. Someone to tell me I'm not losing my mind."

"You're not losing your mind." A beat. "You're just in trouble."

"Helpful. Thanks."

He lets out a short laugh. Then, more seriously, "Meet me in ten minutes, the coffee shop by my place. We'll talk it through."

"Yeah," I say, scrubbing a hand over my face. "Yeah, okay."

"See you soon, man."

He hangs up.

And I sit there in my truck, staring at the spot where Harper's car was parked, replaying that moment over and over.

The way she looked at me.

The way she didn't pull away.

The way everything in me wanted to close that distance and kiss her like I've been wanting to since two nights ago.

Please let it be me, I'd prayed.

And for just a moment, in that parking lot, it almost was.

Chapter 24
Harper

I can't sleep.

I've been staring at my ceiling for the past two hours, replaying the day on an endless loop.

Church. Dr. Bailey. The lunch. The parking lot.

The almost-kiss.

Ugh, the almost-kiss.

I roll over, pressing my face into my pillow, and groan.

What am I doing?

This was supposed to be simple. Fake date Micah to the gala. Make Collin jealous. Win him back.

Except Collin's with Jessica now, the girl who fits perfectly into his life in a way I never did.

And I'm lying in bed at 10:47 p.m. on a Sunday night, unable to stop thinking about the way Micah's hand felt against my cheek. The way he looked at me like I was the only person in the world. The way we both leaned in, closer and closer, until that stupid car alarm.

I sit up, running my hands through my hair.

This isn't about Collin anymore.

And that's a problem.

I grab my phone from the nightstand, scrolling mindlessly through Instagram. Ivy posted a selfie with Gray from church this morning—both of them smiling, his arm around her, looking annoyingly happy.

I keep scrolling.

Anna posted a picture of her and Tim at brunch.

Dr. Bailey shared a photo of the church building with the caption: **Found our new Sunday home!**

Everyone looks so settled. So sure of themselves.

And here I am, 27 years old, single, confused about everything, and exhausted from trying to hold it all together.

I toss my phone aside and swing my legs out of bed.

I walk to my desk and see the photo booth pictures from the gala, still sitting where I left them.

I pick up the strip, studying each frame.

The silly faces. The laughter. The third one where we're trying to look serious but failing.

And the fourth one.

The one where we're looking at each other.

Not at the camera. At each other.

Like nothing else existed.

I set the photo strip down and notice the journal lying next to them.

The brown leather journal Micah gave me before the gala.

I pick it up, running my fingers over the cover, then open it to the first page.

His handwriting stares back at me.

HARPER,

MAY THIS BE A SPACE WHERE YOU CAN BE HONEST WITH GOD, YOURSELF, AND THE JOURNEY AHEAD.

PROVERBS 3:5-6

"TRUST IN THE LORD WITH ALL YOUR HEART, AND DO NOT LEAN ON YOUR OWN UNDERSTANDING. IN ALL YOUR WAYS ACKNOWLEDGE HIM, AND HE WILL MAKE STRAIGHT YOUR PATHS."

- MICAH

I flip through the pages, finding my sermon notes from this morning.

Pastor Jack had asked us to make a list of everything we needed to accomplish this week.

I started to write it down. Underlined it. Then stared at it for the rest of the sermon because I already knew my answer.

He'd talked about Psalm 42. The deer that's parched and longing, desperate for water—not wandering toward it, not thinking about it, but aching for it. And how the psalmist, exhausted and under pressure, doesn't cry out for relief, or answers, or rescue. His deepest cry is just for presence. For God Himself.

I'd written that down too. His innermost desire is for God.

But now, staring at the notes, I realize I don't actually know what that feels like.

Desire.

Longing.

Not because you're supposed to. Not because it's on the list.

I know the words. I've heard them my whole life.

But how do you actually want that?

Because I've been trying. God knows I've been trying.

I'm a nice person. I don't judge others, at least not to their faces. I volunteer in children's ministry nearly every weekend—not because I feel called to it, but because I'm good at it and it's easier than sitting in a pew and actually listening. I know the Bible inside and out—or at least I used to, from the Scripture overload of my childhood. I can still recite verses on command like a party trick.

I add Scripture to all my social media posts. Encouraging ones. The kind that gets saved and shared. I pick them the same way I pick a good caption—for the aesthetic, if I'm being honest.

I've never missed an Easter or Christmas service in my life. Not once. Not because I couldn't wait to get there, but because not going would feel wrong in a way I can't fully explain. Like breaking a rule nobody wrote down.

I tithe. I bow my head when someone prays out loud. I know exactly what to say so that I sound like I mean it.

All the things my parents taught me good Christians do.

But that's the thing Pastor Jack said that I can't shake loose. God isn't waiting at the bottom of your productivity list. Spending time with Him isn't the reward you get after you've performed well enough. It's the thing you're supposed to actually want.

And I don't know if I've ever wanted it. Not really. Not the way the psalmist wanted it. Not like someone parched and desperate and willing to say so out loud.

I've wanted to be good. I've wanted to look good. I've wanted to feel like the kind of person who has it together spiritually.

I close the journal and press it against my chest, sinking onto the edge of my bed.

What's wrong with me?

Micah makes it look so easy. His faith seems so, effortless. Natural. Like breathing.

He doesn't struggle like I do. He doesn't second-guess everything. He just...believes.

And I don't know how to do that.

I glance at my phone. 10:52 p.m.

It's late. Too late to call anyone.

But I could text.

My thumb hovers over Micah's contact.

I shouldn't.

I really, really shouldn't.

But I'm spiraling, and he's the only person who might understand.

I type quickly before I can talk myself out of it.

HARPER

If you're awake, can you talk?

I hit send and immediately regret it.

It's almost 11 p.m. He's probably asleep. Or getting ready for bed. And now I've bothered him with my existential crisis about faith and—my phone rings.

Micah's name flashes on the screen.

My heart jumps into my throat.

He called. He didn't text back. He just... called.

Instantly.

I answer, pressing the phone to my ear. "Hello?"

"Harper?" His voice is alert, concerned. Not groggy at all. "Are you okay?"

"I—yeah. I'm okay. I'm sorry, I know it's late—"

"It's not too late. I was up."

"Really?"

"I don't sleep much," he says, and there's a hint of amusement in his tone. "Four, maybe five hours a night. I've been that way since college."

"That can't be healthy."

"Probably not. But it gives me more time to get things done." He pauses. "What's going on?"

I stand up, pacing my bedroom. "I just... I had a question. About something Pastor Jack said this morning."

There's a pause.

"Okay," he says slowly. "What's the question?"

I look down at the journal in my other hand, at the notes I took, and suddenly I don't know where to start.

"He talked about grace," I begin. "About how we can't earn God's love. That it's a gift. But I don't... I don't understand how to actually live that."

"What do you mean?"

"I mean—" I pace faster. "I've been trying, Micah. I really have. I volunteer. I try to read my Bible. I pray before meals. I do all the things I'm supposed to do. But I still feel like I'm not good enough. Like I'm missing something."

"Harper—"

"And it's easy for you," I continue, the words tumbling out faster now. "You're perfect. You've got your faith all figured out. You don't struggle like I do."

"Harper, I'm not—"

"You are!" My voice cracks. "You lead Bible studies. You run children's ministry. You probably haven't sinned since you were twelve."

He laughs.

And I don't know whether to be offended or relieved.

"Harper," he says, and there's warmth in his voice. "I sinned this morning when I got annoyed at the guy who cut me off in traffic. And yesterday, when I judged someone for their Instagram post. And last week when I snapped at Marcus for eating my leftovers from the church fridge."

Despite everything, I smile. "Okay, fine. But you're

still... good. You don't mess up like I do. You're always doing the right thing."

"That's not true."

"It is—"

"Harper." His voice is firmer now. "I'm the furthest thing from perfect. And if you think I've got my faith all figured out, you're wrong."

I stop pacing, sinking back onto the bed.

"Then why does it seem so easy for you?"

He's quiet for a moment. "You want to know the difference between us?"

"Yes."

"It's not that I'm better. It's that I stopped trying to manufacture fruit on my own."

I grab the journal and flip to a blank page, reaching for a pen. "What does that even mean?"

"There's this passage in John 15," he says. "Jesus says, 'Remain in Me, and I in you. Just as a branch is unable to produce fruit by itself unless it remains on the vine, so neither can you unless you remain in Me.'"

I scribble down the reference.

John 15:4

My handwriting messy and rushed.

"Okay," I say. "John 15. Got it. But I still don't understand what that has to do with me."

"Everything," Micah says. "Harper, you're exhausted because you're trying to be the vine and the branch. But you're not the vine. Jesus is."

"So what am I supposed to do? Just... sit around and hope good things happen?"

"No. You stay connected. You remain in Him."

I press my palm to my forehead, frustration building. "Micah, I don't know what that means. I don't know how to do that."

"Okay, let me explain it better." He takes a breath. "Picture a grapevine."

"Got it."

"The vine is the main part—the trunk. It's strong, rooted, the source of life. And then there are branches growing out of it."

"Okay."

"The branches don't produce the grapes. The vine does. The branches just have to stay connected to the vine. And when they do, the life of the vine flows through them, and fruit grows naturally."

I'm writing now, trying to capture everything he's saying.

"So... Jesus is the vine," I say slowly.

"Right."

"And we're the branches."

"Exactly."

"And the fruit is... what? Love? Joy? All that stuff?"

"Yeah. The fruit of the Spirit. Love, joy, peace, patience, kindness, goodness, faithfulness, gentleness, self-control. All the things you've been trying so hard to produce on your own."

I set down my pen, pressing my hand to my chest. "So you're saying I've been doing it wrong."

"No." His voice is so gentle it makes my throat tight. "I'm saying you've been trying to do it alone. And that's exhausting."

"It is," I whisper. "It's so exhausting, Micah."

"I know."

"I feel like I'm constantly falling short. Like no matter how hard I try, it's never enough."

"That's because you're striving instead of remaining."

I pull my knees to my chest, the phone still pressed to my ear. "What's the difference?"

"Striving is about effort. It's about working harder, doing more, trying to prove yourself. Remaining is about connection. It's about staying close to Jesus and letting His life flow through you."

"But how do I do that?" My voice cracks. "I don't know how to stay connected. I don't even know what that looks like."

There's a pause, and I hear him shift—like he's settling in for a longer conversation.

"It's not as complicated as you think," he says. "Remaining means talking to Him like He's real—because He is. Reading His Word not to check a box, but to hear His voice. Spending time in His presence because you want to, not because you have to."

"But I've tried that. I read my Bible app daily. I pray. And I still feel... empty."

"Because you're doing it to earn something," he says gently. "You're reading your Bible to prove you're a good Christian. You're praying to check off a spiritual to-do list. But Harper, God doesn't want your performance. He wants your presence."

The words hit me like a punch to the chest.

My hand fumbles with my phone, and suddenly the screen lights up.

Switching to FaceTime...

Oh no.

"Wait, I didn't mean to—"

And then Micah's face fills the screen.

Chapter 25
Harper

He's in his bedroom, I think. Sitting against his headboard, wearing a gray t-shirt, his dark-rimmed glasses slightly crooked, hair messy like he's been running his hands through it.

And he's looking at me.

"Oh my gosh, I'm a mess," I blurt out, immediately trying to angle the phone away.

"Harper, stop." His voice is firm but kind. "You're not a mess."

"I literally look like I've been crying."

"You have been crying."

"Exactly. So I'm a mess."

"No." He adjusts his glasses, leaning slightly closer to the camera. "You're being honest. There's a difference."

I pause, the phone still half-angled away from my face.

"Besides," he continues, a small smile tugging at his lips, "I saw you at your worst the other morning after the gala. Mascara everywhere. Missing an eyelash. You can't get much messier than that."

Despite everything, I laugh. "Thanks for the reminder."

"You're still beautiful, Freckles."

The words catch me off guard, and I feel my cheeks heat.

I finally angle the phone back, looking at him properly through the screen.

"Hi," I whisper.

"Hi."

We just look at each other for a moment, and something about seeing his face—even through a screen—makes me feel less alone.

"Your parents taught you that faith is about following rules," Micah says, picking up where we left off. "Checking boxes. Looking the part. But that's not what Jesus taught. Jesus said, '*Remain in Me*'—not '*Try harder.*' Not '*Be perfect.*' *Just stay close.*"

Tears prick at my eyes. "I don't know if I've ever done that. Stayed close. I think I've just been... performing."

"Then it's time to stop performing and start being present."

A tear slides down my cheek, and I quickly wipe it away.

"What if I'm not good at it?" I ask. "What if I try and I still feel empty?"

"Then you keep showing up. You practice. And slowly, you'll notice that you're not striving anymore. You're just... connected. And the fruit? It grows on its own."

I look at him through the screen, and I instantly see it. The thing that sets Micah apart.

The peace. The steadiness. The quiet confidence that comes from being rooted in something bigger than himself.

And I want that.

I want that so badly.

"I'm so tired of trying to be enough," I whisper.

Micah's expression softens, and even through the phone, I can see the emotion in his eyes.

"Then stop trying," he says, his voice breaking slightly. "Just remain."

The tears come in earnest now, and I bury my face in my free hand.

"I don't know how to do this, Micah. I don't know how to let go of all the striving and just... be."

"You don't have to figure it all out tonight," he says quietly. "You just have to take the first step. And the first step is being honest. With God. With yourself."

I nod, still crying.

"Can I tell you something?" he asks.

"Yeah."

"For a long time, I thought being a Christian meant checking boxes too. Church attendance. Bible reading. Volunteering. All good things. But I was doing them to prove I was good enough. And I was miserable."

I look up at the screen, surprised. "You were?"

"Yeah. I burned out completely. Stopped going to church for a while. Stopped reading my Bible. Just... shut down."

"What changed?"

"I realized that Jesus didn't want my performance. He wanted my heart. And once I stopped trying to earn His love and just started receiving it? Everything changed. I wasn't perfect. I still messed up. But I wasn't striving anymore. I was just... connected."

"And that's when the fruit started growing."

"Exactly."

I wipe my eyes, taking a shaky breath. "I want that. I want to stop performing and start actually knowing Him."

"Then you're already on the right path."

We sit in silence for a moment—him in his bedroom, me in mine, connected by a screen and a conversation that feels more real than anything I've experienced in months.

"Can I ask you something?" he says.

"Anything."

Micah's expression softens even more. "Can I pray for you?"

I nearly lose the ability to speak. I manage a breathless, "of course."

I set my phone down, propping it against a pillow so I can still see him, and I close my eyes.

And then, through the phone at almost midnight, Micah prays.

Not a long, performative prayer.

Not a checklist of requests.

Just honest, genuine words from his heart to God's.

"God, thank You for Harper. Thank You for her honesty. Thank You that she's asking real questions and wanting more than just performance. I pray that You would help her learn what it means to remain in You. To stay connected. To let go of striving and just rest in Your love. Help her know that she doesn't have to earn Your approval—she already has it. Not because of what she does, but because of who You are. Give her peace. Give her clarity. And most of all, give her a deep, abiding relationship with You. In Jesus' name, amen."

When he finishes, I open my eyes, and he's looking at me through the screen with such tenderness.

"Thank you," I whisper.

"Anytime, Freckles."

I pick up my phone again, holding it close.

"Micah," I whisper.

"Yeah?"

"Earlier today. In the parking lot."

His jaw tightens slightly. "Yeah."

"We almost—"

"I know."

We sit like that for another minute, just looking at each other, until Micah finally glances at something off-screen.

"I should let you get some sleep," he says reluctantly.

"Yeah. You're probably right."

But neither of us moves to hang up.

"Harper," he says, his voice rough. "I'm really proud of you. For being honest tonight. For asking questions. For wanting more than just going through the motions."

"I couldn't have done it without you."

"Yes, you could. You just needed someone to remind you that it's okay to not have it all figured out."

"Thank you. For everything."

"Get some sleep," he says softly. "And tomorrow? Try talking to God like you talked to me tonight. Just honest. No performance."

I nod. "I will."

"Good night, Freckles."

"Good night, Dimples."

He smiles—that soft, genuine smile that makes my heart do stupid things—and then the screen goes dark.

I set my phone down and sit there for a moment, processing everything.

Then I grab the journal and a pen.

For a long moment, I just stare at the blank page.

And then I start writing.

> *God,*
>
> *I don't know if I've ever really known You. I*

think I've been so busy trying to impress You that I forgot to actually talk to You.

I'm tired of performing. Tired of trying to be good enough. Tired of feeling like I'm failing.

Micah said I need to remain in You. To stay connected. And I don't really know what that means yet, but I want to learn.

I want to stop striving and just... be.

Help me, God. Help me figure out what it means to remain.

- Harper

I set down the pen and close the journal.

And for the first time in a long time, I don't feel empty.

I feel... hopeful.

Like maybe I'm finally on the right path.

Not because I have it all figured out.

But because I'm finally willing to admit that I don't.

And maybe that's enough.

Chapter 26
Micah

I'm still staring at my phone ten minutes after Harper hangs up.

The screen is dark, but I can still see her face in my mind—tear-streaked, vulnerable, beautiful. The way she looked at me through the camera after I prayed for her. The way her expression shifted from exhausted to hopeful.

I want to stop performing and start actually knowing Him.

Those words.

Man, those words.

I set my phone on my nightstand and lean back against my headboard, a smile tugging at my lips despite the late hour.

This is what I live for.

Pointing someone to Jesus. Watching the light come on. Seeing someone realize that faith isn't about striving—it's about staying connected.

Harper Mitchell is starting to understand what it means to truly have a relationship with Jesus.

And I got to be part of that.

Biscuit appears from his tunnel system, chittering softly as he climbs up onto the bed.

"Hey, buddy," I say, scratching behind his ears. "Big night."

He tilts his head, like he's asking for details.

"Harper called. Well, texted first. Then I called. Then we accidentally FaceTime'd." I pause, replaying the moment. "She's wrestling with her faith. Really wrestling with it. Not just going through the motions anymore."

Biscuit climbs onto my chest, settling in.

"And yeah, I know what you're thinking. I'm falling for her. Hard. But tonight wasn't about that. Tonight was about pointing her to the source. To Jesus. Not to me."

Biscuit chitters again, like he's skeptical.

"Okay, fine. Maybe I'm also falling for her. But that's secondary. Her relationship with God comes first. It has to."

I close my eyes, replaying the conversation.

The way she admitted she's been performing her whole life. The way she broke down when she said she's tired of trying to be enough. The way she looked at me after I prayed—like maybe she was starting to believe that God's love isn't something she has to earn.

This is why I do what I do.

This is why I run children's ministry, why I lead Bible studies, why I stay up late answering questions about faith.

Because watching someone encounter Jesus—really encounter Him—is the most beautiful thing in the world.

Even if it's complicated by the fact that I'm completely in love with her.

I open my eyes and look at Biscuit. "I'm in trouble, aren't I?"

He squeaks in agreement.

"Yeah. That's what I thought."

I glance at the clock. It's almost midnight.

I should sleep. I have a meeting with the children's ministry team at 9 a.m. tomorrow, and then curriculum planning in the afternoon.

But I'm too wired. Too full of adrenaline and hope and this overwhelming sense of gratitude that God let me be a part of Harper's journey tonight.

So instead of sleeping, I grab my Bible from the nightstand and flip to John 15.

I read the passage slowly, letting the words sink in.

"I am the vine; you are the branches. The one who remains in Me and I in him produces much fruit, because you can do nothing without Me."

I think about Harper—about how exhausted she's been, trying to produce fruit on her own. Trying to be good enough through sheer effort.

And I think about how freeing it will be for her when she finally lets go and just stays connected.

"God," I whisper into the quiet of my room. "Thank You for tonight. Thank You for giving me the words to say. Thank You for opening Harper's heart to hear them. Please keep working in her. Help her learn what it means to remain. And help me..." I pause, swallowing hard. "Help me love her well. Even if that means just loving her as a friend."

Biscuit nuzzles against my hand, and I smile.

"Alright, buddy. I should probably try to get some sleep."

I set the Bible aside, turn off the lamp, and settle under the covers.

Biscuit curls up on the pillow next to me, and I close my eyes.

And for the first time in weeks, I fall asleep with a smile on my face.

Not because I think Harper's falling for me.

But because she's falling for Jesus.

And that's infinitely better.

I'm in the church supply closet on Wednesday afternoon, taking inventory of craft supplies for this weekend's curriculum, when my phone buzzes in my pocket.

I pull it out, expecting a text from Marcus about Sunday's setup or maybe Gray asking if I want to grab lunch.

But it's Harper.

HARPER

SOS

I freeze, craft supplies forgotten.

SOS?

My mind immediately spirals. Is she okay? Did something happen? Is this about her faith? About Collin?

I'm about to hit call when another text comes through. Followed by several others.

HARPER

Friday night

Bowling

You

Me

And all the elementary staff at my school

Including Collin

It's couples' team building night

You in??

I stare at the screen.

Then I start grinning.

Like, full-on, can't-stop-myself grinning.

She's asking me to attend another fake dating event.

Which means she's not done with this yet.

Which means I get to spend more time with her.

"Why are you smiling like that?"

I jump, nearly dropping my phone, and turn to see Gray standing in the doorway of the supply closet, arms crossed, smirking.

"I'm not smiling," I say automatically.

"You're definitely smiling. You look like someone just told you Christmas is coming early."

"I'm just—" I gesture vaguely at the shelves. "Happy about the googly eyes. We have a lot of googly eyes."

Gray raises an eyebrow. "Googly eyes."

"Yep."

"That's what's making you smile?"

"Absolutely."

He steps into the closet, closing the door behind him and crossing his arms. "Try again. Who texted you?"

I hesitate. "Harper."

He already knows. I can see it on his face—the slight lift of his brow, the way he's clearly trying not to smile. "And?"

"She asked me to go bowling Friday night. With her coworkers."

"Ah," he nods slowly. "Collin going to be there?"

"Well...yeah."

"So she wants you to show up and play the part."

"Yeah."

Gray is quiet for a second, studying me with that look he gets when he's choosing his words carefully. We talked about all of this over coffee. He knows about the almost-kiss, knows about the fake dating, knows exactly how sideways this has gotten.

Which is probably why he doesn't look surprised. Just concerned.

"And you said yes."

"I'm about to."

"Even though—"

"Even though it's fake. I know, Gray."

He exhales. "Micah. A few days ago you called me from a parking lot because you almost kissed her. Now you're grinning at your phone like a teenager because she wants you to go bowling." He tilts his head. "You see how this looks, right?"

"It's just bowling."

"That's not what your face is saying."

I shove my phone into my pocket. "I'm fine. It's one more event. No big deal."

"Micah."

"What?"

"You're lying."

I open my mouth to argue.

Then close it.

Because he's right.

It is too much. It's been too much since the gala. Since the kiss. Since Sunday, when we almost kissed again. Since last night when I prayed with her over FaceTime and realized I'd do anything to help her grow closer to Jesus—even if it means watching her chase after someone else.

But I can't say that to Gray.

Because if I say it out loud, it becomes real.

And I'm not ready for it to be real.

"I'm handling it," I say finally.

Gray doesn't look convinced. "Are you?"

"Yes."

"Because from where I'm standing, it looks like you're setting yourself up to get your heart broken."

"I know what I'm doing."

"Do you?"

"I can't abandon her, not now." I meet his eyes. "She's figuring out her faith, Gray. She called me late last night, and we talked for over an hour about what it means to remain in Jesus. She's wrestling with real questions. She's done performing. And I got to be part of that. So yeah, maybe the fake dating thing is complicated. Maybe it hurts sometimes. But if it means I get to walk alongside her while she discovers what a real relationship with God looks like? It's worth it."

Gray is quiet for a long moment.

Then he sighs. "You really care about her."

"Yeah."

"Like, more than just friends."

"Yeah."

"And she has no idea."

I shrug. "Probably not."

"Micah—"

"I know, okay? I know this is a terrible idea. I know I should tell her how I feel. But right now, she needs a friend. She needs someone who's going to point her to Jesus, not distract her from Him. And if that means I have to keep pretending for a little while longer, then that's what I'll do."

Gray studies me for another moment, then shakes his head. "You're a better man than I am."

"That's not true."

"It is. When I was falling for Ivy, I couldn't keep my feelings to myself for more than five minutes. You've been doing this for weeks."

"Because it's the right thing to do."

"Maybe. Or maybe you're just scared."

The words hit harder than I expect.

"I'm not scared," I say, but it sounds weak even to me.

"Keep telling yourself that, man." Gray pushes off the shelf.

He opens the door and steps out into the hallway, then pauses and looks back. "For what it's worth? I think she's lucky to have you. Even if she doesn't know it yet."

Then he's gone, and I'm left standing in the supply closet, surrounded by construction paper and googly eyes, wondering if he's right.

Am I scared?

Maybe.

But I pull out my phone anyway and type back a response.

MICAH

I'm in. What time?

Three dots appear immediately.

HARPER

Pick me up at 6pm!

MICAH

Sounds good, Freckles.

HARPER

Thanks, Dimples. You're the best.

She has no idea.

No idea that I'd do anything for her. No idea that every time she calls me Dimples, I feel it everywhere. No idea that I'm completely, hopelessly in love with her.

And maybe that's for the best.

Because right now, she needs to focus on Jesus.

Not on me.

So I'll keep pretending.

I'll keep showing up.

I'll keep being her fake boyfriend while she figures out her real relationship with God.

And when it all ends, I'll deal with the heartbreak then.

But for now?

I'm going bowling.

Chapter 27
Micah

The bowling alley is loud.

Music blasting from overhead speakers, the crash of pins, kids screaming in the arcade section, the smell of pizza and nacho cheese permeating everything.

And I'm standing at the entrance with Harper, who looks adorable and determined in jeans and a New Chapter Church hoodie.

"Okay," she says, scrolling through her phone. "We're in lane 7. With Anna and Tim, and..." She pauses. "Collin and Jessica."

Of course we are.

"You okay?" I ask.

"Fine. Totally fine." She's not looking at me. "This is going to be fun. Bowling is fun."

"Harper."

She finally looks up, and I can see the nerves in her eyes. "I'm fine. I just need to... prepare myself."

"For bowling?"

"For Collin and Jessica being all couple-y. They're always couple-y. It's annoying."

I bite back a smile. "So we're going to be more couple-y?"

"Exactly." She grabs my hand, lacing her fingers through mine. "Game face, Dimples. Let's do this."

She pulls me toward lane 7, and I follow, trying very hard not to think about how natural her hand feels in mine.

Anna spots us first, waving enthusiastically from where she's changing into bowling shoes.

"Harper! Micah! You made it!"

"Wouldn't miss it," Harper says brightly, and I can hear the forced cheerfulness in her voice.

Tim is already lacing up his shoes. "You guys ready to get destroyed? Anna and I have been practicing."

"Practicing?" I raise an eyebrow. "For couples bowling?"

"We take team building very seriously," Anna says, grinning.

And then I see them.

Collin and Jessica, sitting side by side on the bench, his arm around her shoulders, her head tilted toward him as she laughs at something on his phone.

Harper's hand tightens in mine.

"Hey, Harper," Collin says, glancing up. "Micah. Glad you could make it."

"Wouldn't miss it," Harper repeats, her smile too bright.

Jessica waves. "Hi! I'm so excited about this. Collin's been teaching me how to bowl. I'm terrible, but he's such a wonderful teacher."

She gazes up at Collin like he just invented fire.

Harper's grip on my hand is borderline painful now.

"Well," I say, squeezing back gently, "Harper's an excellent bowler. She's been teaching me all her tricks."

Harper blinks at me. "I have?"

"You have," I confirm, playing along. "Can't wait to show everyone what I've learned."

"This is going to be fun!" Anna looks delighted. "Okay, what do you want your team name to be? Tim and I are Team Newlyweds. Collin and Jessica, what are you?"

"Team Lovebirds," Jessica says immediately, and I watch Harper's jaw tighten.

"Of course they are," Harper mutters under her breath.

"And you two?" Anna asks.

Harper looks at me, and I can see her brain working.

"Team Meant to Be," I say before she can overthink it.

Harper's eyes widen slightly, and then a real smile breaks across her face. "Yeah. That's perfect."

We get our shoes and enter our names into the system, and I'm acutely aware of how close Harper is standing to me.

Closer than necessary.

She's leaning into my side, her hand still in mine, and when Collin glances over, she laughs at something I didn't even say.

She's performing.

I know she's performing.

But it still does something to me.

The game starts, and Anna goes first, getting a respectable seven pins.

Tim picks up the spare.

Jessica goes next, and her ball veers into the gutter almost immediately. She turns around, pouting, and Collin stands to give her a hug.

"It's okay, babe. You'll get it next time."

"I'm so bad at this," Jessica says, and he kisses the top of her head.

Harper stiffens beside me.

Then Collin goes, getting a strike, and Jessica cheers loudly, throwing her arms around him.

"You're so good at this!" she gushes.

Harper lets out a slow breath, and I can practically see her resolve hardening.

"Your turn, Freckles," I say gently.

She stands, grabbing a ball, and turns to look at me. "Wish me luck, Dimples."

"You don't need luck. You've got this."

She grins, then heads up to the lane.

And proceeds to get a strike.

"Yes!" She spins around, arms in the air, and I'm already standing to celebrate with her.

She runs back and jumps into my arms—literally jumps —and I catch her, laughing.

"That's my girl," I say without thinking.

And then I realize what I said.

Harper's eyes meet mine, something flickering in them, but before either of us can say anything, Anna says, "your turn Micah!"

I grab a ball and try to focus.

I roll the ball, and it veers slightly left, taking out eight pins.

"Good job!" Harper calls out.

I pick up the spare on the second roll, and when I sit back down, Harper slides next to me.

Very next to me.

Like, thigh-to-thigh next to me.

By the third frame, the competitive energy has ramped up.

Anna and Tim are in second place. Collin and Jessica are in third, mostly because Jessica keeps guttering. And Harper and I are solidly in first.

Harper is thriving.

Every time she gets a strike or spare, she celebrates with me—hugs, high-fives, at one point she even does a little victory dance that makes me laugh so hard I almost choke on my soda.

But I also notice something else.

Every time Collin and Jessica get affectionate—his arm around her, her hand on his knee, a kiss on the cheek—Harper escalates.

She scoots closer to me.

Rests her hand on my arm.

Leans her head on my shoulder when it's not our turn.

And I know—I know—it's all for show.

But it's killing me.

Because I like it.

Lord help me, I like it.

We're in the seventh frame when Harper leans close and whispers, "Kiss my cheek."

Everything in me goes still.

"Harper—"

"Collin's watching." Her voice is steady but quiet. "Please."

I glance over. She's right. He's looking directly at us, jaw tight, something flickering behind his eyes that looks a lot like regret.

I look back at her.

She's already tilted her head slightly, the smallest invitation, like she's trying to make it easy for me. Like she hasn't just asked me to do something I've thought about more than I should admit.

I take a slow breath.

Then I dip my head and press my lips softly to the curve of her neck, just below her jaw.

She goes perfectly still.

I feel the moment her breath catches — the slight tremble she tries to hide — and it takes everything I have to pull back casually, like that didn't just cost me something.

I straighten and let my arm settle around her shoulders, pulling her into my side.

She melts against me without a word.

"You good?" I murmur into her hair.

She nods. A beat too late.

"Yeah," she says quietly. "I'm good."

She's lying.

I know because I am too.

She tilts her head up to look at me, and we're so close I can see the flecks of gold in her green eyes.

"You're really good at this," she whispers.

"At what?"

"The whole fake boyfriend thing."

Right.

Fake boyfriend.

I force a smile. "Just trying to keep up with you."

She grins, then turns her attention back to the game.

But my arm stays around her shoulders.

And she doesn't move away.

By the ninth frame, it's close.

Anna and Tim are only ten points behind us. Collin and Jessica have fallen further back, but Jessica doesn't seem to care—she's more interested in taking selfies with Collin than actually bowling.

Harper, on the other hand, is locked in.

"We can win this," she says, standing up for her turn. "I just need a strike."

"You've got this," I say.

She grabs her ball, lines up, and rolls.

Strike.

"Yes!" She spins around, and I'm already on my feet.

She runs back, and this time when she jumps into my arms, I spin her around.

"That's my girl!" I say again, and this time I don't even care that I said it.

She's laughing, her arms around my neck, and when I set her down, we're standing so close I can feel her heartbeat.

"Your turn, Dimples," she says breathlessly. "Bring us home."

I grab the ball, my hands slightly shaking from adrenaline.

Or maybe from holding Harper.

I line up, take a breath, and roll.

The ball glides down the lane, hits the pocket perfectly, and—strike.

"Yeah!" Harper screams, and suddenly she's on me again, arms around my neck, jumping up and down.

"We won! We won!"

I'm laughing, my hands on her waist, steadying her as she bounces.

"We did it, Freckles!"

"That was amazing!"

Anna and Tim are clapping. Even Jessica is cheering.

And then Harper looks up at me.

And the world goes quiet.

Her arms are still around my neck. My hands are still around her waist. We're chest-to-chest, breathless, grinning.

And then—she kisses me.

It's quick. Spontaneous. Born from adrenaline and celebration, and the heat of the moment.

But it's also real.

Her lips are soft and warm, and for half a second, I forget that this is fake. Forget that we're supposed to be pretending. Forget everything except the fact that Harper Mitchell is kissing me again, and I never want it to stop.

But then she pulls back.

Her eyes are wide, startled, like she didn't mean to do that.

"I—" she starts.

And I don't know what to say.

Because that didn't feel fake.

Not even a little bit.

"Harper—"

"I gotta go to the bathroom," she blurts out.

And then she's gone.

Just turns and speed-walks toward the restrooms, leaving me standing in the middle of the bowling alley, my lips still tingling, my heart racing, and absolutely no idea what just happened.

Anna appears at my side. "Uh... you okay?"

"Yeah," I manage. "Fine."

"That was some celebration."

"Yeah," I gesture vaguely toward the restrooms. "I should check on her."

"Maybe give her a minute?"

I nod, but I don't move.

Because I can still feel her lips on mine.

And I don't know if that kiss was part of the act.

Or if—for just a second—it was real.

Collin walks past, heading to return his shoes, and I catch his expression.

He looks... unsettled.

Good.

That was the point, right?

Make him jealous. Show him what he's missing.

Except right now, I don't care about Collin.

I only care about the girl who just kissed me and then ran away.

Tim claps me on the shoulder. "Congrats on the win, man. You two killed it."

"Thanks," I say automatically.

But I'm not thinking about bowling.

I'm thinking about Harper.

And the fact that I have no idea what happens next.

Chapter 28
Harper

I'm hiding in a bathroom stall at a bowling alley.

Which is definitely a new low.

I press my hands to my face, trying to slow my breathing.

What did I just do?

I kissed Micah.

In what was supposed to be part of the act. Part of the show. A celebratory kiss between a couple who just crushed the competition.

Except it didn't feel like an act.

It felt real.

So real that my lips are still tingling. So real that my heart is still racing. So real that I panicked and literally ran away like a teenager.

Get it together, Harper.

I take a deep breath, then another.

It was just a kiss. A quick, spontaneous, heat-of-the-moment kiss. It means nothing.

Except, I think it did.

This whole thing was supposed to be about Collin.

About making him jealous. About winning him back.

But standing there with Micah's arms around me, celebrating our win, I wasn't thinking about Collin at all.

I was just thinking about Micah.

And how right it felt to be in his arms.

I hear the bathroom door open, and someone walks into the stall next to mine.

I need to get out of here.

I can't hide in a bathroom forever.

I flush the toilet even though I didn't use it, wash my hands, and stare at my reflection in the mirror.

My cheeks are flushed. My eyes are too bright. I look like someone who just kissed a guy she's not supposed to have feelings for.

It's fine. Everything is fine. Just go back out there and act normal.

I smooth down my hoodie, take one more deep breath, and push open the bathroom door.

And almost run directly into Collin.

"Oh!" I step back. "Sorry, I didn't see you—"

"Harper." He's standing right outside the women's restroom, hands in his pockets, and there's something in his expression I can't quite read. "Can we talk for a second?"

My stomach drops. "Um. I really should get back—"

"Just for a minute. Please."

There's something in his tone, it's almost desperate—that makes me pause.

"Okay," I say slowly. "What's up?"

He glances around, then gently takes my elbow and guides me a few steps away from the bathroom entrance, toward a quieter corner near the arcade.

His hand lingers on my arm.

Not aggressively. Not inappropriately, in an obvious way.

But it feels wrong.

He has a girlfriend. I technically have a boyfriend.

And yet his thumb is brushing against the inside of my elbow in a way that feels far too familiar.

"I've been wanting to talk to you," he breathes.

"About what?"

"About us."

My heart stutters. "But what about...Jessica."

"I know." His hand is still on my arm, his touch soft, almost caressing. "But watching you tonight with Micah... it made me realize something."

"What?"

"I miss you."

The words should feel like victory.

This is what I wanted, right? For him to notice. To regret letting me go. To realize that he made a mistake.

But instead, I just feel...icky.

Because he's touching me while his girlfriend is thirty feet away.

Because he's saying he misses me while dating someone else.

Because nothing about this feels right.

"Collin—" I step back, and his hand falls away. "You can't say that. You're with Jessica."

"I know, but—"

"And I'm with Micah."

He looks at me, something conflicted in his expression. "Are you really?"

"What's that supposed to mean?"

"I don't know. There's just something about the way you two are together. It feels... I don't know. Almost...fake."

My throat tightens. "We're very happy."

"Are you?"

"Yes."

But the word comes out too defensive.

Collin studies me for a long moment, and I can see him processing, calculating.

"I just—" He runs a hand through his hair. "I made a mistake, Harper. With us. I shouldn't have ended things the way I did."

"You're right. You shouldn't have."

"So maybe we could—"

"No," the word is firm. Final. "Collin, I need to get back. Micah's probably wondering where I am."

I turn to leave, but Collin catches my wrist.

Not hard. Not painful.

But enough to stop me.

"Harper, wait—"

"Let go."

He does, immediately, his eyes widening slightly. "I'm sorry. I just—"

"I really need to go."

I don't wait for a response.

I just walk away, my heart pounding, my skin crawling where he touched me.

I did it.

The plan worked.

Collin noticed. Collin's jealous. Collin misses me.

Mission accomplished.

So why do I feel like I need a shower?

I turn the corner back toward the bowling lanes, and see Micah walking toward me, clearly heading for the bathrooms, and when he sees me, relief floods his face.

"Harper, there you are. I was just coming to check—"

And I don't know why I do it.

Maybe it's because I'm flustered from Collin. Maybe it's because I'm still reeling from the kiss. Maybe it's because I don't want Micah to see how shaken I am.

But I plaster on the biggest, brightest smile I can manage.

"Hey! Sorry, there was a line. You know how it is."

Micah stops, studying my face. "Are you okay?"

"Fine! Totally fine. Just needed a minute."

"Harper—"

"We won!" I say, my voice too loud, too cheerful. "Can you believe it? We actually won. Team Meant to Be for the win."

He's still looking at me like he can see right through the performance.

And maybe he can.

Because his expression shifts—concern mixing with something else. Something that looks almost like hurt.

"Yeah," he says quietly. "We won."

There's a beat of silence.

I should say something. Should acknowledge the kiss. Should explain why I ran.

But I don't.

I just keep smiling that fake smile and say, "We should get back. I'm sure Anna and Tim are waiting."

"Harper—"

"Come on, Dimples."

I loop my arm through his and start walking back toward the lanes, ignoring the way his body has gone tense.

Ignoring the way he's looking at me like I'm a puzzle he can't solve.

Ignoring the fact that I had just lied to him.

Because that's what I do, right?

Perform. Pretend. Put on a show.

Even when the person I'm performing for is the only one who's ever made me want to stop.

When we get back to lane 7, Anna is packing up her shoes.

"There you are! We were wondering if you'd fallen in."

I laugh. Too loud. "Nope! Just a long line."

Anna glances between Micah and me, her expression skeptical, but she doesn't push.

"Well, congrats again on the win. You two were unstoppable."

"Thanks," I say brightly. "It was so fun."

Collin and Jessica are already at the counter returning their shoes. Jessica has her arm looped through his, chattering away about something, completely oblivious.

And Collin glances back at me.

Just once.

But it's enough.

Enough to confirm that the plan worked.

Enough to confirm that he's second-guessing everything.

Enough to make me feel absolutely hollow inside.

Micah's hand finds the small of my back—gentle, grounding—and I have to resist the urge to lean into him.

"You ready to go?" he asks quietly.

"Yeah. Let's go."

The drive back to my apartment is quiet.

Way too quiet.

Micah's hands are on the steering wheel, his jaw tight,

and I can tell he wants to say something but doesn't know how.

I stare out the window, watching the streetlights blur past, replaying the night in my head.

"Harper," Micah says finally.

"Yeah?"

"About earlier. The kiss—"

"It was just the heat of the moment," I blurt. "We won. We were celebrating. It meant nothing."

I can see him tense out of the corner of my eye.

"Right," he says, his voice carefully neutral. "Heat of the moment."

"Exactly."

Silence.

"Did something happen?" he asks. "In the bathroom? Or after?"

"No. Why?"

"You just seem... off."

"I'm fine."

"Harper—"

"Micah, I'm fine. Really. Just tired. It's been a long night."

He doesn't push.

But I can feel the weight of his concern pressing against me.

When we pull up to my apartment, I'm unbuckling my seatbelt before he's even put the truck in park.

"Thanks for tonight," I say, forcing brightness into my voice. "We make a pretty good team."

"Yeah. We do."

I reach for the door handle, but his voice stops me.

"Harper."

I look back.

His eyes are searching mine, and there's something in his expression that makes my chest ache.

"If something's wrong—if you need to talk—I'm here. Okay?"

And that's the problem.

He's here. He's always here.

Patient and kind and steady and everything Collin never was.

And I'm using him.

Pretending with him. Lying to him. Kissing him and then running away because I'm too scared to admit that it felt real.

"I know," I whisper. "Thank you."

Then I get out of the truck and walk to my apartment without looking back.

Because if I look back, I might cry.

And I don't even know why.

Inside my apartment, I lock the door and lean against it, closing my eyes.

What am I doing?

The plan worked. Collin misses me. He's jealous. He's second-guessing his relationship with Jessica.

I should be celebrating.

I push off the door and walk to my bedroom, sinking onto the edge of my bed.

The photo booth picture from the gala is still on my nightstand.

I pick it up, studying the last frame again.

The one where we're looking at each other.

And I realize something that makes my stomach drop.

I'm not trying to win Collin back anymore.

I haven't been for a while now.

I've just been too scared to admit it.

Because admitting it means acknowledging that what I feel for Micah isn't fake.

And I don't know what to do with that.

So I set down the pictures, grab my phone, and open the group chat with Ivy and Olivia.

HARPER

I kissed Micah. Again.

Three dots appear almost immediately.

IVY

Yay!

OLIVIA

Finally!

HARPER

No. Not finally. It was a mistake.

IVY

How was it a mistake?

HARPER

Because we're FAKE DATING.

OLIVIA

Was the kiss fake?

I stare at the question, my heart pounding.

HARPER

I don't know.

IVY

Oh Harper...

HARPER

It felt real. But it can't be real.

OLIVIA

Why not?

HARPER

Because Micah doesn't like me like that.

IVY

Harper that boy has been in love with you since the day he laid eyes on you.

I don't have a response for that.

So I toss my phone aside and bury my face in my hands.

Chapter 29
Harper

I barely sleep.

Every time I close my eyes, I see it all on replay.

The kiss. Collin's hand on my arm. The way Micah looked at me in the truck when I lied and said I was fine.

By 6 a.m., I give up on sleep entirely and drag myself out of bed.

I make coffee. Strong coffee. Then I sit on my couch with the journal Micah gave me, staring at the blank page.

I should pray.

That's what I'm supposed to do, right? When I'm confused and don't know what to do?

But I don't even know where to start.

So I just sit there, holding my coffee, staring at the page, and finally I just start writing.

> *God,*
> *I don't know what I'm doing anymore.*
> *Collin said he misses me. Which is what I*

wanted. That was the whole plan. But when he said it, I just felt... gross.

And then there's Micah.

I kissed him last night. And it felt real. Too real.

I'm so confused. I thought I knew what I wanted. I thought I had everything figured out. But now I don't know anything.

Micah told me I need to stop striving and just remain in You. But I don't know how to do that when I feel like everything is falling apart.

I want to control this. I want to fix it. I want to make everything work out the way I planned.

But I can't. And I don't know what to do with that.

Help me, God. Please.

- Harper

I set down the pen and stare at what I wrote.

It's honest. Raw. Not a surface-level "*bless this day*" kind of prayer.

Just...real.

And for the first time, I feel like I'm actually talking to God.

Like He's listening.

I take a shaky breath and close the journal.

Then I grab my phone and open the group chat.

HARPER

Can we do lunch today? I need to talk.

IVY

Yes. Absolutely. Where?

HARPER

That cafe on Elm? The one with the good sandwiches?

OLIVIA

I can do 12:30?

HARPER

Perfect.

I set my phone down and take another sip of coffee.

I don't know what I'm going to say.

But I know I can't keep doing this alone.

The cafe is busy when I arrive, but Ivy and Olivia have already snagged a corner table.

Ivy waves me over, her smile warm, and Olivia's nursing an iced coffee.

"Hey," I say, sliding into the seat across from them. "Thanks for coming."

"Of course," Ivy says. "What's going on?"

I open my mouth, then close it.

Where do I even start?

"I kissed Micah," I blurt out.

Olivia grins. "We know. You texted us last night, remember?"

"Right. Yeah." I run my hands through my hair. "But it's more complicated than that."

"How so?" Ivy asks gently.

I take a breath. "Collin told me he misses me. Last night. At the bowling alley. He pulled me aside and said he made a mistake breaking up with me."

Ivy's eyes widen. "Wait, what?"

"Yeah. And he was touching my arm in this way that felt... wrong. Because he has Jessica. And I have Micah. Except I don't actually have Micah because we're fake dating and—" I stop, pressing my hands to my face. "I'm a mess."

"Okay, slow down," Ivy says. "So Collin said he misses you. How did you feel about that?"

"Icky."

"Icky?"

"Yeah. Like, that was the whole plan, right? Make him jealous. Win him back. But when he actually said it, I didn't feel happy. I just felt...gross."

Olivia leans forward. "Because you don't actually want him back anymore."

The words hit me like a truck.

"I—" I pause. "Maybe."

"Harper," Ivy says gently. "You kissed Micah. And it felt real. Right?"

I nod, my throat tight.

"So maybe the plan changed," Ivy continues. "Maybe what you thought you wanted isn't what you actually want anymore."

"But I," I say, my voice breaking slightly. "But now everything's different, and I don't know what to do."

Ivy reaches across the table and takes my hand. "Harper, can I be honest with you?"

"Please."

"You're struggling because you're trying to control the

outcome. You made a plan. You executed the plan. But now the plan isn't giving you what you thought you wanted, and that's terrifying because it means you're not in control."

I stare at her, tears pricking at my eyes. "Yeah. That's exactly it."

"But here's the thing," Ivy says. "You were never in control. None of us are. And the sooner we surrender that—the sooner we stop trying to orchestrate every detail and just trust God with the outcome—the freer we become."

"But what if I don't like the outcome?"

"Then you trust God knows better than you do."

I let out a shaky laugh. "That's easier said than done."

"I know." Ivy squeezes my hand. "Believe me, I know. When I first started dating Gray, I tried to control everything. How fast we moved. When we said 'I love you.' When we'd meet each other's parents. And I made myself miserable. It wasn't until I let go—until I stopped striving and just trusted God—that everything fell into place."

"But you and Gray worked out," I say. "What if I let go and it doesn't work out?"

"Then it wasn't meant to," Olivia says quietly.

I look at her, surprised.

"Not everything is supposed to work out the way we plan," she continues. "Sometimes the best thing that can happen is for our plans to fall apart. Because that's when we realize we were chasing the wrong thing all along."

I wipe my eyes. "I just... I want to be different. I want to be the kind of person who trusts God. Who doesn't have to control everything. Who isn't constantly performing." I pause. "I want to be an '*I see Jesus in her*' kind of girl."

The words hang in the air.

And then Olivia says, so softly I almost miss it, "I see Jesus in you, Harper."

I blink. "What?"

"I see Jesus in you," she repeats, her eyes glistening. "In fact, watching you this past year has encouraged me greatly."

My throat closes up. "Olivia—"

"No, I mean it." She sets down her coffee, her hands trembling slightly. "You don't realize it, but you've changed. You're asking proper questions now. You're being honest about your struggles. And that's... that's what faith looks like. Not perfection. Just honesty."

Ivy's eyes are shining now, too. "Olivia..."

Olivia takes a shaky breath. "I haven't been to church in weeks. I've been avoiding Bible study. Avoiding small group. Avoiding all of it."

"We noticed," I mumble.

"I know." She looks down at her hands. "I've been pulling away because I'm angry. At God. At the church. At... everything."

"What happened?" Ivy asks.

Olivia is quiet for a long moment.

Then she starts talking.

"When I was growing up, my parents weren't believers. But I had friends who went to church every Wednesday night, and sometimes on Sundays, and they'd give me rides. So I started going with them. Middle school, high school—I was there all the time."

"I didn't know that," I say.

"Yeah. I loved it at first. The youth group felt like a family I never had at home. Everyone was so welcoming. So kind. And I really believed it all—that God loved me, that Jesus died for me, that faith was about relationship."

She pauses, her jaw tightening.

"But then I started noticing things. The girls I went to

church with—the ones who raised their hands during worship and had all the pretty notebooks and colored pens —they were mean. Like, really mean. At school, they'd ignore me. Talk about me behind my back. Exclude me from things. And then on Wednesday nights, they'd act like we were best friends."

Ivy's expression is pained. "Oh Olivia..."

"And it wasn't just them," Olivia continues. "My youth leader—this woman I really looked up to—she preached all the time about authenticity and being real with God. But then I found out she was having an affair with someone at the church. And when it came out, she blamed everyone else. Said the church was judgmental. That God understood her heart."

My chest aches. "I'm so sorry."

"It confused me," Olivia says, her voice breaking. "Why were all these people being two-faced? Why were they showing off their faith on social media but not living it out in real life? Why did they talk about loving your neighbor and then treat me like I didn't matter?"

"That's not what faith is supposed to look like," Ivy says quietly.

"I know that now. But back then? I just thought maybe God wasn't real. Or if He was real, maybe His people didn't actually believe in Him. So when I went to college, I left. I stopped going to church. Stopped reading my Bible. Stopped trying."

Tears are streaming down her face now, and I reach across the table to grab her other hand.

"And then I met you two," Olivia says, looking between Ivy and me. "And you were different. Ivy, you were brand new to faith. You didn't pretend to have it all figured out. You asked questions. You struggled. You were honest. And when you and Gray were dating, you took a break to focus on Jesus. You put Him first. And that was... that was so inspiring."

Ivy's crying now, too.

"And Harper," Olivia continues, turning to me. "You grew up in the church. You know all the right answers. But you're still willing to admit you struggle. You're still willing to say, 'I don't have this figured out.' And watching you be real about that—watching you wrestle with your faith instead of just performing it—it's made me want to try again."

I can't speak. I can only cry.

"You two are the reason I even came back to church," Olivia says. "Because you showed me that faith isn't about being perfect. It's about being honest. It's about showing up even when you don't have all the answers."

Ivy gets up and moves to Olivia's side of the table, wrapping her arms around her.

And I join them, the three of us crying in the middle of a crowded cafe, not caring who sees.

"I'm sorry you went through that," I whisper. "I'm sorry the church hurt you."

"It's not your fault," Olivia says.

"But I'm still sorry."

We sit like that for a long moment, just holding each other.

Then Olivia pulls back, wiping her eyes. "I don't know if I'm ready to come back all the way. But I think... I think I want to try."

"That's all God asks," Ivy says. "Just try. Just show up."

"And we'll be here," I add. "Every step of the way."

Olivia smiles through her tears. "Thank you."

We settle back into our seats, all of us a little tear-stained and puffy-eyed.

"So," Olivia says, her voice lighter now. "Back to you and Micah."

I laugh, wiping my face. "Right. That."

"What are you going to do?" Ivy asks.

"I don't know," I admit. "I kissed him. And then I ran away. And then I told him it meant nothing."

"But it did," Olivia says.

"Yeah. It did."

"So tell him that."

"I can't."

"Why not?"

"Because—" I pause. "Because what if I'm wrong? What if I tell him how I feel and he doesn't feel the same way? What if I ruin everything?"

"Or," Ivy says gently, "what if you tell him how you feel and it's the best decision you ever make?"

I stare at her. "You make it sound so simple."

"It's not simple. But it's the right thing to do. Harper, you can't keep pretending. Not with Micah. Not with yourself. And definitely not with God."

"She's right," Olivia says. "You said you want to stop performing. So stop. Be honest. Tell Micah the truth."

"What if he doesn't feel the same way?"

"Then you'll know," Ivy says. "And you can move forward. But if you don't tell him, you'll always wonder. And that's worse than knowing."

I take a shaky breath. "I hate that you're right."

Ivy grins. "Get used to it."

"But what do I even say? 'Hey, Micah, remember how I said that kiss didn't mean anything? I lied. It meant everything. Also, I think I'm falling for you. Sorry for the confusion.'"

Olivia laughs. "That's actually not bad."

"I was being sarcastic."

"I know. But it's honest. And that's what matters."

I drop my head into my hands. "I don't know if I can do this."

"Yes, you can," Ivy says firmly. "You're stronger than you think, Harper. And you're not doing this alone. You have us. And you have God."

"Remain in Him," Olivia says softly. "Isn't that what Micah told you?"

I look up at her, surprised. "How did you know that?"

"You mentioned it in the group chat. About the vine and the branches."

"Yeah. He did say that."

"So do it," Olivia says. "Stop trying to control the outcome. Just stay connected to Jesus and trust Him with the rest."

I take a deep breath, letting the words sink in.

Remain in Him.

Trust Him.

Stop striving.

"Okay," I say finally. "I'll talk to Micah. I'll tell him the truth."

"When?" Ivy asks.

"Soon. I just...I need to figure out what I'm going to say first."

"Don't overthink it," Olivia warns. "Just be honest."

"I'll try."

"That's all you can do," Ivy says. "Just try."

Chapter 30
Micah

Monday morning, I wake up to a text from Harper.

HARPER

Quick question...how do you know if you're actually hearing God's voice or if it's just your own thoughts?

I stare at the screen, still half-asleep, and smile.

MICAH

Good morning to you too, Freckles.

HARPER

Good morning, Dimples. Now answer the question.

I sit up against my headboard, Biscuit immediately climbing onto my chest to investigate.

MICAH

It's a good question. Honestly, I think it's about alignment. If what you're "hearing" aligns with Scripture, if it leads you toward love and peace rather than fear and chaos, if it builds up rather than tears down, then that's probably God. Our own thoughts tend to be more self-focused.

Three dots appear, then disappear, then appear again.

HARPER

That makes sense. Thanks.

MICAH

Anytime. Is everything okay?

HARPER

Yeah. Just thinking about a lot of stuff.

MICAH

Want to talk about it?

HARPER

Maybe later. I'm processing.

MICAH

I'm here when you're ready.

HARPER

I know. That's why I texted you first.

I set my phone down and look at Biscuit. "She's texting me faith questions."

He chitters.

"I know. It's a good sign. She's engaging. She's thinking about this stuff. She's not just going through the motions anymore."

Biscuit squeaks, like he's skeptical.

"What? I'm being objective."

He gives me a look that clearly says, sure you are.

"Okay, fine. Maybe I'm also falling harder. But that's secondary. Her relationship with God comes first."

Biscuit climbs off my chest and disappears into his tunnel system, clearly done with this conversation.

My phone pings again.

HARPER

Another question. What does it mean to abide in Christ? Like practically. In everyday life.

I lean back against the headboard, thinking.

MICAH

It means staying connected. Like the vine and branches thing. Practically, it looks like starting your day talking to Him. Reading His Word. Bringing Him into your decisions, your worries, your celebrations. Making Him part of your everyday life.

HARPER

So, like...talking to Him the way I'd talk to a friend?

MICAH

Exactly like that.

HARPER

That feels too simple.

MICAH

The best things usually are.

HARPER

Thanks, Dimples. You're really good at this.

MICAH

At what?

HARPER

Making faith feel less scary.

I stare at those words for a long moment, my throat tight.

MICAH

That's literally my favorite compliment anyone's ever given me.

HARPER

Well, it's true.

MICAH

Harper?

HARPER

Yeah?

MICAH

I'm really proud of you.

Three dots come and go across the screen.

HARPER

Thanks. That means a lot.

I set my phone down and try to refocus on the day ahead of me.

But all I can think about is the fact that Harper Mitchell is texting me first thing in the morning asking about faith. Real questions. Deep questions.

She's seeking. She's growing.

And I get to be part of it.

Even if it's killing me that I'm also completely in love with her.

I'm in the middle of meal-prepping for the week when Gray texts.

GRAY

Guys night. My place. 7pm. Mandatory attendance.

MICAH

Who else is coming?

GRAY

The usual group. Ivy's going to Harper's with Olivia. So you have no excuse.

MICAH

I wasn't making excuses.

GRAY

Good. Bring snacks.

I show up at Gray's house at 7:03 with a bag of chips and some guacamole.

Adam and Marcus are already there, sprawled on Gray's couch.

"Micah!" Marcus calls out. "Finally. We were about to start without you."

"Start what?" I ask, setting the chips on the counter.

"Guy's night," Gray says, emerging from the kitchen with a pizza box. "Which apparently means we eat junk food and pretend we have our lives together."

Adam laughs. "Speak for yourself. I'm thriving."

"You told me this morning you forgot your anniversary was this weekend," Gray says.

"Yeah, yeah." He says, grabbing a slice of pizza.

I grab a plate and settle into the recliner while everyone else argues about what to watch.

We end up with a basketball game on in the background, but nobody's really watching it.

"So," Marcus says, pointing a chip at me. "What's going on with you and Harper?"

I nearly choke on my guacamole. "What?"

"Gray mentioned you're helping her out with some...situation?"

I shoot Gray a look. "Did you tell them?"

"Tell them what?" Gray says innocently. "That you're fake dating a girl to make her ex jealous while simultaneously falling in love with her? No, I kept that to myself."

Adam's eyes widen. "Wait, what?"

"It's complicated," I mutter.

"Clearly," Marcus says. "Explain."

So I do. I tell them about the gala, about the fake dating arrangement, about how it was supposed to be one night and now it's turned into this whole thing.

I don't tell them about the kiss. Or the almost-kiss. Or the way my heart races every time she texts me.

But I think they can tell, anyway.

"Man," Adam says when I finish. "That's rough."

"It's fine."

"Is it?" Marcus asks.

"Yes."

"Because from where I'm sitting, it looks like you're setting yourself up to get your heart broken."

"I'm aware of the risks."

Marcus leans forward. "But why are you doing it? If you know it's going to hurt, why keep going?"

I'm quiet for a moment, trying to find the right words.

"Because she's growing," I say finally. "Her faith. She's asking questions now. She's wrestling with what it means to follow Jesus instead of just performing Christianity. And if playing the fake boyfriend helps her feel safe enough to do that, if it gives her space to figure things out, then it's worth it."

"Even if she ends up with the ex?" Adam asks.

The question hits harder than I expect.

"Even then," I say, though my voice wavers slightly.

Gray is watching me with an expression I can't quite read.

"You really care about her," Marcus says. It's not a question.

"Yeah. I do."

"Have you told her?"

"No."

"Why not?"

"Because she needs to figure out her relationship with God first. Without the complication of me confessing feelings and making everything about us instead of about her and Jesus."

"That's very noble," Adam says. "And also probably going to destroy you."

"Thanks for the encouragement."

"I'm just being honest."

Gray stands up, grabbing another Pepsi from the fridge.

"Okay, enough about Micah's complicated love life. Who else has updates?"

"I got a second date with that girl I told y'all about last month," Marcus says.

"That's great, man," I say. "Congrats."

"Thanks. I'm nervous, but also excited to see where this goes."

Adam grabs another slice of pizza. "Lilly and I are looking at houses. Finally outgrowing the apartment."

"That's huge," Gray says. "Any luck?"

"A few contenders. We'll see."

There's a pause, and then Marcus looks at Gray. "What about you? Any updates?"

Gray sets down his drink, and something shifts in his expression. "Actually, yeah. Ivy and I have been talking about it for a while, and we decided...we're trying for a baby."

The room goes silent.

Then Marcus practically jumps off the couch. "What?"

"Seriously?" Adam grins. "Gray, that's amazing!"

"Yeah." Gray runs a hand through his hair, looking equal parts excited and nervous. "We decided back in December, right after Christmas. We figured, why wait, you know? We're married. We're stable. We want kids. So...yeah."

"How long have you been trying?" I ask.

"Few months now. January, February. No luck yet, but we're trusting God's timing."

Marcus claps him on the shoulder. "Man, that's incredible. You're going to be a dad."

"Hopefully," Gray says. "If it happens."

"It'll happen," Marcus says confidently. "You and Ivy are going to have the cutest kids."

"Assuming they get Ivy's looks and not mine," Gray jokes.

"Hey, you're not that bad," Marcus says. "Slightly above average."

"Wow. Thanks."

I'm still processing. Gray and Ivy. Trying for a baby.

"That's really great, man," I say. "I'm happy for you guys."

"Thanks, Micah." Gray looks at me, and there's something meaningful in his expression. "We'd love for you to pray with us about it. If you're willing."

"Of course."

"Actually," Gray says, glancing around. "We should probably do prayer requests. That's what guys night is supposed to be about, right? Not just eating pizza and talking about basketball?"

"I thought that was exactly what guys night was about," Marcus says.

"Come on. Five minutes. Let's actually be intentional."

We all settle back into our seats, and Gray starts.

"Okay. I already shared mine. Ivy and I are praying for a baby. Pray for patience. Pray for trust. Pray that we don't get too anxious about the timing."

"Got it," I say. "I'll add that to our list."

Marcus goes next. "Pray for my dating life. Oh, and for my little sister—she's going through a rough breakup and it's hitting her hard."

"On it," I say.

Adam shifts. "Lilly and I are praying about the house situation. That we'd find the right place at the right time. And also that I can plan something special for our anniversary this weekend."

We all laugh.

Then they look at me.

"What about you, Micah?" Gray asks. "What can we pray for?"

I hesitate.

Because the honest answer is: *Pray that I don't completely fall apart when Harper doesn't choose me. Pray that I can walk alongside her in her faith journey without making it about my feelings. Pray that I can be okay with just being her friend if that's all God has for us.*

But I don't say that.

"Just... pray for wisdom," I say finally. "With Harper. With the whole situation. That I'd know when to step back. When to speak up. How to point her to Jesus instead of to me."

Gray nods slowly. "We can do that."

"And maybe pray I don't completely lose my mind in the process," I add with a weak laugh.

"Definitely praying for that," Marcus says.

Gray stands. "Alright. Let's do this."

We gather in a loose circle, and Gray leads us in prayer.

Later, after Adam and Marcus have left, Gray pulls me aside.

"You doing okay?" he asks.

I sigh. "I don't know, man. She's been texting me all week. Asking questions about faith. Genuine questions. And it's amazing. I love that she's seeking. I love that she's growing. But it's also..."

"Hard," Gray finishes.

"Yeah. Because every time she texts me, I want to believe it means something. Like, maybe she's thinking about me too. But I know she's probably just processing. Figuring things out. And I'm just the guy who can help her do that."

Gray is quiet for a moment.

"You know what Ivy told me the other day?" he says finally.

"What?"

"She said Harper's been different. That she's been opening up more. Being more honest. Asking harder questions." He pauses. "And she thinks it's because of you."

"That's not because of me. That's God."

"Maybe. But you're the one who's been walking with her through it. You're the one she keeps coming back to."

"Because I'm safe. I'm the friend who knows about faith stuff."

"Or," Gray says carefully, "because she trusts you. And maybe that means more than you think."

I want to believe him.

But I can't let myself hope like that.

Not when I know how this could end.

"Just be careful," Gray says. "I know you're trying to do the right thing. I know you're putting her first. But don't forget to protect your own heart too."

"I know."

"Do you?"

I don't answer.

Because the truth is, I stopped protecting my heart the moment Harper Mitchell asked me to be her fake date.

And there's no going back now.

Chapter 31
Harper

Monday morning, I walk into my classroom and immediately see it.

A coffee cup sitting on my desk.

Starbucks. Vanilla latte. My order.

There's a sticky note attached.

Thought you could use this. Hope you have a great day. - C

My stomach twists.

I pick up the cup, feeling the warmth through the sleeve, and glance toward the door.

Collin's not there. He must have dropped it off before I arrived.

Which means he went out of his way. Got to school early. Brought me coffee.

And left a note.

I crumple the sticky note and toss it in the trash, but I keep the coffee.

Because I'm tired. And it's Monday. And I need the caffeine.

But it still feels...wrong.

By Tuesday, the texts start.

COLLIN

How's your day going?

Saw your class in the hallway earlier. They're lucky to have you.

Let me know if you need anything. I'm here.

I don't respond to any of them.

But they keep coming.

Wednesday morning, I'm in the teacher's lounge making copies when he walks in.

"Harper," he says, smiling. "Hey."

"Hey." I focus on the copier, willing it to work faster.

"I wanted to ask you something."

Please don't.

"What's up?" I say, trying to sound casual.

"There's this new coffee shop that opened downtown. I thought maybe we could check it out sometime. Catch up."

I freeze. "Collin, you have a girlfriend."

"I know. I just meant as friends."

"Friends don't get coffee alone when they're both in relationships."

"Right. Yeah." He shifts his weight. "I just thought—"

"I'm actually really busy this week," I cut him off. "The art showcase is Friday, and I'm drowning in prep work. So... maybe another time."

It's a lie.

Well, half a lie.

I am busy with the art showcase. But I would never say yes to coffee with him. Not now. Not after everything.

"Oh. Okay." He looks disappointed. "Maybe after the showcase, then?"

"Maybe." Another lie.

The copier finally finishes, and I grab my stack of papers. "I really need to get back to my class. See you later."

I don't wait for a response.

Just walk out of the teacher's lounge, my hands shivering, the ick settling deep in my stomach.

This is what I wanted, right?

Collin noticing me. Collin regretting his decision. Collin showing interest again.

So why does it feel so gross?

By Wednesday I'm barely hanging on.

"Miss Mitchell, I don't like my sun."

I crouch down next to Ethan, one of my kindergarteners, and look at his painting. "What's wrong with your sun?"

"It's too yellow."

"Suns are yellow, buddy."

"But I want it to be orange."

"Then make it orange."

"But you said suns are yellow."

I take a deep breath, reminding myself that this is why I love teaching kindergarten. The logic. The creativity. The absolute chaos.

"You know what? Your sun can be any color you want. Orange sounds beautiful."

Ethan beams and immediately starts painting over the yellow with orange.

Crisis averted.

I stand up, surveying the classroom. Twenty-two kindergarteners, all working on their final art pieces for tomorrow's showcase. Paper everywhere. Glitter somehow on the ceiling. One kid eating a crayon.

"Charles, we don't eat crayons," I call out.

"But it's grape flavored!"

"It's purple. That doesn't mean its grape. Spit it out, please."

Anna appears in my doorway, laughing. "How's it going in here?"

"I've confiscated three crayons, two glue sticks, and a pair of scissors. So, about average."

She steps into the room, carefully avoiding a paint puddle. "Are you ready for tomorrow?"

"Define ready."

"Like, do you have all your hallway displays done?"

I gesture to the back table, where approximately forty pieces of art are drying. "Almost. I still need to mount half of them and hang everything in the hallway. Which I'll probably be doing until midnight."

"Need help?"

"You're the best, but I know you have your own class to prep. I'll be fine."

"If you change your mind, text me."

"I will."

She glances at her phone. "Oh, also—did Collin ask you to coffee?"

My stomach drops. "How do you know about that?"

"He mentioned it in the break room. Said he wanted to catch up with you, but you were too busy."

"Yeah. I am busy."

Anna gives me a look.

"What?"

"You don't have to explain yourself to me. But...are you okay? With him being so friendly lately?"

"I'm fine."

"Because if he's making you uncomfortable—"

"He's not." The lie comes automatically. "It's fine. We're fine. Everything's fine."

Anna doesn't look convinced, but she doesn't push. "Okay. But if you need to talk, I'm here."

"Thanks."

She leaves, and I'm left standing in a classroom full of kindergarteners, wondering why "fine" feels like the biggest lie I've ever told.

By the time school ends, I'm exhausted.

I spent my entire lunch break hanging art in the hallway. Then I had to troubleshoot a last-minute printing issue with the programs for tomorrow night's showcase. Then one of my students had a meltdown because his painting got accidentally smudged, and I had to help him create a whole new one.

Now I'm sitting at my desk, staring at my to-do list, and trying not to cry.

Finish hallway display
Organize student take home folders
Grade sight word tests
Prep for parent teacher conference meetings next week.

I just want to go home. Lay on the couch and eat an entire pint of ice cream for dinner.

My phone buzzes.

IVY

Are you coming tonight?

HARPER

To what?

IVY

Bible study, our house?

Oh no.

I completely forgot about Bible study.

HARPER

I can't make it. I'm still at work.

IVY

Awe man! Well, we will miss you!

I set my phone down and drop my head onto my desk.

I love teaching. I love my students. I love seeing their creativity come to life.

But right now, I'm so tired I could cry.

And all I want is to talk to Micah.

Which is ridiculous.

Because Micah is probably at Bible study right now, hanging out with Gray and everyone else, having a great time.

And I'm here, alone, mounting kindergarten art on foam boards.

I grab my phone and pull up our text thread.

The last message is from this morning.

MICAH

How's your day going, Freckles?

HARPER

Chaotic. Kindergarteners + paint + glitter = disaster zone.

MICAH

Sounds about right. Hang in there.

I should text him. Tell him I'm overwhelmed. That I could use some encouragement.

But I don't.

Because I don't want to bother him.

So I set my phone down, grab another foam board, and get back to work.

I'm three spoonfuls into a pint of cookie dough ice cream when my phone buzzes on the cushion beside me.

Micah's name lights up the screen.

A video call.

I look down at myself. Oversized hoodie, hair piled into a bun that stopped being intentional two hours ago, probably a stress line permanently etched between my brows at this point.

I let it ring once.

Twice.

Then I pick up anyway.

"Hey," I say, angling the phone slightly away from the ice cream.

He's sitting back on his couch, relaxed. The kind of easy that only exists when someone has nowhere else to be.

"Hey." His eyes move over my face for just a second. "I missed you tonight."

I go still.

Something in my chest does a slow, traitorous tilt.

He clears his throat. "I mean—we all missed you tonight. Bible study wasn't the same without someone dramatically sighing every time Gray wouldn't stop talking."

"I don't dramatically sigh."

"Then what would you call it?"

"I exhale with intention."

The corner of his mouth pulls up. "Right." He settles deeper into the couch. "How bad was it today?"

And just like that, something in me unravels.

"Okay, it was a lot," I say, pulling my knees up to my chest. "The showcase is tomorrow night and I still have to finish the display boards, and the projector in my classroom has been glitching all week so I had to borrow Mrs. Patterson's which means I have to figure out her remote which has like forty buttons, and three of my kids still haven't turned in their artist statements, and I promised the parents it was going to be this whole beautiful thing and now I'm sitting here eating ice cream at nine-thirty wondering what I was thinking."

Micah doesn't try to fix it. Doesn't jump in with solutions or tell me it's going to be fine in that hollow way people do when they just want you to stop spiraling.

He just listens.

"The projector thing is genuinely stressful," he says when I finally stop. "Everything else? You've got it. You've been building up to this all semester."

"You don't know that."

"I've watched you wrangle a room full of preschoolers at church with the focus of someone planning a military operation." He raises an eyebrow. "You can handle a parent showcase."

I laugh despite myself, pressing my face into my hoodie sleeve for a second. "I just want it to be good for them. The kids worked so hard."

"Then it's already good," he says simply. "The rest is just logistics."

I don't have anything to say to that. So I just sit there for a second, phone propped against my knee, ice cream forgotten.

This is the thing about Micah that I can't quite figure out. Talking to him feels like setting something heavy down. Like I didn't realize how much I was carrying until he was there and I wasn't carrying it anymore.

A beat of comfortable silence settles between us.

"What are you eating?" he asks, nodding toward the pint in my hand.

I tilt it toward the camera. "Cookie dough ice cream."

"Out of the carton?"

"It's been a long week, Micah."

He nods slowly, like that's a completely reasonable medical decision. "Fair enough."

I pull my knees tighter to my chest. "What are you doing?"

"Watching TV." He glances off screen. "Nothing good."

"Then why are you watching it?"

"Because it's on and I'm tired." He looks back at me. "Very complex reasoning."

I smile. "Sounds about right."

He shifts slightly, propping his elbow on the armrest. "How are your students feeling about tomorrow?"

"Nervous. Excited. Camo is convinced his painting is going to be in a real museum someday."

Micah's mouth curves. "Camo?"

"Cameron. He told me on the first day that only his grandma calls him Cameron so," I shrug. "Camo it is."

"And is he right? About the museum?"

I think about the painting in question—chaotic, bold, inexplicably featuring three dinosaurs and what I'm pretty sure is a self-portrait in the corner. "Honestly? Maybe. The kid has zero inhibitions. That's half of what makes great art."

Micah is quiet for a second, just looking at me with that expression I can never fully read. "You really love this, don't you?"

It's not quite a question.

"Yeah," I say, a little surprised by how easily it comes out. "I really do."

He smiles then. Not the polite one, not the amused one. The real one. The quiet kind that does something completely unfair to my ability to think straight.

By the time we hang up, it's almost eleven, and I feel measurably more human than I did an hour ago.

I set my phone down and stare at the ceiling.

It's been almost a week since I've seen him in person. No fake dates, no manufactured reasons to be in the same space. Just texts here and there, easy and low pressure.

And yet somehow that call just felt more real than half the actual dates I've been on in the last two years.

I reach for the ice cream again, frowning at nothing in particular.

He said he missed me. And really, I miss him too.

I'm still thinking about it when I pick up my phone to set an alarm, and out of habit my thumb drifts to Facebook.

Where I end up scrolling.

Where I end up seeing something that literally stops my scroll.

Collin Matthews went from In a Relationship to Single.

I stare at it for three full seconds.

Then my phone buzzes in my hand.

COLLIN

Hey Harper, how's your night going?

I throw my phone across the couch cushion.

Then I sit there, ice cream melting, staring at the wall.

Crap.

I press both hands over my face.

What have I done.

Chapter 32
Micah

I'm standing in the parking lot of Harper's Elementary School at 4:47 p.m. on a Friday, holding a to-go coffee cup and a devotional, having a full on debate with myself about whether or not this is a terrible idea.

It's a terrible idea.

I should go home. Feed the ferret. Prep Sunday's lesson. Do literally anything other than drive across town to a kindergarten art showcase for a woman who is, by every definition that matters, not mine.

But she sounded stressed last night. And I remembered her coffee order. And the devotional practically jumped off the shelf at me, which I'm choosing not to read too deeply into, even though I absolutely am reading too deeply into it.

Lord, if you're trying to tell me something, I'm going to need you to be more specific.

I take a breath and walk toward the entrance.

I follow the signs that lead me to the Kindergarten wing. The hallway is quiet when I step inside.

A hand-lettered banner stretches across the entrance.

Welcome to the Kindergarten Art Showcase.

Warm string lights are woven through the ceiling tiles, and the hallway itself stops me mid-step.

Every inch of wall space is covered. Painted handprints border the doorframes. Crayon self-portraits hang in crooked rows, each one labeled in careful teacher handwriting. Paper Maché animals perch on shelves. Watercolor sunsets fill the windows. Clay sculptures line a kraft paper table, each with a small name card in front.

I smile and keep walking.

Halfway down the hall, I find a small chalkboard sign on an easel outside the last door on the left, written in loopy handwriting:

Miss Mitchell's Kindergarten Classroom

I lean against the doorframe.

She hasn't seen me yet.

She's at a table along the far wall, back half-turned, fussing with a spread of refreshments—straightening napkins, nudging a cookie tray an inch left, then an inch back. Her hair is down, which surprises me. She's wearing a soft yellow dress, and the string lights she must have spent hours hanging make the whole room glow.

She looks nothing like someone who was stress-eating ice cream on the phone with me twelve hours ago.

She looks completely in her element.

I stay there longer than I should.

Then I clear my throat.

She looks up, and her eyes go wide. "Micah? What are you doing here?"

I hold out the coffee. "You mentioned the showcase last night. You sounded stressed. So I thought—" I pause. This sounded more coherent in the car. "I don't know. I thought maybe you could use this."

She stares at the cup like I've handed her something sacred.

"You brought me coffee?"

"Vanilla latte. Extra shot."

"How did you—" she stops. "You remembered."

"Of course I remembered."

Her fingers brush mine when she takes it, and I lose approximately four seconds of my life.

"And this." I hold out the devotional.

Rooted: growing deeper, living fuller.

"I saw it and thought of you. That's all." That's not all. But it's all I'm saying.

She looks at the cover, and something in her expression shifts—soft and a little undone. "Micah." Her voice catches. "This is perfect."

"Yeah?"

"Yeah."

Then she sets both things down and hugs me.

I freeze for exactly half a second, where my brain registers what's happening and tries to remind me of seventeen reasons why this is complicated—and then I wrap my arms around her and none of those reasons matter.

She smells like coffee and dry-erase markers and something floral that is very specifically Harper.

"Thank you," she whispers against my shoulder. "For coming. For this. For everything."

"Anytime, Freckles."

She pulls back, hands still on my arms, cheeks flushed. And then I watch realization move across her face like a cloud passing over the sun.

"Wait," she glances around. "There's nobody here. To see us." She drops her hands, stepping back. "I'm sorry. I shouldn't have—there's no one around, so I didn't need to—"

"Harper," I catch her hand gently. "I wasn't putting on a show."

She looks up at me.

"I'm genuinely proud of you," I say. "All of this—" I gesture to the hallway, the lights, the little name cards. "You made every single one of these kids feel seen. That's not nothing. That's everything. And I wanted to be here for that. Not for Collin. Not for anyone watching. Just for you."

Her eyes are shining now, and I'm actively praying she doesn't cry because I have absolutely no plan for that.

"Micah—"

"Miss Mitchell!"

A small boy with wild, curly hair barrels down the hallway and crashes directly into Harper's knees. His mother is jogging behind him, already apologizing.

"I showed my mom the orange sun painting!" he announces. "I told you orange was better than yellow!"

Harper crouches down immediately. "You were absolutely right. Orange was the perfect choice."

He beams. Then he notices me. His eyes narrow. "Who are you?"

I glance at Harper.

"This is Mr. Sanders," she says. "He's my...friend."

"Your boyfriend?" the kid asks. No hesitation. No filter. Just facts.

Harper's face goes red. "Actually..."

"Yes," I say. Because apparently I have no self-preservation instinct whatsoever. "I'm her boyfriend."

Ethan considers this for approximately one second. "Do you like art?"

"I love art."

"Do you want to see my painting?"

"Absolutely."

He grabs my hand, like we've known each other for years, and starts towing me down the hallway. I glance back at Harper, who has her hand over her mouth, shoulders shaking to hide a laugh.

"Go ahead", she mouths.

So I let this five-year-old drag me through the kindergarten art showcase while he delivers a passionate scientific argument for why orange is objectively superior to yellow.

When we reach his painting, I crouch down and study it seriously, the way it deserves. "Ethan. The orange sun is without question the right call."

"That's what I said!" He turns to his mom. "Miss Mitchell's boyfriend agrees with me!"

His mom gives me an apologetic smile. I wave her off.

"Are you a teacher?" Ethan asks.

"Sort of. At a church. I run the children's ministry."

His eyes go wide. "So you're like Miss Mitchell but for church?"

"Exactly like that."

"Cool." He turns to Harper, who has caught up to us. "Miss Mitchell, your boyfriend is cool."

"I'm glad you think so," she says, in a tone that suggests she is barely holding it together.

"Can he come to show-and-tell?"

"We'll see."

"That means no," he says, devastated.

"That means maybe," I correct, crouching back down to his level. "And if Miss Mitchell invites me, I'll bring something really cool."

"Like what?"

"That's a surprise."

He accepts this with great solemnity and allows his mother to steer him away.

Harper watches them go. Then she turns to me with an expression I can't quite categorize. "You didn't have to promise him that."

"I know."

For the next twenty minutes, she walks me through the hallway and tells me about her kids.

The girl who decided cats are purple with green spots. The boy who spent three weeks changing his mind before landing on a dinosaur riding a rocket. The kid who cried for ten minutes over spilled glitter and then recovered to produce the most glitter-dense piece in the entire showcase.

I try to pay attention to the art.

I mostly pay attention to her.

The way she gestures when she talks. The way she remembers every detail about every single kid. The way her whole face changes when she talks about teaching—like something in her just opens up.

She loves this. Really, truly loves this.

You're in trouble, I think. *You are so deeply in trouble.*

I know what this is. I've been trying to talk myself out of

it for weeks—been praying about it, reasoning through it, reminding myself of all the relevant facts. She's working through her feelings for someone else. I volunteered for this. I knew the terms.

"You're really amazing at this."

"At what?" she asks.

"Teaching. Connecting with kids. Making them feel seen." I gesture to the hallway. "You did all of this, Harper."

"It's just kindergarten art."

"It's not just anything." I pause, because I mean this and I want her to hear it. "You're changing their lives. Even if you don't realize it."

She's quiet for a moment. Something vulnerable moves through her expression.

"Thank you," she says softly. "That means a lot."

And I almost say something I shouldn't.

Instead, a little girl with pigtails appears out of nowhere and grabs Harper's hand, and the moment dissolves.

I step back and find a spot along the wall while Harper takes photos with her students—crouching down to their level, pulling them close, laughing at something a little boy says right before his mom snaps the picture. She's fully present for every single one. No distractions, no rush.

But in between each photo, she glances over.

At me.

Every time, I hold her gaze for just a second before she turns back. And every time, I look away first and tell myself to stop cataloguing the way she smiles at me like that.

It doesn't work.

"Harper!" I hear a familiar voice down the hallway.

I watch Harper's posture shift—subtle, barely noticeable—and I know what it means. We're back on. Performance mode.

I move to her side before she has to ask, my hand settling at the small of her back.

"Mariah. Shawn." I extend my hand. "Good to see you both."

"It's so sweet you came to support Harper," Dr. Bailey says, with the particular warmth of someone who has fully bought into this narrative.

"I wanted to be here," I say. "She's been working nonstop all week."

Dr. Bailey looks between us with a knowing smile. "Harper, you're lucky to have someone so supportive."

"I know," Harper says as she leans into me slightly. I keep my expression neutral and my hand steady and remind myself that I am a functional adult who is completely fine.

I walk with them through the hallway. I answer questions. I say the right things. I play the part.

I'm getting too good at this.

When Mariah and Shawn finally say their goodbyes and head toward the exit, Harper exhales slowly.

"You okay?" I ask.

"Yeah. Just..." She glances up at me. "Going from real to fake so fast is weird."

I'm quiet for a beat. "Yeah. It is."

She looks at me like she's waiting for me to say something else.

I don't.

Because what I want to say is *it didn't feel fake to me.* But that is not information she needs right now.

So instead I say nothing, and the moment passes, and I tell myself that's the right call.

It probably is.

Probably.

Chapter 33
Harper

"Where are we going?" I ask as Micah opens the passenger door of his truck.

"You'll see."

"That's not an answer."

"Correct."

I narrow my eyes at him, but I get in anyway.

Honestly, I don't have a lot of room to argue. My stomach growled three times during cleanup—loud enough that Anna heard it from across the room and gave me a look—and when Micah asked if I'd eaten lunch, the answer was technically no but I had half a granola bar around two o'clock which I feel should count for something.

He disagreed.

So now I'm in his truck at eight o'clock on a Friday night, still in my yellow dress, hair probably doing something unhinged, being driven to an undisclosed location by a man who remembered my coffee order and brought me a devotional and spent his entire Friday evening looking at kindergarten art.

I stare out the window.

Don't make it weird, I tell myself. It's not weird. This is just what Micah does. He's a helper. It's his whole thing. You are a friend in need of a meal and he is a friend with a truck. This is completely normal.

My stomach growls again.

Okay. Moving on.

He drives us through downtown, past all the chain restaurants, past the trendy spots I've eaten at approximately a thousand times, and then pulls into a parking lot in front of a tiny, unassuming building with a hand-painted sign that reads Angelo's.

"What is this?"

"My favorite restaurant in Dallas." He cuts the engine and looks at me. "Best Italian food you'll ever have. I promise."

We walk inside, and it's small and warm and smells like garlic and fresh bread and something that makes my stomach do an immediate, embarrassing sound of approval. Red-and-white checkered tablecloths. Vintage photos on the walls. And behind the counter, an older man who spots Micah and looks genuinely overjoyed about it.

"Micah! My boy!"

"Angelo." Micah grins. "I know, I know. It's been too long."

"You work too much." Angelo comes around the counter and pulls him into a hug like he's a returning soldier. Then he spots me, and his entire face rearranges itself into something delighted. "And who is this beautiful girl?"

"This is Harper," Micah says. "She's—" A half-second pause. "A friend. She's had a long day and she needs feeding."

"Then you are in the right place." Angelo waves us

toward a corner table like he's been expecting us. Micah pulls out my chair before I can grab it, and Angelo nods approvingly. "Such a gentleman."

"Don't encourage him," I say.

Angelo laughs and disappears into the kitchen.

I look around the table. Then at Micah. "He didn't give us menus."

"Nope."

"Are we supposed to...ask for them?"

"We're not getting menus, Harper."

I stare at him. "So how do we order?"

"We don't."

"Micah."

"Angelo knows what to make." He says it with the complete calm of a man who has fully surrendered control of this situation and made peace with it. "You just trust him."

"That's not how restaurants work."

"This one does."

"What if I'm allergic to something?"

"Are you allergic to something?"

"Not currently. But I'd like the option to be."

He looks at me for a long moment. "Harper."

"Micah."

"Have you smelled this place?"

I pause. Garlic. Fresh bread. Something with herbs that I cannot identify but would like to be closer to. "Yes."

"Then trust the process."

I lean back in my chair and cross my arms. "I just want it on record that I had concerns."

"Noted." He adjusts his glasses. "For what it's worth, in four years Angelo has never once made me something I didn't love."

"Fine." I unfold my napkin with what I feel is appropriate skepticism. "But if he brings out something weird, I'm blaming you."

"Completely fair."

Angelo returns with bread and water and launches into a breathless explanation of what he's making us. I catch maybe sixty percent of it—fresh pasta, his grandmother's sauce, something about a specific imported cheese—before he's gone again.

Micah leans back in his chair, completely at ease, and I'm struck again by how he does that. How he just settles into a room. No fidgeting, no scanning, no wondering if he's in the right seat. Just present.

I have never once in my life felt present. My brain is usually about four topics ahead of wherever I actually am.

Right now it's cycling through: the showcase, whether I remembered to tell Anna where the extra tablecloths go, the devotional Micah gave me that's currently sitting in my bag, the way Ethan announced to the entire kindergarten wing that Micah was my boyfriend with the confidence of a tiny CEO, and also what is happening to my hair right now because I can feel it doing something and I don't have a mirror.

"So," Micah looks at me. "How are you feeling? Now that it's over?"

I tear off a piece of bread. "Exhausted. Relieved. Really proud of my kids." I pause. "Also, I think I'm getting a second wind, which is genuinely inconvenient because I should be tired."

"That tracks."

"Classic ADHD. My body doesn't get the memo until about an hour after everyone else's."

He smiles. "Your kids were incredible tonight."

"They really were." I feel the warmth of it settle in my chest—that particular feeling that makes every chaotic, glitter-covered, superglue-adjacent moment worth it. "Seeing their faces when their parents walked in. That's the whole job, right there."

"You're great at what you do."

"You said that already."

"Because it's still true." He says it simply, with no performance behind it. "Watching you tonight—with your kids, with their parents—you're in your element, Harper. It's something."

My throat does a traitorous tightening thing. "Stop."

"Stop what?"

"Being so nice to me. I don't know what to do with it."

He leans forward slightly, and his expression shifts into something that is unfairly sincere. "You deserve people being nice to you. You know that, right?"

I look down at my bread and change the subject.

"Tell me something I don't know about you."

He raises an eyebrow. "Random."

"I'm a random person. Humor me."

He thinks for a second. "I wanted to be an astronaut."

I nearly inhale my water. "I'm sorry?"

"Astronaut. NASA. The whole thing. Had it completely mapped out—engineering degree, pilot training—"

"Please tell me there's more."

"Three summers at space camp."

I put my hands flat on the table. "Micah Sanders went to space camp."

"Three times."

"What happened?"

"Turns out I'm terrified of heights."

The laugh that comes out of me is not cute or dignified. It is full and loud, and I don't even care. "You wanted to go to space and you're afraid of heights?"

"I was twelve. The logic wasn't fully developed."

"So then what—you just pivoted to children's pastor?"

"Close enough." He grins. "Still trying to reach for the stars. Just differently."

I shake my head. "You're such a dork."

"You like it."

"I really do."

The words are out before I can review them, and something flickers across his face—quick and soft and gone before I can name it.

"Yeah?" he says quietly.

"Yeah."

We look at each other for a beat too long.

And that's when it happens. I panic.

I clear my throat. "Is this a date?"

He blinks. "What?"

"This. Us. Dinner." I gesture vaguely at the checkered tablecloth, the candle, Angelo's general romantic-Italian-restaurant energy. "It feels like a date."

Something moves across his face. Complicated and fast, like he's doing math he didn't expect to have to do tonight.

Then he's quiet.

Not a normal quiet. A considered one. The kind where you can almost see someone choosing their words carefully, stacking them up and checking them before letting them out.

He leans back. And when he finally speaks, it comes out just a little too smooth. Just a little too easy.

"No, Harper. This is just a friend making sure a friend

eats something other than showcase cupcake leftovers." He motions to me

"Right." I force a laugh. "Of course. Friends."

"Friends," he repeats.

And I smile, because that's what you do, and I file away the fact that it took him three full seconds to say it — rehearsed and deliberate, like he'd already written that answer out somewhere and just had to find it.

I don't read into it.

I'm not going to read into it.

Friends.

Fine. That's fine. That is the correct and reasonable answer, and I am a reasonable person who is totally fine.

Because honestly—why would he want to date me?

Micah is steady and grounded, and has his whole life organized in a way that suggests he has never once made an impulsive decision based on a feeling he hadn't fully thought through. And I am a woman who forgot to eat lunch, whose kindergarteners had to be stopped from putting glitter in the classroom hamster's cage this week, and who agreed to a fake dating scheme as a legitimate life strategy.

We are not the same.

He would never actually want this—want me, the real version, not the showcase version in the yellow dress. The version that loses her keys twice a week and hyper-focuses on weird random topics at eleven p.m. and cries at dog food commercials.

He deserves someone steady. Someone who matches him.

And I am many wonderful things, but steady has never been one of them.

"You bring her back, yes?" Angelo says, gripping Micah's arm. "She is good for you."

"I'll try," Micah says.

"Don't try. Do."

Angelo hugs us both with the intensity of a man sending people off to war, and then we're back in the truck.

Micah was right. Angelo absolutely knows what he's doing.

He'd brought out two bowls of pasta—wide, silky ribbons in a sauce that tasted like it had been simmering since sometime last Tuesday, topped with fresh parmesan and herbs I couldn't name but fully intended to think about later. Garlic bread that should not have been as good as it was. A small side salad that I ate mostly out of obligation before returning to the pasta with my full attention.

The conversation had been easy but minimal, mostly because I was stuffing my face. At one point he'd just watched me eat with this expression that was somewhere between amused and satisfied, like a man who had made a correct decision and knew it.

I didn't even have the energy to be embarrassed about it.

By the time Angelo cleared our plates, I was so full I briefly considered just living at this corner table forever.

When Micah pulls into the school parking lot—my car exactly where I left it, alone under a single light—he puts the truck in park but leaves the engine running.

I unbuckle my seatbelt. Then I stop. "Micah?"

"Yeah."

"You're not just a good fake boyfriend." I look at him. "You're a genuinely good person. And I'm really glad you're in my life."

Something moves through his jaw—a tightening, quick and controlled. He nods. "Me too, Harper."

I get out of the truck.

I walk to my car, and I can feel him watching until I'm safely inside and my engine turns over.

He waits until I pull out first.

Of course he does.

On the drive home, I can't stop thinking about the hesitation.

Five seconds of thought. Three seconds of silence. Then — just friends.

And even that's a stretch, honestly. Micah and I were never friends. We bickered constantly. He got on my nerves every time he simply took a breath in my general direction.

And now I'm sitting here wishing he'd said yes, it's a date.

"Lord, I am so confused!" I smack the steering wheel. "Why am I catching feelings for a guy who doesn't even like me like that? Why can I not just be content with Collin — who I actually wanted back in the first place?"

No answer. Just Dallas at night sliding past my windows.

I pull into my parking lot, shut the engine off, and sit there staring at my building.

"I don't know what to do," I say finally, quieter. "I don't even know what to ask you. I just..."

I shake my head.

"I don't know."

Chapter 34
Micah

"I can't do this anymore," I pray. "I can't keep pretending. Not with her."

Silence answers me, pressing in from all sides. Heavy. Intentional. Like it's waiting to see if I actually mean it.

I've been on my knees for forty minutes. I know because I started before nine and my phone says 9:43 and my legs are reminding me I am a thirty-one-year-old man and hardwood floors are not as forgiving as they used to be.

I'm falling for her. Hard.

The thought isn't audible, but it might as well be. It echoes in the quiet of my room, undeniable and two years in the making.

I can't fake this anymore. Can't keep pretending this is just an arrangement.

"I need wisdom here," I say. "Because I don't trust myself anymore. I'm saying yes to things I should say no to. I'm letting myself hope for something that isn't mine to hope for. And I don't know how to stop."

The conviction settles over me—not crushing, but firm.

The particular kind of clarity that only comes after you've stopped arguing with it.

I need to end it. Tell her the arrangement is over. Give her a proper reason or a vague one, doesn't matter, just enough to create the distance I should have created weeks ago. Before I get any deeper. Before she figures out that none of what I've been doing has been performance.

Before I get hurt worse than I already am.

I pray until the panic in my chest slows into something that almost feels like peace. Then I push myself up from the floor and sit on the edge of my bed and stare at nothing for a moment.

Tomorrow. Church tomorrow. I'll end it right after.

From the kitchen, I hear Biscuit knock something off the counter—a soft plastic thud, followed by the particular scrambling sound of a ferret who has done something and is not sorry about it. I get up and check. He's sitting beside the now-empty paper towel roll with the composure of someone who has no idea how it got there. I refill his food bowl. He ignores me pointedly until the bowl is full, then ignores me with the addition of eating.

"Rough night for both of us," I tell him.

He doesn't respond.

I lean against the kitchen counter. The house is quiet in that specific Saturday morning way—not lonely, just still. I've lived alone long enough to know the difference. This is the quiet you can breathe in.

I'm still standing there with that thought when the doorbell rings.

I freeze.

It's almost nine. No one comes over unannounced this early. Especially not to my house. Gray texts. My mom calls. Amazon leaves things on the porch and runs.

The doorbell rings again.

I pull the door open.

It's her.

Harper stands on my porch like this is the most normal thing in the world. Wind-tousled hair. Oversized hoodie. Leggings. Sneakers. Her cheeks are pink from the cold, and she's slightly out of breath.

"Hi," she says brightly.

I blink at her.

"Hi," I manage. "Why are you here?"

She shrugs, completely unfazed. "I was on a walk."

"You live twenty minutes away."

"Yeah, I was deep in thought." She gestures vaguely behind her. "Just kept walkin'."

I stare at her.

"And ended up at my house."

"Yep." She rocks back on her heels. "I realized I was like three streets over and thought, huh...Micah lives near here. And then I thought, I wonder what he's doing. And then I thought, I should just go say hi."

She smiles like this is airtight logic.

"You typically just show up at people's houses?"

"Only yours," she winks.

My heart stumbles.

Before I can respond, a blur of brown and white shoots between my legs.

"Ah!" Harper shrieks. "What is that?"

Biscuit skids to a stop at her feet, sniffing her shoelaces like she's the most interesting thing he's ever encountered.

"That," I say carefully, "is Biscuit."

She stares down at him. "There is a rodent on your porch."

"He's not a rodent."

"He looks like a rodent."

"He's a ferret."

She looks up at me slowly. "You have a ferret."

"Yes."

"And it just roams."

"He lives here."

She looks back down at Biscuit, who has now begun climbing her pant leg with alarming determination.

"Micah," she whispers, eyes wide. "It's climbing me."

"He likes you."

"Why does it like me?"

"I don't know. You're chaotic. He respects that."

She snorts.

Biscuit reaches her knee and pauses, nose twitching. Harper hesitates for exactly half a second before crouching down.

"Oh my gosh," she breathes. "Hi."

She holds out her hand. Biscuit sniffs her fingers, then immediately climbs into her palm like he's known her his entire life.

Her face softens in a way I'm not prepared for.

"Your kind of adorable," she murmurs.

I cross my arms, leaning against the doorframe.

"You just called him a rat."

"I was uninformed." She looks up at me. "His name is Biscuit?"

"Yes."

She gasps like I've said something holy. "That's precious."

"He's named after a failed attempt at baking."

She settles onto the porch step like she has all the time in the world. Biscuit climbs onto her shoulder, wraps around the back of her neck, and perches there proudly.

She squeals. "He's wearing me like a scarf!"

"He does that."

She turns her head slightly, trying to see him. "Hi, Biscuit. I'm Harper. I've heard nothing about you."

Biscuit chirps softly.

"Oh, he talks," she says reverently.

I watch her sitting on my porch, laughing at my ferret like this is the most natural place for her to be.

She fits here.

That realization hits harder than it should, specifically because I just spent forty minutes on my knees deciding to end this. There is a particular kind of irony available to a man who prays for clarity and then opens the door.

"So," she says after a moment, still absently scratching behind Biscuit's ears. "Random question."

Of course.

I brace myself.

"My friend Becca is having a baby shower tomorrow," she continues. "Just games and food and chaos. I was wondering if you wanted to come."

"Aren't baby showers for women?" I ask.

"Sometimes, but this one is a couples shower."

Right. Collin. The whole reason any of this started. I almost forgot for a second, standing here on my own porch with her wrapped in my ferret, which tells me everything I need to know about the state of my judgment.

This is the perfect opportunity to say no. To end this fake relationship.

I just decided I was done.

I just prayed about it.

But I watch her instead. She's still on my porch step, Biscuit now fully draped around her shoulders like he's claimed her. She's smiling at me, hopeful but not calculating. Not performing. Just Harper, asking me a question she actually wants the answer to.

"I—" My brain lags behind my mouth. "Yeah. I'll come."

Her face lights up.

"Really?"

"Yeah."

She stands, brushing off her leggings. Biscuit clings stubbornly to her hoodie.

"Do you want coffee?" I hear myself ask, motioning inside my house.

She studies me for half a second, then shrugs. "Okay."

I step aside and hold the door open.

She walks in like she belongs here.

And that's a problem.

She kicks off her shoes without asking and pads into the living room, Biscuit still curled around her shoulders like a living scarf. I head to the kitchen to make our coffee. From the living room, I hear her voice drop into that soft register she uses with kids.

"Hi, Biscuit. You're very dramatic."

The warmth that spreads through my chest is immediate and unwelcome.

I pour the coffee slowly, willing my heartbeat to steady. It's just a cup of coffee. It's what friends do. There is nothing about this situation that requires me to feel what I'm currently feeling, and I would appreciate it very much if my chest got the memo.

I carry the mugs back in and hand one to her. Our fingers brush.

It shouldn't feel like anything.

But it does.

She curls into the corner of my couch, tucking one leg beneath her. Biscuit immediately claims her lap like he's been waiting for her to arrive all evening, which, knowing Biscuit, he probably has.

"He likes me," she says smugly.

"He likes chaos."

She grins at that. We sit in quiet for a moment. The lamp beside the couch casts everything in warm light. Outside, the neighborhood is still.

"Can I ask you something?" she blurts.

My guard rises automatically. "Sure."

She stares into her coffee for a second, like she's deciding whether to say it out loud.

"How do you actually feel it?" It comes out less like a question than something she's been carrying around and finally set down. "God. All of it. How does it get from your head to the rest of you?"

That wasn't what I expected.

I sit back in the armchair across from her.

"That's a big question for a Saturday morning."

"I'm serious." There's frustration in her tone. "I've been reading. Studying. Going to church. Volunteering with the kids. I'm doing all the things, Micah. But I still don't feel it. Not the way Ivy does. Not the way you do."

She looks almost embarrassed admitting that, and something in me softens immediately.

"What are you looking for?" I ask gently. "Like, what would make it feel real to you?"

"Connection. Something that reaches past my brain and actually lands. I can know all of it and still feel nothing, and I don't know what I'm doing wrong."

"You're trying to think your way into it."

"Well, yeah." She crosses her arms. "That's how I process everything. I need to understand something before I accept it."

I nod slowly.

That's Harper. Brilliant. Analytical. Perpetually building a case.

"You can study theology until your brain hurts," I say carefully. "You can memorize Scripture, understand the historical context, read every commentary that's ever been written. But knowledge isn't the same thing as relationship."

She looks up at that.

"Then what is?" Her voice cracks slightly. "Because I feel like I'm standing outside looking in. Watching everyone else experience something I can't access."

I lean forward, elbows on my knees.

The honest answer surfaces quickly, the way it does when you've been turning something over for years. And underneath it, quieter and less comfortable, is the awareness that I am sitting here about to tell her that faith requires surrender—that you have to stop white-knuckling the outcome and just let go—while I am doing exactly the opposite with every feeling I have in this room. Praying for clarity with one hand and reaching for more time with the other.

I know what surrender looks like. I've just been avoiding it too.

"Can I be honest?" I ask.

"When are you not?"

A faint smile pulls at my mouth.

"Faith isn't about having all the answers. It's about surrender. Letting go of control and trusting Him even when it doesn't make logical sense."

She flinches slightly. "But that's terrifying."

"I know."

"You think I'm overthinking it."

"I think you're brilliant," I say immediately. "Your brain

is one of your greatest gifts. But God doesn't need you to figure Him out, Harper. He just needs you to stop holding Him at arm's length."

Her eyes glisten.

"What if I don't know how to stop?"

"You can learn. But you have to stop trying to earn it. Stop trying to prove you're smart enough or good enough or faithful enough." I pause. "Just be. Let Him do the rest."

She goes quiet at that.

"I don't know how to surrender," she admits.

"Start with honesty. Tell God you don't know how. Tell Him you're scared. Tell Him you want to feel close to Him but don't know how to let go."

"That's it?"

"That's it."

She huffs out a breath that's almost a laugh. "You make it sound simple."

"It is simple. We're the ones who complicate it."

She looks at me then, and I can feel the shift in the room. This isn't fake. This isn't performance. This is her letting me see the part she doesn't show anyone. Which is the exact thing I told myself I was going to walk away from, and I am sitting here in my own living room completely unable to do it.

She sets her mug down eventually and stands.

"I've got a long walk back."

"I can drive you."

"No," she pauses, then smiles. "I always do my best thinking on walks. I want to sit with this a little."

I walk her to the door and pull Biscuit off her shoulder, which he objects to by making a small sound of protest that Harper finds deeply moving.

"Bye, sweet little squishy thing." She pets his head with

complete sincerity. "I'll miss you so much. Make sure Micah gives you extra treats."

She hesitates at the door. Something moving through her expression that she doesn't quite say.

"Harper."

She turns.

"For what it's worth," I say, meaning every word of it, "I think you're closer than you think."

Something moves across her face. Not certainty. But openness — the particular kind that happens when someone has stopped arguing and started actually listening.

She nods once. "Bye, Micah."

"See you tomorrow."

I wait in the doorway until she reaches the corner, and then I close the door.

The house settles around me. Biscuit, denied his new favorite human, drapes himself across my feet with quiet drama.

She showed up at my door. Walked twenty minutes because she was thinking and her feet brought her here without asking the rest of her.

I close my eyes and lean back against the door.

One last thing. One last performance. After the shower tomorrow, I end it, and then I figure out how to be her friend in a way that doesn't cost me everything, which I am told is possible and currently cannot imagine.

I push off the door and head down the hall.

"God," I mutter quietly. "You really have a sense of humor."

Chapter 35
Harper

The house is packed.

Music plays somewhere in the kitchen. Someone is laughing too loudly near the gift table. The smell of vanilla cake and barbecue sliders hangs in the air.

"Harper! You made it!"

Becca barrels into me, nearly knocking the wind out of my lungs.

"You act like I moved states," I laugh.

"Wait." Her eyes widen dramatically as she spots Micah beside me. "Is this the famous Micah?"

Micah stiffens slightly next to me.

"I'm so glad you're here!" Becca grabs his hands like she's known him forever. "Harper talks about you constantly."

My cheeks go hot instantly. "I do not—"

"Yes, you do!" She grins wickedly and turns back to him. "She shows us your Instagram all the time. She also said you—"

"Okay!" I cut in quickly, grabbing Micah's wrist and

dragging him toward the dining room. "You have other guests to harass."

Becca just laughs and waves.

I don't stop walking until we're halfway across the room.

"You talk about me all the time, huh?" Micah asks quietly.

There's something in his tone I can't quite read.

I shrug, trying to play it cool. "You're very talk-about-able."

"That's not a word."

"It is now."

He studies me for a second, like he's trying to decide something.

"You showed them my Instagram?" he presses.

"It was one time."

He huffs a soft laugh, scanning the room full of people around us.

"Looks like Collin isn't here yet."

I blink. "What?"

"Collin." He gestures vaguely. "He's not here."

"Why would he be here?"

He looks genuinely confused now. "You said this was a couples shower."

"It is."

"And he's not coming?"

"He's not friends with Becca," I say slowly. "He wasn't invited."

The expression on Micah's face shifts.

Something between confusion and frustration.

"But I thought—" He stops himself. Runs a hand through his hair. "I thought this was...you know."

"What?"

He exhales sharply.

"A fake dating event. To make him jealous."

Oh.

I stare at him.

"Micah," I whisper. "I didn't invite you to make him jealous."

He goes still.

"I just..." I swallow. Why is this suddenly hard to say? "I wanted you to come."

He blinks like I've spoken another language.

"You wanted me to come?"

"Yeah." My voice drops. "I didn't want to go alone. And I enjoy hanging out with you. It doesn't always have to be strategic."

He searches my face like he's looking for the catch.

"We're friends, right? Friends go to things together. It doesn't always have to be—"

I stop.

It doesn't always have to be fake.

The air shifts between us.

He looks almost...wrecked.

Not angry.

Not relieved.

Just undone.

For a second, I think I've said something wrong.

Before I can ask, Becca's sister stands in front of the room. "Time to open gifts!"

Micah straightens instantly, that steady public composure sliding back into place.

But something has changed.

I can feel it.

By the time we leave the shower, I'm starving.

The cucumber sandwiches, and mini cupcakes weren't exactly filling. Micah and I both pretended we were full, but the second we stepped outside into the warm April air, he looked at me and said, "Burgers?"

I didn't even hesitate. "Immediately."

Ten minutes later, we're sitting in a vinyl booth at a burger joint just down the road, the kind with a buzzing neon sign and a jukebox that hasn't been updated since 1998.

The food arrives fast. Greasy, glorious, life-saving food.

Micah takes a bite of his burger and studies me over the top of it.

"Becca really loves you," he says.

I glance up. "She loves everyone."

"No," he shakes his head. "The way she talked about you—she thinks you're going to be an incredible mom someday."

The words settle over me like a blanket.

"She said that?"

"While you were getting another cupcake." A faint smile touches his mouth. "She said you're a natural with kids. That she sees it every day at school."

He pauses.

"Do you want kids?"

The question hangs between us.

It shouldn't feel heavy.

But it does.

This is the kind of thing fake boyfriends don't usually ask.

Then again...nothing about today feels fake.

"Yeah," I say quietly. "I do. Like...a lot of them."

His expression shifts—surprise mixed with something softer. Something almost hopeful.

"How many is a lot?"

"I want four." I watch his face carefully. Most guys flinch at that number. "Maybe more. I know that sounds crazy, but I grew up an only child and I always wished—" I stop, suddenly unsure how exposed I want to be. "I always wanted a big family. The chaos and the noise, and the love that just keeps multiplying. I want that."

He's quiet for a long moment.

I brace myself for the usual response.

That's a lot.

Wow.

Are you serious?

Instead, he smiles.

"I want six."

I blink. "Six kids?"

"At least." He shrugs like that's perfectly reasonable. "I'm one of four. Growing up, it was loud and messy, and there was always someone in your business, but I loved it. I want that. The full house. Big holidays. Soccer games where you need a spreadsheet to keep track of whose game is when." He leans forward slightly, his eyes brighter now. "I want the chaos."

Something in my chest cracks open.

"Most people think I'm crazy when I say four."

"Most people are boring."

I laugh, surprised by how easily it bubbles out of me.

"Okay, but real talk—six kids? That's a lot of diapers."

"That's a lot of everything," he says easily. "A lot of diapers. A lot of college tuition. A lot of noise." His grin widens. "A lot of love."

"A lot of love," I repeat softly.

The way he's looking at me when he says it makes my pulse race.

Not like we're joking anymore.

Not like this is hypothetical.

Like he can see it.

Like he's picturing it.

Micah wipes his hands on a napkin and leans back in the booth, studying me with that thoughtful look he gets when he's about to ask something deeper.

"So," he says casually, "growing up an only child... what was that like? I bet you got all the attention from your parents."

I let out a small laugh.

"You have no idea."

He smiles. "Perks of being the only kid."

I pick at a fry.

"Yeah," I say slowly. "All the attention."

He tilts his head slightly. "Why do I get the feeling it wasn't a positive thing?"

I hesitate.

Because this is the part I don't talk about.

"Yeah," I admit quietly. "All the attention was not always ideal."

I glance up at him.

His expression shifts immediately. Softer. More alert.

"What do you mean?"

I sigh and lean back in the booth, crossing my arms over my chest like I need something solid between us.

"My parents are good people," I say quickly. "They

really are. They love God. They love me. They provided for me. They never missed a recital or a game."

I pause.

"They were just... strict."

"How strict?"

"Very." I let out a humorless breath. "Very religious. Very by the book. If there was a rule, we followed it. If there was a verse, we memorized it. If there was a gray area, we avoided it."

He doesn't interrupt.

That almost makes it worse.

"I wasn't allowed to go to sleepovers. Or dances. Or youth group events unless my parents personally knew every parent in attendance." I shrug like it's no big deal. "No dating. Ever. Not even in high school."

His brows knit slightly.

"That must've been hard."

"It was normal," I say quickly. "To me, at least."

The music from the jukebox hums faintly in the background. The booth suddenly feels smaller.

"They believed holiness meant separation," I continue. "From everything. From culture. From people who didn't think like we did. From anything that might even look questionable."

"And you?"

I swallow.

"I was the example at our church. The one who couldn't mess up. The one everyone watched."

His jaw tightens slightly.

"So yeah," I say lightly, forcing a small smile. "All the attention."

But not the warm kind.

The measuring kind.

The evaluating kind.

"I was always trying to be good enough," I admit quietly. "Good enough for them. Good enough for church. Good enough for God."

Micah goes still.

"And if you weren't?" he asks carefully.

I stare at the table.

"You couldn't not be," I say.

The words sit between us.

Heavy.

I shrug again, defensive now. "It's fine. They weren't cruel. They weren't abusive. They were just... intense."

"And you think that's why faith feels hard now?" he asks gently.

The question hits deeper than I expect.

"I think," I say slowly, "that when you grow up being told exactly how to believe and exactly how to behave and exactly how to measure your worth... it's hard to know what's real and what's just performance."

The word hangs there.

Performance.

I didn't mean to say it.

But I did.

Micah's eyes search mine.

"You were never allowed to just...be," he says quietly.

Something inside me tightens.

"That's not fair," I say automatically.

"To who?"

"To them." My voice sharpens. "They were trying to protect me. They thought they were doing the right thing."

"I'm not questioning their motives," he says calmly. "I'm just asking about the impact."

That lands.

I look away.

"It's all in or all out." I admit finally. "And I don't know how to be all in without feeling like I'm twelve again trying not to disappoint someone."

The confession feels like it scrapes something raw.

Micah doesn't rush to fix it.

Doesn't quote Scripture.

Doesn't correct me.

He just sits there with me.

And somehow that's the thing that undoes me most. Not the scripture he didn't quote. Not the advice he didn't give. Just—him, steady across a vinyl booth, holding space for something I've never said out loud to anyone, and not flinching from the weight of it.

I clear my throat. Pick up a fry I have no intention of eating.

"Okay," I say, mostly to change the subject. "Your turn. Deepest, darkest secret. Go."

He huffs a soft laugh. "Not sure I can top that."

"You absolutely can. You went to space camp three times. There's more where that came from."

The tension in the booth shifts, not gone, but gentler. He steals one of my fries. I pretend to be outraged. The jukebox cycles to something old and vaguely country, and neither of us comment on it.

By the time we leave, the parking lot is dark, and the air has cooled to that particular mid-April temperature that can't decide between jacket and no jacket. I pull mine tighter. Micah walks beside me toward where we parked, hands in his pockets, unhurried.

We stop at my car.

"Hey." His voice is different. Quieter. The particular

tone he uses when he's been sitting on something and has finally decided to say it.

I look up.

"Can I ask you something?"

My stomach does a small, inconvenient thing. "Sure."

He tilts his head slightly, studying me with that expression that always makes me feel like he's reading several pages at once. "Why did you invite me tonight?"

"I told you, Becca's shower, couples event, I didn't want to go—"

"Collin wasn't here," he says. Quiet. Not accusing. Just true. "He wasn't invited. There was no one here who needed convincing of anything." A beat. "So why did you invite me?"

I open my mouth.

Nothing comes out.

The parking lot is quiet around us. A car passes on the street. Somewhere nearby, a wind chime goes off briefly, then stops.

Why did I invite him?

I reach back through the last two weeks, looking for the calculation. Looking for the moment I thought through the logistics, weighed the optics, asked myself how Collin would read it if he found out. That's how this works. That's how it has always worked. Every event, every appearance, every call—there's always been a reason that starts and ends with Collin.

I can't find it.

I invited Micah because I wanted him there.

That's the whole thing. I didn't think about Collin once. Not when I picked up my phone, not when I typed the message, not when I saw Micah walk through Becca's front door and something in my chest did that stupid warm thing it keeps doing. Not once during the whole afternoon. Not during the burgers or the kids' conversation or the booth or the part where he just sat there and let me be a mess without making me feel like one.

Not once.

The realization lands in stages, each one slightly more alarming than the last.

"I just..." My voice comes out smaller than I intend. "I should go." I reach for my door handle. "It's late and I have a full week of...there's a lot happening with my class right now and I need to—"

"Harper."

"Thank you for tonight." I get the door open, which is a victory. "Seriously. The burgers were good. You were right about the onion rings."

"Yeah, of course," he says, but his voice is gentle. Watching me go.

I get in. I close the door.

I don't look at him through the window because I already know what I'll find, and I cannot deal with whatever that expression is doing to me right now. I start the car, back out, and keep my eyes on the road pulling away.

Chapter 36
Harper

I've been home for forty minutes, and I've rearranged the throw pillows on my couch three times.

This is a known symptom. I know what it means. I do it when my brain is moving faster than my ability to process what it's moving about, and right now it is moving very, very fast about something I am not ready to name out loud in my own apartment with no one watching.

I wanted you to come.

I said that. To Micah. With full eye contact and absolutely no strategic reason attached to it. Then, I bolted. Left him there in the parking lot after lunch.

I move the pillow on the left two inches to the right.

It doesn't help.

I go to the kitchen. Fill a glass of water I don't drink. Stand at the counter staring at the fruit bowl—still empty, still waiting on fruit I keep meaning to buy—and try to do something useful with the feeling currently occupying my entire chest.

My phone buzzes on the counter.

I look at the screen the way you look at something you're not sure is safe.

Collin.

I pick it up slowly.

COLLIN

I broke up with Jessica. I've been doing a lot of thinking. I miss you, Harper. Can we get coffee this week? I think I made a mistake.

I read it once.

I set the phone face-down on the counter.

I pick it back up and read it again, waiting for the feeling. The flutter, the spike, the complicated rush of vindication that I would have expected—two months ago, even two weeks ago—to hit me somewhere around the word mistake. I built an entire architecture around this moment. A dress, a gala, a fake boyfriend, a performance sustained across weeks of dinners and events and carefully managed impressions. All of it pointed here, toward exactly this message, this confirmation that he saw what he let go.

I feel nothing.

That's not quite right. I feel something. But it isn't about Collin.

I set the phone down again, and this time I leave it.

I make it to the living room. The throw pillows are in slightly wrong configurations from my earlier intervention. I look at them for a moment and then I look at my Bible on the coffee table and my journal beside it—the brown leather one with the cracked spine, the one Micah gave me—and then I do the only thing that makes any sense.

I sit down on the floor.

Not a composed, folded, presentable sit. Cross-legged on the rug with my back against the couch, in my going-out top and jeans from today, and I close my eyes.

"Okay," I say. Out loud, because apparently that's where we are. "I don't know how to start this."

Silence. The apartment hum. A car passing outside.

"I've been pretending for so long I don't know what's real anymore." The words come out rough, slower than I expect. "I started all of this to get Collin back. I didn't ask You. I didn't think to ask You. I just...grabbed the wheel, made a plan, and told myself it would work out."

I press the heels of my hands against my eyes.

"And now he texted me and it's exactly what I thought I wanted and I feel absolutely nothing. Except—" My voice breaks slightly on the word, which is embarrassing and also apparently unavoidable. "Except I can't stop thinking about a man who went to three space camps and has a ferret named Biscuit and remembered my coffee order and sat across a vinyl booth with me tonight while I told him things I've never told anyone. And I don't know what to do with that."

I drop my hands. The ceiling is neutral about all of this.

"I don't know how to want something I didn't plan for," I admit. "I don't know how to trust something I can't see the end of. I've been performing faith the same way I've been performing everything else—doing all the right things so nobody looks too closely at what's underneath. And I'm tired." I exhale slowly. "I am so tired of it."

The quiet settles differently after that. Not empty. Just still.

"I don't know how to let You in," I say. "But I think...I think I want to try. Actually try. Not the streak version." I pick up the journal from the coffee table and hold it without opening it, just the weight of it in my hands. The inscription inside the cover, which I have read enough times I could recite it.

MAY THIS BE A SPACE WHERE YOU CAN BE HONEST WITH GOD, YOURSELF, AND THE JOURNEY AHEAD.

"I'm trying," I say. "That's all I've got right now. I'm trying."

It isn't dramatic. No lightning, no sudden warmth, no audible answer. Just the particular peace of having put something down that's been too heavy to carry alone, and the apartment around me, and the journal in my hands, and somewhere across the city a man who asked me why I invited him tonight and actually waited for the real answer.

I pick up my phone.

I don't text Collin back.

I open my contacts instead, scroll to the group chat.

HARPER

Are y'all free tomorrow? I need to talk. And possibly shop.

Three dots appear almost immediately.

IVY

Don't you have work?

HARPER

It's a bad weather makeup day we didn't use. So no school.

IVY

Gotcha. I'm open!

OLIVIA

I only have one client in the morning. Brunch first then we'll drag you to every store in the Galleria until you feel better.

IVY

Also Gray and Micah are playing at The Parish tomorrow night. Y'all wanna come?

I stare at that last line for a long moment.

OLIVIA

Sure, why not.

HARPER

I guess.

I set the phone down, pick up the journal, and open it to the first blank page.

I start writing.

Brunch is Ivy's idea of emotional triage, which means we're at a table by the window at her favorite spot in Uptown with overpriced lattes and a bread basket that appears before we've even ordered, and she's watching me with the particular expression she reserves for situations she has already diagnosed.

"Talk," she says.

So I do.

I tell them about the parking lot. The question Micah asked. What I said back and the way I just—bolted, because apparently my response to any genuine emotion is to locate the nearest exit and take it at speed. I tell them about the Collin text. I tell them about sitting on my floor and praying, which I say quickly and sideways because I'm still figuring out how to talk about that part without it feeling fragile, like something that might break if I handle it wrong.

When I finish, the bread basket is significantly emptier.

Ivy is crying. Quietly, controlled, dabbing under her eye with a napkin. "Sorry, I'm just so proud of you, Harp."

"You're crying because I prayed on my floor?"

"I'm crying because *you* prayed on your floor. Do you understand how long I've been—" She fans her face. "Never mind. Keep going."

"That's it," I say. "That's the whole thing."

"The whole thing," Olivia repeats, in the specific tone she uses when she wants me to hear how wrong I am. She has her coffee cup in both hands, legs crossed, the picture of calm. Olivia always looks like she's taking notes, even when she isn't.

"So you've realized you have genuine feelings for Micah, you've had your first honest conversation with God in what sounds like years, and your response is to call it 'the whole thing' like it's a parking ticket."

"Olivia."

"I'm just naming what I'm observing."

"That's literally what you always say."

"Because it's literally always what I'm doing." She sets her cup down. "So, tell him."

I pick at the edge of my napkin. "It's complicated."

"It's not, actually. You feel something, he probably feels

something, you tell each other, that's communication, it's a straightforward process that humans have been doing for ages."

"It started as a fake arrangement," I say. "I recruited him to pretend to be my boyfriend so my ex would be jealous. That's the foundation we're working with."

Olivia considers this. "Okay, that complicates communication slightly."

"Thank you."

"But it doesn't make it impossible. It just means the conversation starts one step earlier."

Ivy, who has successfully stopped crying and is now dismantling a piece of sourdough with the calm focus of someone who has been waiting to say something for a while, looks up. "He's going to be at the show tonight."

"I know."

"You should come."

"I was already going to come, Ivy."

"Good." She puts her sourdough down. "And when you see him, you don't have to say anything enormous. You just say you want to try dating for real."

The words land the way they always do when they are true.

"Working on it," I say.

"I know you are." She reaches across the table and squeezes my hand once. "That's the whole point."

Olivia picks up her latte. "For what it's worth, the fact that you prayed last night is not a small thing, Harper. That's not nothing. That's you actually showing up instead of just going through the motions."

I look out the window at the street. "It felt like nothing. I don't even know if I did it right."

"You did it," Olivia says simply. "That's what right looks like at the beginning."

We shop for three hours, which is exactly the amount of time it takes for Ivy to develop opinions about every piece of clothing I hold up and Olivia to evaluate each one with the measured neutrality of someone on a panel. I find a top I like on the second floor of a store we almost didn't go into, deep burgundy, soft fabric that looks effortless and takes six minutes to find the right earrings for.

"That one," Ivy says, the second I hold it up.

"You said that about the last three."

"I meant it every time. I mean it more now." She tilts her head. "Wear it tonight."

Olivia, who has been holding a jacket she has looked at from four angles without committing to, finally hangs it back on the rack. "I'm not buying anything today. I'm in a very specific relationship with my budget right now, and retail therapy is not covered."

"Chris mentioned there might be a few more people coming. From Gray's old college group." A pause that has too much space in it. "Apparently James will be there."

Olivia's expression doesn't change. This is a skill she has developed professionally and personally, the ability to keep her face exactly where she wants it. "That's fine."

"He asked about you."

"People ask about things all the time. I ask about things. It doesn't mean anything."

"Olivia—"

"I have seventeen active clients, a waiting list, and a lease renewal coming up." She adjusts the strap on her bag with complete composure. "I am not in a position to be asked about."

Ivy looks at me. I look at Ivy. We do the silent conversation.

"Noted," Ivy says pleasantly, and drops it.

For now.

I'm standing in front of my bathroom mirror at six-fifteen with the burgundy top on and my hair doing something that required three attempts and is still only cooperating at about sixty percent.

The thing I'm trying not to think about is that tonight I get to see Micah. I'm about to walk into a room where he'll be on a stage with a guitar, and I will have to exist somewhere in his line of sight and act like a functional person.

I can do that.

I put my mascara on.

I can absolutely do that.

I don't actually want to act anymore. That's what Sunday night on the floor was about, in the end. Not just Micah. Not just Collin. The whole pattern, the whole exhausting architecture of performing the right version of myself for whoever's watching. I'm tired of it.

But knowing a thing and doing a thing are different, and right now I'm standing in my bathroom trying to make my hair cooperate while every nerve in my body is running a quiet rehearsal of what it might look like to just be honest.

My phone lights up on the counter.

IVY

We're outside. Ready?

I look at my reflection one more time, grab my jacket off the chair and head for the door.

Chapter 37
Micah

At church, I'm the children's ministry director. Responsible. Organized. The guy who color-codes his volunteer schedule and brings backup markers to craft night. The guy parents' trust with their kids and their chaos and their questions about whether Jesus liked dinosaurs.

Here, at this dive bar on a Monday night, I'm just the guy with the guitar who hasn't figured out a better way to spend a Monday.

"You're tuning it too tight," Gray says, not looking up from his own guitar.

"I'm tuning it correctly." I adjust the G string. "These are two very different things."

"Sounds like you're strangling it."

"Sounds like you should mind your own instrument."

Chris, behind the kit running a lazy warmup beat, snorts loud enough to be heard over both of us. "Every time. Every single time."

Gray grins. I grin. This is fine. This is what Monday nights look like when the three of us drag ourselves out of our respective corners of responsible adulthood and remember we used to do this for fun.

The venue is small—more pizza counter than stage, honestly. A handful of mismatched tables, string lights strung along exposed brick, a stage that's really just a corner of the room with better acoustics and a modest PA system someone's cousin clearly installed with good intentions and limited expertise. It smells like garlic and old wood and something faintly sweet from whatever they were baking earlier. I love it unreasonably. There's something about a room that doesn't try too hard that I've always found more honest than places that do.

"Song order?" Gray asks, finally looking up.

I pull the set list from my back pocket. We spent exactly fourteen minutes putting it together via text yesterday, which is roughly twelve more than usual. It starts with a Relient K deep cut, wanders into some early Switchfoot, a couple of original worship songs we're telling ourselves we're playing for fun and not because Gray literally cannot stop writing music even when he tries, and ends with a chaotic detour into some mid-2000s emo that Chris lobbied for aggressively and we caved on immediately.

"Looks good," Gray says, handing it back.

I'm mid-chord checking when the door opens.

I look up.

Ivy first, hair down, laughing at something on her phone. Olivia beside her, already scanning the room with that calm, assessing quality she carries everywhere, the kind of attentiveness that makes you feel like she's cataloguing you whether she means to or not.

And then Harper.

Harper, in jeans and a jean jacket over a burgundy top

with her red hair loose, who steps through the door last and looks up at exactly the wrong moment.

Or the right one, depending on how you're keeping score, which I'm not. Obviously.

Our eyes meet across the room.

I smile. Because that's what normal people do when they see a friend. A normal friend. Someone they're friends with in a completely standard, uncomplicated way. I raise my hand in a small wave.

She looks—breathless. For about half a second. And then she nods, that sharp little dip of her chin, and looks away and lets Ivy steer her toward a table two rows back from the stage.

I turn back to my guitar.

"You good?" Gray asks, casually, not looking at me.

"Great," I say. "Let's play."

Between songs, the bar fills in a little more. A few people pull chairs around. Someone orders the garlic knots and the smell hits with such force that three different tables seem to perk up in unison.

I'm enjoying myself. I genuinely am.

Except.

I'm also hyperaware of exactly where Harper is sitting in this room. Two tables back, slightly left of center. She's laughing at something Olivia said, her head tipped back slightly. Her jean jacket is off now, draped over the back of her chair. She's got her elbows on the table, and she's leaning in toward Olivia's voice.

She hasn't looked at the stage in approximately four minutes.

Not that I'm tracking this.

Gray leans into the mic for the next song, that easy performance smile sliding into place. "This one's about a guy," he says, "who took way too long to figure out something pretty obvious."

Then he starts playing, and I recognize the chord progression immediately, and I nearly close my eyes because the lyrics are about a guy watching a girl across a room and understanding, with sudden, inconvenient clarity, that he has completely miscalculated his feelings.

I keep my expression neutral through main strength of character.

I also, at no point, look at Harper.

This is a significant personal achievement and I feel it deserves recognition.

We cycle through the set. The Switchfoot songs land well. The worship ones always have this moment, halfway through, where the energy in the room shifts—not everyone, not even most people, but a few. A couple near the back who close their eyes for a verse. A guy at the bar who sets down his drink and just listens. It's quiet and strange and good, the way those moments always are. Like dropping something true into a noisy room and watching it ripple outward without asking permission.

The emo detour in the final slot causes exactly the amount of chaos Chris hoped for, which is significant.

Through all of it, song by song, I am aware of her. Aware that the last time I saw her, she bolted. That things were getting real, and she left.

I play the last chord of the set, and Gray says something

charming into the mic about garlic knots, and the table up front cheers.

Dinner is loud and comfortable in the way that only happens when everyone at the table has known each other long enough that silence isn't weird and interrupting each other mid-sentence is a love language. Two long rectangular tables shoved together, paper plates, pizza, a pitcher of Mountain Dew that Chris requested unironically.

Gray and Ivy are in the middle of the table, which means they're at the center of everything, which is where they always end up without trying. Ivy's eating carefully around the peppers on her slice and Gray keeps moving them to his plate without her asking, without even interrupting the conversation. I notice this and try not to let it make me feel anything.

Olivia is telling a story about a situation at work and it's the kind of story that gets funnier the further in you get, building toward something that makes Marcus inhale his drink at the punchline.

Harper laughs so hard she has to set down her cup.

"I don't believe you," she says.

"Every word," Olivia says, entirely composed.

"There is no way that's how it ended."

"It ended exactly like that."

"That cannot be legal."

"Legally ambiguous," Olivia says. "Which is its own category."

Ivy is already laughing again, one hand on her stomach.

Gray watches her laugh, and there it is again—that thing in his expression I have long since stopped pretending I don't see. Like she is genuinely, constantly, the most interesting thing in any room.

I take a long sip of my drink and look at the ceiling for a second.

I'm at one end of the table. Harper is at the other.

I tell myself it doesn't matter and then proceed to find my eyes drifting to that end of the table with a frequency that is, objectively, embarrassing.

She's talking to Olivia. Laughing at something that makes her tip her head back slightly.

Then, as if she feels it, she looks up.

Directly at me.

I don't look away.

She doesn't either.

There's this strange, suspended moment where we're just looking at each other across this long, chaotic, noisy table, and I genuinely don't know what's happening in her head. Her expression is unreadable in a way it rarely is, Harper is usually broadcasting something, even when she thinks she's not, but right now it's just quiet, and direct, and I feel it somewhere in my sternum.

She blinks first and looks back down at her plate.

But then she looks up again almost immediately, like she can't quite help it.

I take a very composed sip of my drink.

She looks back down.

This happens four more times over the next fifteen minutes. Look. Look back. Look away. Repeat. It is excruciating in a way that is also somehow sort of funny, or would be funny in maybe three to five years when I have sufficient emotional distance to find it amusing.

Gray catches the third or fourth round of it and I watch him bite down on a grin from across the table. He says absolutely nothing. It's the most gracious thing he's done for me in recent memory.

Olivia, however, is looking at me with an expression of quiet, forensic interest that I find significantly less comfortable.

I'm mid-sentence talking to Marcus when I see Harper lean toward Ivy. Whisper something. Olivia glances over. The two of them do a brief, wordless exchange that has the particular quality of a conversation conducted entirely in expressions, the kind of shorthand that only develops after years of friendship.

Then Harper reaches for her jacket. And her purse.

I watch her stand up.

And then she's weaving through the chairs toward the door, and the whole thing takes about thirty seconds, and then she's gone.

I'm pushing back from the table before I've made any conscious decision to do so.

"Where are you going?" Gray grabs my arm, half-laughing, half-something else. His eyes go to the door and back to me, and I can see him working to keep his face completely neutral, which he is only partially succeeding at.

"I don't know," I say.

Completely honest. I genuinely don't know. I just know that Harper Mitchell has walked out of a room and my body has apparently decided that's information requiring a response.

Gray's hand drops. He shakes his head slowly, but there's something in his expression that isn't quite exasperation.

I head for the door.

Outside, the air is cooler than inside—sharp with the particular edge of late April after dark, the kind of cool that feels less like temperature and more like a reminder that the night is still happening out here regardless of what goes on in that room.

She hasn't made it to her car yet. She's standing near the edge of the parking lot with her jacket half on, not quite at her car, and she turns when she hears the door. The amber streetlights catch her hair, the red of it going warm and gold, and for a second we just look at each other, and I don't have a single prepared sentence for this moment because I didn't plan to be in this moment.

I'm not sure what I planned. Just that I couldn't stay at that table.

I move toward her. She watches me.

And then I step in front of her, between her and her car, close enough that she has to stop.

She does.

Neither of us says anything.

She looks up at me. I look down at her. The string lights from the bar window throw just enough light out here to see by, warm and low, and the night is quiet in the particular way that means we are the only two people in it right now. Her chin lifts slightly, the way it does when she's trying to hold something together, and her lips part like she's about to say something and then doesn't.

I don't say anything either.

There's no version of what I want to say that comes out right. Everything true feels like too much. Everything safe feels like a lie. So I just stay where I am, and she stays where she is, and neither of us moves.

She breathes in. I watch her eyes go soft and then complicated, the way they do when she's processing something she didn't expect. She looks down briefly. Then back up. And I think she might be about to say something real, something past the deflection, something I would actually be allowed to hold onto.

Her phone rings.

The sound is jarring and immediate and wrong, cutting through whatever the air between us was building toward. She flinches, just barely. Her hand moves to her jacket pocket automatically, a reflex, pulling the screen out into the amber light.

She looks at it.

I watch her face change.

She raises her eyes to mine.

And I see it. The apology. The conflict. The impossibility of whatever she's working through that she has not let me anywhere near, and I know, with the kind of certainty that settles in the chest rather than the head, that I am looking at the shape of something I am not going to be able to fix tonight.

"Harper." My voice comes out lower than I intended. Rougher. "Please."

She shakes her head.

It's small. Barely anything. But it lands with the weight of something much larger, and she already knows it, I can see that she knows it, and she is doing it anyway.

She steps around me. Walks to her car. The door opens and closes and the engine turns over in the dark, and the headlights sweep a wide arc across the lot as she pulls out.

I stand there until the taillights disappear.

Chapter 38
Micah

I wake up at six forty-three and I am done.

Not done in a dramatic, everything-has-crumbled kind of way. Done the way you feel when you've finally found your keys and they were in your jacket pocket the whole time. Like, yes, obviously. Of course.

Harper Mitchell is not a woman I can keep pretending to date without eventually losing my mind, and Monday night proved it.

I've been patient in a way that would make the most self-controlled man I know look like he's in a hurry, and it is time to stop. Because she matters enough to stop pretending otherwise.

I'm going to tell her. After church tomorrow. I'm going to find her, and I'm going to say the thing I have not been saying for roughly six weeks, and then whatever happens, happens.

I get up, make coffee, feed Biscuit, and feel so resolved about this that I'm halfway through the mug before I realize I have absolutely no idea how I'm going to do it.

Time to pull out my handy dandy notebook.

I use a standard composition book. Black and white cover, college-ruled. I've had three of them this year because I go through them fast—children's ministry curriculum takes up a lot of real estate, and I have a habit of working things out on paper when they're too complicated for my head alone.

I open to a fresh page. Write the date. Then, at the top:

HARPER PLAN.

Then I stare at it for a second, because seeing it written in actual ink makes it the most real thing in the room.

I keep going.

OPTION A: TEXT HER SOMETHING LOW-PRESSURE BUT CLEAR.

I write three versions in the margin. The first is too casual. The second sounds like the opening line of a complaint. The third is actually decent until I read it again and realize it could be interpreted as asking about her availability for a volunteer shift, which is not the impression I'm going for.

Scratch all three. Moving on.

OPTION B: SHOW UP AT HER DOOR.

I write this, look at it, and immediately write *not this*

next to it and draw a box around it so I don't accidentally talk myself into it later.

OPTION C: TELL HER AFTER SECOND SERVICE. CATCH HER BEFORE SHE MAKES IT OUT TO THE PARKING LOT.

This has some merit. Church gives us a natural reason to be in the same place. It also gives her the option of getting distracted by twelve separate conversations and a snack table before I can get to her. The problem with Option C is it still puts me intercepting her on the way out, which has the energy of an ambush more than an invitation.

OPTION D: ASK HER TO GET LUNCH. JUST US. MAKE IT CLEAR THAT'S WHAT I MEAN.

I write this one and underline it.

This is the move. *Hey, can I take you to lunch?* That is a sentence I am fully capable of saying. And once we're at lunch, I can say the thing.

I make a second column:

WHAT I'LL ACTUALLY SAY:

I get three sentences in before Biscuit climbs onto the table.

"I'm working," I tell him.

He steps directly onto the notebook, turns in a small circle, and sits down on Option D—the lunch option—with the full intention of staying there.

"Biscuit."

He looks at me, blinks once, and tucks his feet under

himself in that way that means he is settling in for the long haul, and no amount of gentle nudging will change this.

"You're doing this on purpose."

He does not confirm or deny.

"I have to say, your timing is terrible." I look down at the notebook, at his paws folded over the word lunch like he's signed off on it.

He chirps.

I slide the notebook out from under him at an angle, careful not to disrupt his center of gravity.

"You've met her once." I tell him.

He chirps again, lower this time.

"I know," I say. "She is pretty great."

I go back to the notebook.

Option D it is. After second service. Ask her to lunch. Say the thing.

I cap the pen and look at what I've written.

It's a solid plan. Clear. Specific. It gives her room to respond without putting her on the spot in the middle of a crowd.

I flip back to find where I wrote the actual words again.

HARPER, I'VE BEEN SHOWING UP TO EVERYTHING EXCEPT THE ONLY CONVERSATION THAT MATTERS. WOULD YOU CONSIDER DATING ME FOR REAL?

I read it twice. Scratch out the first sentence, eager to get to the point.

Better. Specific without being a speech. Open without being wishy-washy.

I close the notebook.

Then I sit with the quiet for a minute, coffee warm in

my hands, Biscuit settled somewhere behind me making small, satisfied ferret sounds at nothing.

"Okay," I pray. "I think I have a plan. I'm going to do it."

A pause.

"I'm aware this is not news to You. I'm also aware I've been a little slow to get here." I look at the kitchen table, at the notebook that holds my plan.

The quiet is the same it always is. Present. Not empty.

"I'm asking You to go ahead of me," I say. "Tomorrow. I'll do the part I can do. The rest is yours."

I sit there for another minute. Then I put the mug in the sink, go to the bedroom, and pull out my running shoes.

The air outside is exactly what it always is on a Texas April morning before nine—cool enough that you need it, warm enough that you don't have to fight it. I start at a walk, let my legs figure out what they're doing, and settle into a pace.

I left my headphones on the counter on purpose.

I've been spending a lot of mornings inside my own head and not enough of them in the actual world, and the actual world is happening, regardless. The Hendersons' dog is getting its walk. Two houses down, a kid is already on his bike, executing some kind of ambitious maneuver off the driveway curb. The entire neighborhood is out here being fully operational while I've been sitting in my kitchen writing out a plan in my notebook.

Left foot, right foot. The pace settles.

I'm finally going to tell her.

Tomorrow, after second service, I am going to find

Harper Mitchell and tell her that I'm done pretending, and if that goes sideways, then at least I'll know. Certainty in either direction is better than six more weeks of analyzing parking lot eye contact.

The park comes into view on my left, and I take the familiar turn.

The path runs along the west side, past the big oak that always looks borrowed from another century. A couple with a stroller. An old man on a bench with a newspaper that he is not reading. A kid near the pond, throwing bread at pigeons.

My calf starts arguing around the eight-minute mark. I slow my pace.

And that's when I see her.

About thirty yards further down the path. On a bench near the pond, red hair loose around her shoulders, scarf pulled up despite the weather not entirely requiring it. Head tilted down slightly.

I go completely still.

She hasn't seen me.

Tomorrow. The plan was tomorrow.

Well.

The plan was also supposed to involve less sweating.

I take one breath. And then I start walking toward her.

Chapter 39
Harper

I've been sitting on this bench for twenty minutes and I still haven't figured out what to do.

Which tracks, honestly. Sitting on a cold park bench crying has solved exactly zero of my problems historically, but here I am, doing it again, because apparently I am a woman who learns nothing.

The park is quiet for a Saturday morning. There's a kid near the pond throwing bread at pigeons with the focused intensity of someone conducting a very important experiment. A couple with a stroller. An old man with a newspaper he's not reading. The whole thing is peaceful and pretty and I am ruining it by crying into my scarf.

I don't even know why I'm here, exactly. I left my apartment to clear my head, started walking, and somehow ended up on this bench because apparently my feet made a decision my brain wasn't consulted about.

The girls tried to help. I'll give them that.

I'd called Ivy on Thursday, mostly incoherent, trying to explain that whatever I'd been chasing for the last several weeks wasn't even important anymore. That I'd finally gone to meet Collin, told him I didn't want him back, that I was not interested, that he should please move on with his life and leave me alone, and it had taken eleven minutes, I timed it.

And then I'd made the mistake of saying Micah's name out loud, just once, and Ivy had gotten very quiet.

"So tell him," she'd said.

Which is easy for Ivy to say. Ivy, who got dared to hold a stranger's hand in New Orleans and somehow ended up married to him. Some people just trip and fall directly into their happy ending.

I'd called Olivia too, because I wanted a second opinion, which was possibly a mistake because Olivia's second opinion was identical.

"Communication," she'd said, in the calm, infuriating voice she uses when she knows she's right and is being patient about it. "That's it. That's all you have to do."

"And if he doesn't feel the same way?"

"Then you'll know. And you'll survive knowing."

Which is objectively true and also completely unhelpful to me right now, sitting here on a park bench in a scarf I didn't need, spiraling with slightly better scenery than my apartment.

I wipe my face with the back of my hand and stare at the pigeon nearest to me. It stares back, unimpressed.

"Don't look at me like that," I tell it.

It walks away.

I drop my head back and close my eyes.

Lord, I have no idea what I'm doing. I've tried the lists and the plans and the color-coded strategy, and none of it helped. I keep running from the thing right in front of me, and I'm tired. If You could send me something. A sign, a clue, anything—now would be a great time.

I sit in the quiet. The wind picks up off the water and cuts right through my jacket, and somewhere nearby a bird calls once and goes still.

Then I hear footsteps on the path.

Breathing harder than the pace warrants, getting closer, and there's something about the rhythm of it that moves through me before my brain catches up. I open my eyes.

Micah.

Running clothes, slightly out of breath, his glasses catching the morning light as his pace slows—because he's seen me. He stops about ten feet away, chest still rising and falling, and for one suspended second we just look at each other across the quiet Saturday park.

He is so unfairly, inconveniently, completely him.

I asked for a sign, and God sent me a man who has been standing right in front of me for two years while I looked absolutely everywhere else.

I stand up.

I don't plan to. My body just does it, the same way my feet brought me to this park this morning—some part of me making a decision before the rest catches up. I'm on my feet, and now we're facing each other, and there's nowhere to hide behind the scarf and the bench and the pigeon.

He takes a few steps forward. His eyes move over my face and something shifts in his expression, careful and quiet.

"Harper," his voice drops. "Why are you crying?"

"I'm not crying."

He gives me a look.

"I *was* crying. Past tense. I'm done now."

He tilts his head, something caught between concern and the very specific expression he gets when he finds me funny and is trying not to show it. "You're sure about that?"

"I'm completely fine."

"You've got—" He gestures vaguely at his own cheek.

I wipe my face. My hand comes away damp. "That's just the wind."

"It's not that windy."

"Well, my eyes are very sensitive."

"To what?"

"Micah."

"I'm just asking."

"To emotions," I say, which I did not intend to say, and he bites down on a smile, and there, in the corner of his mouth, the dimple appears, and I feel my entire argument evaporate.

This is exactly the problem.

"Okay," he says, and his voice has shifted into that unhurried, low register he uses when he's actually paying attention to something. Not teasing anymore. "What happened?"

I look at him. He's close enough now that I can see the morning light catching in his glasses, the slight flush from the run still in his face. He's not moving. Not checking his phone, not scanning the park, not doing anything except standing here like he has exactly as much time as I need and the rest of the world can work itself out.

It is extremely inconvenient to be known by someone.

"I went to meet Collin," I say.

He goes still.

"I told him I didn't want him back. That I wasn't interested. That he should move on." I press my lips together. "It took eleven minutes. I timed it."

A pause. Something in his expression I can't quite read.

"You timed it?"

"I was very efficient."

He exhales, slow, and looks out over the pond. Then back at me. "And you're crying because—"

"Because I'm an idiot." The words come out before I can stop them. "I made everything so complicated when it didn't have to be complicated. I had Ivy telling me to communicate and Olivia telling me to communicate and apparently the entire population of people who know me have been watching me avoid the obvious thing, and I walked out here to clear my head and instead I've just been sitting on that bench being an idiot with better scenery."

He's quiet for a moment.

"You're not an idiot."

"Micah—"

"You're complicated," he says. "There's a difference."

I look at him. He says it so simply, like it's not even a compliment, just a fact he's catalogued alongside everything else he knows about me.

I have been running from this man for months.

"What's the obvious thing?" he asks. Quiet. Careful. His eyes steady on mine, his lips forming into a knowing smile.

And there it is again. In the corner of his mouth. The faintest pull.

The dimple.

Something in me completely snaps.

"Because I love you!" The words come out entirely too loud and I immediately want to walk into the duck pond. "And those stupid dimples of yours."

Micah goes very still.

"I meant..." I backtrack immediately, feeling my face go hot. "I meant the dimples. Specifically. The dimples are the problem. Whenever I'm mad at you one of them just appears in the corner of your mouth and it completely derails me and I forget what I was saying. It's been happening for months and it's very distracting and I resent it."

"You said you loved me."

"I said I loved the dimples."

"Harper," his voice is quiet. Careful. "You said you loved me."

Chapter 40
Micah

"I meant the dimples—"

"No." I take a step toward her, and I'm close enough now to see exactly what's happening on her face, which means she can see exactly what's happening on mine too. "No, Harper. I don't think you did."

She opens her mouth.

Closes it.

Harper Mitchell, who has never once in her life been at a loss for words, is standing here with nothing.

So I say it.

"I've been in love with you for two years." It comes out steady, which surprises me a little. Like something that's been under pressure for a long time finally finding a clean release. "Long before you asked me to do any of this." I pause. "I thought I was doing a good job of keeping it contained, but in the interest of communication..."

Something flickers across her face at that word. Like she knows exactly where it came from.

"There it is," I finish.

She stares at me. "Two years?"

"Two years."

"And you didn't—you never said—"

"You were in love with someone else." No bitterness in it. Just the truth. "And then you weren't, but I didn't know for certain, and then the whole arrangement made it impossible to tell what was real and what was performance, and I —" I stop. Look at her directly. "I didn't want to be one more person making things about himself when you were already carrying enough."

The expression on her face does something I've been hoping for for two years.

"Dimples," she says.

"Freckles."

"You are the most aggravating person I have ever met."

"I know."

"I mean it. You are genuinely, deeply, specifically aggravating."

"I know that too."

And I can feel it happening, the smile pulling at the corner of my mouth before I can stop it, and I watch her eyes drop to exactly that spot and then lift back to mine with an expression that looks a lot like surrender.

"You're doing it," she says.

"I'm just standing here."

"You're doing the dimple on purpose."

"I have no control over the dimple, Harper. I've told you this."

"It's not fair." Her voice has gone softer. "It's genuinely not fair that you can just do that."

I lean forward slightly. "Say it again."

"I'm not saying it again."

"Harper."

She looks at me for a long moment, and the park is quiet

around us, the little boy with the pigeons has moved on, a jogger passes on the far path, and Harper Mitchell is looking at me like she's finally decided to stop running from something.

"People are staring at us," she says.

She glances past my shoulder, and I can see it in her face, the flicker of self-consciousness. Old instinct. The worry about being too much, taking up too much space, making a scene.

"I don't care," I say.

She looks back at me. "I'm chaotic."

"Yes."

"And loud. And a complete mess half the time."

I take another step toward her.

"Micah, I'm being serious—"

"I know you are." I stop in front of her, close enough that she has to look up at me, and I reach down and take her hand, and now there's almost no space between us, and she's looking up at me with those green eyes. "Harper. I know you're chaotic. I know you're loud. I know you are, on any given day, a magnificent, beautiful disaster."

"That's not—"

"And I love that about you." The words come out quiet and sure. "I love that you rearrange furniture when you're anxious and that you made a color-coded itinerary for a Bible study, and that you cry at kindergarten art showcases." I watch her face, the way her breath has gone uneven. "And I love that you filled out my background check out of spite." A beat, just for that one. "I love all of it, Harper. All of you. Even the parts that drive me absolutely crazy."

"Micah," she whispers.

"I've loved you since the day you stormed into that hallway at church." My hand finds her face, thumb brushing her cheek. "Hair everywhere, fire in your eyes, ready to argue with a complete stranger at nine in the morning because a kid needed help. I didn't stand a chance." I pause. "That was almost two years ago."

Something in her expression breaks open. "You've been fighting it the whole time?"

"The whole time," I confirm. "And when you asked me to be your fake date, I thought..." My heart aches at the memory, but I let it show, because she deserves the whole truth. "I thought that would be my only chance to ever stand next to you like I mattered. My only shot at being in that space, even if none of it was real."

Her eyes are bright now.

"But it turns out," I say, and I lower my forehead slowly until it rests against hers, her warmth finding mine, her breath catching in a way that does something irreversible to my ability to think clearly, "that I don't have to pretend anymore."

She makes a small sound, almost a laugh, almost something else. "I don't like you."

"I know," I say. "You love me."

And she does the most Harper thing she has ever done.

She rolls her eyes.

I go still and observe the way she looks at me like she's done fighting the inevitable.

She rises onto her toes, wraps her hands in my hair, and brings her lips to mine.

And I kiss Harper Mitchell. For real. For the first time.

She kisses me back like she's been waiting just as long as I have, and I wrap one arm around her waist and pull her in, and I think, *oh*. So that's what it was supposed to feel like. All those times I stood next to her and kept my hands to myself and called it enough. It was never enough. It was just all I had.

This is what it feels like to kiss her for real.

When we finally pull back, she keeps her hands around my neck, and I keep mine around her waist, and she's smiling up at me in a way I've never actually seen before—the full version, no performance in it, nothing held back.

"Hi," she says, a little breathless.

"Hi."

She bites her lip, trying to contain the smile and failing spectacularly. "So, this whole thing started with a dare."

"It did."

"Ivy dared me to find a fake boyfriend. Which led to you. Which led to—" she gestures vaguely between us with one hand, "all of this."

"Technically it led to a lot of unnecessary suffering that could have been avoided if either of us had just communicated."

She points at me. "Do not be reasonable right now."

"Sorry."

She settles back against my chest and I rest my chin on top of her head, and the park is very nice, actually. Very peaceful. I understand why she came here.

"Micah."

"Yeah."

"I dare you." She tilts her head up to look at me, and her eyes are bright, and her hair is a mess from the wind and she is the most beautiful thing I have ever seen. "I dare you to stop fake dating me."

"And start dating you for real."

"And start dating me for real," she confirms.

"Harper Mitchell," I say, "that is the easiest dare I have ever accepted in my life."

She smiles. "Yeah?"

"Yeah," I press a kiss to her forehead. Then one to her cheek. Then I rest my forehead against hers and close my eyes, and for a moment I just breathe her in, and I think about two years of standing in hallways and sitting across tables and watching her laugh from the other end of a room, and how none of it was ever going to be enough.

"I would have said yes to anything you ever asked me," I say quietly. "You know that, right?"

She's quiet for a second.

Then, soft enough I almost miss it. "I know. I just finally asked the right thing."

Chapter 41
Harper
Six Hours Later

I have been on eleven fake dates with this man.

Eleven.

I have held his hand and danced with him and sat across from him at a candlelit table and convinced an entire room of people that we were deeply, genuinely in love.

And I am currently standing in my bathroom having a complete emotional crisis about what to wear to our first *real* date.

"You're spiraling," Olivia says from the doorway. She has her arms crossed and her therapist expression on.

"I'm not spiraling. I'm curating."

"You've changed your earrings four times."

"Earrings are important, Olivia. They frame the face."

From my bedroom, a sound that is unmistakably Ivy trying not to cry.

I lean around the doorframe. "Ivy. Are you crying?"

"No." She fans her face with both hands.

"You're crying because I'm going on a date?"

"I'm crying because you're going on a date with *Micah.*" She says his name like it's an entire sentence. "Do you understand how long I have waited for this? Do you have any idea—"

"Ivy."

"He's Gray's best friend." Her voice wobbles. "My best friend is dating my husband's best friend."

Olivia and I exchange a look.

"Olivia is your best friend too," I say.

"I know." Ivy presses her fingertips under her eyes. "But you know what I mean."

I walk back into the bedroom and sit beside her on the edge of the bed and wrap an arm around her shoulders. "Okay. Deep breath. You're going to ruin your mascara."

"I don't care about my mascara. I care about you." She turns to look at me, eyes bright, genuinely emotional in that way she's been lately where everything hits twice as hard. "You deserve this. You deserve someone who has been crazy about you the whole time and just waited and was patient and never made you feel like too much." She grabs my hand. "You deserve Micah."

I open my mouth. But no words come out.

Because there is genuinely nothing I can say to that.

"Okay," Olivia says from the doorway, apparently deciding the emotional portion of the evening has run its course. "Back to the earrings. Gold hoops. Final answer. You've been on eleven dates with this man, Harper. You don't need to impress him."

"This is different."

"How."

"Because those didn't count." I stand back up, returning to the mirror. "This one counts."

Olivia tilts her head slowly. "Does it feel different? Or does it feel exactly the same, except now you're allowed to admit what it actually is?"

I stare at my reflection.

The gold hoops catch the light.

"Both," I say finally. "It feels like both."

Olivia nods, satisfied. "Gold hoops. Dark jeans. The green top. Go."

He knocks at exactly seven o'clock.

Not 6:58. Not 7:04. Seven o'clock precisely, which is so completely Micah that I actually have to take a breath before I open the door.

When I do, he's standing there in dark jeans and a navy button-down with his glasses on, hair slightly damp from a shower, and he looks exactly like himself. No gala suit, no performance version. Just him.

He looks at me for a moment without saying anything.

Then, "hi."

"Hi."

"You look—" he stops. Starts again. "You look really beautiful, Harper."

My face goes warm. "Thank you."

He smiles. The dimple appears.

"Don't," I say.

"I'm not doing anything."

"You're doing the dimple."

"I literally cannot control—"

"Let's go," I say, grabbing my jacket, because if I stand here looking at that dimple for one more second, I am going to say something embarrassing.

Behind me, from the living room, I hear Ivy make a sound that is definitely crying.

I know where we're going before we even turn onto the street.

Something about the direction, the familiar route, the way he's not offering any dramatic hints because he doesn't need to. He's completely calm in the driver's seat, one hand on the wheel, the Dallas night sliding past the windows, and I'm watching the city and doing the math and then I see the sign.

Angelo's.

The hand-painted sign is welcoming in the window.

"Micah."

"Yeah."

"You brought me back to Angelo's."

"I did."

I turn to look at him. "You planned this."

He glances over, the corner of his mouth pulling up. "I've been planning this for a while, actually."

"Of course you have," I whisper.

"Is that okay?"

"That is extremely okay."

Angelo, when he sees us walk in together, does not immediately come around the counter. He stops. He looks at Micah. He looks at me. He looks at our hands, which are linked at my side because somewhere between the truck and the door that just happened.

Then he presses both hands to his chest and says something in Italian that I don't catch but that makes Micah laugh.

"What did he say?" I whisper.

"He said he *knew* it," Micah says. "He claims he called it the first time I brought you here."

I pause. Then I turn to look at him fully. "Wait."

"What?"

"You understood that."

"Yes."

"You just...understood what he said. In Italian."

"That is what understanding a language means, yes."

"Micah." I stop walking entirely. "Do you speak Italian?"

"Reasonably well," he says, with the complete calm of a man who does not understand why this is newsworthy.

"You speak Italian and you never told me this?"

"You never asked."

"That is not a defense! That is the kind of thing you lead with! '*Hi, I'm Micah, I run children's ministry, I speak Italian*'—"

"That would be a weird way to introduce myself."

"It would be a great way to introduce yourself!" I stare at him. "How? When? Why?"

"I took it in high school," he says, steering us gently toward the corner table because Angelo is now watching this exchange with visible delight. "And I studied abroad during my sophomore year of college. Torino. Four months."

"You studied abroad in Italy?"

"I did."

"You lived in Italy."

"For four months, yes."

"Micah Sanders." I sit down at the table and point at

him as he takes the seat across from me. "What else don't I know about you?"

He picks up his water glass, completely unbothered, the dimple making its inevitable appearance. "We have time."

Angelo, still watching from across the room, says something else in rapid Italian. Micah responds without missing a beat, which causes Angelo to laugh loudly and disappear into the kitchen.

"What did he just say?" I demand.

"He said you're even more fun than he expected."

"And what did you say back?"

Micah looks at me over his water glass. "I said, I *know*."

Angelo disappears with the confidence of a man who has somewhere to be and food to make and no need to take our order because he already knows.

I look across the table.

"Hi," I say, because we seem to be doing this again.

"Hi," he says.

"This is our first date."

"It is."

"Even though we've been here before."

"We have." He leans forward slightly, elbows on the table, completely at ease. "Does it feel different?"

I look around at the checkered tablecloth, the candle, the vintage photos on the wall.

"Yes," I say. "It feels like everything is finally the right way around."

Something in his expression settles. Deepens. "Yeah," he says quietly. "It does."

Angelo brings bread first, which I fall on immediately, and then pasta that is as devastatingly good as I remembered, and Micah watches me eat with that same amused, satisfied expression from last time except now I don't have to pretend I don't notice it.

We talk the way we always talk, easy and sideways, circling big things through small ones. He tells me about a kid in children's ministry who told him this week that he wanted to be a "church guy" when he grew up, delivered with complete sincerity at snack time, and I tell him about Camo's latest artistic development, which involves exclusively painting things in orange regardless of what color they are in real life.

It's easy. That's the thing. It has always been easy, underneath the bickering and the performance and the weeks of not letting myself look directly at what this actually was. Underneath all of it, it has just been this. Two people who fit, talking about children's ministry and kindergarten art and the things that matter.

I tear off a piece of bread and look at him across the candlelight.

"Okay," he says, setting down his water glass. "Serious question."

I look up from my pasta. "That face is not a serious question face."

"It's a serious question."

"Micah."

"How long," he says, calmly, "do you think a couple should date before they start talking about marriage?"

"Three months," I say immediately.

He blinks. Clearly he expected more resistance.

"Minimum," I continue, twirling my fork. "Long enough to really know each other. Make sure neither are serial killers or anything like that."

"You think three months is sufficient time to rule out a serial killer?"

"It's a starting point. You look for patterns. Consistent behavior. Whether they're nice to waitstaff." I point my fork at him. "You've been very nice to Angelo, for the record. That's a good sign."

"I've known Angelo for four years."

"Even better. Character reference built in."

He's trying very hard not to smile. "So three months. That's your official position."

"That's my official position."

He nods slowly, like he's filing that away somewhere.

We eat in comfortable silence for a moment. Then he sets his fork down and says, "I should tell you, I was kind of joking when I asked that. Trying to be funny."

I look up at him.

"Trying to lighten the mood a little," he adds.

"Micah." I set my fork down. "There is nothing funny about true love."

He stares at me.

"This is serious business," I continue. "Marriage. Futures. These are not joke topics."

"Right," he says carefully. "I see that now."

"Good." I pick my fork back up. Then, because I'm already here and the pasta is incredible and something about Angelo's makes me feel like I can say the real thing: "Besides, I'd like to be married with at least two kids by the time I'm thirty."

I say it simply. Plainly. The way you say something you've known for a long time but haven't said out loud to the right person yet.

And when I look up at him, he's smiling.

Not the polite one. Not the amused one. Not even the dimple one, though that's there too. It's the full version—

quiet and certain and so completely unguarded that it almost takes my breath away.

"I really like that plan," he says.

And the way he says it—like it isn't hypothetical at all, like he's already folding it into something he's been building in his head for a long time—makes my heart do something it has absolutely no business doing over pasta on a first date.

I take a sip of water.

"Good," I say, trying to sound casual.

When Angelo comes back to clear our plates, he looks at our joined hands on the table and nods with solemn satisfaction.

"You come back," he tells me. "Next time I make the gnocchi."

"I will absolutely be back," I say.

He points at Micah. "You. Good job. Finally."

Micah ducks his head, laughing. "Thanks, Angelo."

Angelo hugs us both on the way out, which takes longer than expected, and then we're back in the cool April air, standing on the sidewalk beside his truck, and I tilt my face up at the Dallas sky and breathe.

No agenda. No performance to maintain or impression to make.

Just this.

"Thank you," I say. "For tonight. For—" I pause, at a loss for words.

For waiting. For being patient. For showing up at a park bench on a Saturday morning looking slightly out of breath and refusing to leave.

"Harper." He tucks a strand of hair behind my ear, his hand lingering at my jaw. "You never have to thank me."

"I know. I wanted to anyway."

He looks at me for a long moment.

Then he drops his hand and reaches for his keys. "The date isn't over yet."

I blink. "It's not?"

"We still have dessert." He pulls open my door, and the dimple appears in the corner of his mouth, devastating as ever. "Get in."

I get in.

He closes the door, walks around to the driver's side, and starts the engine. The city opens up around us as he pulls into traffic, Dallas lit up and alive, and I lean back against the seat and watch the lights go by.

I am not performing. I am not managing an outcome or running a plan or waiting for the other shoe to drop.

I am just here. In this truck. With this man who has been quietly, patiently, stubbornly in love with me for two years while I figured out how to be brave enough to feel it back.

And I think about a dare that started in a boutique dressing room with a emerald green dress and a terrible plan. About everything that dare set in motion.

Maybe the bravest thing I ever did was dare to fall for someone real. And then, when I was already falling, dare to say it out loud.

I glance over at him. He's got one hand on the wheel, the other resting on the console between us, and without thinking about it at all, I reach over and take his hand.

He doesn't say anything.

He just holds on.

I have absolutely no idea where he's taking me.

His hand is warm in mine. The city is bright outside the window. And I think about the dare, the one that started all of this.

I lean my head back against the seat and close my eyes for a second, and I pray.

Thank You for teaching me that remaining isn't the same as staying stuck. That abiding isn't passive. That sometimes it looks like sitting still on a bench long enough for something real to finally find you.

His thumb traces a slow circle against my hand, unhurried, like he's got nowhere else to be. Like this is exactly where he planned to end up.

I think I'm finally doing it.

Chapter 42
Micah

I just took Harper Mitchell to Angelo's for our first official date.

And I'm not ready for the night to end.

Which is why, when I pull away from the curb with her in the passenger seat, I don't head toward her apartment. I head toward the other side of Dallas. The quiet side. The side I haven't taken her to yet.

"Where are we going?" she asks, watching the familiar streets give way to less familiar ones.

"It's a surprise."

She turns to look at me. "You already did the surprise thing tonight. Angelo's was the surprise."

"That was the first surprise."

"There's a limit, Micah. You can't just keep surprising people indefinitely. It's a lot of pressure."

"You'll survive."

She crosses her arms, but she's smiling. I can see it in my periphery, that smile she gets when she's pretending to be annoyed and isn't, the one I've been cataloguing without meaning to for two years.

I make the last turn and pull into the parking lot.

"Why are we at a Chinese restaurant for dessert?"

The sign above the door is not impressive. The parking lot has exactly four other cars in it. The neon light in the window is the kind that flickers every few seconds like it's considering retirement.

"Because they have the best vanilla ice cream in Dallas," I say.

She stares at the sign. Then at me. "Vanilla ice cream."

"Yes."

"From a Chinese restaurant."

"Yes."

"Micah." She turns fully toward me. "We just came from Angelo's. Angelo, who makes his grandmother's pasta from scratch and imports his cheese specifically. And now you're taking me to a strip mall Chinese restaurant for vanilla ice cream."

"Correct."

"That's insane."

"You haven't tried the ice cream yet."

She looks back at the flickering sign. I watch her face cycle through skepticism, curiosity, and then that particular Harper expression where she's already decided she's going to do the thing but needs a moment to pretend she hasn't.

"Fine," she says. "But I want it on the record that I had concerns."

"Noted." I open my door. "That's also what you said at Angelo's."

"And I was wrong at Angelo's." She gets out of the truck. "This is different."

"It really isn't."

The woman behind the counter knows me, which Harper clocks immediately with an expression of complete delight. I order two vanilla ice creams in paper cups without looking at the menu, which makes Harper make a sound somewhere between a laugh and disbelief, and four minutes later we're back outside in the cool April air with plastic spoons and paper cups and the quiet Dallas night opening up around us.

Harper takes one bite.

She stops walking.

"Okay," she says.

"Yeah."

"This is so good."

"I know."

"How?" She looks at the cup. "How is this the best vanilla ice cream I've ever had? It's vanilla. It's the most boring flavor in existence. How is it doing this?"

"I don't know," I say honestly. "I found this place by accident three years ago after a late church event, and I've never been able to explain it. I just know it's the best."

She takes another bite. Closes her eyes briefly.

"Okay," she says again. "You win. You win completely."

"I usually do."

She points her spoon at me. "Do not get smug about the ice cream."

"I'm not smug. I'm satisfied."

"That's the same thing."

We fall into step beside each other, moving away from the parking lot toward the quieter street that runs alongside it. It's the kind of block that empties out at night—a hardware store, a dry cleaner, a little stretch of sidewalk with old brick buildings on one side and a narrow alley that opens up toward the city skyline on the other. No crowd. No noise except our footsteps and the distant hum of Dallas being Dallas.

It's exactly what I wanted.

She finishes her ice cream and holds the empty cup in both hands, and I watch her from the corner of my eye the way I've been watching her for two years. Except tonight it's different. Tonight I don't have to pretend I'm not looking.

We toss our empty cups in a trash can and stop at the mouth of a narrow alley between two old brick buildings; it belongs in a different decade. The city glows faintly at the far end, just enough light to see by, warm and low. Quiet. Nobody here but us.

Harper leans back against the brick wall, tilting her face up toward the sky.

I lean against the wall beside her, close enough that our shoulders nearly touch.

For a moment, neither of us says anything.

Then she says quietly. "Can I tell you something?"

"Always."

She looks at the sky, not at me. "I didn't know what real faith was supposed to feel like until you." She pauses. "I grew up in church. I knew all the right words. All the right behaviors. I could perform Christianity better than almost anyone. But it was all surface. I was checking boxes for my parents. For the version of myself I thought I was supposed to be."

I don't say anything. I just listen, the way she once told me nobody did.

"You were the first person who made me think it could actually be real," she says. "Not rules. Not performance. Just...actually knowing God." She finally looks at me. "You did that. You pointed me there when you didn't have to. When it cost you something."

"It didn't cost me anything," I say.

"Micah."

"Walking alongside you was never a cost."

She holds my gaze for a long moment. "You know what I mean."

I do. I do know what she means. And she deserves the honest answer.

"Okay," I say. "I have a confession to make."

She waits.

"Do you remember the night of the gala? When you'd had too much champagne and I drove you home?"

"Vividly. Against my will, but vividly."

"You fell asleep." I look at the city at the end of the alley, finding my words. "And I sat there for a while. Just praying. Because I was already in it, already completely gone for you. And I knew you were trying to get back with someone else, and I was trying to figure out how to just—" I stop. Start again. "I prayed a pretty specific prayer that night."

She's very still beside me.

"I prayed," I say slowly, "*Lord, let it be me.*"

The silence between us is the softest kind.

"That's it," I say. "No fancy language. No theological depth. Just that. Four words. Every night for a long time."

Harper is quiet for a moment. When she speaks, her voice is distinct. Lower. "You prayed that for how long?"

"A while."

"How long is a while, Micah?"

"Almost two months. Give or take."

She exhales. Looks at me with an expression I feel all the way through. "You prayed *let it be me* the entire time we were fake dating while acting completely normal around me."

"I didn't always act completely normal."

"You acted completely normal."

She turns to face me fully, her back against the brick, and looks up at me the way she did on the park bench this morning, except now there's nothing uncertain in it. Just her. Just this.

She's quiet for a moment after I finish. Just looking at me with that expression I still can't fully read, the one that makes me want to say everything and nothing at the same time.

"Can I ask you something?" I say.

"Go for it."

"Is it weird?" I hold her gaze. "That I prayed that specifically. For that long. About you." I pause. "Serial killer vibes?"

She bursts into a laugh that isn't graceful or contained, and that I would do basically anything to keep hearing for the rest of my life.

"Micah Sanders," she says, still laughing. "Did you just use my own bit against me?"

"I'm asking a legitimate question."

"You quite literally just told me you prayed *let it be me* for several months and your follow up is whether that gives off serial killer energy?"

"It's a valid concern."

"It's not weird. It's actually—" she stops. Like she's deciding whether to say the real thing. Then she does. "It's the most anyone has ever quietly, consistently, patiently been in my corner without me even knowing it."

Something in my chest goes completely still.

"So no," she says again, quieter. "Not serial killer vibes." The corner of her mouth pulls up. "I love that you're obsessed with me."

I let that land for exactly one second.

"Good," I say. "Because I really am."

Then she reaches up, grabs the front of my shirt, and pulls me in.

And I kiss her in a dark alley in Dallas with nobody watching and no room full of people to perform for and nothing between us except the truth we've been carrying toward each other for two years.

It's not careful. It's not calibrated. It's the kind of kiss that happens when two people have been patient long enough and finally don't have to be anymore.

When we finally pull back, her hands are still in my hair and mine are on her face, and she's looking at me with bright eyes and slightly uneven breathing and the best expression I have ever seen on another human being.

"Hi," she says.

"Hi."

"That was—"

"Yeah."

She laughs, dropping her forehead against my chest, and I wrap my arms around her and hold her there in the alley with the city glowing at the end of it and the night wide open above us.

Thank You, I think. Not for the first time today. Not for the last time in my life. *For letting it be me.*

Chapter 43
Harper

I'm in the middle of doing absolutely nothing productive, sitting cross-legged on the floor in my living room eating cereal for a late lunch when my phone rings. I look at the screen.

Mom.

I chew. Consider. Answer on the third ring because anything before two rings communicates too much availability and anything after four communicates avoidance, and with my mother, both are equally dangerous.

"Hi, Mom."

"Harper." The way she says my name—not warm, not cold, just efficient, like my name is an item on a checklist she's moving through. "Your father and I are coming through the city tomorrow evening. We'll be there at five. Sharp."

Not *can we come over?*

Not *would that work for you?*

"Oh," I say. "Tomorrow."

"Is that a problem?"

"No." That's always the answer. "No, of course not. I'll...yeah, that's great."

"Make that pasta dish your father loves. The one with the sausage."

"The rigatoni."

"Yes. That one." A pause that has the texture of her looking at a list. "We just got back from the coast this morning. I picked up something for Collin while we were there—one of those specialty hot sauces he's always going on about. I got it at the market in Jamaica, near the pier."

My cereal spoon stops mid-lift.

"That's—really thoughtful, Mom."

"Well, I try to pay attention." Another pause. "Is he coming to dinner? You can let him know we have a gift."

I set the spoon down in the bowl.

The thing about hard conversations is that I have been putting this one off for a very specific reason: I knew exactly what my mother would say, and I have been quietly, deliberately not giving her the opportunity to say it. I'm good at this. I've had years of practice building the particular skill of managing my mother's expectations by controlling the information she receives.

I've been managing the Collin situation on a strictly need-to-know basis since February.

She does not, technically, need to know.

Except she has a hot sauce with his name on it.

"Mom." I stand up from the floor. "Collin and I broke up."

Silence.

The particular quality of my mother's silence is its own form of communication. This one is twelve seconds long and feels like being held underwater.

"When," she says. Not *what happened or are you okay or I'm sorry, sweetheart.* Just, *when.*

"February. A couple of months ago."

"February." She repeats. "And you're just telling me now."

"I didn't want to...I was figuring things out. It's been a process."

"Harper." There it is again. My name like a period at the end of a sentence that isn't finished yet. "What did you do?"

And there it is.

The assumption already in place, already settled, that whatever went wrong went wrong because of me. Because it always does. Because I'm the variable in the equation, always have been—the one who laughs too loud, talks too much, makes things messier than they need to be. Collin was tidy and professional and he had a five-year plan, and of course something with that kind of structure couldn't survive me for long.

"We just weren't right for each other," I say. My voice is steady. I have years of practice at this too. "It was mutual."

"Collin was a very good man."

"I know."

"He had a plan. A future. He treated you well."

"I know, Mom."

"Men like that don't grow on trees, Harper."

The back of my eyes sting. I will not do this. I am a grown woman standing in my own apartment and I will not stand here and cry on the phone over a relationship I don't even miss.

Especially when I have a new one that is way better.

I walk to the window. Stare at the street below. Take a breath.

And I say it before I chicken out.

"There's someone new."

Silence again. Shorter this time.

"Already?"

"It's—yes." I take a breath. "And Mom, he's great. I really want you to meet him. I think..."

"Doubt it."

The word lands flat and certain.

I close my eyes. "Mom."

"I've met your exes, Harper. I know the kinds of men you're drawn to."

"This is different."

"That's what you always say."

I don't have an answer for that. Partly because she's not entirely wrong about the pattern.

"Invite him tomorrow," she says, and her tone has shifted back to logistics, which is how she closes conversations she's finished having. "We'll see."

"Okay."

"Five o'clock."

The line clicks.

I stand at the window for a long moment, phone in my hand, watching a dog trot past on the sidewalk below.

I try Ivy first.

Voicemail.

I try Olivia.

She picks up, which is a minor miracle and a major complication, because Olivia has therapist instincts that activate in the presence of any emotional situation and I cannot afford a full therapeutic intervention right now, I need a best-friend intervention, and after thirty seconds of her saying *okay*, and *how does that make you feel*, I tell her I'll call her back and hang up.

I pace my living room.

Okay. The situation is this: my parents are coming to dinner tomorrow at five. I have told my mother I am dating someone wonderful. The difference is that this time it's true —I am dating someone wonderful.

He should know that she's going to compare him to Collin, out loud, at the table, and probably not subtly.

I find his contact, look at his name on the screen for a moment, then press call.

It rings six times before it goes to voicemail.

You've reached Micah Sanders. Leave a message and I'll call you back. Unless this is about the parking lot situation at church, in which case, that is out of my control.

The beep sounds and I just stand there for a second with my mouth open and nothing coming out, because even his voicemail has dad joke energy, and I have been dating this man for less time than it takes to grow a houseplant and I am already so completely gone for him that his voicemail greeting makes my chest feel warm, and I hang up without saying anything and throw myself facedown on the couch.

This is fine.

I am fine.

I'm just trying to prepare my actual boyfriend for dinner with my parents. And praying he can make it.

I pull a throw pillow over my head.

My phone rings.

I come up from under the pillow so fast I nearly tip off the couch.

It's a FaceTime. From Micah. Not a call—a FaceTime, which means he wanted to see my face, which is a thing I have recently realized he prefers. I answer immediately.

He's somewhere outdoors. I can see sky behind him, he's slightly out of breath from something, glasses on, and the second the call connects his whole demeanor shifts. Whatever easy expression he answered with sharpens into something focused and alert.

"Harper." His voice is different. The easy tone gone, something more direct underneath it. "What's wrong? Where are you? I can be on my way right now."

I stare at him.

And then, despite everything—I laugh. It comes out real and slightly startled and I press my hand over my mouth.

"What," he says.

"You answered a FaceTime and immediately offered to be on your way somewhere. You don't even know what I'm about to say."

"You called and hung up without leaving a message, which means something's wrong. And you look all frazzled." He motions toward the screen. "Are you okay? Where are you?"

"I'm on my couch."

He exhales slightly. Some of the sharpness comes down. "Okay. Good." He adjusts his glasses. "What happened?"

"My parents are coming to dinner tomorrow night." I sit up and pull my knees to my chest. "They called this afternoon. That's just how they operate—they don't really ask, they just tell you when they'll be there and what you should cook."

"Okay," he says.

"And she called to tell me she got Collin something on their trip." I watch his face. "So I had to tell her. About the breakup. And she was..." I stop. Reorganize. "She was my mom about it. Which is a specific thing."

"The *what did you do assumption*," he says.

I blink. "How did you—"

"You told me. Burgers, after the shower. You said she always assumes you're the variable."

He remembered that. Of course he remembered that.

"Yeah," I say quietly. "That one."

He nods, just once. Not trying to fix it. Just acknowledging it landed the way it always does.

"So I told her there was someone new," I continue. "And she said..." I hesitate, because this is the part that still stings even though it shouldn't, even though I know who he is and she doesn't yet. "She said doubt it. Before she even knew anything about you. Just flat out, doubt it."

Something moves through his expression. Calm, but with something steady underneath it.

"And then she said she wants to meet you tomorrow," I finish. "Which is, I know it's fast. I know we've only been..." I gesture vaguely. "This. For a minute. And I would completely understand if—"

"Harper."

"—you wanted more time before doing the whole meet-the-parents thing because it is a lot and my parents are specifically a lot—"

"Harper."

"—and my mom is going to compare you to Collin at the table and not even try to be subtle about it, and my dad communicates primarily through silence which reads as disapproval even when it isn't, and the pasta has to be exactly right or—"

"Harper." His voice is patient but firm, the same tone he

uses when he's redirecting a five-year-old who is very committed to a bad decision. "Take a breath."

I take a breath.

He waits.

"I want to meet your parents," he says. Simply. Like it's not even a complicated sentence. "That's not a question for me."

Something in my chest does the folding thing. "You don't have to if it is too soon."

"I know I don't have to." He looks at me directly through the small screen. "I want to. They're important to you—even when it's complicated, they're important to you. Which makes them important to me."

I look at the ceiling for a second to get my face in order.

"Besides," he adds, and I can hear the shift into that dry, quiet humor that I have grown to love, "any opportunity to outshine Collin, and I'm in."

The laugh that comes out of me is surprised and genuine and slightly embarrassing. "You barely even knew him."

"I know enough," he says. He's smiling now, the screen highlighting his dimple. "What time?"

"Dinner at five. But could you come a little early?" I pause, because what I actually want to say is *I want to tell you things about them so you're not walking in blind, I want you to understand what you're stepping into so you don't have to figure it out alone in the middle of it.* "I want to make sure you have context. About them."

"I'll be there at four-thirty," he says. "So you're not alone when they get there."

I press my lips together. Look at him through the small screen. The glasses slightly crooked, the evening sky behind him, this man who remembered something I said over burgers at a diner weeks ago and is now offering to show up early to stand next to me at my own dinner table.

"Micah," I say. "I'm nervous."

He looks at me for a moment.

"Yeah," he says. "I know, but we've got this."

He doesn't say *she's wrong* or *I'll prove her wrong* or any of the things that would make this about him. Which is something Collin would have done.

"Does your mom do that thing," he asks then, shifting slightly, "where she asks rapid-fire questions and makes eye contact like she's looking for inconsistencies?"

"She made my prom date write a formal itinerary. With timestamps."

He stares at me. "For prom."

"She wanted to know where we'd be at 9:15 specifically."

"Where were you at 9:15?"

"Micah, that is not the point—"

He's already grinning. "I'm going to make a very good impression on this woman."

He says it with the particular confidence of someone who has already decided how this goes, and something about the certainty of it loosens something in my chest I didn't realize was still wound tight.

"Four-thirty," he says again.

"Four-thirty," I confirm.

"And Harper." His voice settles back into something more even. The something that's always underneath the jokes. "You okay? Everything you didn't say just now—you okay?"

I look at him through the small screen. The glasses slightly crooked. The sky behind him going golden at the edges.

"Yes."

He holds my gaze.

"I love you Harper."

"Love you too," I smile, still not used to the words but overwhelmed with the fact that they feel so right. "See you tomorrow."

"See you tomorrow."

I hang up. Set my phone face-down on the cushion beside me. Sit there for a moment in the quiet of my apartment, the early evening light doing something nice through the blinds.

Tomorrow my mother is going to walk into this apartment already skeptical. She's going to compare him to Collin, out loud, probably by dessert. She's going to look for cracks.

And Micah is going to show up at four-thirty so I'm not alone when they arrive.

Doubt it, she said. The words hanging heavy over me.

So I do the thing I've been trying to do more of; I take my fears and lay them at the feet of Jesus.

Chapter 44
Harper

I have rearranged the living room furniture twice.

I know this is a me thing. I do it when I can't fix the actual problem and need somewhere to put my hands. I have been doing it since I was nine years old and my mother told me we were having company, and I responded by reorganizing my entire bookshelf by color while the actual problem—a sink full of dishes—remained entirely unaddressed. Some things do not change.

The actual problem is that my parents are coming to dinner in two hours.

I leave the armchair where it is and go start the pasta.

Except first I should change out of the bathrobe, so I go to the bedroom to pick an outfit, but on the way I notice the bathroom mirror has a water spot on it and that is genuinely going to bother me all night, so I go get the glass spray and the paper towels, and while I'm under the sink, I remember I meant to replace the cabinet liner in here weeks ago and it's still a little crooked on the left side, so I fix that, and then I'm putting the spray back and I realize I never started the pasta.

I go start the pasta.

The sauce goes on first and then I need to let it come up to heat so I have a few minutes, so I go get dressed, but I pass the entry table on the way and the mail is sitting there from three days ago still in the little pile I made when I told myself I would sort it later, so I sort it now, and there's a card from my aunt and I read it, and then I respond to a text from Olivia who is asking how I'm feeling, and then I'm looking at my phone and seventeen minutes have passed and I can smell the sauce.

I run to the kitchen.

The sauce is fine. It's barely even bubbling, which means I turned it down too low at the beginning because I was worried about exactly this scenario, which means I planned ahead, which means somewhere underneath all of this I am actually a functional adult.

I go get dressed.

I make it as far as the bedroom doorway before I remember I was going to set the table first. I set the table. I light the candles on the table. I light the candle on the bookshelf, and then I'm looking at the bookshelf and my Bible is sitting out, open, and I close it gently and set it on the coffee table instead because it feels like the right place for it tonight.

I look at the time.

I have just under an hour, and I am still in the bathrobe.

I go to the bedroom. I pick up a shirt, decide it's wrong, pick up another one, put the first one back in the wrong drawer, take it out of the wrong drawer, hang it back up, and sit down on the edge of the bed for a second with the second shirt in my hands.

Breath Harper.

The sauce is on. The table is set. It's time to focus on getting ready.

There's a knock on the door at 4:15.

He said 4:30.

I look at myself in the hallway mirror—still in my robe, but at least my hair and makeup are done.

I answer the door.

Micah is standing on my welcome mat holding two bouquets, and for a second I just take him in the way I'm still getting used to being allowed to.

He's in a navy dress shirt that does something unfair to his shoulders, sleeves pulled up, collar sitting just right. Glasses straight. He smells of cedar and something clean and faintly like the warm air outside.

He is, objectively, a very good-looking man. He has always been a very good-looking man. The difference is that I am now allowed to think that without immediately finding some reason to be annoyed with him.

He is also mine. Which is still the strangest, truest thing.

He opens his mouth.

Nothing comes out.

He just looks at me. His eyes track from my hair, which is in loose curls, down to the robe covering my body and to my bare feet on the wood floors. For one full second, Micah Sanders, who always has something to say, has absolutely nothing to say.

Then he clears his throat.

He sets both bouquets carefully on the entry table. And then, without a word, he reaches over and pulls the shoulder of my robe up where it's slipped down, and tugs the knot at my waist until it's actually secured.

He takes a small step back.

"There is a specific scenario," he says, in a very measured tone, "that men who aren't married should avoid."

I raise my eyebrows. "And what's that?"

"Alone in an apartment with a woman in a robe." He keeps his expression entirely neutral. "I'm going to assume you have nothing on under that, which means my brain is currently going places an unmarried man has no business going."

I stare at him.

Then I turn around and walk back to the stove and pick up the wooden spoon.

"Well," I say, giving the sauce a stir, "you know what you could do about that."

"Harper..."

"Put a ring on it." I say it lightly, eyes on the pot. "Then your brain can go wherever it wants."

Silence.

I glance back over my shoulder.

He is still standing in my doorway with an expression on his face that I have never seen before. Not flustered, not composing himself—just very, very still.

I face the stove again and say nothing, because that banter was already too honest, and I know it, and the sauce needs attention, anyway.

I hear him step inside; the door closes behind him.

Then I hear him cross the kitchen, and his hand finds my waist and he turns me gently but completely around, away from the stove, and his eyes meet mine.

"Go," he says. And I can hear the desperation in his voice. "Put clothes on. Right now."

"The sauce..."

"I'll handle the sauce."

"But the simmer time..."

"Harper." There is something underneath the patience, warm and certain, and the way he's looking at me makes my whole chest go off balance. "Clothes. Now."

I hold his gaze for one more second. Then I push up onto my toes, kiss the corner of his jaw, and pat his chest once.

"Sauce is on medium-low," I say against his cheek. "Don't let it boil."

Then I go.

I come out in jeans and my cream sweater.

The apartment smells like garlic and herbs and the good kind of warmth.

I walk to the living room doorway and stop.

Micah is standing at the coffee table holding something. He's very still. Careful still, like he's found something he didn't expect.

I see it before I crossed the room.

The photo strip.

My Bible is on the edge of the table, open to the passage I read this morning.

"I use it as a bookmark." I say.

"I can see that."

I cross to him and he holds it out. I take it and look at

the four frames. The first two we're mid-laugh. The third one is posed, barely. And the fourth—the fourth one, neither of us is looking at the camera. We're looking at each other, and whatever was happening in that photo booth was already something, even then. Even before I had words for it. Even when I was still calling it nothing.

"Did you keep yours?" I ask. Like I don't already know.

"Yeah," he says. "I did."

I look up.

He takes the strip gently from my hand and sets it back on my Bible.

Then he closes the space between us, and his hand finds my face as he kisses me.

Not the soft, unhurried kind. The kind that says something. His hand slides from my jaw into my hair and I grab the front of his shirt with both hands and hold on.

When we finally pull back, we're both a little breathless.

He rests his forehead against mine. His hands are still in my hair. My fists are still curled into his shirt.

"Hi," I say.

"Hi." I can hear the smile in it.

We stay like that for a moment, just breathing, and then he says, "Can I pray with you? Before we finish up in there."

"Yeah," I say. "Please."

He pulls back just enough to take my hands, and he bows his head.

"God, we need You in this room tonight." His voice is quiet and completely steady. Not polished, not performed. Just honest. "Give Harper peace right now. Not the kind that makes sense, the other kind. The kind that holds even when things aren't perfect. Help her know she doesn't have to prove anything tonight." A pause. "Let tonight be good. And if it gets hard, let us get through it together. Amen."

"Amen," I whisper.

I stand there for a second with his hands around mine. I think about all the ways I have tried to make myself enough for this moment.

I am the vine; you are the branches.

That verse comes to me instantly and I am reminded to remain in Him.

And for the first time all afternoon, I actually feel like I might be able to.

"Okay," I say. I squeeze his hands and release them. "I need to finish our meal."

He follows me into the kitchen, and I pull the index card from where I tucked it under the edge of the fruit bowl. It's handwritten, front and back.

"Okay," I say, smoothing it flat on the counter. "So the sauce has been going; the noodles just need to finish. Just so you know, the secret to the sauce is this specific brand of sausage and these exact noodles." I point to the brand name, which I have underlined twice and then circled for emphasis.

Micah lifts the card and reads it.

"Your parents will really notice," he says slowly, "if you don't use those exact things?"

"Um," I look at him. "Yes. Absolutely."

He looks at me. He looks at the card. Then he looks back at me.

"Well," he says, setting it down with great seriousness, "let's get it mixed together."

He reaches past me for the colander, and I pull the sauce off the heat, and we finish it together, the two of us moving around my small kitchen until the rigatoni is plated and the salad is tossed.

He carries the salad bowl to the table. I light the two candles I've already lit once today, because they burned down a little while the afternoon happened around them.

It actually looks really nice in here.

I'm standing there looking at it when the doorbell rings.

Micah steps up beside me and reaches for my hand. His fingers wrap around mine, warm and certain.

"Hey." Quiet. Just for me. "You've got this."

I look at him.

He smiles, and then he leans down and presses a kiss to my cheek, slow and deliberate, the kind that says I'm right here even after he pulls back.

I walk toward the door slowly.

Take a breath.

Then open the door.

Chapter 45
Micah

I check the sauce once more, turn it to low, and wipe my hands on the dish towel just as Harper opens the door.

Bill Mitchell is exactly what I expected, although slightly taller than I imagined. His handshake is firm and unhurried, as if he's been assessing people for decades and doesn't need long to do it. I match it, hold his gaze, and say nothing beyond what's appropriate.

He nods once. Takes his glass of sweet tea to the armchair in the living room like a man who has been to this apartment before and knows where he belongs.

I like him immediately.

Carol Mitchell is harder to read. Not cold, the warmth is there, I can see it, it's just organized differently. Held at a specific temperature and released in controlled amounts. She looks at the apartment and then she looks at me, and I see her doing the thing Harper warned me about—the inventory. Quick and thorough, and not entirely concealed.

I cross to her before she can finish it.

"Mrs. Mitchell." I hold out the bouquet. "These are for you."

Lilies, structured and clean-lined. I chose them specifically—not roses, which would be trying too hard. Not something random, which would suggest I hadn't thought about it. Lilies, because they say care and intention and a certain kind of respect.

She takes them.

Her expression shifts. A small recalibration.

"These are lovely," she says.

From across the kitchen I feel Harper watching me. I don't look at her; instead I return to the stove. I hear Carol lean toward her daughter and whisper, "You have him cooking?"

"He volunteered," Harper says.

"I volunteered," I confirm, from the stove. "Harper walked me through her recipe, it sounds delicious."

A beat from Carol. "She taught you?"

"She did. It's a very precise process."

"It is." A pause. "Bill has requested that pasta every time we visit. It's a family recipe."

From the armchair, Bill says nothing.

"Then I'll try to honor the legacy," I say.

"We'll see," Carol says.

Dinner starts quietly.

Bread passed. Plates filled. Carol compliments the sauce, and Bill says nothing, which I am already learning to read as a form of agreement.

Carol, it turns out, has a lot to say.

She starts at the beginning. The birth, the red hair, the

way Harper came into the world loud and hasn't changed since. I eat my rigatoni and listen and piece together the version of Harper that existed before I knew her. The childhood in Ashen Mills. The recitals Carol never missed. The rules Harper tested and the ones she didn't, and Carol's particular tone when she describes each, which tells me more than the words do. I watch Harper across the table, absorbing all of it with the careful stillness of someone who has heard this story many times and has learned exactly where to brace for it.

By the time we reach high school, I have refilled the bread basket once.

By the time we reach senior year I have learned that Harper was the kind of teenager who rearranged her bedroom furniture when she was anxious, which tracks since she does this same thing now as an adult.

Then Carol sets her fork down.

"We weren't entirely sure she was ready," she says. "When she went off to college at UNT."

I keep eating. Harper opens her mouth, thinks better of it, and closes it again. Carol sees the whole thing.

"I'm not saying anything critical, Harper. I'm stating a fact. You had never lived alone. You'd never managed your own finances. You were..."

"Nineteen," Harper says.

"Young," Carol retorts.

My protective instincts kick in.

"She figured it out," I say.

Carol pauses. Fork halfway to her mouth.

"She did," she agrees, in a slightly modified tone. "Eventually."

"The first year is always a learning curve," I say, easy and conversational. "But her career, her classroom, the life she's built here." I shake my head. "That doesn't happen by accident. That happens because someone did the work."

Harper is looking at her water glass.

I pass the bread basket to Bill.

He takes a piece without looking at me. But something in the set of his jaw is different from what it was a minute ago.

We eat. The conversation finds a different current. The drive up. The highway construction outside of town. Carol mentions they finally finished the renovation on their master bedroom and bathroom. Sarah redesigned it, Ivy's cousin, apparently she has a gift for it. That leads to Ashen Mills itself, the way the downtown has been quietly hollowing out, another two storefronts gone since Christmas.

"The only place still holding on with any real life in it," Carol says, "is that little gift shop on Main. Hannah's place."

"Hannah Banana's," Harper says.

"That's the one." Then Carol looks across the table, abruptly changing the subject. "I have to say, Harper, your hair looks beautiful tonight."

Harper glances up. "Thanks, Mom."

"She got the color from Grandma Jackie, you know," Carol says to me. "Her grandmother. My mother."

"I was actually going to ask about that," I say. "Both of you are so dark-haired and Harper is so specifically not."

Carol's expression does something I haven't seen from her yet.

It softens.

"Jackie had the most magnificent red hair you've ever seen," she says. "Wild as anything."

"Wild as anything," Bill echoes. The most he has smiled all evening.

"She sounds incredible," I say. And I mean it.

"She was," Carol says. Something quieter moves through her voice on the word was.

"She had this old van," Harper says. "A red Chrysler minivan, she'd had it since the eighties. It sounded like a dying lawnmower every time she started it."

She's smiling. The real one, not the careful *dinner with her parents version.*

"She'd load all the grandkids in—me, my cousins, whoever was around—and drive to this one empty road outside of town. A long, flat stretch where nobody ever went."

I set my fork down.

"What would she do?" I ask, watching the joy of the memory spread across her face.

"She'd blast the music. Volume all the way up, windows down. And then she'd just weave. Side to side, down the whole empty road, slow enough to be safe and wild enough to feel like anything could happen." She laughs, a little. "We called it *rocking out*. We'd hang onto the seat backs and scream and she'd laugh this big, full laugh you could hear over the music." A pause. "We thought she was the coolest person alive."

I watch her face as she tells it. The careful monitoring she's carried all evening just disappears. She stops checking her father between sentences and stops measuring her words and stops performing the version of herself that fits neatly into her parents' expectations.

I have been watching her learn how to do this for months. Watching her move slowly and stubbornly toward the thing she actually is when she stops trying to be enough for everyone in the room.

This is it. Right here, over a bowl of rigatoni, and she doesn't even know she's doing it.

"I want to be like that when I'm a mom," she says, and it comes out completely unguarded. "I want my kids to think I'm the coolest person alive."

Carol sets her fork down. "Children need structure too, Harper. You can't just..."

"You will be incredible at it."

I say it the way I'd say any fact I'm certain of. Because I've watched her with five-year-olds. I've watched her get down on the floor and remember every single name and the name of every pet and every specific opinion about orange versus yellow. I know what kind of mother she'll be, the same way I know she takes her coffee with an extra shot. I've been paying attention, for a long time, and I know.

Carol looks at me.

I hold her gaze, easy as anything.

She picks up her fork and the conversation moves on.

Somewhere between that and dessert, Harper's foot finds mine under the table.

She doesn't look at me when it happens. She's listening to her mother describe a Kool-Aid hair incident, expression perfectly composed, like she is not currently pressing the toe of her shoe against mine in a way that is entirely deliberate. I leave my foot exactly where it is and reach for my water glass and say nothing.

A few minutes later she looks at me across the table. Not a checking look. Not a monitoring look. Something that has nothing to do with the dinner or her parents, or what anyone else in this room thinks about anything. Just her, looking at me, the corner of her mouth moving in the way it does when she is trying not to smile and losing the battle slightly.

I look back. One second. That's all either of us needs.

Then I look at my plate and eat my pasta and do not grin like an idiot.

This takes considerable effort and I feel it deserves acknowledgment.

"Best batch yet," Bill says. And then, without looking up, "He can come back."

"You know," I say, setting my fork down, "you can follow a recipe exactly. Every teaspoon, every temperature, every minute on the timer, and it'll come out fine. Good, even." I look at Bill's empty bowl. "But the ones that come out extraordinary aren't always the most precisely measured. It's something else. The attention you bring to it. Whether you're actually present in the kitchen or just going through the steps." I pause. "You can't always measure love in teaspoons. But you can always taste it when it's there."

Carol swirls her water glass, slow and thoughtful. Bill nods once. And then Harper reaches across the table and takes my hand. Quiet and deliberate, in plain sight, not hiding it from anyone. For a girl who has spent her whole life managing what her parents see, it is the bravest thing she has done all evening.

I thread my fingers through hers and don't let go.

Her parents leave at 7:43.

Carol hugs Harper at the door—longer than I expected,

long enough that I notice Harper doesn't know what to do with her hands at first, and then figures it out and holds on.

Bill shakes my hand then kisses Harper on the cheek. "Good dinner you two."

Four words. From him, an essay.

And then they're gone and the door clicks shut and it's just us.

We clean up without discussing it, which tells me everything. She washes, I dry, we move around each other like we have been doing this for years instead of this one time. Every few minutes she glances at me over her shoulder and I look back and neither of us says anything because neither of us needs to.

This is what it is going to be like.

I think about that the whole time I'm drying dishes.

When the last dish is dried Harper hops up onto one of the bar stools at her kitchen counter and pats the one beside her.

I sit.

She leans her head against my shoulder and lets out a long slow breath, like she has been holding it since five o'clock and is only now remembering she doesn't have to anymore. I rest my cheek against the top of her head. Neither of us says anything for a while. The candles have burned low. The apartment smells like garlic and something warm and good.

"Thank you," she says finally. Quietly. Into the comfortable nothing between us.

"No need to thank me Harper."

She lifts her head and looks at me. "I mean it."

"I know you mean it."

She holds my gaze for one more second, then tucks back

in, and I rest my cheek against her hair again, and neither of us moves.

This is the problem.

This is exactly the problem.

The apartment is quiet and the candles are low and her parents are gone and she fits here, beside me, in this specific way, and I am a man who made a commitment a long time ago and intends to keep it, which means I need to get my jacket.

I clear my throat.

"I should go."

She tilts her head up. "It's barely eight."

"I know."

"We won't see each other until Wednesday."

"I know that too."

She studies me. "Are you okay?"

"Harper." I exhale slowly. "I can't be alone with you in this apartment."

She sits up. Pulls back slightly. And I can see it immediately—the way she's reading into what I just said.

"That's not... " I stop. Start over. "That came out wrong."

"Did it?"

"It's not that I don't want to be here." I turn to face her properly. "It's the opposite. Which is exactly the problem."

She blinks.

"I don't trust myself," I say simply. "Not because I don't respect you. Because I do. More than I know how to say. But I made a decision a long time ago about how I want to do this, about waiting, and that decision gets harder to hold onto the longer I sit here alone with you."

The room is quiet.

Harper looks at me for a long moment, the defensive

edge coming down, replaced by something softer and more real.

"Micah."

"Yeah."

"I made that same decision." Her voice is quiet. "A long time ago. I've never, you know." She stops, glances down. "I've never been with anyone. And there were moments with Collin where I felt pressured and I held the line and he made me feel like that was wrong and I..." She shakes her head. "I just want you to know that I'm not expecting anything."

"I know," I say. "I know you're not."

"And I made that same commitment. So you don't have to..."

"Harper."

She stops.

"I know." I hold her gaze. "I'm not going anywhere because I think you'd push me somewhere I don't want to go. I'm going because I think I might push myself. And I would rather leave while everything is good than stay until it's something I have to apologize for." I pause. "This matters too much. You matter too much."

"I've never had someone leave because they were trying to protect something." She whispers.

"You have now," I say.

She looks down at her hands. I watch her process it—the thing she's been handed, the shape of it. The fact that this is a man who is choosing the harder thing not because of rules but because of love, and that is possibly something she has never been offered before.

She looks up.

"Wednesday," she says. "Bible study at Ivy and Gray's."

"Wednesday," I confirm.

I get my jacket and she walks me to the door. When I turn around she is right there, and I cup her face in both hands and kiss her the way I've been wanting to kiss her since somewhere around the salad course. Slowly. Like neither of us is in a hurry, even though I am absolutely leaving right now. Her hands find my jacket and hold on and I feel her exhale into it and I think, not for the first time, that this woman is going to be the best thing that ever happened to me.

I make myself pull back.

"Wednesday," I say again. Slightly less steadily than before.

"Wednesday," she says. Eyes still closed.

I open the door. Step out. She leans against the door-frame and watches me go, and I make it approximately six steps down the hall before I stop.

I turn around.

She's still there, watching me with that expression—the fond, certain one, slightly amused. Like she knew.

"One more," I say.

She raises her eyebrows. "One more what?"

"You know what."

She pushes off the doorframe, walks the three steps between us, and goes up on her toes, and I meet her there, and it's just one more, just one, which somehow takes a significant amount of time.

When we finally separate she is smiling in the way she does when she's too happy to manage her face, which is my favorite version of her.

"Wednesday," I say.

"Go home, Micah."

"Yes, ma'am." I wink.

Chapter 46
Harper

"You're doing the thing," he says.

"I'm not doing anything."

"Your left knee is bouncing."

I press my hand flat against it. "That's just how my knee sits."

He glances over, and even in the dark of the truck cab I can see that he is absolutely not convinced. "Harper."

"I'm fine." I look out the window. "I'm just thinking about whether we should have texted first. Should we have texted first? Like a heads up. Something like, 'Hey, by the way, we're coming as an actual couple now, please adjust your expectations accordingly.'"

"Ivy knows."

"Ivy's one person."

"Gray knows."

"Gray doesn't count; he knew before we did." I tug at the strap of my bag. "And Olivia might not even be there. She said maybe, but she's been saying maybe for months, and since we'll be announcing our relationship status to a room full of people we should..."

"Harper."

"What."

"We survived dinner with your parents," he says it easy, like he's noting the weather. "I think we can handle a Bible study."

I close my mouth.

He reaches over and takes my hand off my knee and holds it, and I let him, because apparently this is something we do now.

We pull onto Ivy and Gray's street.

"Okay," I say.

"Okay," he agrees.

He parks the truck and neither of us moves for a moment.

"You know what's funny," I say, mostly to the windshield. "I have walked into that condo approximately two hundred times. I have a key. I once let myself in at six in the morning to steal their waffle iron and Ivy didn't even wake up."

"And this time feels different?"

"It does. Tonight I am genuinely considering sitting in this truck until the meeting is over and just texting everyone that I got a flat tire."

He laughs, which is not the reaction I was looking for, but I feel myself relax slightly anyway. "Come on, Freckles." He squeezes my hand once and opens his door.

The night air is warm for early May, the light is on in every window of Ivy and Gray's condo. I can hear the low, indistinct sound of voices from outside.

We walk up the path.

Micah reaches for the door.

I grab his arm.

He looks back at me, patient, not rushing it.

"Just," I start, and then don't finish, because there isn't a clean way to say *this is the first time I'm walking into something as myself, without a plan or a performance, and I want to remember what that feels like.*

He seems to understand anyway.

I take one breath and nod.

He opens the door.

The room is buzzing when we walk in. There are drinks and snacks on the kitchen counter, and at least three different conversations are happening at once, and for approximately two seconds nobody notices us.

Then Ivy looks up.

Her face does something I have never seen it do before. She goes completely still, and then she exhales, and her eyes fill up so fast she barely gets a hand over her mouth in time.

Gray, who is standing beside her, follows her gaze to us and then looks down at our hands, connected right there in the doorway, and his entire face breaks open in this quiet, enormous smile.

And then Marcus, who is sitting on the couch and has no filter whatsoever, says loud enough that the rest of the room turns to look, "Finally!"

Someone starts clapping.

I don't know who starts it but it spreads fast and suddenly six people are clapping and someone lets out a low whistle and Ivy makes a sound that is mostly laugh and mostly sob and crosses the room in about three steps, and she wraps her arms around both of us because we're still standing close enough together that she can reach, and I feel her shaking slightly against my shoulder.

"I am so happy," she says, muffled, into the general vicinity of my collar. "I am genuinely so happy right now."

"Okay," I say, laughing, embarrassed and warm all at once. "Okay, we know."

"Two years," Gray says, over her head, looking at Micah with that look. "Man, two years I've been waiting for this moment."

Ivy pulls back, wiping under her eyes with her thumb, and I am doing a very competent job of not crying.

I look across the room.

And then I stop.

Olivia is standing near the window.

She has her iced coffee in one hand and her arms loosely crossed, and she is watching me with an expression that is, for Olivia, completely unguarded.

She doesn't cross the room. She doesn't have to.

I hold her gaze for a moment, and she tilts her head once, the smallest possible acknowledgment, and I feel the full weight of what it means that she is standing in this room.

Olivia is here.

At Bible study.

It takes all of me not to make a big deal of it, because that's the thing about Olivia. You don't hold a spotlight up to her. You just make room and let her be there, and you act like it is the most normal thing in the world for her to show up, because if you make it into a moment she will turn it into a joke and disappear.

So I just look at her, and she looks at me, and then she raises her iced coffee in a small toast and says, from across the room, "to dating for real."

I laugh before I can stop it.

She grins, satisfied, and goes back to her conversation.

Someone hands me a drink.

The evening settles.

Ivy and Gray's living room holds more people than it technically should, but nobody minds because that's always been true of this group. We drag chairs in from the dining room. A few people sit on the floor without being asked. The lamp in the corner keeps the light warm and low, and I end up on the couch with Micah, tucked against his side like that's just where I go now, his arm easy around my shoulders.

The passage tonight is from Philippians. It's the last week of the series they've been working through since February.

Philippians 4:11-13.

Marcus reads it slowly, which is not his usual pace, and I follow along on the page in front of me.

"I have learned, in whatever state I am, to be content. I know how to be abased, and I know how to abound. Everywhere and in all things I have learned both to be full and to be hungry, both to abound and to suffer need. I can do all things through Christ who strengthens me."

I have heard this verse approximately four thousand times in my life. I could have told you the book, the chapter, the verse number if pressed. I won a Bible drill ribbon with it in sixth grade, stood at a microphone in a church fellowship hall and recited it with my hands flat at my sides, loud and clear and perfectly correct. I have seen it on coffee mugs and phone cases and little framed prints in church hallways, the last line lifted out on its own, standing alone like a motivational poster.

I can do all things through Christ who strengthens me.

Meaning: you can do hard things.

Meaning: push through.

Meaning: the point is the achievement.

I never read the two verses before it though.

I never noticed that the whole passage is not about strength at all.

It's about learning to let go of the outcome.

I look back down at the page.

I have learned, in whatever state I am, to be content.

I have spent twenty-seven years treating contentment like a destination. Like something I would finally arrive at once the list was finished, once everything was organized and approved and accounted for. Once I had checked the right boxes and volunteered the right number of hours and performed the right version of faith in the right rooms with the right people watching. I thought it was something you earned by doing enough.

I thought the point was the achievement.

I did not know it was something you received by releasing your grip.

It's not about winning the ribbon. Not the color-coded itinerary. Not the Bible app streak or the perfectly timed verse caption or the right answer in the right room.

It's not about the doing good. It's about the fact that the source is not in me, has never been in me, and the moment I stopped trying to manufacture it from the inside and started letting it come from somewhere else, something changed. Something in me that has been braced against the next thing for as long as I can remember.

I exhale slowly.

Micah's hand finds mine without him looking down.

Someone across the room asks a question about

suffering and what it means to be content in the hard seasons, the ones that don't resolve cleanly. Gray answers carefully. Others add things. The conversation moves the way it does in this group, honestly, without anyone needing to have the right answer before they speak.

I don't say anything tonight. I just listen.

And for the first time in my life, that is exactly enough.

Because I spent twenty-seven years trying to earn contentment through performance, and somewhere in the last two months I started learning what it actually means to just be where you are. To not strive toward the next thing that will finally make you feel like enough.

To remain.

I think about how Olivia is in this room right now.

I find her across the space. She's standing near the window, same place she was when we came in.

She blinks, looks down at her coffee, and when she looks back up she catches me watching her.

She holds my gaze for just a second.

Then she smiles.

I glance sideways at Micah.

He's listening, his chin resting in one hand, completely at ease. He doesn't perform attention. He just pays it, freely, like it costs him nothing.

He must feel me looking because he turns his head slightly, and when he sees my face he softens, just for a moment, before he mouths, *love you.*

I grip his hand tighter.

Ivy is scribbling the last of the prayer requests in that little notebook she keeps. I watch her flip back through the pages to make sure she got everyone's.

She caps her pen and looks up at Gray with a small nod.

He clears his throat once, not loud, but the room settles anyway because that's just what happens when Gray Bennett asks for a room's attention.

"Before everyone heads out," he says, "I want to close us out in prayer."

Heads bow. The room goes quiet, and Gray starts to pray.

He thanks God for the study, for the people in this room and the way they keep showing up for each other. His voice is low and unhurried, the same voice he uses on Sunday mornings, like he is not performing prayer but simply having a conversation he knows will be heard.

And then he pauses.

Just for a beat.

"And Lord," he says, and something in his voice shifts, rougher at the edges, "we ask Your blessing over the sweet baby growing in Ivy's belly."

The room detonates.

Chapter 47
Micah

Gray and Ivy are going to have a baby.

Marcus and Olivia are already on their feet before I lift my head from prayer, and Ivy has both hands pressed over her face, completely undone, and Gray is standing there with the smile of a man who has been carrying something beautiful for weeks and has finally gotten to set it down in front of the people he loves most.

Harper and I stay on the couch.

She is tucked against my side with her head on my shoulder and my arm around her, and I am aware of every small point of contact. The way she fits there. I have imagined this specific thing more times than I will ever admit to anyone, Harper Mitchell simply leaning against me like that's just where she goes.

We watch the room love our friends well.

"Is it bad that I'm a little jealous?" I say. Low, just for her.

She tilts her head up to look at me, and I can already see the thing happening at the corner of her mouth, the tell she has when something is coming that she finds funnier than she wants to let on.

"That they get to do the act that makes babies," she says, entirely composed, "or that they're going to have a baby?"

I laugh before I can stop it, and I duck my head and press my lips to the side of her neck without thinking, just a brief warm press against her skin, and I feel her breath catch, just slightly.

"Both, for sure," I whisper against her ear. "But my mind was actually going more toward the fact that Gray gets to be a dad."

Which is true. Both things are true simultaneously.

She settles back against my shoulder, and I feel her look across the room toward Gray, who has one arm around Ivy and is shaking someone's hand with the other, his face doing that thing, the enormous uncomplicated joy I have watched him grow into over the last several years.

"He's going to be so good at it," she says.

"Yeah," I agree. "He really is."

Gray catches my eye over the top of Ivy's head.

He looks at Harper, tucked against me. Looks back at me.

He nods once. The specific nod that covers everything we would need fifteen minutes to say out loud.

I nod back.

Harper stirs beside me, lifting her head. "We should go congratulate them."

"Yeah, we should."

She untangles herself and stands, holding out her hand, and I take it. We cross the room together, and I watch her make it about three steps from Ivy before something in her face gives, and Ivy sees it and opens her arms, and Harper walks straight into them and holds on.

I stop a few feet back and let her have it.

"Harper," Ivy says her name like she is gathering it up carefully.

"You're going to be the best mom."

"Stop."

"I mean it. That baby is so lucky."

Ivy pulls back and cups Harper's face in both hands, and Harper is crying in that way she would absolutely deny if asked about it later, and Ivy is looking at her with twenty-something years of friendship in her eyes.

"You're going to be the best auntie," Ivy tells her.

Gray appears at my shoulder.

I put my arm around him without looking, and he grabs the back of my neck, and we stand there like that watching our girls fall apart in the best possible way, and neither of us says a word, because some moments are not improved by commentary.

After a while I pull back and look at him.

"A dad," I say.

He exhales, slowly, the biggest smile on his face. "Yeah."

I shake my head once, not because I'm surprised, but because some things deserve a moment before you move past them. Gray Bennett is going to be a father. I have watched this man pray over strangers, lead rooms full of people, sit with people in the hardest seasons of their lives and not flinch. I have watched him love Ivy with a steadiness that made the rest of us quietly recalibrate what we thought we were capable of.

"You're going to be incredible," I tell him.

He looks at me. Nods once, the way he does when something lands and he doesn't want to make a production of it.

We turn, almost at the same time, and find them.

Harper has both arms around Ivy and she is crying, and Ivy is holding her like she's been waiting to tell her for weeks, which she probably has. They are talking in that fast, overlapping way they do, half sentences finishing each other's thoughts.

Gray watches Ivy the way he always watches Ivy. Like she is something he has been given and has never once taken for granted.

I watch Harper.

She pulls back and Ivy cups her face in both hands and says something that makes Harper laugh again, messier this time, and I feel the full weight of the last several months settle into something quiet and certain in my chest.

I spent a long time being careful about this. Afraid that I had read it wrong. That what I felt was mine alone. That the right thing to do was to keep it contained and managed.

Gray shifts beside me. "You're staring."

"I'm aware."

He smiles, slow, and says nothing else, which is one of the things I have always appreciated about Gray Bennett. He knows when the point has been made.

The hallway is quiet and the light is low and Harper Mitchell is pressed against her front door with my hand on her cheek and my fingers in her hair and I am kissing her the way I have wanted to kiss her for two years.

She is not complaining.

When I finally pull back, we are both a little unsteady,

which I find deeply satisfying, and her eyes take a second to open.

"I don't want to leave," I say.

It comes out more honest than I intend it to, which seems to be a recurring condition around her.

She laughs softly, her hands still in my jacket. "I never understood why Ivy struggled so much." A pause. "Now I know." She tilts her head, something mischievous moving across her face. "Are you sure you don't want to just go to the courthouse tomorrow morning?"

"Who says I wanna marry you?"

She swats my arm.

I look at her for a moment. "Harper."

"I'm just saying. It's efficient."

"You deserve a proper proposal," I say. "And a beautiful wedding with your friends and your family and probably a color-coded seating chart that takes you three weeks to finalize."

"Four weeks minimum, actually."

"And we are not going to rush it."

She sighs. Dramatically. Rolls her eyes toward the ceiling. "Fine."

"Fine," I agree.

"You're very annoying."

"You've mentioned that."

"Deeply, profoundly annoying."

"And yet you love me."

"I do," she repeats, quieter, looking back at me.

I lean down and kiss her once more, slower this time, and she makes a small sound against my mouth that I am going to be thinking about for the rest of the night, and when I pull back I rest my forehead against hers for just a moment.

"Inside," I say.

"You can't tell me what to do."

"Harper."

She sighs again, less dramatic this time, and turns and opens the door. She steps inside and leans against the frame looking up at me.

"Lock it," I say.

"I always lock it."

"Lock it while I'm standing here."

She gives me a look that is somehow both exasperated and fond, which is essentially her natural resting expression around me, and reaches back and turns the deadbolt. I hear it click.

"Satisfied?" she says through the door.

"Very much, thank you."

"Good night, Dimples."

"Good night, Freckles."

Acknowledgments

To my Lord and Savior, Jesus Christ—thank You reminding me that there is nothing I need to do to earn my place in your kingdom besides laying it all at your feet, and remaining in You.

For those of you who don't know, I was previously published as a steamy romance author. But I finally listened to the convictions the Lord placed on my heart and unpublished those books to step into this new pen name, as a Christian Romance Author.

There are so many people I want to thank. First, to my husband—for always being supportive when I need to lock myself away to focus on edits. For encouraging me everytime I ramble about turning this dream of being a full time author into a reality.

To my kids—thank you for being excited about seeing my social media graphics and book covers. For being my mini fans and so eager to read my books one day

To my sister Ashlynn—you always support me no matter what, even from 5,000+ miles away. I can't wait to write a book on your terrace in Italy.

To my friends and family—for cheering me on even when I'm terrible at texting back. Specifically, to my Home Group ladies: I couldn't do this life without you. Thank you for keeping me on track every time I "squirrel."

To Jordan Riley—for always listening to my crazy long Marco Polos, and for sending equally long ones back. I'm so thankful I have you as an author friend to bounce ideas back and forth.

To my beta readers—you have blown me away, again! I hope, as you read the final version of this book, you can see the ways your feedback helped me shape the first draft into this story I'm so proud of. I can't wait to work with you again on Book 3.

And finally, to my readers—the fact that you picked up this book means the world to me. I've prayed over every page of this story, and I've prayed over you, too. Thank you for supporting me as a debut Christian Romance author and coming back for the second book in this series.

About the Author

Hey y'all, I'm Amber!

A christian romance author writing swoony love stories that honor faith, purity, and heart.

If you're looking for stories that stir your soul and point to something deeper, you're in the right place.

And if you love kisses-only romance with all the swoony moments, check out my other pen name, Erin Renee!

authorambernicole.com

Follow me on social media
@authorambernicole

Want more of Harper and Micah?

A Season To Fall ~ A Summer Novella

After three months of dating Harper Mitchell, Micah Sanders has a ring in his pocket and a plan in his head. Three months, after all, is exactly how long Harper once told him someone needed to date before they got married. And Micah Sanders has never been one to argue with Harper Mitchell.

He just has to ask her. Easy enough. Except they're spending the Fourth of July in Ashen Mills, Texas, at the small-town festival Harper has never once missed in her life. And between sketchy carnival rides, sticky funnel cake, and Harper's wide-eyed campaign to show him every corner of her hometown, every perfect moment Micah plans keeps slipping right past her. He's been waiting two years to ask this question. What's a few more hours?

***A Season to Fall* is a clean, faith-filled Christian summer romance filled with hometown charm, swoony proposal mishaps, and a love that points straight to Jesus. Perfect for readers who**

love small-town settings, patient heroes with a plan, sunshine heroines worth chasing, and the kind of forever worth waiting on. A heartwarming novella of faith, family, and finally finding the right moment to fall.

Read A Season To Fall available exclusively in ebook format on my website! www.authorambernicole.com

Want more of Harper and Micah?

A SEASON TO FALL
EBOOK

www.ingramcontent.com/pod-product-compliance
Lightning Source LLC
La Vergne TN
LVHW010627110826
845149LV00014B/2796

9798989793990